DAWN OF FATE AND FIRE

Also by Mariely Lares

Sun of Blood and Ruin

DAWN OF FATE AND FIRE

MARIELY LARES

HARPER
Voyager

Harper*Voyager*
An imprint of
HarperCollins*Publishers* Ltd
1 London Bridge Street
London SE1 9GF

www.harpercollins.co.uk

HarperCollins*Publishers*
Macken House,
39/40 Mayor Street Upper,
Dublin 1
D01 C9W8
Ireland

First published by HarperCollins*Publishers* Ltd 2025
1

A catalogue record for this book is available from the British Library.

ISBN: 978-0-00-860960-3 (HB)
ISBN: 978-0-00-860965-8 (TPB)

This novel is entirely a work of fiction.
The names, characters and incidents portrayed in it are
the work of the author's imagination. Any resemblance to
actual persons, living or dead, events or localities is
entirely coincidental.

Set in Adobe Garamond by Palimpsest Book Production Limited, Falkirk, Stirlingshire

Printed and bound in the UK using 100% renewable electricity by CPI Group (UK) Ltd

This book contains FSC™ certified paper and other controlled sources
to ensure responsible forest management.

For more information visit: www.harpercollins.co.uk/green

Para mi mamá, que espera con ilusión el día en que pueda leer esta historia en español. Te amo.

THE BASIN
OF MEXICO

MARKET OF
TLATELOLCO

SANTIAGO
TLATELOLCO

TACUBA CAUSEWAY
TO CHAPULTEPEC

SANTA MARÍA
CUEPOHPAN

CATHEDRA

LA
TRAZA

PLAZA
MAYOR

SAN JUAN
MOYOTLAN

SAN JUAN
TENOCHTITLA

N

N

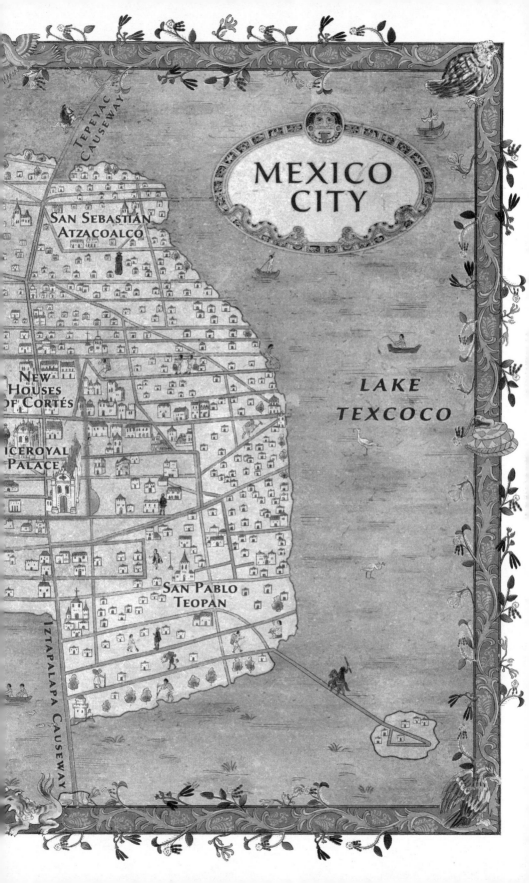

MEXICO CITY

TEPEYAC CAUSEWAY

SAN SEBASTIÁN
ATZACOALCO

NEW
HOUSES
OF CORTÉS

VICEROYAL
PALACE

SAN PABLO
TEOPAN

IZTAPALAPA CAUSEWAY

LAKE
TEXCOCO

INSIDE THE DUOLOGY. . .

Sun of Blood and Ruin

Leonora is a mestiza woman known by her Spanish name, Leonora; her Nahua name, Tecuani, and her alter ego, the masked vigilante Pantera. Trained as a child in the paradisal realm of Tamoanchan, she can transform into a panther, draw power from the sun, and wield her tonalli, her vital force. Armed with a magical sword, she battles against the oppressive Spanish colonial rule, aligning herself with an Indigenous group called La Justicia.

As the Nahua face the prophecy of the End of the Fifth Sun— foretelling the world's end through earthquakes and the demonic Tzitzimime—the Spaniards launch a brutal attack on the Nahua stronghold at Snake Mountain. Leonora discovers her divine heritage and defeats the queen of the Tzitzimime, causing her army of demon goddesses to collapse. During the battle, an imposter seizes control of Snake Mountain by murdering his brother, the rightful king. The war with the Spaniards is declared over, and an alliance is struck between them and La Justicia.

With the remaining survivors of La Justicia and allies, Leonora vows to avenge the slain king and continue fighting evil, human or otherwise, with the mask of Pantera if need be.

Part 1: Tozoztontli

Little Watch

CHAPTER 1

La Sequía

The battlefield is the place,
where one toasts the divine liquor in war,
where are stained red the divine eagles,
where the jaguars howl,
where all kinds of precious stones rain from ornaments,
where wave headdresses rich with fine plumes,
where princes are smashed to bits.

Nezahualcoyotl, King of Texcoco

For everything there's a season; there's a time for sowing and a time for harvest, a time for toil and a time for rest, a time for living and a time for dying.

Tonalco, the dry season, is a time for war.

The gods Tlaloc and Huitzilopochtli together command the natural cycle of the year and the changing days. Before the Spaniards came, two shrines topped the Great Temple in the center of Tenochtitlan. Tlaloc's faced north, the god of rain bringing fertility to the earth. The other toward the south for Huitzilopochtli, the god of war who scorches the land with battle.

The seasons reveal a proper time for all things to happen. The solar calendar with its eighteen months of twenty days. Each celebrates a festival honoring a different god.

In the hunting season of Quecholli, a great feast honors the god of the chase, Mixcoatl. Other months are dedicated to Tlaloc, such as Tozoztontli. Under the old ways, pipiltin, the nobility, queens of Nahua cities, kings of kings, journeyed to the summit of Mount Tlaloc to offer prayers and sacrifice, ensuring the rains would come again.

As far as any can tell, the last Tozoztontli was performed successfully.

As far as *I* can tell, that must've been a long time ago.

Now, the air scorches, the land parches.

Tlaloc may be the god of rain, but even he can't manage all the watering alone. That's why his little assistants, the Tlaloque, carry immense clay pots to fill and, when Tlaloc tells them, they break those vessels all over the land, lakes, and seas.

However, they have done no such thing in months.

In the dry season, hiding is not easy. Catching prey, less so. Though I have black spots—all jaguars do—the rest of my fur is also dark. I don't blend in with my surroundings.

Stay quiet. Stay out of sight. Those nosy howlers in the treetops will alert the entire forest that I'm on the hunt. They can see me coming a far distance away. The oldest and largest of the troop, one bearded male with thick and full hair, is the leader. He's the worst of them.

I am not larger than the bull, bigger than the bear, heavier than the whale, not as clever as the snake, but here the jaguar reigns supreme, and when I show up, the howlers sound the alarm.

Tonatiuh bright in the sky is my ally, creating shadows. The ideal cover. I keep to the shade as I pad along, careful, listening for movement. Within me, a deep pit of hunger festers. It's been days, weeks, of eating scraps. The natural does not always come naturally. Despite not having enemies, except perhaps the raucous monkeys, I have had to learn how to live in the forest, how to survive.

4

The backwaters, hidden in the heart of chaneque territory, offer some relief. This part of the river holds water year-round, even during the dry season.

No screeching calls. All is going well so far.

Silently, I swim in, my senses attuned to every ripple and current, looking for sunshiny creatures. I'm not a fussy eater. Anything along the river, or in the river, will do.

On the bank, two blue-green pits glint like jewels. A caiman's nostrils, followed by the whole snout. It lies motionless, cloaked in mud. Perfect camouflage.

A shiver of elation starts in my paws, races up my legs, and quivers through my body. Nothing is more exciting than that first glimpse of your prey. The caiman is magnificent—about my size, its craggy skin spotted almost like mine. Here we are together, bound as one in this wonderful moment of life and death. My heart starts racing.

I paddle in the water with practiced silence, eyes locked on my target. Every muscle in my body is taut with focus as I choose my angle of attack.

Just a little closer.

One bite is all it takes. Then the monkeys can howl all they want.

Closer.

Closer.

Now.

I pounce.

My jaws snap shut, piercing the soft underbelly of the neck, where the scales are thinner. The caiman wriggles—a desperate attempt to escape. But in less than a heartbeat, its struggle ceases. I start pulling it to the tree line, and the howlers start their screaming chorus, harsh and savage.

Too late, my friends.

Death in the forest is quick.

We predators can afford no mercy.

The howlers continue their ungodly alarm, but their song almost immediately dies away. They will sing again, of course, in an hour or two, but from a different place, for the monkeys must always travel between songs. Otherwise, it would be an easy matter for enemies to find them among the branches.

The clawing hunger finally subsides as I feast on the caiman's entrails. My belly swells with its flesh; delicious meat, my snout splattered with hot sweet blood.

I swivel my ears. A rustle of leaves behind me betrays a presence, though it was their scent I caught first from a distance.

My fur rises on end, tail twitching furiously. Then, baring my bloody fangs, I let out a growl, a threat, a promise of pain. I tighten my muscles, bend my hind legs, and just as I am about to leap, a pushing pressure inside forces my form to change.

I don't remember the last time I was human.

I'm curled up on the forest floor, my skin bare against the dead leaves and twigs. Everything hurts. My muscles are like knotted ropes, my limbs a pair of willowing reeds. I cough, spitting out bits of flesh and guts stuck between my teeth. The more I move, the more my body aches. I struggle like an insect caught in a spider's web. I try to push myself from the ground and find that I'm covered in blood. I turn and vomit, again and again, until I think my ribs will crack, and I cannot bring up anything more. I'm completely empty.

Everything is bright and loud and spinning. My eyes are heavy, my head dull, disoriented. Changing forms is worse than waking up from a drunken binge. I am aware of myself, but I have no control. I wonder if this is what babes feel when they enter the world. I blink, once, twice, and then again before shaking my head, trying to clear the mist in front of my eyes. Dazedly I try to make sense of what just took place. I didn't start the shift. It was spontaneous, like sneezing.

This isn't the first time it's happened. Many times before, the Panther has urged the shift, as if my skin will split open if I don't.

But never have I involuntarily reverted to my human form. What went wrong?

I'm looking at my answer now. It takes my mind a second to recognize that distinctive chaneque smell.

"*You.*" I orient myself to uttering words again. "You did this to me."

Zyanya stands over me, all three feet of her, face petulant. She's grown a shock of white hair, exposing pointy ears. A brown mantle makes her short body look longer than it truly is. Talons allow her bare feet to cling to trees and move easily through the rough terrain.

"Aren't you going to say anything?" I ask.

"I'm waiting," she says.

"Waiting for what?"

"You're in your nagual head," she says. "The mind is always last to return to normal."

My stomach cramps again. Clutching it, I hack up a fist-sized, soggy clump of undigested fur.

Zyanya sighs. "You did this to yourself. I warned you not to abuse your power. Staying in your nagual for too long has consequences. It's dangerous not to be able to shift on command. If you lose focus, you'll find yourself somewhere in between, stranded, with no tonalli to help you complete the change. Is that your wish?"

I wipe my mouth with the back of my hand.

"You can't live in chaneque territory forever, Pantera," Zyanya says.

"And where should I go?" I snap. "Neza is dead. Snake Mountain has fallen. Ichcatzin would sooner kill me than allow me to live in his midst. My brother would burn me at the stake the moment I set foot in the capital. I am not wanted anywhere."

Her bright yellow eyes, large and rounded, soften. She shakes her head as if pitying a fool.

"I've protected you, have I not?" I ask her. "From the dangers in the forest."

"Yes, but not from yourself. You are welcome here, but you are a guest. And guests show respect. Guests have *manners.*"

She looks behind me, where the caiman carcass lies partly eaten.

"We make use of the forest," she says, "but we take care of it. You'll have to make a new home for yourself. Elsewhere."

I'm reminded that though I've befriended the belligerent chaneques, the little creatures are protectors of the forest. Upon intrusion, they will throw stones, pull hair, weave disorienting illusions. Frighten by any means at their disposal. Some have power over nature. Once spooked, a person's tonalli will come flying out of their body, at which point the chaneque will steal it. And, as I all too well know, without tonalli, you die.

"What will you have me do, Zyanya?" I say defeatedly. "Beg to Ichcatzin? I will not beg."

Before Zyanya can answer, the wind whispers against the strands of my hair, a susurrus of sound. Voices . . . noises that seem to come all at once and wrap around me.

I turn around slowly, listening to every sound in the distance.

"What is it?" Zyanya asks.

A deep growl escapes my throat. "Your friends are doing this. Make them stop."

It's a cacophony, each sound inside the other, all competing to be heard—wild laughter, mosquitoes buzzing, the tread of many feet, the flight of an eagle, the rushing water crashing against the rocks, the angry call of howlers and chachalacas and a hundred other animals. A deafening tempest.

"Make them stop." I raise my hands to my ears. "Stop it. *Stop* it!"

Zyanya rushes to me and takes my hands. "Listen to me. Breathe. Shut it out. You know how to do it. Focus. Do you hear me? Focus only on my voice."

Her words are far away. A great pain goes through my head, and I cry out, *"Quiet!"* The ground trembles as a destructive force of tonalli frees itself out of me, flying in all directions. It picks up Zyanya like she is nothing, tossing her across the clearing, and everything else with it.

Trees strain against the onslaught as tonalli continues to burst from me, unrestrained and unyielding. I fall to my knees. I can't make it stop.

I squint my eyes to keep out the violent dust, but amid the eddying debris, I make out Zyanya held against a tree. She struggles to lift a hand, curling fingers at me, and to mouth words.

The devastation finally dies as my vital force is taken from the crown of my head.

I awaken, swaying. My head is in a dizzying spiral. As I sit up, stifling a groan, I realize I'm dangling in a hammock strung in the corner of Zyanya's hut. I grip its edges and try to free myself, squirming like a worm. One of my legs is caught in the rope, and the hammock swings violently. I roll around, drop, and hit the earthen floor with a loud thud.

"The legendary Pantera." Zyanya shakes her head.

Her hut has a reed bed padded with feathers, chairs, tables, and a cooking area, where Zyanya sits crushing herbs in a molcajete. It's quiet, too quiet. I don't hear much of anything. How can I? She took my tonalli.

Clumsily, I sit on a chair too small for me. "I didn't mean—I'm sorry. That's never happened before. Well, not like *that*."

"Your power is growing." Zyanya looks down at her belt, where a dangling green stone glints with my vital force in an intriguing swirl. "I can feel it. And the proof of that is evident," she says, eyeing my hair. It's been a long time since I've seen my reflection, but as my fingers brush through the strands, I realize it now falls well below my waist.

"What do you mean growing?" I ask.

"Learning," she says. "Responding to the demands you make upon it."

"How can that be?"

"You're the daughter of the Feathered Serpent." I've spoken of this with no one, and Zyanya must see the look of surprise on my face because she explains, "Your tonalli told me."

I frown. "Told you?"

"The gods manifest their power in circling motions," she says as if that makes any sense. "You're not human, Pantera. Not entirely. What you did that night when the Tzitzimime came . . . it was one of the greatest things I've ever seen."

I hardly recall my past human life. After months of living as the Panther, the mind stops thinking like a human. Every sorcerer knows: stay in your nagual for too long, you risk losing touch with reality or getting trapped as an animal forever.

I shrug. "If you say so."

"There's no denying you're a sorceress. This is what you trained for. But you have god tonalli. You must learn to center your vital force inside, where it can be held and harnessed. With increased tonalli, the path becomes more slippery. Order cannot exist without chaos and chaos cannot exist without order. There must be balance in this world, and within you. Until then, you are dangerous. To yourself . . . and others."

Leonora . . . A male voice comes from a distance.

"No, no, no. Not again," I say frantically, shooting up from the chair. "It's not possible. I don't have my tonalli. I can't be hearing things!"

Zyanya turns her head. I sag with relief; she heard the voice too.

Someone is calling me, and for a moment, I don't realize it's my name. Then my human mind clears, and at once, I think, *Leonora?* Why *Leonora?*

The name sounds too odd, too unfamiliar to my ears. Pantera would have been so much better. After all, it is *his* voice.

I haven't heard his voice in what seems like years. Since the victory at Snake Mountain, where we fought the Spaniards and the Tzitzimime, and won. He made a great slaughter, and I, too, did my part. At the battle's end, I faced the Obsidian Butterfly, and the Sword of Integrity sent her to the blackness of the heavens. After, we lay together on the hillside, watching Tonatiuh rise, and we ran as fast as our paws could take us. Then, he returned to his people, the Tlahuica, and I went my way.

What I should have done, what my heart told me to do, was give him the truth of who he is—a god. It's a secret unknown to himself, revealed to me by his mother, the Precious Flower, Xochiquetzal. I should have told him about my true father, Quetzalcoatl, and my mother, Tlazohtzin, the woman who, through my birth, became a goddess and a servant of the Obsidian Butterfly.

I should have gone with him. He asked me to. Instead, I remained in chaneque territory with Zyanya.

I have not seen Tezca since that day.

He calls my name again. I go to look for him, following his voice.

My human legs have not been used in a long time, and they feel unnatural; I can barely get my knees to bend. I stumble forward, no longer able to stand erect. Unsteadily, I brush the dirt from my knees and push myself back up.

The forest isn't kind to bare feet, but I pick up speed, leaping over fallen trees, pushing through bushes. More in control. More like myself. I reach a mossy clearing. It undulates, the vegetation floating atop water that bubbles beneath.

"Pantera, wait!" Zyanya trails behind me. "Stop!"

I'm ready to leap, but she grabs my shoulders and pulls me back. We teeter on the spongy edge for a moment, about to fall together.

"Look." Zyanya points.

His voice calls to me again.

CHAPTER 2

La Amenaza

It's not Tezca. It is Rayo, the ahuizotl, mimicking his speech. He's a terrifying creature, a tricky one too. He has the ability to imitate sounds and voices, using them to lure victims near so he can snatch them with his sinuous tail claw.

Amalia and Eréndira jump off the ahuizotl, and Amalia tosses the flesh of a dead animal toward the eager Rayo, who surges to catch it in the air, then plunges back into the water.

Eréndira greets me with a nod. "Still alive, Pantera?"

"Still alive, princess."

"Good. I'm glad. I didn't think we'd find you."

"I told you she would find us," Amalia says, pleased. "It's good to see you, Leonora." She opens her arms, coming for an embrace. Her golden hair is braided, and she's dressed in a simple blouse and pants. The most ornate thing about her is the beaded cross encircling her neck.

"You are changed," I tell her.

"You are *not*," she says with a chuckle. "When was the last time you washed? You reek of death."

I grin. "The forest becomes you."

"Yes," she says, looking up at the trees. "It's been a good place

12

for me to grow. I would not have done so with my mother's coddling."

"It'll be dark soon," Zyanya warns. "We should return to Tozi."

If you ask a chaneque, they will say: chaneques don't live in the forest; chaneques *are* the forest, as much as the trees, plants, and animals. They're constantly moving, like the forest. When not frightening intruders and stealing tonalli, they gather in different communities of between twenty and thirty, foraging, hunting, and building their homes which, for a wandering group of little creatures, is an interminable process. Chaneques have been known to set up their huts in a couple of hours, but they are constantly adding rooms, repairing doors, strawing and re-strawing the roofs. Sometimes, for reasons I have yet to understand, they will take down their huts and begin again.

If there's one thing chaneques hate more than intruders, it's being thought of as children. They might look like children, but they're not. They're not even human—not anymore.

We pass several round bamboo huts lined up one next to the other, some clustered in small areas, a few standing alone like tiny islands.

Such is the village of Tozi.

The chaneques flock about us, and soon, Amalia has a crowd around her. They tug on her hair and push her sleeves up so they can examine her skin more closely. They spit on her freckled forearms and rub, wrinkling their noses in disgust when her freckles don't come off. Other chaneques are fascinated with her pockmarked face, thinking Amalia is a great warrior. They're not wrong. She battled and conquered the pox.

The eldest in the community, twenty-six, a very respectable age for a chaneque, introduces himself to Amalia and Eréndira as Itzmin. He's no taller than my shoulder, but he expresses himself confidently, recognized as the leading authority by all the chaneques in Tozi. Though his face is considerably lined, Itzmin still possesses the glow of a child's countenance, keen yellow eyes, floppy ears, and sparse, white hair.

"Niltze," Amalia greets. "Notoca Amalia." She's been learning Nahuatl from Eréndira. It's far from perfect, but it's sufficient to make herself understood.

"I am Eréndira," she says, taking a step forward. "We have come to—"

"We know, Owl Witch," says Itzmin. "We've been expecting you."

To chaneques, dreams are a different form of reality. They begin each day with a ceremony where they share their dreams from the previous night, from the youngest member to the eldest, and based on those dreams, the village decides what they will do that day. Sometimes the dreams are so long, they dictate full months.

They must have dreamt of Eréndira and Amalia's arrival.

Eréndira and Amalia trade perplexed glances but simply nod their gratefulness.

"You come to Tozi," Itzmin says. "Good. Rest your worries. You're safe. We dance and drink tonight."

Amalia arches an eyebrow. "Aren't they a little too young to drink?"

Though Amalia murmurs this to me, barely above a whisper, her question is met with a resounding silence and glares. Chaneques have flawless hearing, perhaps even more than I do. With their flopping ears moving to and fro, they can discern the slightest sound.

Itzmin narrows his eyes. "Settle in. Zyanya will show you where," he says with some asperity, before he walks away.

"What did I say?" Amalia asks innocently.

"You were doing so well," Zyanya says, humor lacing her tone. She gives Amalia a playful pat on the back. "Come, countess."

A look of displeasure flits across Amalia's face. Eréndira chuckles.

"What did I say?" Zyanya taunts.

"Don't call me that," Amalia protests, though her voice lacks any real heat.

"Call you what? Countess?"

"It's not who I am anymore."

"Sorry, countess," Zyanya says, her lips curved upward. "Whatever you say, countess."

Still smiling, Zyanya heads toward her hut, and Amalia exhales sharply.

"She's just teasing you," I assure.

"Why?"

"I'm not sure," I say, thinking of the many times I've been the recipient of Zyanya's jests. "I think she gets pleasure from it. It's harmless. Well, most of the time. Unless you remind her of her age. She doesn't like that. None of them do."

Metzli, the Lady of the Night, has not yet risen when the chaneques start gathering in a circle. Musicians pick up their instruments and immediately the village comes alive. Every chaneque takes part, bursting into a bright and merry song, clapping their hands and shaking the rattles on their feet.

There is music, then there is chaneque music.

The sound is extraordinary, a very full and rich form of singing, accompanied by the mesmerizing sounds of the drum, the conch, the flute, the whistle, the horn, all wonderfully blended into the melody.

Long ago, when the earth was a quiet and joyless place, Tezcatlipoca gave humans the gift of music.

It was an agreement between Tezcatlipoca and Quetzalcoatl. In the dawn of the Fifth Sun, the Thirteen Heavens were filled with music. Although humans had lush vegetation, flowers of all colors, and much beauty to behold, Tezcatlipoca noticed they weren't truly happy. And Quetzalcoatl wished for his people to have all the riches of life, so Tezcatlipoca, with his help, awakened the world. For the first time, people sang, and so did the trees and birds, whales, crickets, and frogs. Ever since, music has filled our souls.

The moon now illuminates the sky as it climbs above the trees. The song drifts into the night, melting into the sounds of the forest.

"Well?" I say, offering Amalia a cup of pulque.

She takes the drink and sips it, licking her lips afterward. "Well, what?"

"Are you going to tell me why you have come?"

"What if I said I simply wished to see you?"

"I would say you're lying."

Amalia drinks, hiding a smirk.

Eréndira approaches us, her expression grave.

"What is it?" I ask.

"We've come because of Ichcatzin," Eréndira answers. "He rules Snake Mountain with an iron hand. He has some kind of plan to restore Mexico to its former glory. Chipahua has been made high general. He plays along for now, but Ichcatzin doesn't trust him. He knows Chipahua is loyal to Neza."

Nezahualpilli. Once the king of Snake Mountain and Sin Rostro, the head of La Justicia, though this he never admitted. A brave man, a good and just man. He believed in a better life for his people with rights and privileges, where all persons live in harmony and with equal opportunities. It was an ideal he hoped to live for and achieve, and he was prepared to die for it. But a lesser man, his own brother, Ichcatzin, drove a sword into his back. I wept for his death.

"Chipahua is working to find out Ichcatzin's plan without arousing suspicion," Eréndira continues. "He has a few allies. Most are too afraid to openly oppose Ichcatzin. But when Ichcatzin falls—and he *will* fall—Chipahua shall take his place."

Chipahua, a king? As a Shorn One, his duty is to the battlefield, not to lead. Yet, he is Neza's cousin, a nobleman, and he has the strength and wisdom needed to guide Snake Mountain.

"Ichcatzin's plan—you think it involves shedding blood?" I know the answer before I ask the question.

Eréndira nods somberly. "Ichcatzin didn't just murder Neza to seize power. He isn't just some false king on the throne. He has a larger plan, Chipahua is convinced. I think we should find out what he's up to." A bitter breath. "This should never have happened. I wasn't paying attention. If only Neza—"

"Neza's death wasn't your fault," Amalia reassures her. "Ichcatzin is to blame."

For a moment, Eréndira seems to fade, trapped in her memories and emotions. She is not usually lost for words. She looks tired, a different kind of tired. An angry kind of tired.

I drink my pulque, watching Zyanya dancing with the other chaneques. "What will you do?"

"Fight," Eréndira says without hesitation. "Fight like I always do. For Neza. His death will not be in vain."

Amalia huffs as if the world is giving her a headache. "Aren't you forgetting something? Tell her, Eréndira. Tell her the other reason why we're here."

"Quit telling me what to do," Eréndira moans.

Amalia crosses her arms. "Quit acting like you need to be told! You're always saying how Snake Mountain is a people, not a city. What is the point of taking back the city if we don't have a people?"

Eréndira makes an effort to collect herself. "We're dying," she confesses finally. "We're dying of the white demon's disease. Our remedies cannot cure it. The tribes are scattered. Our great warriors are gone. We need a place to heal. To stay alive, away from Ichcatzin's wrath. And after, to rise again, and avenge what has been lost."

"I know what this disease is, and I know how to treat it," says Amalia. "I myself have been cured of it. I know how to help. There is medicine in the capital to manage the symptoms."

She means the palace.

She wants me to go to Jerónimo.

"I'm sorry. I can't go back," I say hoarsely.

"What? Why not?" Amalia asks.

"Jerónimo knows I am Pantera," I tell her. "He made it clear he never wanted to see me again."

"Leonora, please," Amalia says. "You have to try. We can't watch helplessly while the plague rages and people continue to die. You're the viceregent of New Spain."

"I doubt it," I say. "I've been gone too long."

"Jerónimo listens to you. He doesn't listen to me. He takes your advice."

"Except when he remembers who I am, or he is angry about something, or when things are going badly, or I don't go to Mass, then he does not." I look at Eréndira. "He will give you an audience. After the battle with the Tzitzimime, Jerónimo made his promise to work with La Justicia."

"Neza is dead," Eréndira snaps. "So is La Justicia." Her hands fist at her sides, fingers pressing into her palms as if that might somehow keep her grief at bay.

"The promise didn't die with Neza. You shook hands with my brother," I remind her. "Neza's beliefs live in you, in me, in everyone who stood beside him. We are *all* La Justicia. One face. One voice. La Justicia is alive within us."

Eréndira glares at me, struggling between the pain of anger and loss. "My people need me," she argues. "I can't leave them. We've tried to contain it, but it spreads quickly. We travel at night, and we carry the sick on litters. Those who can still walk take turns carrying those who can't. When we stop, we dig pits to burn the clothing, keep the children far from the sick. Even with every precaution, the pox keeps claiming more of us. We can't go on like this forever, Leonora. We're camped not far from here, but if Ichcatzin finds us, he won't let us escape. Snake Mountain isn't safe. We can't make the long trip to the capital." She pauses, her breath unsteady. "We have nowhere to go."

In that, we share the same struggle.

"You heard Itzmin," I say. "There's room for everyone, and chaneques aren't vulnerable; they don't succumb to the pox."

Amalia shakes her head in disbelief. "You will not help?"

I sigh. "It's complicated, Amalia. There are things you don't know and wouldn't understand."

18

"Like what? Why don't you explain them to me?"
She waits for an answer. It doesn't come.

The dancing begins to wind down late into the night. Soon after, the chaneques withdraw to sleep, and Zyanya finds me brooding inside her hut. She carries my mask, my attire, my dagger, my belt, and the Sword of Integrity, which is nearly her length, and she has to drag it about. This tells me she knows what has been asked of me—either because Amalia or Eréndira told her, or because the trees did.

Zyanya drops all my belongings at my feet. My eyes glaze as I close a hand around the blade's hilt. It's been a while since I've held her.

"I'm not going back to the capital," I say.

She exhales one deep breath from the exertion. "Then don't."

I give her a puzzled look. "My power is growing. I must be careful. Isn't that what you told me?"

"Yes."

"Nine Hells, Zyanya, just say what you want to say and be done with it."

She comes closer and sniffs the air. "Amalia was right. You *do* smell. Your stench is invading my senses."

I only barely stop myself from rolling my eyes. "Is it wise to return to the palace while my tonalli swells unrestrained within me?"

"No."

"Then why advise me to leave, if I'm so unstable?"

She considers this, fondling the green stone on her belt with my vital force.

"You wish to restrain my tonalli?" I ask when she doesn't answer. "Keep it under control? Is that it?"

"No, not restrain it," she answers. "Protect it."

"From *what*?" I nearly shout.

"From those who might try to take it for their own benefit. I have a responsibility to maintain the—"

19

"The balance. Yes, yes, I know. And what about me?" I say irritably. "Without my tonalli, I'm vulnerable."

"With it, you're dangerous."

"I'd rather be the predator than the prey."

"Yes, it's your nature."

"Zyanya," I say, "I have known the loss of tonalli. I would begin to deteriorate, forget. I could get lost, not knowing what to do next."

"Oh, yes, I agree," she says idly as if we're chatting about the weather. "Better leave now. You don't have a lot of time."

"You're just trying to get rid of me. Go on. Admit it."

"I should be so lucky." She snickers at her joke. "Believe it or not, I am on your side. And you're missing the point."

"What is the point?"

A silence follows, and I shift uncomfortably under her stare. "Are you even listening? The point is," she says, "tlaalahua, tlapetzcahui in tlalticpac."

A Nahua saying. The words of a tlamatini, a wise one. They are a reminder that the earth is a perilous place and one can easily fall. This means that the ideal path to walk is the one in balance, in the nepantla—the middle—where the tlalticpac is not slippery.

Order can become suffocating. It can halt progress, stunt growth. Chaos is more liberating, but it can get out of hand and become destructive.

Thus the nepantla is necessary. The space between two worlds.

I must make order out of chaos and throw a little chaos into order.

I pick up my mask, understanding that a person's life is not always their own. There is duty and obligation.

The padded guard around my chest feels heavy because I have grown unaccustomed to clothes. My belt which carries my dagger is also a little too big for me as I have become slimmer roaming the forest. I slide the Sword of Integrity in her scabbard and carry her on my back. I cast Zyanya an uneasy glance. She gives me a reassuring nod.

"I see you've reconsidered," Amalia says as I emerge from the hut.

She smiles one moment but frowns the next. "Wait. You're leaving now? It's the dead of night."

"I know how to walk in the darkness."

"Of course, you do." Amalia smiles but rather feebly. "I will stay to help the sick. It can't hurt me. The pox doesn't visit you twice."

I look around. "Where's Eréndira?"

A screeching cry comes from above, and I tilt my head back to see the Owl Witch in the air, her great white wings flapping. Before I lower my gaze, Amalia manages to wrap her arms around my neck. "Gracias, Leonora." My eyes bulge at the assault, and I wheeze for air as she nearly smothers me, but when she is about to let go, I tighten my grasp. Her comforting warmth is a reminder that I'm without my heat, my vital force.

Tonalli is so complex and confusing that even the tlamatini, the knowers of things, the philosophers—puzzle over it. It resists fitting into one meaning in particular. It's impossible to fully grasp or describe. At least, not without a lot of effort and by reason alone.

God tonalli, however—how do I even begin to understand?

I force the thought to the back of my mind. The urgency of returning to the capital overtakes me. Mexico City was once my home, and I used to believe my brother would protect me if he ever learned my identity.

Will Jerónimo turn me away now?

Tezca haunts my mind. More than a year is a long time to be apart, and yet he's never far from my thoughts. He is a shadow, present but always just beyond my reach.

And Ichcatzin—he was already an enemy. I witnessed his ambition in Snake Mountain, his hunger for power. If Chipahua and Eréndira are convinced that he harbors a dark plot for Mexico, then we must heed the threat.

I have work to do.

CHAPTER 3

El Inspector

My first stop in Mexico City is at the inn Los Tres Pablos, just south of the palace, for rest and nourishment. The innkeeper's wife, a kindly woman, prepares a stew of beans and fresh tortillas. I eat like a condemned woman facing her last meal—slowly, savoring each bite, making the food spend an eternity on my tongue. Each morsel is better than anything I hunted on my best day. My belly full, I indulge in a hot bath to rid myself of the grime and stench of travel.

In the morning, I procure a simple dress from the market, a pair of soft gloves, slippers, and a cloak perfect for concealing my sword. It's not what one might expect of the viceregent of New Spain, if I even hold the title still, but it'll have to do.

I unbraid my dark hair and let it fall in loose, wavy strands. It's longer and more untamed, a reminder that my tonalli has grown alongside it, just as Zyanya said.

I redden my cheeks and lips with achiote, then look at myself in the mirror, seeing the woman I used to be.

Today, I pretend to be that woman again.

The innkeeper's wife can hardly believe I'm the same disheveled person who arrived late last night covered in filth and weariness. Neither can I.

Jerónimo, when he sees me, is just as bewildered.

"Leonora . . . is it truly you?" He rises from the dining table placed in his antechamber.

I step inside and lower my hood. "Excelencia." He admires the sweep down to my knee and the grace with which I rise.

"Oh, my prayers have been answered!" Jerónimo says exaltedly. Quickly, he moves around the table and comes to me. "The viceregent has returned from her expedition! Go! Spread the good news!" He motions to his guards, who promptly obey.

"Expedition?" I ask once they are gone.

"You've been absent for a year. I had to say something, didn't I?"

To my shock, he pulls me to him and embraces me tightly. "God's truth, I am overjoyed to see you, sister." Before I can comprehend what is happening now, he lets go, grinning. "I have been deeply troubled these past months. Are you well?"

I frown, not expecting this warm welcome. "I am."

Jerónimo has grown a short beard that makes him look older. Although he's lived fifteen years, he seems closer to forty. With a large crucifix hanging from his neck, he looks more like a man of the cloth than the viceroy of New Spain.

"God has brought you home," Jerónimo says, glowing with happiness. "This is a sign of his favor! And a cause for rejoicing!"

Under different circumstances, I would say that this isn't my home, and God has nothing to do with my return, but that would make me petulant, and careless.

"I've been praying for you," he says. "I prayed for your safe return, and now that you're here, we must thank God."

"I thought . . . you didn't want to see me."

"Nonsense! You're family. Please, sit, sit." He entwines his arm with mine, leading me to the chair closest to his. "Are you hungry? You must be hungry."

I take my seat, glancing at the feast spread across the table. A platter of Iberian ham, empanadas stuffed with meats, olives with cheese, orange tarts.

"Gracias, Dios," Jerónimo says, clasping his hands together, "for saving Leonora. Give her the strength to live as a Christian would. Help us both to do your will every day. Thank you. In Jesus's name. Amen."

I squint at him as he beckons a servant, who pours white liquid from a carafe. Despite my thirst, I can barely drink the obnoxious pulque that tastes like slime and chalk mixed into a nasty brew. The sour bite clings unpleasantly to my tongue.

"Pulque blanco," Jerónimo says with a satisfied smile. "Wonderful, isn't it?"

It isn't.

"Good for thirst. Good for the stomach. Oh, Leo. How I've missed you so."

"Did you just call me Leo?"

"Let me speak bluntly," he says, leaning back and folding his hands. "There is something I need you to do for me."

"I've only just arrived, and you're offering me a job?" I say with barely concealed suspicion.

"An opportunity. I could use someone of your . . . talents."

And there it is.

"Talents?"

"Your ability to . . . how shall I put it . . . manage difficult situations. You have a way of getting things done, Leo."

His eyes linger on me, as if he's already decided what I'm capable of.

"The Northmen have been raiding our caravans along the King's Highway," he says, "inflicting great loss of life, stealing food supplies, horses, and other valuables. Unfortunately, we have been unable to quell the growing rebellion."

Possibly, out of all the peoples in New Spain, the Spaniards fear the Northmen—Chichimeca—the most. The different tribes are spread across the northern mountains and deserts, an area the Spaniards call La Gran Chichimeca. They've never been able to subdue them, and maybe that's why they call them Northmen, as if that might lessen the threat. It almost softens them, making them seem less formidable, less dangerous.

It was on the King's Highway not long ago, that Martín and I were ambushed by the best archers in the world, and the Panther butchered them in a bloody frenzy.

Jerónimo continues. "The conflict has proved much more difficult and enduring than we anticipated. The more pressure we apply, the more fearsome the Northmen grow. I want you to go there, put down the revolt, and negotiate peace talks."

I consider the perils of making such a journey. Zyanya keeps my tonalli safe and Eréndira's people are sheltered in Tozi, but I don't have a moment to waste. "There are many others you could send on this mission."

"Yes, I know, but I wish to handle the matter quietly," Jerónimo replies. "You're the only one who can go and live to see another day. No one who isn't heavily guarded makes their way safely along the King's Highway. Hundreds are dead. Morale isn't high."

I take a sip of my drink. "Nothing some good pulque can't fix. The *real* pulque. Not . . . whatever this is."

Jerónimo is quiet, fondling the cross about his neck. "Some of the men don't seem to like the new captain general. They think him weak."

"Why?"

"Because he prays for his enemies."

I snort. "Then the new captain general *is* weak."

"*I* am the new captain general, Leonora."

Oops. "Oh."

"Jesus prayed for His enemies. He teaches us to do the same."

25

"Why not go there yourself then? Give them your heart and surround them with your love."

"Do not play with me, Leonora," Jerónimo snaps. "I cannot go. There is much to do here. The moment I leave the palace, Don Martín, the marquess of the Valley of Oaxaca, will want to claim the viceroyalty for himself. Mother sends word that he is now advised by his brother, Martín the Bastard. Those two are of too vast an ambition. I need to keep their desires in check."

This is news. I've not seen Martín since Snake Mountain fell. I didn't know he lived or that his path—like Vicereine Carlota's—had taken him to Cuernavaca, though it's not a shock. He suffered great grief in the death of Neza, which distance might make him forget. He loved him truly and mourned his loss.

"And what will you do about Cortés's heir?" I ask carefully.

Jerónimo exhales. "I don't know yet. I am waiting for Mother's correspondence. She keeps me informed of all matters concerning Don Martín."

This tells me what I need to know: that Jerónimo is not aware that Martín the Bastard is Cortés's *true* heir. He was legitimized by the pope. Martín trusted me with this secret. He warned me that if anyone found out, it would end badly for him.

"Don Martín is not of age," I say, feeding his unawareness. "He's not a threat to you."

Jerónimo slams his hand down on the table between us. "Yes, he is!" The words burst out of him. "Don Martín has numerous encomiendas as well as an extensive estate, making him the wealthiest man in New Spain. Look around, Leonora. Hernán Cortés built this palace. It belongs to his heir. How long do you think it will be before the enemy is tearing down our doors?" He leans back in his chair to rub his chin. "I must stay here. So I need you to go to Royal Road. Negotiate a peace initiative with the Northmen. Do so quickly and quietly. Don't let anyone see you. Well, not . . . *you.*"

He wants me to wear the mask of Pantera. He wants my sword

to be at his command. That Jerónimo would persecute and condemn me and now turn to see my value fills me with indignation. The hypocrisy of it.

"You hesitate. Why?"

"Their leader, Prince Xico, fell to your sword that night in battle. The Northmen would sooner roast you on a spit than agree to a peace treaty," I say, thinking they must seek revenge.

Jerónimo's reaction is one of restrained surprise, almost as if this is the first time he learns of it, but then a servant glides out of the shadows to fill his cup with more of that dreadful pulque, and his expression clears.

"You seem to forget Pantera is a wanted criminal," says Jerónimo. "Criminals face judgment. It's not something I *want* . . . but, well, I must abide by the law."

A threat? He would reveal my identity?

"Would you deny you've committed your fair share of crimes? Murder? King Carlos received a letter, a rather odd confession from Captain Nabarres right before he fell in battle, and my suspicion is you were somehow involved."

"I didn't kill Nabarres if that's what you're implying," I say. "All I did was sever his sword arm."

"That's not what his page says."

"You're going to believe a page? I'm telling the truth."

He sighs as if I'm tiresome. "You think the truth makes any difference? If the capital falls to the Northmen, we'll *all* be looking for a way to stay alive."

I raise my chin. "Fine. But I want medicine for the pox—to help with the symptoms."

"The pox?" Jerónimo asks with wide eyes. "Leonora . . . don't tell me—?"

"It's not for me. You will also release me of my court duties. After this, I am dead. Find yourself another viceregent. If you agree, I will negotiate your peace."

"I can't."

"What do you mean you can't? You're the viceroy of New Spain."

"I'm sorry, Leonora. We can discuss this another time."

What other time? I want to ask, but it's Sunday, and Jerónimo can't be late for Mass, so I'm unable to argue. I have to settle for a look of pure scorn.

This was no sweet family reunion. I rage at myself, thinking Jerónimo might have been worried for me these past months. He was only glad to see me because my arrival was opportune. Were it not for the fact that Jerónimo needs Pantera, he would've turned me away. Or worse, he would've turned me in. This was business, nothing more.

Anger simmering within me, I push open the door to the chamber that used to be mine a little unwillingly, hardly daring to breathe, knowing Inés won't be inside. I expect to find it in the deepest shadow, reflecting her death, but the curtains are open, and the room is light and airy.

An eternity passes as I stand there in the middle of the room. The pain of her loss stabs through me. Everything reminds me of her. A book still open on the table, left next to her sewing needles; her clothes; the chair she favored. I lie back on the bed, inhaling the faint but sweet scent of her on the pillows. I clench my eyes shut and sniff, desperately trying to capture it.

She is everywhere and nowhere.

I knew returning to the palace would open wounds I thought I'd healed. But like a fresh-torn scab, the pain was brought to the fore.

In my nagual, far away from the madness of the capital, I can live fully, free from past regrets and future worries. A jaguar doesn't wonder about the opinion of his prey, nor does he fumble during an attack. A jaguar never doubts himself. He knows exactly what to do. There's no room for pride or indecision in a jaguar's life.

It's far more difficult to be Leonora. To be human means dealing with doubts, bitterness, and resentment that claw at the scab. I belong to a world that doesn't exist. Neither here nor there. But I *know* the Nagual Path requires walking in the "in-betweenness."

I have no desire to squabble with Jerónimo or negotiate peace with the Chichimeca. There's a reason for my presence, however, and I'm not leaving until I get what I came for.

Sunday means the halls are filled with lords and ladies filing to Mass. The crowd parts as I stride through, heads turning and whispers trailing in my wake. Some curious, others less welcoming. Without my tonalli, I can't distinguish the murmurs, but I can imagine them: *Is that . . .? Oh my god, it is! I thought she was dead!* I nod at a few faces.

"Viceregent Leonora?"

My brisk stride is halted by a black-bearded man with sunken eyes. He doesn't seem old, but his face is lined with the burden of someone who does too much. His voice carries a note of authority, cutting through the hum of the hall.

"Yes?" I say, my voice uncertain.

The man comes to me with a sure gait. "I was informed of your return to the capital this morning, my lady. I understand you were away on official duties."

I search his grim face but see no familiarity there. I smile apologetically. "I'm sorry, señor, you are not known to me."

"My name is Rosendo Corona," he utters in a clipped tone. "I'm investigating reports of lawbreaking and corruption in the colony. There is to be a trial in a fortnight, and you are to come before the Audiencia."

"I am to do what?" I ask, sure I've misheard him.

"You're required to give an account of your actions." His voice is harsh and void of warmth, although he doesn't raise it above a whisper. "Lady, this is not a request."

"You have been terribly forward, señor," I say, undaunted. "I will be taking this up with Viceroy Jerónimo."

"You misunderstand, my lady. I have been sent by His Royal

Majesty the Emperor King Carlos. The viceroy is cooperating in this matter."

Cooperating? Jerónimo concealed this from me? This must be why he wants me to deal with the Chichimeca quietly. I bristle.

"You'll excuse me, señor," I say cordially, "I haven't time to converse."

"You have a lot to answer for, Lady Leonora," he says to my back as I walk away, now raising his voice. "Taking the identity of the witch Pantera . . . colluding with the Prince of Asturia's imposter."

Upon hearing this, I pause. How? How in the Nine Hells does he know anything? Who is this man?

I finally turn around, looking to see who is within hearing distance. This Rosendo Corona has chosen to humiliate me in front of half the court, all of whom crane their necks, trying but failing not to make it obvious they are staring.

"How dare you, señor?" I breathe out.

"We have a witness."

"You will mind your words and remember to whom it is you speak." My voice strikes like a lash. "I am the viceregent of New Spain. You attack my character, and I have done nothing wrong." Recently. "If you were the Prince of Asturias himself—you could not make me go anywhere."

"I am the Prince of Asturias," a low voice says without a flicker of amusement.

What in the Fifth Sun is this?

CHAPTER 4

La Visita

A man approaches us, finely dressed, in a black doublet with golden embroidery and ribboned shoes. On his fingers, there are many rings, and a bejeweled cross hangs over his heart, showcasing his faithful loyalty to the One True Church.

Felipe of the House of Habsburg, son of Carlos V, heir apparent to the Spanish throne. The man whom Martín impersonated, and surely, whose ears have heard of it.

This can't be good.

"The lady has said she is innocent of these accusations, Inspector Corona." He speaks softly, but his voice carries an icy calm. His mere presence fills the main hallway with command. Power will do that.

"Alteza," I say demurely.

"Felipe de Habsburgo is King of Chile," Inspector Corona corrects me.

"Majestad," I amend, dropping into a curtsey.

"Leave us," the king orders Inspector Corona.

The man nods, but there is no satisfaction on his face. He disappears out of sight.

The displeasure melts from Felipe's expression. "I hope you take no offense for Inspector Corona's boorish behavior, my lady, and I am very sorry for this unseemly introduction. I won't fail in courtesy toward you, I assure you."

A man who can apologize? Rare. A king who apologizes? Rarer still.

I don't have to stretch my imagination to see the resemblance to Martín. He is attractive, though not exactly beautiful; fair-skinned, with pale blue eyes and a protruding jaw, which I've heard to be a Habsburg inheritance. His hair is a light shade of blond, covering both his head and his chin in a short beard. It's not their faces that closely resemble each other's, but strangely, I see in him Martín's reflection.

"Sois muy justo, mi señor," I say with my head lowered, unsure whether to address him as a prince or a king.

"Thank you, my lady. Pray God I am always just."

"I . . . you have taken me somewhat by surprise," I say, trying to sound sheepish. "I was not informed of the honor of this visit. This is not a welcome fit for a king. I'm not wearing my best brocade."

Felipe pulls a rueful face, almost as if he is ashamed. "Forgive me, dear lady. This isn't how I planned our first encounter. I would've preferred a ball, a hunt, or even a corrida to mark the moment, but I confess I couldn't wait longer in my impatience to see you."

"Oh?"

"You were to become my queen," he murmurs. "It's no fault of yours, and it's all in the past. I am betrothed to another now."

"If anyone is at fault, it's the imposter, Your Majesty. We all thought he was you. He copied you well. He fooled us, and he's a traitor. Each person is responsible for their own behavior, are they not?"

"True, my lady," he says simply, "true. The impersonator will be brought to justice, whoever he is. And the one they call Pantera. I have heard of her fabled dealings all the way in Spain. She has caused quite a reign of terror."

I smile. A smile that says, *how silly*, and *I know nothing*. I've never been to Spain, but the thing about legends . . . they have a way of

32

going places. I absorb the compliment for a delicious moment. "Put your mind at ease, Your Majesty," I say stoutly. "You have nothing to fear. Pantera is dead."

"She is?"

"Well, I don't delight in gossip. I find it a horrible pastime . . . but it's the talk of the town."

"Praise Him," he says.

"Yes, praise Him. I'm sorry, Your Majesty, for the troublesome events that led to your gracious visit."

He sighs. "Indeed. My father tells me it's not easy being king."

"Felipe, it's time for your siesta," the man behind him says.

"Ya sé, ya sé," says Felipe, waving his hand. "This is my advisor and dear friend, Don Ruy Gómez de Silva. He has an uncanny knack for anticipating and catering to my desires. He's been serving my mother since he was ten."

I nod politely, but I'm barely listening. I'm thinking of how I will free myself of this predicament.

"I've had many pages throughout my youth, but Don Ruy was there when I was born," Felipe goes on, then abruptly says, "I should so like to hunt. Do you have land to hunt on?"

Now I'm alert and interested. "Oh, yes. In Chapultepec. Shall we have the horses readied?"

Felipe chokes on a laugh. "I am the Crown Prince, lady dear. I always travel in a coach with the curtains drawn."

"As you command, Your Majesty."

He gives me a sly grin, blue eyes shining. "Un favor os he de pedir. Llamadme Felipe."

"Felipe," I say coyly.

This can't be good at all.

Jerónimo stands in Mass surrounded by his closest advisors. All those men turn as I throw open the church doors.

Fray Anonasi is submerging the heads of several native men in holy water as he conducts a series of baptisms. At seeing me, he crosses himself as if to ward off some evil spirit, then looks at Jerónimo. The rest of the priests murmur amongst themselves, scowling.

Bartolo de Molina turns and hurries toward me. "Lady Leonora," he whispers so as not to disturb the service. "They said you were dead."

"Who said I was dead, Don Bartolo?"

Fray Anonasi glares at me with a familiar viciousness. He's never been fond of me because he thinks me a pagan. Well, I think him rather a fanatic. "She should be punished, excelencia," he mutters to Jerónimo. "She takes no interest in our holiness or our rites. She doesn't even notice your exceptional piety."

"Was it Fray Anonasi? Did that shriveled walnut say I was dead?" I spread my arms. "I am obviously not dead!"

Jerónimo's face is twisted with hostility. Don Bartolo tries to calm me with a soothing voice. He has proven himself to be a decent man, one of the few in Jerónimo's council. "My lady, please," he mumbles. "This is a house of prayer, not a tavern. Now isn't the time to bicker."

But I'm in the mood to bicker.

"Let's discuss this outside," he says.

"Let's discuss this right here."

"Please," he says, hurrying me away, and I begrudgingly follow him outside, down the steps, and toward the gardens of the cathedral.

"I have met la visita, Don Bartolo," I say with more serenity, walking through a row of pines. "I'm to be questioned before the Audiencia. Did you know?"

"Did I know? My lady, I believed you dead a moment ago." He releases a breath. "Inspector Corona was sent to investigate complaints lodged in the government in Madrid. It was a surprise to us all."

"Complaints? Against the viceroyalty?"

"Of course," he says as if I am a fool to ask. "The king has grown concerned over written testimonies of abuse and corruption in the New World. Not to mention, his own son was impersonated."

The Crown has kept busy with their troubles in Spain, until now it seems.

"Rosendo Corona is the king's inspector general," Don Bartolo says, "and you, or I, or Viceroy Jerónimo, can do nothing about that, my lady."

Jerónimo barges out of the church, barely containing his anger. He dismisses Don Bartolo as he flounces toward me.

"I will forgive you for this sacrilege," he says harshly, "but you will do penance."

I scoff. "Penance?"

"You will go and tell Fray Anonasi that you have defiled the Lord's house; therefore, you have sinned, and will do such penance as he may lay on you, and then perhaps God will forgive you."

My fury grows. "Is your God a ghost? I didn't see Him there."

"I will not stand here and listen to you speak blasphemously of God, Leonora. God is everywhere. In everything."

He pushes past me, fuming.

Jerónimo loves his Nailed God, his White Christ, his Church. It's who he is. And he loves order. The problem is, he thinks I'm chaos. I'm not a Christian. I wasn't born in Spain. I have an Indigenous mother. I don't know Latin. I speak different Spanish.

I can never be what my brother wants me to be.

Later, in my bedchamber, as I'm failing to fasten the row of buttons on the back of my bodice, a butterfly flies in through the open window. It swirls about for a moment, fluttering its orange and black wings, then hovers on my hand. I hold it gently, and it draws closer and closer until it comes to my outstretched finger. She is so beautiful. I watch her slowly resting her wings, and I smile, for I know Inés is with me.

"Do you require assistance with your buttons?"

The butterfly haphazardly flaps away as I give a startled jump, whirling around to find Felipe standing in the antechamber. My bodice slips, but I manage to grab it before it falls. "Your Majesty—"

He is smiling. "I didn't mean to frighten you."

"You didn't."

"Then why did you gasp?"

"That's quite silly. I'm not a gasping sort of woman."

"Where are your handmaids, my lady?" He arches a fair eyebrow. "You don't dress yourself, do you?"

"Is that so scandalous?"

"If you have no servants, how do you get people to wait upon you?"

"I'm quite capable of buttoning myself," I say, trying not to sound irritated. "Tell me, Your Majesty, do you make a practice of barging into ladies' chambers?"

His lips twitch slightly. "Ah, I have intruded where I should not. I hope you will forgive me. The servants told me you were in your quarters, but you didn't answer when I knocked. For a moment, I thought of planning to mount a rescue party."

"A rescue party?" I parrot. "Nonsense, Your Majesty. Where else would I be if not in my room?"

"Indeed," he says. "I will join you for breakfast if I may. I'm starving. And then we must take the dogs out and go hunting. You will come, won't you?"

"I have confession," I answer quickly, saying the first thing that slips into my mind.

"Ah, very well. We will break our fast and hunt after confession then."

I nod, biting the inside of my lip to keep from making a displeased face. "His Majesty may want to consider a change of wardrobe."

"Why?" He gives his clothing a look. "What's wrong with what I'm wearing?"

"Well, nothing, if you're accustomed to the heat. I suppose you never get used to it, just learn to accept it."

"I see," he says. "Lady, do you make a practice of telling newcomers how to dress when they arrive in town or is it just me you're finding fault with?"

"No—"

He laughs. "I'm only jesting, my lady. El calor no me asusta. It can get quite warm in Castille in the summer, though it's not as humid, I'll admit." Before he leaves, he says, "You should lock the door."

"Why? Am I in danger?"

He holds my gaze for a long minute as if considering the matter, looks as though he is going to say something—but then shakes his head, one small, quick jerk, like a horse twitching its ears to be rid of a fly. "I will see you at breakfast."

Fray Anonasi opens the mesh screen of his confessional booth. "Lady Leonora, have you had an awakening?"

"Forgive me, father, for I have sinned. It's been . . . I don't remember the last time I confessed."

"Do you know the words of contrition?"

"I do, but I don't speak Latin."

"Say them."

"How can I say them if I don't know what they mean?"

"What matters is God looks into your heart. He will know."

I say the prayer, and Fray Anonasi beams, pleased.

"Tell me, for what do you ask God's absolution?"

"My list of sins is long, Padre. I don't think we have enough time for all of them."

I'm not sure Fray Anonasi could survive that long in a little wooden box with no food or water at his disposal. But, then again, maybe he sits there all day munching bread and drinking wine.

"Go ahead," he says.

Whispering my sins through a screen is ridiculous. I haven't been to confession since I was a little girl. I used to go dragging my feet and scowling like a demon.

"I'm not sure where to begin. I have troubling thoughts, Padre. See, I didn't plan to live this long. I didn't expect to see past my nineteen years. I've been close to death more times than I can count. But here I am. Still alive, and . . . I'm not certain where my path leads. It's hard to secure a future for yourself when you don't think you have much time to live. Do I thank God? Of course. But if we're being honest right now, there is something wrong with me, something that gets in the way."

Fray Anonasi yawns. I can tell he's tired. Baptizing so many pagans today. "This weighs on you," he concludes.

"Sí, Padre." I nod. "I can't really live. I can't really die either. Do you see my problem?"

"You are at war with yourself, child, because you think your survival depends on this. You want to be who you are, and you aren't quite sure if you can do that."

"Yes . . ." I say, a little shocked. "I'm a fragment of myself."

"Except you're filled with resentment because you know you are in the wrong, and shame because you know you can do better, and fear that because of this, you're not at peace. You're stuck, but you don't know what to change because you don't know any different."

I'm stunned silent. Fray Anonasi has greatly surprised me. That he would understand my affliction and offer some guidance. A Christian priest of all people.

"It's time to let God's peace rule in your heart and to end this battle with yourself. The war is over. What else, my child?" he probes.

"That's really all I think about. Just life and death. Gracias, Padre, I feel so much better!" I say, rising to my feet.

"Niña . . . niña . . . but you have confessed no sin."

"But . . . I'm in the confessional, and I confessed my truth."

He makes a sound like a moaning sigh. "Let's try again. What are your sins?"

Why do I have to tell some man my sins? What affair is it of some priest what I did wrong? He's not God. He's a man. A sinner just like me. He's probably worse than me. That's another thought I can add to my record of sins.

"I disrespected the house of God," I say.

"Yes . . ."

"I have deceived, sworn, missed Sunday Mass, fingered the confections. I do so like the confections, Padre. The churros. The puddings. The custards. Oh, and the fruit and honey tamales."

Fray Anonasi's long face is creased with disapproval at my gluttony, but that's his usual expression.

"I haven't been completely honest," I say.

"Go on."

"I think that is enough."

"Tell me."

"I mean, is a lie a lie even if you only tell it to yourself?"

"Lying is lying, child," he says. "How many lies have you told?"

"It's the same lie to others as to myself, Padre. It's one big lie. I'm not who everyone thinks I am. I'm pretending."

"Many people feel that way," he says. "God knows who you really are. He knows the real you. Continue."

"Do you need more?"

"Take your time. Everything you say remains between you, me, and God," he reassures.

"You're saying you can't tell anyone?"

"The sacrament of confession is sacred," he says. "It's utterly secret."

"Padre," I say, "there's a guilt inside me."

"Guilt is the heaviest of all burdens. For what are you guilty?"

"The blood on my hands. I've killed people."

Silence. Fray Anonasi clears his throat and leans forward behind the screen. I can actually feel his breath on my face. "Were they . . . indios?" he asks in a whisper. He's probably heard the confessions of men who have gone to battle and carried out their duty, and so my confession doesn't surprise him—I think he may even be a tiny bit curious.

"Some of them," I say regrettably.

"Were they a threat?"

"Yes."

"And this troubles you?"

"Deeply, Padre."

"There's no sin in that, child."

"But . . . doesn't your god, I mean God, forbid murder?"

"A justified killing is based on love," he answers. "God makes exceptions to His commands."

"Love?" I balk. "What does love have to do with it?"

"Everything," Fray Anonasi says. "Evil exists in this world, and until evil is done away with, it must be fought against to bring peace. It's permitted to protect ourselves against an unjust aggressor."

Leave it to Christians to twist the truth to their own benefit.

"So that's it? I'm forgiven?"

"If you wish to be forgiven, you must be contrite, express your sorrow, and promise that you will not commit the sin again."

"Oh, I don't know if I can do that, Padre," I admit. I am the daughter of Quetzalcoatl, a servant of Huitzilopochtli, a disciple of Tezcatlipoca. It's in my blood to be tempted by unholy things, or as Fray Anonasi calls it, Satan's luring.

"Tell me that you are sorry, and the sacrament can be completed. Say the words and you will be forgiven."

"Yes, yes. I'm sorry. I do repent of my sins. I do!" I say exuberantly.

"Ego te absolvo a peccatis tuis in nomine Patris et Filii et Spiritus Sancti. You will go to Mass, and there you will say three Paternosters."

"Gracias, Padre."

"Go in peace."

I scoff. What an absurd thing to say.

Fray Anonasi offers his hand for me to kiss. His aging fingers glitter with jeweled rings. This angers me. The Franciscan friars are vowed to poverty.

"Padre," I say. "There is one more thing I wish to confess."

"Yes?"

"I am Pantera."

"Enough!" He slams his hands into his thighs. "Enough. No more! Get out!"

"That didn't take long." Felipe rises from a small dining table set for two as I enter his private quarters.

"Your Majesty?"

"You must have no great sins to confess!" he says, quite content. "A woman of holy purity, just like my mother."

The servants bring around grapes, figs, and sliced mangos. Felipe glances toward Don Ruy, who is standing behind him uncomfortably close, quietly regarding the floor beneath his boots. "I shall talk privately with Lady Leonora," he says. "You may go."

Don Ruy bows and the rest of the servants sweep out after him. I push half a fig into my mouth and bite down ravenously, flooding my mouth with juice.

"You're very beautiful," Felipe declares. "Your eyes. Your gaze. Your smile."

I fidget about in my chair.

"You must have known that I desired you," he says, "when I came to see you this morning in your bedchamber? In truth, I desired you from the moment I first saw you."

The last thing I'm in the mood for is to be courted like some weak-kneed debutante who swoons in the presence of powerful men.

"Sorry, am I making you uncomfortable?" he asks.

"You're a king . . ."

"I'm certain you're a virtuous lady."

"His Majesty is betrothed."

"So?"

"So," I say, "I am neither a man nor a king."

For a moment, I think he will argue, but he understands that I would be shamed.

"She's my aunt, you know," he says. "My father considered marrying her himself, but since I am younger and more likely to have children,

41

he decided it would be better for Mary to marry me instead. She will be the queen of England. Ours will be a marriage of political convenience. Nights can be lonely. Are you not, lady?"

"What?"

"Lonely."

I flush with indignation. "Your Majesty."

"*Felipe*," he corrects. "Can you say you don't want me now?"

"I will not dishonor my name. I won't be your mistress."

"But do you want me?"

I clear my throat, more and more astonished at his persistence. A lady is to always behave with courteous dignity. "I . . . can't say you're an easy man to refuse, but this is most wrong."

Felipe wants so much to believe that I want him that he says nothing else, perhaps fearing that he might get an answer he doesn't like.

Coward.

Felipe's pompous coach rattles over the rough terrain. We are swaying furiously. I press an unsteady hand to my temple, feeling the beginnings of a headache.

"Do you hunt, my lady?" Felipe moves to sit beside me.

"As in chase a creature and slaughter it?" *Yes, yes, I hunt.* "No, no, I don't hunt."

"I could teach you," he says. "Would you like to learn?"

"Ladies do not hunt, Your Majesty."

"*Felipe*. How many times must I tell you?"

Accommodating him is getting very tiring. Men must always be more clever, stronger, taller, funnier than women. A king, more so. I'm expected to treat him with grace and good manners and, if engaged in conversation, talk on a wide range of topics—and, of course, under no circumstances form an opinion. Feminine humor is acceptable, but only men joke or laugh loudly, and even they can only do so when in the company of other men or, at most, of women of ill-repute.

"Why are you not married yet, lady?" Felipe asks.

"I have been cursed enough in life," I say, sliding to put distance between us.

"Dear lady," he says. "Please. Be kind to me."

"I told you I would not lie with you. I meant it."

"May I ask for a favor then? Might I smell your neck?"

His audacity surpasses belief.

"I know. I know. I'm sorry," he says, looking deeply into my eyes. "I can't help it. I'm utterly drawn to you. All I can think of is smelling your sweet fragrance."

"Felipe, stop it. You can't say such things."

"I can say whatever I like. I'm the king's son."

I wish to cry out that I'm not some whore behind a haystack. But, instead, I pretend to almost faint, fanning myself rapidly. "My smelling salts. I need my smelling salts!"

"Oh, my lady. I humbly apologize," says Felipe. "I mean no disrespect. If I weren't already promised to another, I would offer for your hand right this moment."

His words make my head shake, each sentence more outrageous than the last. "What about the trial?"

"What about it?"

"I'm to be questioned before Inspector Corona and the Audiencia. I have been accused of wrongdoings, and though I'm innocent, I wouldn't want His Majesty's good name besmirched by keeping company with me."

"Oh, but I find your company most invigorating." The coach jerks to a halt. Felipe draws back the curtains. "It seems we've arrived." He dismounts and holds out his hand to help me down. "Shall we?"

"I would like to remain in the coach."

"What is the matter?"

I fan myself more vigorously. "I'm feeling rather lightheaded, and I'm comfortably seated here."

"My lady, you can't remain alone in the coach. Come, take my hand."

I grit my teeth and take it.

Felipe spends almost the entire day chasing after a rabbit that jumps with great strides through the woods of Chapultepec.

A rabbit.

I maintain a decorous quiet during the whole affair, surveilling the trees for any sign of the Northmen. It's the only reason I came. I don't have the slightest interest in watching Felipe chase bunnies. If the Chichimeca do decide to attack, I plan to allow myself to be captured and negotiate their withdrawal from Royal Road. The sooner I do that, the sooner I can return to Tozi.

A broken arrow on the ground tells me they are here, somewhere.

"Lady Leonora," Felipe says behind me.

I turn around.

"You shouldn't wander alone in the woods. It's easy enough to get lost during the day."

"It's a good thing you found me then," I say.

Finally, the hounds bring the rabbit down in a stream. Felipe goes into the water, laughing.

"Victory to King Felipe!" Don Ruy shouts, and there is a burst of trumpets.

"I always win," Felipe says. He approaches me cheerfully, holding the dead rabbit by the ears. "I have caught it! My lady, you bring me luck."

"Well done. His Majesty has demonstrated superiority over a rabbit," I say tartly.

Felipe smiles and then frowns at my comment, not entirely sure what to make of it. A stream of red blooms around him, staining his clothes and hands. "I'm sorry about all this blood. You need not be frightened, my lady."

"Why would blood frighten me?" I ask. "Women see a lot more blood than this." I take the animal's blood and smear it across my forehead. "A badge of honor."

Felipe is silent. Perhaps he's at a loss at the abruptness of my reply or my bold behavior.

"I think her very pleasing, Ruy," I hear him say as I walk ahead. "She has the wits to match her exquisite beauty."

Much to my dismay, it goes on like this all day.

I don't have time for this nonsense. Every time I find a moment to take my leave, there he is, offering an arm, a word, a smile. He's exhausting to the point of incapacitation.

When, finally, I can lie in bed, I'm numb and blank-brained, cursing him. I shiver from a sudden chill. My skin is icy cold.

It's starting. The symptoms of tonalli loss.

I slink deeper under the covers. I imagine a nice warm soup. Tonatiuh. A fire. Something far. The desert.

Tezca . . .

CHAPTER 5

El Acuerdo

"You are *encouraging* this?" I spit out in disbelief.

Jerónimo sits in his study over a parchment, furiously writing, so absorbed in his task that he barely acknowledges me. Occasionally, his head rises, but only to dip the quill in ink. He has received word of at least fifty of his men slaughtered by the Chichimeca in the outpost of San Miguel de Allende, forcing its abandonment.

"He's a prince," Jerónimo says flippantly. "And a king."

"And so I must not keep him at arm's length? He is to wed Mary Tudor, Jerónimo."

"A spinster."

"I'm confused. Is adultery not sinful? Is it not immoral in the eyes of your Nailed Christ to fool around with another woman's man?"

"Betrothed isn't married," he says. The quill stops moving, and I think he will look up, but he reaches toward the inkwell instead.

"You're not even *listening* to me."

He puts the parchment down and gives me a weary look. "I don't have time for this! The Northern warriors continue to ravage the land. Raids. More raids." He holds up letter after letter. "An opportunity has arisen, Leonora. If King Felipe has taken a liking to you, then bewitch him."

"I'm sorry. Did you say, 'bewitch him'?"

"You are a witch, yes? Enchant him."

"I will not be his whore," I retort.

He sighs, his patience dwindling. "Leonora."

"Is that what you want?"

"You can think of it as a game of deception. And who better than you to play it? You are my cross to bear, sister, and I offer you up in my prayers. But you are indeed good at playacting. It's no wonder you were able to fool everyone so easily . . . Pantera."

I'm not above using flirtation to good advantage. I've done plenty of worse things to survive. But this is absolute folly, and I can't believe my brother is blind to it.

"You need his favor," Jerónimo counsels. "With Inspector Corona's investigation, having the king's son vouch for you could save your life. Or is it your wish to be burned at the stake?"

"I'd fight," I say, considering it.

"And then what? Well, tell me. What are you to do? You can't fight all the time."

"So, your solution is that I should open my legs instead?"

"For God's sake, Leonora. You know what he wants. You can use that for your own gain."

I would shout, except I can't manage it. I'm tired. Every second without my tonalli is a second closer to death.

"You know, there is no eleventh commandment," Jerónimo says. "Perhaps it never made it down the mountain with Moses. But if there was, I believe it would say, 'Thou shalt appease the king.'"

"He's not *the* king. He's *a* king," I say stubbornly. "The only reason he's a king is because he was given the title to the distant kingdom of Chile by his father to make him more regal to Mary Tudor, heir to the English throne. You say I'm good at pretending? Felipe is nothing but a prince playacting as a king. And what about you, Jerónimo? Is this all an act of holiness?"

Anger flashes across his face. "You dare suggest I'm playing at piety?"

"You tell me. I'm no Christian. It seems you're picking and choosing which commandments to obey and interpreting them to suit your needs."

"I read my Bible for two hours every day," Jerónimo says. "I go to Mass three times a day. I take Communion every Sunday. I pray so much that the skin of my knees is becoming hard. I'm not yet sixteen, but I have the knees of a saint."

"Then I pray, dear brother, your God does not give you the end of a saint too."

I leave the room in a fury. I know how to anger Jerónimo—ever since we were children—and I may have succeeded in provoking him far more effectively than he did in irritating me, but he's the viceroy of New Spain. I need him. Much is at stake. Much is in danger.

A moment later, I storm back into his study. He's pouring wine into his cup, and my sudden entrance startles him enough that a little sloshes over the rim.

"I have to pretend all the time that I enjoy his company," I say indignantly. "And I have to go on walks with him. And listen to him. And amuse him."

Jerónimo thumps the wine jug onto the table with an irritated clatter. "Felipe is the greatest debauchee in court. They've dubbed him the 'Babymaker' for a reason."

"And?"

"And you have childbearing hips."

I give him a scathing glance.

"King Felipe wants an heir. Or rather, a spare. His last wife died due to complications of childbirth. He has a son, but rumors in the Spanish court have given rise that he is a mentally feeble child."

"I don't care what he wants," I say, my voice rising shrilly. "Don't be fooled by my dress, Jerónimo. I'm not a lady. I'm a warrior. You wanted me to settle your peace, yes? We're wasting time. The

48

Chichimeca are wanderers spread across the entire valley. If a war breaks out, it will be a war to the end of the world."

He sits back in his chair, pensive. "What do you suppose is behind his visit?"

"Who?"

"King Felipe."

I shrug. "Someone impersonated him. He wants the truth."

He scoffs. "You believe King Felipe would cross oceans just for the truth?"

"Do you have a better explanation?"

"I can't say for certain why he's here, but one thing's clear: this investigation could drag on for weeks . . . or even months."

Months? A cold wave of dread washes over me. I don't have that long.

"Visitadores generales cause problems," Jerónimo continues. "Inspector Corona is a representative of the king and has powers superior to mine, military as well as political. He can demand to see any documentation, interrogate anyone, investigate all sorts of conditions. If he finds even the smallest sliver of offense and believes the viceroyalty involved with illicit activities, he will report directly to the king. And then may God help us all."

"Oh, Jerónimo," I say. It's all making sense now.

Jerónimo couldn't agree to my terms because, so long as Inspector Corona remains in Mexico, *he* is in power.

"It's temporary," Jerónimo assures.

"Why didn't you just tell me?"

He shrugs as if it's of no matter to him one way or the other. Either way, he has limited authority. Either way, he mustn't intervene with the investigation. Either way, the Chichimeca continue to cause trouble.

"Why are you so afraid of this investigation?" I ask. "Of Inspector Corona?"

"I'm not afraid of him. I simply don't want him here. The sooner the Northmen leave the King's Highway, the sooner we can breathe easier about Inspector Corona's presence. He must not find out that we're in the throes of a rebellion. We must all retrace our steps and show ourselves loyal subjects of the Crown. Do you understand?"

The viceroy serves at the pleasure of the Crown. Few have lasted more than five years. Jerónimo is smart, yet he's young and inexperienced. And though the law says that Jerónimo is just as Spanish as peninsulares, in truth he is not. He speaks their language, professes their religion, and even thinks of life on their terms. Nevertheless, he was not born in the Mother Country, and that makes him inferior, weak even, for the New World climatic conditions somehow have an enervating effect, physically, mentally, and morally. That's what the cosmographers claim.

For the moment, I realize, we need each other.

"Very well," I say. "I will do this. But after Inspector Corona is gone, you will provide what I have asked for, and I will be free of my responsibilities as viceregent. Do we have an agreement?"

He nods rather feebly.

"Tell me we have an agreement."

"Yes, fine. We have an agreement. Now get to work."

CHAPTER 6

La Muerte

My heeled slippers carry me with great purpose all the way to Cortés's private headquarters. The last time I was here, Martín made himself at home. I didn't know he was Cortés's son then, posing as the king's son. It seems like years ago.

Don Ruy ushers me inside, where Felipe is twirling knives, then throwing them at a target on the wall with surprising accuracy.

"Can you not see that I am busy, Ruy?"

"My king, it's—"

"Whatever it is can wait until I'm finished."

I clear my throat. He turns around and sees me standing in the antechamber.

"My lady. How did you get in here?" There's a subtle edge to his voice.

"I was announced," I say, "but it seems His Majesty was lost in thought and failed to hear Don Ruy."

He flicks his fingers, a gesture for Don Ruy to leave us, while never taking his gaze from me. His eyes seem tired.

"Why are you here, my lady?"

"I wished to see you," I say warmly. "You seem distraught. Is something troubling you?"

He clenches his teeth, then throws another knife.

"Felipe, I hope you will not refuse my friendship."

"Yes, well, you've denied us any carnal pleasures . . ."

Another knife. Another throw.

"Perhaps we can find something more stimulating for you to do," I say.

"I can think of several stimulating things to do."

I look down at my slippers as if in an agony of embarrassment. That's what a modest woman would do.

He shakes his head as if awakened. "I've been unforgivably rude. I'm sorry, my lady. It's not you. It's my son. Carlos." He walks to his desk and holds up a piece of parchment. "This letter arrived today from Spain. They tell me Carlos held a dagger to a cardinal and hurled a shoemaker out the window." He lets out a breath, inhaling another to calm himself before speaking. "My poor son. He endures some physical abnormalities. I can attest to his good memory and wit, yet he's given to outbursts of violent temper . . . unpredictable."

"Is there anything I might do to help?"

"You're too kind, my lady," he says with a watery smile. "Keep him in your prayers."

If he has no sons, Felipe has no legacy.

"I will do that. You have my promise," I say. "Perhaps . . . another Habsburg heir will ease many worries?"

"My lady?"

"Surely, his Majesty must feel the need to have more royal princes of your blood to ensure the succession. It's both wise and prudent, for your sake as well as your father's own peace of mind."

Felipe laughs shortly and sends another knife flying, hitting the wooden board. "Believe me. I am trying," he says. "My father wishes me to stop taking lovers. María is not yet my wife. But I do what I have to do. I don't skimp my duty."

I move closer to him, letting my fragrance infuse his senses.

"Are you?" I say in a low, sultry voice. "Trying?"

The seed has been planted. It begins to take root and is now growing, being tended to. I water it several times that day, little flirtatious exchanges here, a sultry smile there. I know the seed is showing signs of bearing fruit when Don Ruy arrives at my bedchamber the next day carrying a gift from Felipe. A bracelet heavy with pearls and purple stones fashioned into a cross design.

Jewelry. How revolutionary.

"Return it," I demand.

"My lady?"

"Return it."

Don Ruy blinks confusedly then leaves.

Two times more, Felipe sends a gift. The second is a black and yellow embroidered cloak, the heraldic colors of the House of Habsburg, the fabric stunning. On the third occasion, after returning a carved bust of Felipe himself, I hear him snap from the bottom of the stairs.

He finds me on the second floor, under one of the balcony arches.

"Felipe," I say quietly.

"Why did you return my gifts?"

I look away, trying to appear timid. "Your attentions are flattering, and you will make a wonderful husband to Mary Tudor, but I'm a devout Christian, full of faith and virtues and honor. I can't be anyone's mistress, no matter . . . how I feel for you."

Another seed.

"Sheer lunacy, Leonora!" Jerónimo rages. "I can't believe what I'm hearing. You were to entertain him."

"He is entertained," I say slyly.

*

I expect Felipe's visit, so I wait. Like a damn fool, I wait. I have to wait, lest he finds that Lady Leonora has disappeared from the palace. That would be unseemly. And suspicious.

To my surprise, he doesn't visit all day, but I'm sure he will come, and I prepare myself to keep him interested but under control.

This is reckless—reckless and stupid. What am I doing? I should be negotiating a peace treaty, I should have my tonalli returned to me—something, anything—not sitting around, planning to lead Felipe on, to keep him dancing at arm's length.

When he doesn't come, I realize I am anxious to see him. Not for desire, of course, but because the trial is to begin soon.

Two days elapse. I start to wonder if I've truly offended him, if Jerónimo was right and I have lost him. I can't think. Did he say he was going somewhere? Did he say anything?

I try hard to remember, but there is numbness inside my head like a penetrating fog. This morning, I saw a bird in my bedchamber circling above me, before it precipitously dove to the bed. I screamed. It was my imagination.

"Have you seen Felipe?" I ask Jerónimo as we break our fast.

He frowns. "You asked me that already."

"I did?"

"Just a moment ago. I told you I haven't seen him." Jerónimo notices that I'm pushing food around my plate, hardly eating. "Are you unwell, sister?"

I swallow past the ache in my throat. "I'm merely tired."

"In the middle of the day?"

"My night was disturbed." The quiver in my hand reminds me I'm dying. The fork slips from my fingers, clattering onto the table. How can I hope to bend Felipe to my will when I can't even hold a fork? "It's just a passing condition. I've been through this before."

"Sleeplessness, dullness, poor appetite . . ." he says. "Is your blood coming regularly?"

I groan in response. A pale female needs a male they say. Such are the signs of being labelled a sufferer from green sickness, the disease of virgins. "I'm *fine*," I say, sliding my shaking hands under the table. "Where do you think he is? Why would Felipe court me and then not come at all? I know what you're thinking. Don't say I told you so."

"You must take care of yourself, sister. Remain abed and mend. Perhaps he will come tomorrow."

But he doesn't. Another day goes past, and then another.

Finally, on the fifth day, Don Ruy, running ahead of his master in the interior courtyard, announces him. "¡El rey Felipe!"

I have to feign emotion, to look vigorous, like a woman in love.

"Good day, Lady Leonora," Felipe says.

I curtsey. "I should like to be alone with His Majesty," I tell Don Ruy. "You may go."

Felipe chuckles lightly. "You command very smoothly. You could have been my queen. We would have ruled Old and New Spain together. You and me."

If I had wedded him. If Martín hadn't impersonated him. If I was a Spanish lady with a duty to the Crown. Alas, I am not enamored by a king who is not yet the king.

"Indeed, Felipe."

I want to ask where he's been, but I'm afraid he'll be confused, since we've been together all week—I just don't remember it.

"Is there something else, my lady?"

"I find your company most invigorating," I say, tossing his own words at him.

"May I suggest a stroll through the gardens? It might lift my spirits, with the investigation soon to commence."

"Of course," Felipe agrees and steps forward to lead the way. "You need not worry. You are blessed, Lady Leonora. You will overcome."

I say "Amen" with conviction, but I can feel the tiredness inside me like a worm, slowly but deliberately sapping my life.

We walk in silence for a moment, with the scent of pine and the delicate perfume of dahlias. Tonatiuh's breath, warm and gentle, stirs the leaves and teases the aromatic oils from the bushes.

"When I was a little girl," I say, "there used to be a guanábana tree here. I have always liked the taste. It's one of the fruits that has always fascinated me, certainly one of my favorites. Chirimoyas too."

"What of the tree?" asks Felipe. "What happened to it?"

The image of the tree is vivid in my mind, though it's long gone now, like so many other things from my childhood. "I'm not sure. They don't grow quickly. About three or four years to bear fruit. I used to climb it, despite the protests of my father. He would scold me for dirtying my dress or risking a fall, but I never listened. I would perch up there for hours, hidden among the leaves."

"You were a fearless child, then."

Those were simpler times, when my greatest concern was whether I could sneak a guanábana before dinner. The Panther within me yearned for freedom.

Felipe plucks a flower from a dahlia bush and brings it to my nose. "Do you know there's never been a woman before you who refused me?"

"It was not you whom I refused. I refused your gifts."

He throws his hands up in defeat. "Great God above, you push me away and then you draw me in. I am undone, my lady. I am mad for you."

"Felipe."

"I *know*. I have given you offense. I'm sorry. My life has been difficult lately, and I have been forward in my attentions to you. I sent you those gifts as a means of making amends, to show you that there is great depth to my feeling for you."

I actually feel the sincerity in his words.

"That first time I saw you with Inspector Corona," he says, "I watched you for a moment before you saw me, and I thought to myself then, if I should let her, there is a woman who can easily break my heart."

Such a riveting speech. So dignified, so perfect, so sweet. Truly, Felipe's path lies in politics.

"What are you thinking?" he asks.

"I'm thinking you'll make a great king."

I look down at the dahlias, open, beautiful, red, the color of fire and blood. It makes me think of the Precious Flower, Xochiquetzal. I can't go anywhere without being reminded of Tezca. That is how it is with the gods who rule the skies, the soil, the wind. They demand to be seen.

"One day, Lord willing," Felipe says, looking at the garden. Then he looks back at me with the saddest expression. "But I want more."

"What more could you possibly want?"

"What I want is to feel loved as a man is loved, not as a king is coveted for what his position affords. It was like this for my father. He married my mother with great joy and fell in love with her. When I grew older, I began to understand that they felt a real desire for each other—it was not just a powerful partnership of two great monarchs. They say I was conceived during their honeymoon in Granada. It happened during a hot siesta, weary from the hunt. It was their love, their lust, which drove them. Almost as much as God."

"You're a passionate man."

"Indeed. I come from passionate stock—and what about you, my lady?"

"What about me?"

"Have you known love?" he asks.

I've worn my mask for so long that my lying breath comes quickly. Not the mask of Pantera, of course. The real me. My real feelings buried so deep. "I'm unmarried. I've no experience in such matters. I must defer to your familiarity with the subject."

"My first wife Manuela . . ." he says. "She was the mother of my son. There was respect and mutual understanding. Not love. I'm not talking about marriage, my lady. I'm talking about true, unlimited passion, the most burning carnal desire you could ever dream of. I'm talking about wanting to be with someone so much that you can't think of anything else. Love began with God when he created the world and us. And what is love if not holy? Do we not worship the people we love?"

He sounds tortured, miserable, and perhaps my mask of deception is slipping because I am quiet, thinking on his words. His voice is filled with the lament of someone who has loved and lost. I know this pain because I too have known desire and longing. "You are in love. I can't say I have an inkling of what you're suffering."

"Once," he says, "a long time ago."

Even without my tonalli, I can see through the lie. His voice falters just slightly at the end. The wound is far too fresh. It sounds like he's trying to convince himself as much as me. "What happened?"

He hesitates. "They betrayed me in the worst way."

"How?"

"They made promises. Spoke of loyalty, trust, a future. I believed them . . . I thought . . . we could change the world together." He lets out a bitter laugh. His hurt radiates like heat off a flame. "But they betrayed every word, every vow. Gave what we'd built to my enemies, as if it meant nothing."

He closes his eyes, as if trying to shut out the memory. When he opens them again, he pastes on a forced smile, one that doesn't reach the depths of his gaze. "It's all insignificant now," he says, his words rehearsed, as if he's told this story over and over to keep from feeling the pain beneath it. He then leans in, his hand reaching up to brush a strand of hair from my face. "I wish very much to kiss you." His head lowers to do just that.

"You must really stop this," I say, looking away.

Felipe releases a weary breath, his hand still hovering. "Why? Because I'm betrothed? Is that your reason?"

"Yes." *I have a cold?* Too feeble. He'll never believe it. I should make a fuss, be indignant, make him feel guilt. *Shame on my family? Dishonor?* "Because—because I have deployed your lust and covetousness. This is a sin. A sin of vanity and sin of pride." He turns around, inhaling sharply. "And, because . . ." I reach for his hand, waiting, careful with how I approach this very dangerous act. "I feel the same."

He faces me again. My eyes are downcast, but slowly, in the silence, I look up at him. When my face is upturned to his, he can't resist the unstated invitation. He bends and kisses me.

I take his kiss. He overpowers me with the touch of his lips. In his embrace, the kiss deepening, I feel nothing. With my eyes closed, his arms firmly around me, I slip into a pit where there is only darkness . . . and Tezca. It terrifies me, and I shudder as Felipe's tongue sweeps inside my mouth. I can feel his desire for me rising so strongly that I let him go at once.

As I step back, a man plummets from the sky with a sickening thud.

I freeze, the horror jolting me from the moment I was wrapped in just before. The man's head hits a large rock with a brutal, bone-crunching impact, the force splitting the skin open like an overripe fruit.

A cold dread sinks into my chest. I'm no stranger to corpses, but this one strikes me differently. I stagger to the side, thinking of how quickly everything can change.

Someone screams. Someone faints. Someone makes the sign of the cross.

Felipe stretches his arm across me, grabbing blindly at his weapon. "My lady, stay back."

Fray Anonasi has fallen to his death.

Tongues are quickly loosened throughout the palace.

"Did you hear about Fray Anonasi?"

"Sounds gruesome. I wonder if he did this deliberately."

"There was no note. And why would a priest take his own life?"

All of court titters with conversation. Four or five versions of his death circulate, depending on who you ask.

The first is that Fray Anonasi's heart failed, which resulted in his fall. This is the least fanciful version. But there is disbelief that such a pious and gentle man could succumb to a sudden seizure of the heart. His physicians can't account for it.

The second version is somewhat similar but adds an intent to die.

He was in his bedchamber, feeling like an insect about to be crushed by the world. He felt disconnected from his Church, his God. He walked to the balcony and looked down. He was in a desperate struggle. He jumped.

The third version represents an evolution of the second.

Fray Anonasi is very distressed, because he stood accused of breaking the confessional seal. A charge that, if proven, would lead to his disgrace and shunning. He couldn't cope with Inspector Corona's investigation into his conduct, the details and the source for which he was never told. He refused to eat, drink, even pray. He jumped.

The fourth version was built on the second and third versions, but with a new detail: mushrooms.

Specifically, teonanacatl.

The intoxicating "flesh of the gods" excites the consumer with bliss and visions, some laughable, others frightful. The work of Satan unquestionably. The missionaries had attempted to destroy all records and evidence of the use of teonanacatl. Nevertheless, Fray Anonasi ingested the mushroom to escape his tortured mind. Out of his senses, he heard Jesus Christ calling him, he saw serpents, his legs full of worms eating him alive. He flailed helplessly out of his bedchamber, wanting to be rid of them, and at the peak of his intoxication, he fell.

The fifth and final version is the only one that absolves Fray Anonasi and points to someone *else*.

This version talks about different theories for murdering a Franciscan missionary: revenge, frustration, perhaps he knew something he wasn't supposed to? One of his servants, whose job it was to wake Fray Anonasi every morning for Mass, swears a chest filled with great value disappeared from his room. The man had taken a vow of poverty, though he did not own little.

There is just no evidence to support that version. In fact, there is no evidence to support any version. But there are plenty of rumors. In the palace, gossip is currency.

Inspector Corona reassures court that it was likely a pure matter of natural causes which led to Fray Anonasi's fall. "It was a tragic, tragic end," he says. "May God give his soul eternal peace and a safe resting place. We will pray for him."

Following Fray Anonasi's funeral service, Inspector Corona orders that everyone remain in the palace while his investigation is in progress.

"He can do that?" I ask Jerónimo.

"Yes," he says.

"So what do we do now?"

"Do?"

"Have you forgotten the Chichimeca camp on Royal Road? My condition progresses rapidly. I need my strength if I'm to negotiate with them. What do we do?"

"For God's sake, Leonora, a priest has died! Show some respect."

"There is nothing we can do for the dead. What matters is the future. Best to move on."

"Tell me this wasn't you," he says in a low voice.

"What?"

"Tell me you haven't made a fool of me yet again."

I give a small chuckle. "You think *I* killed him?"

"Everyone knows you hated Fray Anonasi. All of church heard your insults. You called him an old goat."

"I called him a shriveled walnut."

The correction annoys Jerónimo.

"I did hate him," I admit. "When he was alive. But now he's dead. And if God has called Fray Anonasi home, who am I to disagree with His will?"

Jerónimo dares not argue with the will of God.

What I don't tell him, or anyone else, is that Fray Anonasi by the grace of his God survived the fall for a passing moment, sparing me only a fleeting glimpse of his eyes bulging with surprise. They gazed into mine as his mouth spluttered with blood. One word was all he could force to leave his throat: *help*.

At least, that's what I think happened.

Of course, I could be wrong. I question this certainty, telling me that it might all be my imagination. I go to bed wondering whether what I heard was real.

That, or Fray Anonasi wasn't planning on going to his grave anytime soon.

Death is sneaking around me, and I can't afford to be distracted, to let my guard down—not even for a second.

I'm afraid, but by the gods, I will never show it.

CHAPTER 7

La Investigación

While Fray Anonasi's death shocks many, few grieve for him. There is weeping but little. No one truly succumbs to grief. Inspector Corona busies himself with his investigation, Jerónimo can think of nothing but his own worries. Felipe is at the center of everything, and nobody can take his eyes off him. And in this court where everyone sticks to etiquette, schemes for position, and covets the privilege of serving the king's son, Felipe favors *me*.

"May I ask a promise of you?" I ask him.

Felipe reaches out to catch my gloved hand, clutching it between his own. "Anything. I'll make a case for your innocence—whatever you need. I'll speak to Inspector Corona."

"My request is not that His Majesty intercedes . . . but that you pray for me." A tear slips down my cheek, but I hurriedly wipe it away. I look up, my eyes hopeful again. "You are the king's son. Your prayers are anointed. Surely, they will reach Heaven."

"I won't let anything happen to you," he confirms. "I promise."

"My king," I say, fighting a smile.

The Habsburg Empire in the New World is controlled by three heads: first, the authority in Spain itself.

Second, the administration in the New World, through the vice-royalty, governors, and other public servants.

Third, the Royal Audiencia in the city of Mexico, the highest court of justice in the colony. It's comprised of its acting president, Inspector Corona, and four judges to hear cases, render decisions, and dispense justice: Cino Mondragon, Bartolo de Molina, and two others recommended by King Carlos who tragically did not survive the rigors of a trip across the Atlantic Ocean, so I don't have to worry about them.

I stand before these powerful men now in the ayuntamiento, engulfed by a deafening silence.

Inspector Corona breaks it. "We are met to render justice. Lady Leonora," he begins, peering down at me from his raised bench. "You have been accused of taking the identity of the criminal Pantera. How do you plead?"

"Innocent," I say with just the proper note of outrage. Around me, a dozen quills scratch.

"Lady Leonora, you have been accused of conspiring with King Felipe's impersonator. How do you plead?"

I look to Felipe, circled by dons and doñas like wasps around a tart of marmalade. He gives me a courteous nod, and I respond with a confident smile.

"Innocent," I reply.

"You plead not guilty to these accusations?"

"I do."

The wrinkles in Inspector Corona's forehead deepen, as do the crow's feet marking his eyes. "On your wedding day," he continues, "your betrothed confessed to being an imposter." His scraggly black beard touches his sternum when he looks down. "Lady Leonora?"

"That wasn't a question," I say, "so I don't have an answer."

"Did you know he was an imposter prior to his confession?"

My voice remains firm and in control. "No, I didn't. I noticed some oddities from the very beginning, but I kept my thoughts to myself."

"Oddities?"

"Well, I couldn't say for sure, of course. He seemed to know things he shouldn't—I heard him once or twice say a few words in Nahuatl—and yet he was strangely clueless about other matters. He hesitated before answering questions, like he was carefully choosing his lie. And it always seemed like he steered conversations away from anything too personal. But I simply thought them minor quirks. Perhaps I didn't want to believe there was more to it, so I convinced myself they were nothing of real consequence. Our Lord God is merciful and gracious. It was He who planted in me this suspicion like He planted a garden in Eden."

Inspector Corona smiles reassuringly, but his gaze remains cold. "Did God happen to tell you who the imposter was?"

"No, I don't know the imposter's identity. It's not for us to know the infinite knowledge of God, Inspector."

"The imposter never mentioned anything of significance? Nothing at all?"

I shake my head. "Not a word."

"Never said anything against the viceroyalty?"

"I don't believe so, no," I reply. "My memory is sound, and I do not recall."

"It would seem . . ." Inspector Corona says, "that there wasn't anyone closer to the imposter than you, Lady Leonora. And somehow, you know nothing."

His stare pierces me like he's trying to force himself into my thoughts through sheer will. I lift my chin, letting him know I won't be intimidated. I have nothing to fear.

Felipe interjects, "The lady has already answered your questions. Move on to something else, Inspector."

Inspector Corona straightens, his head high. "You weren't born in Spain, correct?"

"That's a strange question . . ." I answer.

"Yes or no?"

"No."

"You're the daughter of Don Joaquín, the former viceroy, and an Indian woman?"

The room buzzes with whispered conversations. The question has nothing to do with the accusations, and yet Inspector Corona asks. He asks because I'm a woman and a mestiza. Neither is much worth in the eyes of a peninsular Spaniard.

Jerónimo is up from his chair. "I must object to this line of questioning. It's well beyond any possible relevance to this trial."

I have to admire Jerónimo's attempt, in the guise of an objection, to redirect the Audiencia's attention.

"This strikes me as highly relevant to bias against Lady Leonora and her views," says Inspector Corona. "Please sit down, Your Excellency. Viceregent, you may answer."

I suppress a grimace. "Yes, my mother was Mexica."

Inspector Corona lowers his head and scribbles on his parchment. After a long moment of quiet, he speaks again.

"There have been reports of Pantera's return to the streets."

Those gathered shift uneasily, murmuring amongst themselves.

"Your information is untrue, Inspector," I say in an even tone. "Pantera has not been seen since the earthquake last year and is presumed dead. If anyone claims they've sighted her, they are surely sighting phantoms."

"I hear many things—such as the claim that you yourself *are* Pantera."

Inspector Corona bangs his gavel to quiet the babble filling the hall.

I tilt my head, letting a small, amused smile slip across my face. "So I am accused of both pretending to be her *and* actually being her? Well, that is just silly, isn't it? I've already made my innocence clear. Surely there are others who would claim to be Pantera. Anyone can don a mask and declare themselves the witch, Inspector. In fact, New Spain could have as many Panteras as it needs."

The room hushes as I continue, my voice calm, indifferent.

"In my view, the mask is merely a reminder, much like the cross I carry around my neck, Inspector." I touch the silver pendant, worn deliberately for this moment. "It reminds me of my faith, and it gives me strength in times of difficulty."

"Are you saying the mask offers the same kind of strength? You would liken defying the law and inciting rebellion to God's promise of eternal life?"

"No, I'm saying you can't chase a belief even with the swiftest horse. It's not the mask that gives strength—it's what it represents. Don't you see, Inspector? The mask is not to hide but to create."

"Create?"

"A symbol," I reply. "And in this way, everlasting. So, what does it matter who the girl was? Or what she did. Or how she lived. Or where she came from. Or what she looked like. What can it possibly matter to us? Pantera, the first one, as far as we know, is dead."

"Is that so?" Inspector Corona looks like he wants to say something else, but he moves on. "Are there any witnesses?" he calls. "Well? If there are any witnesses, would they come forth?"

"That would be me," a young voice declares.

"Speak up, niño," Inspector Corona says, "so we can all hear you."

I turn my gaze to the boy coming forward. I try not to frown as I search my memory. If I've seen him before, I have no recollection of it.

"I was there," he says, "on the battlefield."

The battlefield? *What* battlefield? My mind races, thinking of every battle I've faced. What does this boy know, and why is he here now?

"What is your name, niño?" Inspector Corona asks.

"Tomás," the boy answers. He looks around, awkwardly, like he isn't quite sure what he's supposed to do.

"You are Don Cino's page?" Inspector Corona asks.

The boy—Tomás—nods.

"And before Don Cino?"

"I was Captain Nabarres's page."

My heart is pounding, and I'm having trouble catching my breath. Nabarres's page—I remember him now; he never left his side, and he was there with him when the Tzitzimime came, right up until one of the Cihuateteo snatched him away. I chose not to wear a mask that night. I wasn't hiding.

Tomás saw Pantera's face.

"What did you do for Captain Nabarres?"

Tomás scratches the back of his neck. "I cleaned his armor and weapons, took care of his horse, accompanied him to battle."

"Tell us what happened on the night of his death," Inspector Corona prompts.

"He was killed," Tomás abruptly says. "Pantera killed him in battle." There's an odd lilt to his voice, almost dramatic.

A frenzy of disorder takes over the room. Inspector Corona's gavel comes down once again.

"You are certain of this, niño?"

Tomás nods. "Positively. I saw Pantera myself."

Panic rises. Viceroy Jerónimo stands and harshly says, "Inspector Corona."

Inspector Corona gives him a bored look. "Your Excellency, do you have a question?"

"Yes. That question would be, what is the relevance of this testimony to the matter at hand?"

"The relevance will be apparent when the witness answers my next question," Inspector Corona says, then turns his attention to Tomás. "Do you know the identity of the masked witch?"

"Yes," Tomás replies steadfastly.

I swallow hard, feeling a bead of sweat trickle down my spine.

"Do you see her today?"

"I do."

"Would you point her out for us?"

"No, I'm not going to point her out. She is here."

"Describe where she is. You don't have to point."

"She's in this hall."

"Where in the hall, niño?"

"Somewhere in the vicinity of the hall."

"Why won't you tell us where she is?" Inspector Corona asks, irritated.

Tomás frowns. "There are too many people."

"Can you walk around and have a look?"

"I think so."

The hall remains quiet. All I can hear are Tomás's steps getting close, then retreating, then approaching again. This boy is toying with me. He's proved to me just how far he is prepared to go—or not go. What sort of game is he playing, pretending he doesn't see me in the room? What is he trying to accomplish?

After an interminable amount of time, Inspector Corona says, "Are you finished with the examination of this hall, niño?"

"I'm not sure," Tomás says fearfully. "It's a large room."

"You've looked at everyone."

After some fruitless back and forth, those in attendance rise from their seats, showing and shouting their impatience and disapproval.

"Enough!" Inspector Corona commands. The hall quiets, and he says, "This session is adjourned. We will break for lunch and reconvene in an hour."

The crowd begins to disperse, grumbling as they make their way out of the building.

I have one hour.

"What game is this you play, niño?"

Tomás jumps back as he opens the door, startled by the voice coming from the shadows of Don Cino's antechamber. He wasn't expecting me, though I'd anticipated his return here, where he'd be nearby for whatever Don Cino might need. I step forward into the sunlight streaming through the windows. I'm not wearing my mask;

after his little performance in the hall, there's no need for it. Doubt now clouds every accusation.

But even maskless, Tomás looks at me with awe. "Pantera." He steps inside, closing the door quickly behind him. "I knew you would come," he exclaims, his voice vibrating with excitement. "I knew it. I knew it!"

"I'm not who you think I am."

"I *know* it's you."

"Whatever fantasies you hold about Pantera don't belong to me." I pause, studying him. "What is it you want from her?"

A sly smile. "How do you know I want something? Maybe I'm an admirer and just wished to say hello."

"What is it you want? Is it riches?"

He snorts. "No."

"Did Inspector Corona promise you something?"

"No."

"Then what do you want?"

"I need you to kill my master. Don Cino."

Of all the things I expected, it wasn't this. *"What?"*

"He's cruel to me," he says, his voice trembling with anger. "He—he makes demands I can't meet and punishes me. Just one life. Should be easy for Pantera."

Cino Mondragon. A man of power, a source and dealer of information, fanatical and fearless. He has a reputation for not being afraid to get his hands dirty, at whatever cost. The world probably wouldn't miss him, but his absence might create problems in the colony. He has a meticulously organized web of influence, and the Audiencia is already a fragile authority, weakened by the loss of Nabarres and Fray Anonasi. Removing Don Cino is one thing; the real concern is who would rush to take his place?

I'd rather not find out.

"No," I answer.

"Why not?" Tomás squawks.

"Because I'm not Pantera."

He glares at me, his lips twisting in defiance. "Keep telling yourself that. We both know you are." He inspects his fingernails. "These are my terms."

"You mean threats."

"Yes, but I don't like that word."

He is unbelievable. "How old are you again?"

"Almost thirteen."

I remember when I was twelve. An awful age of transitions and contradictions.

My blood first came. I remember a lot of things—Tamoanchan, my father Quetzalcoatl, Ollin, other Naguals I trained with. I don't remember the moments, but I recall my earnestness, my impatience to advance. To prove myself. To stand in my own light. So desperate to fit in. I can see that same eagerness in Tomás.

I scoff and say, "You are still wet from your mother's womb."

"Do I hear a yes?" he asks, cupping his protruding ears.

I narrow my eyes at him, trying to gauge his seriousness. He's just a boy, but his tonalli is strong. That fire in him could either burn brightly or consume him entirely. "This isn't a game, niño. Even if I *were* Pantera, I can't just assassinate one of the most powerful men in Mexico on your whim. Killing someone, even someone like Don Cino, has consequences. I'd be exchanging one tyrant's grip for another's. It's a terrible idea, so get it out of your head."

"I don't care! He deserves it!" Tomás snaps. "You don't know what he's done to me!"

"There are ways to deal with Don Cino without resorting to killing," I say.

"What ways?"

I consider the question in silence.

"*What* ways?" he repeats more insistently.

"I don't know yet," I say, "but I'll think of something."

His forehead wrinkles as he holds back tears. "I thought you would understand."

"Tomás, I want to help you, but—"

He angrily brushes an arm over his eyes. "Just forget it!" he shouts, barreling past me and sending the door crashing against the wall as he storms out.

CHAPTER 8

El Veredicto

"For God's sake, how can you sit there so glib, toasting your toes?" Jerónimo paces my bedchamber with the nervousness of a caged animal.

I'm by the fireplace, watching the flames dance whimsically. "I find it rather pleasant."

"You must *do* something."

"About Tomás? He's twelve," I say. He's just a boy. A cunning, quick-witted, and resourceful boy. He needs help, but the request he's made is one I can't grant.

Jerónimo whirls on me angrily. "And I'm fifteen. Don't be stupid. He's an enemy!"

"Why don't you sit down? Try to relax."

"*Relax?* Relax she says!" His hands go up in disgust. "What will you do if this page reveals Pantera's identity to Inspector Corona? Are you going to let him do this to you? Does this not alarm you?"

Closing my eyes, I rest my head against the wall. "I have other things on my mind."

"Such as? What is more important than ensuring your head remains on your shoulders? Leonora, you will burn for this. Do you realize into what jeopardy you have walked?"

A chill sneaks into my bones. I wrap my arms around my knees. "Jerónimo," I say, "my life has been in jeopardy since the moment I took my first breath."

"Why must you always be so contrary? You are never willing to stir yourself on my behalf. Aren't you worried?" he asks. "Or at least scared?"

I shrug. "God is in control."

"Oh, please. Save your mockery for the trial." He wipes a hand across his forehead. Sweat is running down his face. "Christ, it is the blast of Hell," he grumbles. He stares down at me slumped on the floor, brows knitting, as if it only now occurred to him that the night is sticky warm, and I have a fire going.

"You're oddly quiet," he says. "Your condition . . . is it easing?"

"It's been a long day, and I need rest," I say to him, blinking to try to reawaken my heavy eyelids.

He draws in a sharp breath. "You look exhausted, Leo. Are you eating enough? I've not seen a morsel cross your lips."

"I'm not hungry. And why do you keep calling me Leo?"

"You're not . . . with child, are you?"

I give him an annoyed look. "You'd love that, wouldn't you?"

"You're my sister, Leonora," he says, his voice edged with a quiet indignation. "Believe it or not, I care for your wellbeing. Something is wrong—I can tell. I'll send for the physician."

"I'm just tired, nothing more," I insist, but Jerónimo is already halfway to the door. "Don't—"

I push myself to stand, but the room sways, and I have to steady myself against a chair.

Jerónimo is at my side in an instant, gripping my arms. "I'm not taking any chances, Leonora. The physician will know what to do."

"No physician can help me. I just need to sit by the fire."

Jerónimo nods rather reluctantly. He gently lowers me onto the chair and pulls another chair to sit beside me. I exhale, feeling warmth, both from the fire, and my brother's presence.

"I'll be all right," I whisper, more to myself than to him.

Even though he doesn't know what ails me, I'm grateful that he's with me—that he's trying.

I wait for the members of the Audiencia to deliver their judgment, I pray to the gods that the seeds I have planted and nurtured will bring harvest.

"You told this governing authority you knew the identity of Pantera," Inspector Corona says. "Are you changing your story from what you stated earlier?"

Tomás lifts his chin and looks straight into Inspector Corona's cold, hard eyes. "No, I'm trying to recollect."

"Do you recollect now?"

Tomás takes a deep breath. "It all happened very quickly. I don't remember."

Confusion floods my mind, drowning me in doubt and questions. Why would Tomás threaten me only to change his mind about testifying against me?

Jerónimo bounces to his feet, outraged. "You don't remember? Or did you lie?"

"I didn't—I didn't lie," Tomás mumbles, his face visibly flushed. "I—"

"You *what*?" Jerónimo asks angrily. "You made a mistake? Say it."

Tomás lowers his head. "I . . . made a mistake."

"Indeed, you did," says Jerónimo. "How can we believe anything he has to say? Don Cino, he is your page. He must do what you tell him. I demand you send him away."

Don Cino's jaw tightens. After a moment, he turns on Tomás, fury simmering beneath his expression. "You wretched boy," he says to Tomás. "Get out before I have your innards fed to the hounds."

Tomás glances briefly in my direction, a flicker in his eyes that pleads for some intervention, some sign that he's not entirely abandoned. I remain quiet. Tomás swallows his anger, pride, and perhaps the sting of rejection. His shoulders slump as he turns to leave.

I'm sorry, Tomás.

He's just a child. An innocent. I don't know how to help him without resorting to violence. I appear unmoved, but I am deeply torn.

Inspector Corona holds up a palm. "We have heard enough. Let us vote. As president of the Audiencia, I will go first."

I feel sick; I taste vomit in my throat. My blood drums in my ears, drowning out the few murmurs that echo before being smothered by the thick silence.

"I have reviewed all the evidence presented to me, and based on unforthcoming answers, I find Lady Leonora guilty on both charges," Inspector Corona says with conviction.

Cino Mondragon is the first on his feet, and I will remember that. "Guilty."

Bartolo de Molina believes me to be not guilty.

"Two to one. You're all alone, Don Bartolo," says Inspector Corona. "It takes courage to stand alone."

"Then I will vote again," says Don Bartolo. "Not guilty."

"You already voted, Don Bartolo," Inspector Corona says crossly. "You can't vote twice."

"Don't all members of the Audiencia get a vote?" Don Bartolo quips. "The first vote was from the Minister of Development. The second vote is from the Minister of Treasury. I hold both positions."

The hall bursts into a riot of whispers. More banging of Inspector Corona's gavel. He remains silent, but his face betrays his red-hot rage. "The count is tied."

From the side of the hall, Felipe rises from his seat. "I vote not guilty."

"His Majesty is not a member of the Audiencia," Inspector Corona says.

"I am the king's son," Felipe says, "and the count is no longer tied."

I have sowed.

I have reaped.

CHAPTER 9

El Tesoro

The corridor that leads to my bedchamber is silent, bathed in darkness, save for a flickering candelabra which gleams on the low-arched ceiling. I pause suddenly, seeing a figure cut through the shadows.

"Hello?"

An uneasy breeze blows and grasps me with its chilly touch. *Stop it*, I tell myself, hitting my temple with the heel of my palm. *There is no one.*

Maybe I am losing my soundness, so I pick up my feet, as if I can outrun my own mind, and come barreling inside my room.

"Tomás, what—?"

I stick my head out the door, looking either way to make sure no guards are near. Then I shut it quickly, bolting and chain-locking it.

"What are you doing here? Someone could see you."

"I have my ways of getting around. I can go places . . ." Tomás says. "Hear things . . ."

This isn't the same helpless child I saw in the ayuntamiento. He has that shrewd look on his face. It pains me to see he's had to learn that to survive in the palace.

"So can I."

"Yes, but you can't be everywhere. You need my help."

"Do I now?"

"Yes. And people—*some* people—they're not as truthful as they should be."

"What people?"

"Oh, you know . . . sometimes . . . in the courtyards, in the kitchen and the corridors, behind closed doors, I hear chatter. Complaints, contempt, chisme. People forget that children have ears."

I frown. "You're an odd little boy."

"Gracias."

"That wasn't a compliment."

"My point is, I realized something in the ayuntamiento. I can be your eyes and ears—an important factor what with the likes of Inspector Corona and King Felipe being in the palace. I can make regular reports about Inspector Corona's behavior and the way he conducts his affairs. I can be one of Pantera's associates. I can help you save lives!" he exclaims almost too excitedly.

"This is a very dangerous game you're playing, Tomás," I say. "One that may well cost you your life."

"Think about it. My master is Minister of Intelligence. He knows all. I'll listen, when I'm near, when I can. It's just for you. So you know. So you know when there's a problem beginning. So I can do something to help." He thrusts his chin up. "I will report to you any untoward behavior I notice, any comments I hear or see, any secret activities or private gatherings. Any sort at all. We'll make a great team, don't you think?"

"Do you really believe he won't find out? You said so yourself, your master is Minister of Intelligence."

"He mistakes my age for weakness. That makes him a fool."

I exhale. "It's too risky."

There's a knock on my door.

"Be quiet," I tell Tomás.

It is Don Ruy with a note, written in a hand I'm coming to know well. Felipe is requesting the pleasure of my company at tonight's social affair in the palace. He ends by expressing regret for having caused me any distress and assuring me that I need not fear any unwanted overtures this evening.

I pen a quick reply, acknowledging his invitation, and seal it. I dismiss Don Ruy, feigning sleepiness, and murmur that I wish to take my siesta before dinner. He withdraws without question.

"Can you wield a blade?" I ask, turning back to Tomás.

"Well, I'm no expert," he says, "but I learned a thing or two from Captain Nabarres."

I notice good posture and positioning. He's standing lightly on the balls of his feet.

"Can you write?"

"I'm a page. Of course, I can read and write."

I fold my arms. "And what will your services cost me?"

"Twenty silver ones ought to compensate for my trouble."

"Twenty coins?"

"For skills of such worth? Well, let me see . . . with the discounted price . . . that will be . . . *twenty* coins."

"Get out."

He snorts in annoyance. "You know what I want."

"We've discussed this," I say. "I'm not going to kill Don Cino, Tomás. We have to be smarter than that."

He shakes his head in disgust. "You're no different from him— dismissing my capabilities. I'll show you," he spits.

It's precisely because I see his strength that I'm afraid to let him tread this path. His cunning and resourcefulness is already far greater than his years suggest. This is a boy that has dealt with men like Nabarres and now Don Cino, and that's already beyond what any child should face. I have to guide Tomás carefully, not fuel the flames of his impulses.

As night descends, much of the reception hall's beauty is hidden by the crowd of at least a hundred courtiers. But the grandeur of the space is overshadowed by the social maneuvering—relationships are being made, friends advanced, enemies undermined.

The gossip is the worst.

"I don't know how much of it is true," I catch one señorita's remark, "but they were seen kissing and holding hands."

Jerónimo cuts in. "Lady Leonora is my sister. I assure you ladies that if there was a courtship involved between her and King Felipe, I would be the first to know it."

"Courtship?" says another lady. "Is that what they're calling it these days? Hmph!"

The musicians play a lively tune from Spain, and I go to Don Bartolo who is watching the dancers stomping and leaping the galliard, his face flushed with excitement.

"I wanted to thank you," I say, "for what you did for me. Had you not advocated for my innocence, I would have found myself in vastly different circumstances."

Don Bartolo shakes his head, cutting off my gratitude. "No need to thank me, my lady. Anyone would have done the same."

"Oh, I'm not sure anyone would. So few have ever come to my aid."

"We all need help once in a while," he says. "No one can do it all alone. Not even you . . . my lady."

I pause, take a breath. I certainly don't miss his tone, conveying a deeper meaning. I know exactly which me he is referring to. "You're a good man, Don Bartolo."

The smile that graces his face is sad. He averts his eyes for a moment. "No such thing."

"But you're a Christian. Isn't that what Christians claim? To be good people?"

"We're all bad. Some of us just try to do good."

"Then why do you think yourselves superior? That your faith is better? That you're right and everybody else in the world is wrong?"

"My lady, everyone has some form of delusions they believe to be the truth. Some follow their delusions blindly, others because it comforts them, and others because they believe they'll be damned in the fires of Hell for all eternity if they don't. You understand that, don't you?"

I suppose the difference is Don Bartolo has the honesty to admit it.

As I turn, I collide with Felipe. Don Ruy, who follows Felipe like a dog, steadies him.

"I'm afraid I pushed against you, my lady," Felipe says. "I do beg your pardon. It's like a battlefield in here."

"No harm done," I say, forcing a polite smile. "I hope His Majesty is enjoying the gathering."

"Indeed, my lady. Thank you for accepting my invitation. I must say that dress becomes you. Every time I see you, I have to think of a new word to compliment you."

"Magnificent?" Don Ruy suggests.

"Why, yes," Felipe says. "Tonight, you are magnificent, my lady. You have been through such a trial. I'm sorry that I didn't come to your rescue sooner. But let us trouble ourselves over this no more. You must now put all this behind you and move forward. I have something for you." He snaps his fingers, and at once a servant holds a covered silver dish before me and removes the lid, presenting slices of the soursop fruit.

"Guanábana?" I grin. A pleasant surprise. "You remembered."

"I hope you like them," says Felipe.

"I do, thank you," I say.

"Is something weighing on your mind, my lady?"

"No, it's just—well, it's nothing, really."

"Please," he urges gently. "I'm a good listener."

I weigh my words. "I have a friend in a difficult situation. I'm unsure where to turn for the right kind of help."

"Look no further. I'm the Crown Prince. Whatever the matter, consider it done."

Would I be a fool to trust him with Tómas's predicament? Inspector Corona's investigation into me would have continued if not for Felipe's intervention. The sincerity in his voice hints at his genuine willingness to help. I glance around, making sure no one is listening, before continuing with my guarded tone, "My friend serves a powerful man in court. I fear for their safety."

Felipe's expression becomes serious. "Whoever this man may be, I assure you, he wields no power greater than the king's son. Tell me more about the situation. I promise, I will see to it that your friend is protected. No one should live in fear."

Don Ruy interjects, "Felipe, the viceroy is requesting your presence."

Felipe groans softly. "I will return shortly. Do not worry, my lady, I will handle this," he says, before turning away.

Tomás modestly appears by my side, pouring my cup half full. "He's acquiring land," he whispers to me.

"What?"

"Inspector Corona," he mutters.

"So?"

"So he's doing it the old Spanish way . . . you know, by stealing it."

I glance at Felipe. Our eyes meet across the room, and I offer a subtle salute with my glass. He acknowledges with a warm smile and mirrors the gesture.

Tomás stays close. "There are rumors of a treasure."

"Inspector Corona is stealing land because he's searching for some treasure? That's quite a tale, Tomás."

"I don't think such a treasure exists, but who knows what the missionaries have found in the mines."

That makes me frown. "What mines?"

"The silver mines of the Franciscans are legendary," Tomás says. "You didn't know that? Hah! I told you I could help."

Franciscans? Fray Anonasi was the leader of the Twelve Apostles of Mexico, the order chosen to establish the Christian faith.

Did Inspector Corona murder Fray Anonasi over some fairytale treasure?

Now that I think about it, I look around the hall, wondering who might have had a motive to harm the man. No one took pains to try to hide Fray Anonasi's body. If someone did attack him, they wanted him found. They wanted us to see him. A message.

My thoughts run riot. But why? Who would want a priest out of the way?

"I need you to distract King Felipe," I say discreetly to Tomás.

We watch Felipe, enmeshed in conversation with Jerónimo and members of his father's court. "You don't think he's distracted enough?" Tomás asks.

"If I leave now, he will notice."

His forehead puckers. "But you can't leave. No one can leave. The investigation is not over."

"Indeed. And that is why you have to distract him."

"How exactly am I supposed to do that?"

"I don't know. Tell a joke. Argue. Point at something and say, 'look'. Use your imagination, Tomás. You can do that, can't you?"

He scoffs. "You insult me."

"While I'm gone, Felipe will request an audience with me. He will send letters to my bedchamber. You must be there and respond in my hand. Tell him I've fallen ill and cannot see anyone. Tell him I'm bedridden—anything you like, so long as he thinks I'm still in the palace."

"Where are you going? And how long will you be away?"

"That depends if I am successful."

He swallows. "What happens if you aren't?"

"Let's hope it doesn't come to that."

What I plan is risky, leaving for the King's Highway in the middle of the night. The Chichimeca will be there, and I can make my move. If I'm lucky. My sickness won't complicate matters. If I'm lucky. Don Cino won't be a problem. If Tomás is lucky. I say a little prayer to the gods, asking that I may be successful in my endeavor.

"What's taking so long?" I whisper harshly. "Distract him."

Tomás blinks. "Oh, you meant right now?"

"Yes, *now*."

He smirks. "You need me, then?" He leans in closer, his voice laced with satisfaction. "Wait—no. Pantera needs me. Admit it. Admit you are Pantera."

I groan, glancing over my shoulder to make sure we're still alone. "What difference does it make?"

"None, really," he replies, his smirk widening with each word, clearly enjoying every second of my discomfort. "I just want to hear you say it. You want my help? Say you're Pantera. Because I know it. You know it. Hell, Inspector Corona knows it."

"Yes, fine. I'm Pantera. Now do it. Once I'm back, I will deal with Don Cino."

He tips his head, feigning a gracious nod. "Now, was that so hard?" He straightens, pleased with himself. "Now that we've got that sorted, I'll get to work. But, if you ever tell this story, make sure I sound . . . oh, I don't know . . . heroic."

"Thank you, Tomás."

He holds his hand up, as if he's warding off praise. "No need to thank me—just don't forget to mention how indispensable I was." He straightens his jacket, adopting an expression of innocent charm that's at complete odds with his usual demeanor. "Watch and learn, Pantera. Watch and learn."

He gulps down water and slams down the cup, as if steeling himself for the ordeal, but I quickly realize it is to bathe his throat. Because his distraction is to sing.

The effect of him singing in Latin, the Spaniard's favored language, is apparent. Felipe reacts much the same way the other courtiers do. That is to say, with enjoyment.

Tomás keeps singing, amusing the women, entertaining the men. Then, with a kick of his legs, he is on the stage, doing some spins, throwing his arms in the air, moving like a silk ribbon in the night breeze. Now they are clapping to the rhythm. He continues his little number with an attempt to liberate the women, and they soon join him dancing, which surprisingly works better as a distraction than I could've hoped for.

Given how well Tomás is performing under very adverse conditions, I take my chance and slip away, trying to appear casual.

If anyone asks, I will say I'm unwell. But nobody does.

Part 2: Hueyi Tozoztli

Great Watch

CHAPTER 10

El Camino

At long agonizing last. I'm free again. Sort of.

I deem it too risky to ride a horse; the sound of hooves would carry, and I can't have someone hear me wandering about in the night. And the extra moments I'd need to slip into the stable, choose a suitable horse for the journey, and ready the tack—it's time I don't have. So I go on foot. I go slowly. I go carefully. It's less than a day's trip to the King's Highway. I'm accustomed to walking far longer distances, so the prospect fails to daunt me, though the prospect of death does. Feeling the weight of the Sword of Integrity is my only comfort. The crisscross of leather straps keeping the scabbard high on my back holds the blade safe. I check the side of my belt. My dagger is secure in its sheath.

Walking gives me plenty of time to remind myself of what must be done. What I must do. Recall basic everyday details. Remember who I am, where I am. Eréndira. Amalia. Zyanya.

I follow the vast network of dirt roads that run to the north, twisting through woods and grassland, surrounded by mountains and volcanoes, used as a major means of transport for goods—goods susceptible to be seized.

There's no moon. It's the darkest of nights. I look up at the stars, wondering if they will fall again, the way they did when the Tzitzimime came down to devour us all. I can't see much except the path I'm on, making it almost impossible to judge what direction I'm heading. Still, I know the Chichimeca are near, just as they were when Martín and I were ambushed.

It feels cold. It smells cold. It even sounds cold, the wind rustling. It's not a happy sound. It's eerie. Ominous, like maybe the trees are calling to me, warning not to go any further.

The soles of my feet hurt; my legs beg for a reprieve. The wind keeps moving through the trees, moaning and moaning, groaning and whistling.

My hands are icy to the touch. Shaking, I walk faster. If I run into any sort of danger, I'm not sure how well I can swing my sword while shivering. My mask and robe provide some relief, but without my tonalli, I can't stay warm. Kindling a fire is not an option. If it were day and Tonatiuh blazed in the sky, I could cultivate some heat, just enough to get by.

I come to a place where the road ends and I go to the edge and just listen.

I see them then. They are a bone-chilling sight: twenty or thirty warriors in a small pasture. A company of archers, all of whom can fire with discipline and deadly accuracy. They are stacking kindling, and the first fires are being lit, telling me they plan to spend the night where they are.

Only Chichimeca would feel safe to camp in the open countryside, certain that no Spaniard will attack them. And they are right. Who would dare ambush a group of Chichimeca in the middle of the night?

I come out of the darkness.

In a matter of seconds, my throat is greeted with spears.

"Hold! I come alone," I say in the common tongue. "I bear no threat to you." I say it in Nahuatl too.

They seem to be Red Sparrows, tall and of great strength. They distinguish themselves from other Chichimeca tribes by painting their heads and bodies with achiote, a bloody color. Most are only wearing a breechcloth. Some are covered with animal skins. All look at each other, standing confused at the absurdity of this moment.

The largest of the men, naturally, steps forward. "What do we have here? Have you come to give yourself up to be sacrificed in our fires tonight?"

With a shove, I'm brought to my knees before him. I'm weak in ways they do not know, in ways I dare not show. To display fear would be the surest way to invite death.

"You're not the first person to threaten me this week," I say. "I have not introduced myself, so I won't take this personally. I am Pantera, and I wish to speak to your chieftain."

Hearing such a bold statement, the large man and the rest of the warriors start laughing. A few of them look as if they might fall over from their laughter.

"You have amused us. So we will be generous today. You will go back the way you came, and we will let you live, Pantera," the large man says drolly.

"Your chieftain," I say again.

He comes closer to me, and I see his face hardened by the sun, with the blank, expressionless eyes of someone who has appeased the gods with a lot of blood.

"You are on your knees," he says. "Surely, you know I can cut your throat if I wish it."

"You must know, I'm more of a danger to you than you are to me."

"Is this threat supposed to worry us?"

"I don't issue threats. I offer facts."

No one speaks. The men exchange bewildered glances. The large man looks me up and down, probably judging how well I fight, looking at my mask, my clothes, and noting especially my sword.

"What do you want?" he asks.

I think it a miracle that my head is still attached to my neck, and

I don't believe in miracles. That they don't know about what happened here—that they haven't heard of the one who slaughtered their Chichimeca kin—seems impossible. It wasn't long ago, and it was right here, on this very road, where the ground still feels heavy with the memory of blood.

It's not something I am proud of. I didn't want to kill Prince Xico's men. They attacked me, and in that moment, I chose my own life over theirs. I had no other choice.

But as I look at the faces of the warriors surrounding me now, I'm reminded that the Chichimeca are not a single people; they are many tribes, each with their own customs and alliances. Some are at war with each other, fighting over food, boundaries, honor.

Perhaps, if fate is kind, the Red Sparrows might see me differently. Perhaps, I could become an ally rather than an enemy.

"I'm here to negotiate an agreement," I say. "I propose that you stop any further attacks on the King's Highway. I further propose that your people leave at once. You alone choose what these efforts are worth. What is it you want in return?"

They aren't laughing anymore.

"We will do what we always do," the large man says. He mimes shooting an arrow at my chest, and the other warriors laugh again.

"Talking is better than killing, don't you think?" I ask.

"Depends on who's doing the talking and who's doing the killing."

"You will lose, is that your wish?" I say with more verve. "To lose more of your people? We can resolve this. Name your demands so we may satisfy them. This is Viceroy Jerónimo's promise."

He lifts a brow. "Viceroy Jerónimo you say?"

I nod.

Slipping his breechcloth to the side, he takes a piss in front of my knees. Several of the other men snicker. I'm more annoyed than I am disgusted, but I can't show any sign of weakness or discomfort.

"You're not the chieftain . . ." I sigh. "This is getting us nowhere. It's time for action. Who's really in charge?" I'm already eyeing the warriors, specifically their heads, as the hair is of primary importance in conveying identity, rank, and function.

"I am." A smaller man with insolent eyes calls out. "And I agree," he says. "It's time for action. My bow."

The men start hollering with excitement. They take up a chant— *Tlahuicole, Tlahuicole, Tlahuicole* —crowing that he is the best marksman, his accuracy second to none, even over great distances, and I'm sure that is true. One of them disappears and comes back with a bow and quiver, with a set of some thirty arrows. I'm provided with a second bow.

It isn't my favored weapon. Actually, it's my worst weapon. The sword and the knife—these weapons I can wield, possibly I could even throw a spear, but my archery skills are certainly not legendary, not by any stretch of the imagination. I'm not so arrogant to think I can win against a Chichimeca. But I'm left no choice.

"Are we doing this or not?" I pull an arrow from the quiver and fit it into my bow. It's suited to motion; that is, fighting while moving. Much smaller than bows used by the Spaniards, easier to draw and with greater range. I inspect the tip. The arrowhead is obsidian, knapped into sharped points.

The larger man from before carves a target in a tree.

"Three arrows in the center, or you lose," says my opponent Tlahuicole.

"Lose what?"

He looks at me as if I am foolish to ask. If I win, I live; if I lose, my life is his.

Raising my bow, I take aim, call on the gods, pull the string, and let the arrow slice across the air. It speeds toward the target, but my opponent, in one single fluid motion, lifts his bow and takes a shot so that his arrow strikes mine, deflecting it from its true path, splinters it, then—what in the Nine Hells? That can't be right. But it is. His arrow turns in flight and buries itself deep into the tree, cleanly lodged in the center.

"You missed," Tlahuicole says. "Again."

Once more, I take my stance and release the arrow.

Tlahuicole wheels round, bow drawn. His arrow hits mine a second time, slightly to the left, and it pierces the target off center. He sneers in contempt. "That's disappointing. Again."

Scowling, I quickly pluck the last remaining arrow from the quiver and aim it, straight at his face. He doesn't flinch. He only leans over to spit on the ground in response.

"Enough of your games," I say. "I've not come to cause you harm, but I will not ask again. You will bring me your leader. When your leader and I have made our acquaintance, we can begin to negotiate an agreeable arrangement that is advantageous to all. I think that's very reasonable. I have been reasonable, wouldn't you say? Unless . . . your leader dares not meet with me. Then he is a coward, and you will all suffer for it."

Tlahuicole is amused. "He will kill you," he says slowly and with a curve of his lip, as if looking forward to it.

"He can try," I say.

Tlahuicole jerks his head to the right, then the left, searching. "He must not be far away."

An arrow hisses out of the night. It passes within a hair's breadth of my fingers, nearly grazing the tips. I jerk back my hand with a gasp, dropping the bow.

"I never am," says a deep voice, and the men go silent. The air becomes still, even the fires quiet.

Either I have finally dropped dead, or this is a dream, the work of a trickster or a powerful bewitcher, the intoxicating result of toad skins, the sacred morning glory seed, or other hallucinogenic plants . . .

Or Tezca is truly standing before me.

Shit.

CHAPTER 11

El Engaño

I blink. It's *him*. A more mature, older version of him; nonetheless, him.

I catch my breath, completely unprepared by the suddenness of seeing him again.

My eyes are wide, and I am grateful for the mask that hides them. I can't stop staring at him. The sharp angles of his face, the way he proudly stands, hair tied in a topknot, showing his status as a seasoned warrior. He looks strong, youthful. I can do nothing about my heartbeat, and I'm sure he hears it pounding.

What in the Nine Hells is he doing here? Why is he with the Chichimeca?

I smile, relieved and hopeful that my efforts will be fruitful. Before there was doubt in me, but now I'm certain. He will not try to take my head. He will be an easier man to deal with. He will listen to my proposal, agree to it, and stand down.

But then he says, "I am Tezcacoatzin, and I reject your peace."

I'm silent, stunned in abject shock for several moments. His gaze is hard and unflinching.

"Tez—my lord," I say in a croak. I shake my head out of my daze. "May we speak privately?"

"We are not prepared for dialogue. We are prepared for war."

He nods to one of the men to take me away. Instinct would have me bury the Sword of Integrity in his chest, but I allow him to drag me from their midst. I have been bested.

I'm tied to a tree with the horses. Noble steeds of Portugal, of great spirit and beauty, which the Chichimeca capture and ride in battle.

I push forward, straining at the rope around my waist. When I can sit up, I use the tree's bark to fray it. Nine Hells, this would be so much easier if only I had my tonalli.

Everyone is gathered around the fires, drunk and getting drunker. No one notices as I finally free myself and stand. Neither do they notice that the horses have been freed of their holds. I pat their necks, urging them to flee.

There are two men outside Tezca's tent, but they are in a stupor, half-asleep. Not that he needs guards. He already knows I'm here.

I throw open the tent's door and slip off my mask. I'm soaked in a cold sweat and the cool night air on my face is not a welcome relief.

A dozen questions rise in my mind and stay there. The only thing that manages to emerge is, "Don't *ever* tie me up again."

Tezca sits on a table, absently drumming his fingers on its surface, staring at me. His gaze is intent. He knew I would come. Did he want me to?

"Are you dead?" he asks.

"What?"

"You walk, talk, breathe. You seem to be alive in every way." The muscles of his jawbone flex as he grinds his teeth together. "Where is your tonalli?" He tips his head, regarding me with a cross expression. "Has King Felipe acquired it for himself?"

Ah. He knows Felipe is in Mexico. Of course he knows. But how much does he know?

It takes me a moment to understand his hidden meaning. Tonalli escapes the flesh in sex, especially consumed in lovemaking by someone whose vital force is too low. He thinks I've lain with Felipe.

"It was you who walked away. Not me."

"Is that what you tell yourself?"

"You *left*, Tezca."

"I did what I had to do to ensure the survival of my people. What did you do? Hide, like you always do."

"I didn't hide! I'm not here to quarrel. I'm here because we need a peaceful solution to the conflict with the Chichimeca."

"Fuck your peaceful solution."

"Nine Hells, Tezca. What's the matter with you? You're not yourself. Hasn't there been enough bloodshed?" I say it nearly shouting. "Why must there be more?"

"Not nearly enough, in my opinion." His voice is tight and cold. "We will not stop, we will not relent, and we will not compromise."

"Don't make me an enemy."

He scoffs. "You've done that all by yourself."

We are both angry. Chaos—fighting fire with fire.

I soften and try again. "We won the Long War. The last thing we need right now is another war. In a fight on Chichimeca soil, you might prevail. You know the desert and the Spaniards do not. But war of any kind will be long and costly, in terms of lives and in terms of resources. More people will die. Is that what you want?"

"Why are you speaking to me about war?" he says scornfully.

"You would sacrifice peace? For what, jealousy?"

He laughs at that. "You *have* been busy. Amusing the king's son."

Who told him? Nine Hells, he likely heard it with his own two ears: the coquetry, the stupid courtship game, all of it. "That's no concern of yours . . . my lord."

His nose wrinkles, as if disgusted by a rotten smell in the air. "It's difficult to say where your scent begins and his ends."

He stands and comes toward me. I stiffen like a board.

Tezca looms over me, and as he looks down, his fingers move some of my hair away from my face. They find a few scrapes across my forehead. Beneath his healing touch, the edges smooth, closing, and I shudder with goose flesh.

His lips fall to my ears. "Does he kiss you like I do?"

I know exactly what comes next. I sure wouldn't have to feign my desire for him. With the loss of my tonalli, I can't sense the fullness of his internal heat. My skin is ice cold. I long for his warmth. I'm desperate for it. I'm like a thirsty traveler, wandering hither and thither in search of water, and then I find a river where I can drink my fill. Just a little? Just one tiny sip to sate myself? What could a sip hurt?

What am I thinking? I mustn't lose focus.

It will be my greatest charade yet: fighting my own desire, pretending I don't want him.

"Yes." It is a lie, and it burns on my tongue.

Tezca stares at me for a moment, and I think he'll say more, but then he sighs and takes a step back. I release a breath, grateful for the reprieve.

"Eréndira's people," I say. "They were able to leave Snake Mountain. They're safe from Ichcatzin's wrath, but they've fallen sick to the pox. If you leave Royal Road and cease the attacks, Viceroy Jerónimo promised to provide medicine. They need help. I can't do this by myself. Please, Tezca. Help me help them. Stand down."

"Ichcatzin's wrath?"

I nod. "Eréndira and Chipahua spoke of a supernatural weapon he possesses. And some kind of plan tied to it."

"What weapon?"

"I don't know, but I know I can't uncover it if I'm here quelling a rebellion."

"Walk away, Leonora."

I'm at a loss and I badly wish to scream. "Why are you're being so stubborn?"

Tezca's gaze sharpens, his face etched with lines of barely contained anger. *"Stubborn?"* he spits the word. His eyes are full of fury and craze. "If you've let the Spaniards lull you, then don't expect me to be the one to wake you. That's your problem. Not mine."

"Tezca, *please*."

"They play with the women, forcing them to run behind a horse until they can't any longer and then they fall and are dragged across the desert. I've seen them cut off parts of a body while they are still alive, listened to them scream in agony. The screams that stay with you long after they've stopped. They burn houses with families inside—children burned to ash. Tell me again how I'm being stubborn."

I try to make sense of what he's saying. The Sword of Integrity feels heavy on my back, so heavy that it almost drags me to the floor with it. "What are you *talking* about?"

"Where's the princess?"

"What princess?"

"Leonora. Do not make me force answers from you."

"I swear to you. I don't know what you mean!"

He must be able to tell I'm truly confused because some of his fury melts away. "The Red Sparrows—they follow Princess Nelli," he says. "She's been taken captive by the Spaniards."

"Captive? I . . . I didn't know," I say again. "Tezca, I didn't know."

"But you *do* know, don't you? The abuse. The slaughter. There is death every day. Or did you forget who the enemy is?" His tone is cruel, and it stings. I flinch as if he struck me. "Did you soften in his arms?"

"Tezca," I whisper. My heart aches at the image of torture, the sheer senselessness of it all, the intensity of his pain and rage. I thought I had helped build peace. Not true peace—no. That would be an illusion under Spanish rule. Yet, I had hoped for justice. "I . . . I don't understand. Jerónimo spoke of negotiations, of efforts to build a new alliance with La Justicia. He said whoever broke the peace would face punishment. You were *there*."

"Tlahuica and Chichimeca have never allied," he says. "But I've made a decision to align my actions with my beliefs. I know why I am fighting. Do you?"

"Tezca, I'm sorry," I say, my voice breaking. "I'm sorry I've been away, and I'm sorry about all that's happened. I will speak to my brother, and he will right this."

He shakes his head, as if my words are completely unfathomable. "Perhaps Neza would like to hear about the deep and enduring bond between kin. He can't, can he? He's dead. Murdered. Betrayed by his own brother," Tezca says. "I gave Jerónimo a chance to prove himself because he's Nican Nicah's son. I wanted to believe he was like him. But he is the enemy, yet you defend him. He is a liar who continues to lie."

"He is a child surrounded by snakes whispering in his ear!" This is not his doing. It can't be. I'm sure of it.

"You are either on our side, or you are part of the problem. Choose quickly, Leonora," he says, "while the choice remains."

There is more to say, so much more, but I say nothing. The secrets between us have created a gulf we can't cross. I take a last look at him, and as I make for the exit, he calls after me.

"I needed you," he says. His words are a lash.

CHAPTER 12

El Mentiroso

It's the darkest hour of the following night as I come crawling in my bedchamber through the servants' passageway, writhing like a snake, all the air squeezed from my lungs. My body has become stiff and numb, closing in on itself in an effort to sustain breath. Before I know it, I'm unable to walk or even lift my hands. My legs do not obey me, and my brain scarcely functions.

"Pantera?" Tomás, stretched out on my bed, sits up in a panic. "What are you—? What happened? Are you hurt?"

"Fire," is all I can say.

"What?"

I nod to the lit torch on the wall. "Bring it," I say, my breath coming in wheezing draws. "Bring it to me."

Tomás stands quickly, goes to the torch, and pries at it with both hands. It pops free, and he hurries back to hold it close to me. The welcome heat reaches my skin. My breathing becomes fuller, easier.

"Better," I rasp.

The torch looms in front of his face, brightening the fresh, shadowy bruise under his eye. "Who did that to you?"

"Did what?"

"The injury that you so obviously have. Was it Don Cino?"

101

"No." He shakes his head. "It doesn't matter. Listen, something has—"

"Why did he hit you?"

"Leonora—"

"Why?"

"He just did."

"For no reason?"

"I tried to kill him," he says with a sigh. "I was going to cut his balls off. But he's quicker than he looks."

"Don't lie to me, Tomás."

He rubs a hand tiredly across his eyes. "He was going to read one of the letters for King Felipe. I said it was a letter from my mother. He said I had no mother because I am a God-cursed little bastard. So, I ate the letter." He gives a little laugh as he says that. "I had to do something. He was going to find out—"

"You shouldn't have done that," I say reproachingly. "I told you this was a bad idea. Look what he's done to you."

He shrugs. "He's done worse for far less. How was your trip?"

"Eye opening." I take the torch from him and kindle the fireplace. "Felipe has been receiving my correspondence?"

Tomás nods. "As planned."

"He doesn't suspect anything?"

"No, but Leonora . . . I don't have good news."

"What did you hear?" I ask.

"Well . . ." He rubs the back of his neck, hesitant to talk. "Not only do you have a treasure hunter to deal with, now you must make sure he doesn't go on a warpath. While you were away, I found out Inspector Corona has both land *and* men. He has men in every town from here to Zacatecas and he's recruiting more each day."

"Zacatecas?" I frown. "That's Chichimeca territory."

"What do I know, Pantera? I'm only a kid. I've got years to grow up, many years. But I know there is only one reason to build an army," he says. "War."

I'm quiet.

"What are you thinking?"

"I saw presidios on the King's Highway," I say, catching on. "Like the military outposts along the coast to defend against pirates, smugglers, and foreign invasion. I didn't think anything of them. Many presidios are used as trading centers."

Tomás gives this thought for a moment, and his brows are gathered as he asks, "You think Inspector Corona has been manning the presidios?"

"I must warn the viceroy."

"About that . . . Viceroy Jerónimo has been imprisoned for plotting against the Crown. They called him an enemy of the king."

"Prison? Jerónimo is in prison? You tell me this *now*?" I hurl the words at him.

"I was trying to tell you before!" Tomás squabbles.

"I was only gone for a day. What exactly happened?"

"Leonora, it's been nearly a week. I've penned a letter every day."

"A week?" I say with an incredulous shake of my head. "No, no . . . that's not—that's not . . ."

"Possible?" he quietly suggests. "What did you do? Did you get drunk or something?"

Or something.

A week? It's been a week? Where have I been? So many questions, so many thoughts circling. My fingers jab at my temples while I blink furiously trying to awaken the part of my brain that knows things. This is what I have now. Pieces that are disjointed and not connected anymore. So yes, my mind is still working, but not in the way it should.

I sleep on the floor by the fireside, dreaming of Tezca's warmth. *I needed you.* I repeat those three words over and over again. He needed me, and I wasn't there for him. I make it through the night without shaking from the cold, and when morning comes, Tonatiuh's rays renew my strength, although the tiredness doesn't leave me altogether.

I bask in him like a butterfly sitting in a patch of sunlight. Cold-blooded animals don't generate heat on their own. And butterflies can't fly if they're cold. It's why they have darkly colored bodies.

I miss the Panther.

I miss . . . me.

"The viceregent wishes to speak to a prisoner!" the guard shouts to the gate. As it rises, it reveals another guard, bowing his head in my presence. I walk with him into the darkness. The restless moans of other prisoners echo loudly.

"Quiet!" he barks. "My lady, which prisoner do you wish to speak to?"

"Viceroy Jerónimo."

It gets colder and damper as the guard and I move downward. We reach the bottom of the dungeon and take the right tunnel at the dead end.

I'm furious. Jerónimo is a lying, manipulating child who distrusts me simply because I'm a pagan, because I'm Pantera. But then I see him languishing in the depths of a tiny prison cell, stewing in his own shit, dirtied and tattered, helpless and in despair, and I go weak. I nod for the guard to leave.

"Jerónimo? Jerónimo it's me . . . Leonora. Your sister."

"The crow . . . the crow," he is babbling. "Where's the crow?"

"What crow?" I take steps closer to him.

"The crow covered in flies. It was just here."

"A crow?"

"God has sent me dreams," he says. "Visions. I believe my imprisonment has brought me closer to godliness. God sends signs that will make us take notice. He is speaking to me, and I must listen. Don't you see, Leo? It was an omen."

"An omen of what?"

"Death!" he shouts. "An omen of death!"

"Christians don't believe in omens," I tell him.

"I'm not always a good Christian," he admits.

"It was just a crow, Jerónimo. It means nothing."

He looks upward as high as he can but sees no sign of the crow. "It wasn't just a crow; it flew right up to heaven. Why was it here? What did it want?" he mutters frantically to himself. "Wait. Oh, yes. King Felipe."

"What about King Felipe?"

"He came to see me," Jerónimo explains. "The omen . . . the omen appeared shortly after his visit. Perhaps God speaks—he's come to wreak havoc on us all."

"Jerónimo, you mustn't lose your head over a crow. Listen to me—"

"Leave me. I must commune with God."

I groan. "What you must do is return to power. We must get you out of here and back to the palace. You made a promise, and you must honor it. Are you listening to me?"

He falls to his knees and bows his head in prayer. "My Father in Heaven, please forgive me. Forgive my sins and wash them away. I'm not sure who I am or what I'm supposed to be doing. Father, I know not to test thy Lord, but please send me a sign. Walk with me and talk with me in my times of need. For I have fallen, and I need your strength. Dear God, come into my life." His face is to the ground with his palms outstretched before him, and he is sobbing now, unable to stop the waterfall of tears. "Please, please, forgive me!"

I've never seen Jerónimo like this. It's an overwhelming sight that makes my heart shrivel, and I hold him in my arms, caressing him.

"Leo," he says, pulling back to look at me, "why must I be chosen by God and then neglected by Him? It is not for me to question His will, but why did He choose me if He was just going to leave me here? Abandoned? My God, my God, why have you forsaken me?"

"Don't you think Jesus felt abandoned when his disciples left him to die? You don't think maybe he felt just a little afraid?" I'm desperate. I have to say something to make him see sense. "Jerónimo, being afraid doesn't mean you lack courage. It means overcoming your fears and standing up for what's right. Everyone is scared of something."

"Even Pantera?"

"Especially Pantera."

"What are you afraid of?"

"How much time do you have?" He gives me a crooked smile, and I say, "Don't you think God knows what He's doing?"

"What do you mean?"

"I mean God knows everything, yes?"

"Yes."

"Then He already has this figured out," I say more firmly, trying to restore his confidence and raise more serious matters. "So, what is there to be afraid of?"

He thinks on this for a moment. "You're right," he says, nodding. "I can feel Him working on my heart." He crosses himself and mumbles a prayer of thanks. Finally, he's able to see a little light where there was nothing but darkness.

"You have a duty," I remind. "You can't stay here. I will find a way to prove your innocence."

"Leo, I . . . it's not that simple."

"You *are* innocent, aren't you? Jerónimo, tell me you are innocent."

"Innocent? I don't think so." A female's voice emerges from the shadows. "Make one move," she says to me, "and I'll bleed him to death."

I stand still, irritated by my common ears. I have heard whispered prayers from across the marketplace, tremors beneath the earth before an earthquake, the growth of maize pushing through the soil, the heartbeats of hummingbirds from across a clearing. If I had my tonalli, I wouldn't have missed this approach.

Jerónimo freezes as cold steel kisses his neck. "Who are you? What do you want?"

"You killed Prince Xico, and now I must kill you."

CHAPTER 13

La Princesa

Her hair is red—red in the fashion of the Red Sparrows of the Chichimeca tribe.

"You're the princess . . ." I stammer. She has to be. Tezca spoke of a princess who was captured by the Spaniards. I know little of the Red Sparrows, but her hair tells me she must be their leader. I wager there are not many Nahua princesses whose hair is naturally red.

She tips her head at me, as if she wasn't expecting I would place her.

"My mother was a princess," she says, her voice strong and clear. "I am Nelli Xicotenga."

"You seek to avenge Prince Xico?"

"He was my uncle," says the princess. "The last of my Tlaxcalan family."

I nod. "I see his bravery in you."

"He was fearless!"

"Yes. He was a great warrior," I say. "No one wielded a bow and arrow better than him."

"You *killed* him," she snarls at Jerónimo.

"He fell in battle," I'm quick to say. "He died a warrior's death and earned his place with Tonatiuh. He no longer walks the earth, but he is here. He is the wind in the trees. He is the darkness of night and the light of day."

Her eyes narrow. "Who are you?"

"My name is Leonora."

She lets out a breath almost like a sigh, but shorter and sharper. "Pantera."

I cast an uneasy glance at Jerónimo, then back at Nelli. *How does she know?* As soon as the thought crosses my mind, I know the answer. Tezca. Only Tezca could have revealed this to her. I am seething now.

"*You* are the great warrior they talk about? The powerful sorceress who defeated the Obsidian Butterfly and led a great Nagual army into battle? I think not!"

My face gives no hint of it. "Your name isn't Nelli Xicotenga, is it?"

"Of course it isn't," she says. "My real name is Spanish, like my father Pedro de Alvarado." She turns her head and spits, as if disgusted by this fact.

"You're Tonatiuh's daughter?" I ask. A man of Cortés, Pedro de Alvarado's hair and beard were red, which reminded the Nahuas of the sun god, earning him the nickname. It's known he was ruthless in his dealings with the native peoples he set out to conquer.

"Before you kill me," Jerónimo says, "can I just say one thing?"

"Ah, ah, ah," Nelli tsks. The tip of her blade presses further to his throat. A dot of blood beads from the indent in his flesh.

"Easy . . ." I say evenly. "There is no honor in this. It ill becomes a warrior to slay an unarmed man."

"I am the granddaughter of the last tlahtoani of Tlaxcala. I am a war leader. I have honor!"

"Then drop your sword," I say.

"I will do as I please. You do not give me orders."

"If you wish him dead, then give him a blade so he will give you a warrior's mahuizotl." It means honor, glory.

Jerónimo squawks, "What?"

"No warrior claims victory without battle," I say. "I would hate for you to lose your status, princess."

"No one would know," she says proudly.

"*I* would know." Unless she plans on killing me too, and I would strongly advise against that for her own sake, but I don't need to speak. That's the thing about reputation. It speaks for you. It travels. It goes places. I do not carry it; it carries me. At the moment, it's all I have.

Thankfully, I wield my tongue like a weapon gifted to man by the gods.

"You lay in wait to butcher a boy when he is a prisoner and can't defend himself and then say you have honor," I go on. "You sully the word. I doubt you'd be as brave if you had to face an experienced swordswoman."

A fragile thing, a warrior's pride. Nelli could've chosen the path of her tyrant father and squandered the Alvarado fortune on expensive jewels and extravagant parties, yet the blood of her Tlaxcalan ancestors burns within her like a thousand tiny suns. If I've assessed her correctly, she's a warrior first, a woman second. She dreams a warrior's dream and wears her pride like a suit of armor. She holds high rank in the Red Sparrows. A blot upon her honor would be deep shame.

"Your uncle died a warrior," I say again. "He earned his place in the House of the Sun. If you are your mother's daughter, then you must believe that."

Nelli's face is tight with anger. "He said you would get in my way."

Who said that? I want to ask. *Tezca?* It doesn't matter.

With an infuriated grunt, she lowers her blade, though she keeps it at the ready. "You're no Godslayer," she says. "I see you as someone easily killed, witch. You're just skin and bone that will wither and turn to dust."

"Godslayer?" Jerónimo parrots.

"You know *nothing* about me," I snap.

Nelli argues, "And *you* know nothing about me."

"I was told you were being held captive," I say. "I should like the truth, princess."

She lifts her head, inhaling sharply. "I kill the viceroy. He stops killing my people. That was the agreement."

"He? Who is 'he'?"

Silence, then, "Inspector Corona."

"You made a deal with Inspector Corona to murder Viceroy Jerónimo?" I ask. My head is starting to ache. I bring a hand to the bridge of my nose and rub it with trembling fingers. "He has made a fool of you, princess. Inspector Corona seeks a treasure in your lands."

Nelli's laugh is humorless. "Who do you think told him where to find it in the first place?"

"I'm gathering it was you."

"Inspector Corona agreed to deliver Jerónimo to me *after* I gave him the location," Nelli explains. "He promised our freedom in exchange."

I stare at her in disbelief. "You trusted a Spaniard?"

"What choice did I have? Everyone knows there's silver in La Gran Chichimeca," she says. "Only Chichimeca know where to look. The priests buried it to avoid discovery by the Spanish soldiers."

The priests? The Franciscan priests. This is what Fray Anonasi was murdered for.

"I only gave him one vein," Nelli says defensively. "One, out of many."

"One vein is all they need to bleed the land dry, princess," I tell her. "In trying to save your people, you have doomed them."

Her face falls, anger flickering in her gaze. "You think I don't know the risk I've taken? What was I supposed to do? I had to give him something. If sacrificing a piece of the land was the price for our survival, then I was willing to pay it."

I narrow my eyes, my voice dropping to a harsh whisper. "You sold out. You wanted Jerónimo. You wanted revenge."

"I wanted *justice!*"

I wanted that too. I still do. I let out a bitter scoff, shaking my head. I look at her the same way Tezca looked at me when I told him the war was over, clinging to false hope. I can see it in her eyes, the belief that if she just sacrifices enough, if she fights hard enough, she can force the world to be fair. That's the problem with certainty; it blinds you. I was naive—and so is Nelli.

I glance at my brother. Jerónimo looks not the least bit surprised. "Did you know about this?"

"Well, there are many tales of treasure in New Spain," he says with a dismissing wave of his hand. "It's hardly a secret."

"But did you know about *this*?" I press angrily.

No response.

"Answer me. Now."

Finally, he says, "The mines are worked under a cloak of secrecy to avoid paying the King's Fifth."

My jaw tightens. "What?"

"New Galicia is a province of New Spain. Under Spanish law, one-fifth of all silver mined belongs to the King of Spain," he explains. "This requires full disclosure of the amount of silver mined in Zacatecas. It's then smelted and made into ingots, with the Royal Fifth shipped to Spain for delivery to the king. The galleons sailing to Spain were filled with shipments of bullion. Unfortunately, Caribbean hurricanes sent hundreds of these ships, and their treasures, to the bottom of the sea. At least . . . that's what we've been telling the king."

"You've been stealing from the king?" This is bold. More brazen than I'm used to from him.

"Oh, don't look so shocked, Leo," he says. "People do it all the time. They cheat on their taxes. They hide their coin beneath their beds. Besides, you were there when *La Capitana* sank. Mother held the position of Minister of Treasury. The Crown doesn't support us. From where exactly do you think we've been acquiring coin?" He looks at Nelli. "The mistreatment of your people I had nothing to do with. I swear to you! Since the Long War, there has been peace between Spaniards and the Northmen."

Nelli looks angry and not nearly convinced. "We are the resistance. We will continue to rebel. We will be slaves in our land no longer."

"Slaves?" Jerónimo parrots. "You're Alvarado's daughter. And New Spain has had a partnership with Tlaxcala since the Fall, from which Tlaxcalans have benefited handsomely. My father spoke of your grandfather, Don Lorenzo. You're no slave, princess."

Nelli levels a furious stare at him. "My father can burn in Hell, for all I care. I'm grateful for the horse that crushed him. As for my grandfather," she adds, "it's true. He embraced Cortés. My uncle Xico, however, did not. He never submitted to the authority of Spain, nor will I. And *you* took him from me."

It was I. Jerónimo delivered the strike, but I sent him to Tonatiuh. He was going to kill me. He fought, and he lost.

"That's what you were afraid about, wasn't it?" I say to Jerónimo. "You didn't want Inspector Corona to find out about the silver."

He gives a tense nod. "King Carlos is furious with us. After several years of no shipments of silver, the king dispatched Inspector Corona to try and locate the mines."

"So, you concealed them, fearing you would lose control of the silver," I say. "And you had the priests do it."

"The Franciscans are authorized by the Pope and their founder immortalized as a saint," Jerónimo says. "King Carlos dares not harm them in any way because it would be a sin against God."

"Tell that to Fray Anonasi. What else have you lied about?"

Jerónimo winces at the sting in my words. "Leonora, you have to believe me. I had nothing to do with this. Inspector Corona—as soon as he found out about the silver, he promised death, enslavement, or mutilation to any Northman who resisted his demands. As you might imagine from our northern neighbors, they did not yield quietly. And Inspector Corona, to subdue them, raided settlements and acquired slaves for the mines. He's created a dozen new presidios along the King's Highway. He controls the army, and he has native allies. He is more dangerous than you know."

I assumed, wrongly, that the Chichimeca were attacking the King's Highway purely out of anger over Prince Xico's death. I thought their raids were acts of revenge, driven by the pain of losing a leader.

This wasn't *just* about honor or blood. This was about the silver mines, and the insidious lure of wealth driving the Spaniards. Inspector Corona didn't care about the people who lived there. To them, the territory was little more than a resource, something to be stripped bare to line their own pockets.

"He's coming for La Condesa," Nelli says.

"La Condesa?" I ask.

"The mine. La Condesa is the deepest, and the most important. It's the reason Zacatecas is a province in New Galicia at all. The Spaniard Gascon de Parada discovered it a few years ago. He named the mine after his wife."

Amalia's first husband. "The Countess of Niebla?" I ask.

"Someone you know?"

I look at Jerónimo briefly. "No," I say. I glance back to Nelli. "How many do you lead?"

"Enough," she says flatly.

She doesn't need to say more. The best warriors, the best archers, the most seasoned, the ones who love battle the most. After all, they are Chichimeca.

"And Inspector Corona?" I ask. "How many does he have?"

"I think he has six thousand," Jerónimo says, "at least."

I sigh. "It'll be a bloodbath."

"Like any war," says Nelli. "I don't care about the odds."

"Do you have a plan?" I ask.

"We fight harder," she says. "We fight more ferociously than a million Spaniards."

"Do you have a real plan?"

"The bigger army doesn't always win," she stubbornly says.

"And that's why you need a plan," I say, my voice louder.

"Haven't you ever fought and won when you've been outnumbered?" Nelli asks.

I nod. "I have."

"So why are we doomed?"

"Only a fool seeks a battle against a stronger enemy," I say.

Nelli chuckles. "Only a fool seeks a battle. I don't wish to be outnumbered, but we have little choice. We will have to beat Inspector Corona's army by ourselves. And we *can* beat them. Believe that, Godslayer."

"How will you wage war?"

"Cruelly, of course," she answers with a smirk.

It's not that I think the Chichimeca cannot win. They can. They will fight to the last breath. I admire Nelli's confidence, and I don't distrust her ability, but she is much too eager to battle. To go to war in haste is reckless. It behooves a leader to plan wisely, attack at the right moment, and then maybe her people will live to see another day.

"What if that doesn't work?" I ask.

"Then my uncle Xico will not be alone in the House of the Sun. And you?" she asks. "Where will you be when the Spaniards attack our Northmen? Inside these walls of Mexico?"

"Depends."

"On what?"

"You are right," I say. "I'm just flesh, blood, skin, and bones. I'm a woman like you. I will someday die, and my body will be returned to the earth. But I am Pantera, and I will be where I'm needed the most."

Her face puckered in a scowl, nostrils flared, she takes one deadly look at Jerónimo, then she is gone.

"It would seem you've made a name for yourself," Jerónimo says, "Godslayer."

"As have you," I say, "Jerónimo El Mentiroso."

Tezca was right. He's a liar who continues to lie. I swear a private, bitter oath to myself that I will never, ever let him fool me again.

CHAPTER 14

La Promesa

His Majesty King Felipe gallops into the stable yard, where Pantera waits for him in his horse's pen. As soon as he dismounts, he whirls around, sword drawn with surprising speed.

His blue eyes are afire. "Did you really think you could hide in here without me knowing, witch?"

"I hid nothing, Your Majesty. I'm in plain view." Felipe looks none too pleased as he meets the masked woman in black. Bewilderment spasms across his face. "What's the matter? You look like you've seen a ghost."

"*Are* you?" he asks, his blade still leveled at me. "A ghost?"

"Ghosts are harmless."

His face is carefully neutral; it gives little away. "La Pantera. So, it's true. You're alive. What do you want?" His jaw is so clamped the words barely escape him.

"Where is he?" I ask, my voice vibrant with danger.

"Who?"

"Inspector Corona. Where is he now?"

"How should I know?" he says in an unbothered tone. "I'm the king's son, not Corona's keeper."

With a fluid twitch of my wrist, I step in close, wrench the blade

116

from his grasp, and aim the point of it at his chest. "You lie. Come, your reply. Your life depends on it."

"I *don't* know. I swear that is the truth. May I never speak again if that is not true."

"Your Majesty!" Don Ruy comes running inside the pen and quickly steps in front of Felipe, shielding him with his lithe form. "You can't have him. You'll have to kill me first. I swear to God, I don't care what happens to me. Leave him! Leave him!"

Felipe moves him aside. "It's all right, Ruy. I've not been harmed." His calm appearance belies the rapid pace of his heartbeat. "What is it you want with Inspector Corona?" He looks down at his sword aimed at his chest. "This is unnecessary. You have my attention and cooperation. Now, tell me. What has he done to earn your ire? It must be serious."

I turn the sword about and offer its hilt to Felipe. "Inspector Corona forces his way through the north in search of a great treasure, killing and enslaving the people who occupy the region."

Felipe can hardly find his voice. "How could he? How can such a thing be done? Betrayal. A most terrible betrayal!" bursts out of him, carrying the depth of his shock. "This is an extreme violation. I assure you my father will hear of this matter."

"Are you saying Inspector Corona is acting independently, not on your father's orders?"

Felipe runs a hand over his mouth. "My father has been a shadow of himself since my mother's passing. This cruelty cannot be his doing. I am certain of it. The king's reforms must be upheld, and those who corrupt them must be brought to justice."

Though I'm wearing a mask, Felipe holds my gaze. His voice is steady. He seems to be telling the truth.

"Inspector Corona commands the army," I say. "He means to take control of the mine in Zacatecas. He must be stopped, before he can do more damage."

Felipe exchanges a glance with Don Ruy. "I'm afraid I cannot," he says through thin lips. "As the king's special deputy, Inspector Corona has extensive powers exceeding mine. I have been made a fool. I should have known he would become drunk on his own power. He is a madman."

"Sane or not, he must be given no advantage." I turn to take my leave.

"Where are you going?"

"To find myself an army."

"Wait!" Felipe says. "I can fight."

Don Ruy stares at him, wide-eyed. "Felipe, you're the king's son."

"Remember your place, Ruy," Felipe warns.

"You should remember yours, dear friend. You're the Crown Prince. It's too great a risk!"

"I am a knight, and I have my personal guard. I'll fight," says Felipe. "I'll do it."

"Why would you want to do that?" I ask him.

"It is my duty."

That's true, but is it the whole truth?

"I do not condone rebellion," Felipe says. "When the Spanish settlers rebelled against the New Laws in Peru, my father was in Germany. *I* suppressed the revolt. As the future king, I knew that my actions would set a precedent. Allowing rebellion to fester would weaken the Crown's authority, not just in the Americas but across the empire. If we showed leniency, others might follow suit, thinking they too could defy royal edicts." He takes a breath. "I'll fight because it's my duty, yes. But more than that, I'll fight because I know what's at stake. I will not allow rebellion to undermine the foundations of our empire. Not then, and not now."

"No," I say.

"But you're a woman!" Felipe protests.

"And you're a man."

"I shall be left here to cower behind these walls while you ride off to battle? I don't think so. I've no desire to stay abed," Felipe insists.

"What will men say of me when this is known? I will not—I refuse. I will send my guard to the north and join them on the battlefield."

"Felipe, you're far too valuable to Spain to risk it in battle," says Don Ruy. "What will the king say? If his heir falls? If you fall, so does Spain. It is better if she takes the risk."

"You can't stop me," Felipe says. "I *will* fight. I give you my word on that."

I stop in front of Don Cino's antechamber and softly knock.

I wait and listen, but there's no response. I knock again. And again. I put my ear up against the door, trying to hear something to indicate that I don't need to force my way in. He's usually here. A horrible feeling comes over me. I shove the door with my shoulder, once, twice, and it gives, pitching me forward into the dark interior. No sign of Tomás.

Fearing the worst, I look for Tomás around the palace, in his usual spots, but none of the servants have seen him. The only other place he might be is with Don Cino, who I hear frequents a seedy establishment in la traza where he goes to have a good time.

Sure enough, I find him in a brothel, with a buxom brunette upon his knee. He has lost his trousers, his shirt, and his left boot so far.

Slowly, I unsheathe my dagger, and the woman's laughter cuts off with a strangled gasp. She jumps to her feet with a wild scream, fleeing faster than Don Cino can gather his senses.

The sight of Pantera doesn't seem to faze Don Cino. He leans back, narrowing his bleary eyes.

"What do you *want*? You won't leave here alive," he snarls. "If I give the order, my men will have you in seconds."

For a man in his underpants, he is amusingly defiant.

"I must tell you something. I don't take threats well, Don Cino. And you're an idiot. Your men left a few minutes ago."

"Left? Left where?"

"To Heaven. Or Hell. I really don't know. At your expense, of course," I say. "I'm looking for Tomás. Your page. You remember your page don't you, Don Cino? Dark-haired, protuberant ears, clever wit."

"I don't know. He was here just a moment ago. Isn't he here?"

"My patience will only stretch so far."

"I don't know where he is! The boy is like a rat scooting off and scurrying around the streets."

"And you're the cat? Pestering him. You like beating up little boys, don't you? He's small and easy to pick on. Why don't you try this on for size?" I drive my dagger into the flesh of his knee, pushing deep into the bone.

Don Cino bellows a cry of agonizing pain. The stench of urine pricks my nose. He's pissed himself. "You *bitch*! Damn you! Damn you to Hell!"

I pluck the dagger from his bloody knee, and Don Cino gives a whimper. "Stop. Please stop."

"Do you think Tomás is shorter or taller?" I stab him again, higher up his leg. "Shorter?" I stab again and again, blood spurting, plunging the knife.

"You can't," Don Cino moans. "You can't do this."

"I can."

"I'm a don!"

"Oh, I know what you are. You're a tyrant, Cino Mondragon. I don't like tyrants, any kind of tyrants. I suppose no one does. I especially don't like tyrants in a position of power who seek defenseless targets and get away with it. You see, it frustrates me, and this is the way I deal with my frustration. You wouldn't raise a hand against me, would you? Go on. Try."

He does nothing of the sort.

"Tell you what," I say, slapping his bloody leg, and he winces in pain. "If the boy is alive, I might let you crawl back to the palace to tell everyone how Pantera frightened you. Although . . . I wouldn't want to leave you *entirely* unscathed, because you'll just do it again, won't you?"

"What do you care for a lousy nobody?" With hatred in his gaze, Don Cino attempts to seize me, but his leg doesn't work, and he tumbles forward, rolling close to my feet.

"Wait!" he says, flailing the air. "I have answers. Answers to the questions you must have asked yourself. Must still be asking. I can give you information. After all, I am Minister of Intelligence."

A muscle twitches in my cheek. "Information about what?"

"I can't very well tell you anything if I'm dead. If you kill me," he says, "you'll never know. Do you hear me? Never!"

What I should do is have Don Cino charged and tried before the Audiencia where old men will decide his guilt.

But I'm in no mood for such a tedious process.

"I can live with that," I say, then drive my knife into his skull. He is dead before sound can come out of his mouth.

"Pantera?"

I turn around. "Tomás."

"You . . . killed him," he gasps.

"I . . . I thought he had—"

"You saved me!" He comes to me quickly, wrapping his arms around my waist, and well . . . I don't try to get out of his hold. I welcome his warm embrace, although that's not my natural reaction, but seeing him unharmed and obviously not dead is such a relief, so I go with it.

CHAPTER 15

El Marqués

I head south to Cuernavaca, about a day's ride from the capital. On the way, my travelling coach passes sugarcane fields and the Tepozteco mountains, home to a belt of volcanos and the ruins of the temple-pyramid of Tepoztecatl, the god of pulque. I find the Valley of Morelos fascinating, a lush area I would love to explore.

Alas, I've not come for pleasure.

In the center of Cuernavaca stands the Palacio de Cortés, built on the site of a Tlahuica building that was razed by the Spanish when they first arrived. Cortés himself lived here, and now his sons do. It's a garden spot of great haciendas and an abundance of flowers, a favorite escape of noble Spaniards who vacation in the summer due to its soft and benign climate.

All I can think about in Cuernavaca is Tezca.

His people inhabited this land. It was them who found the area to be fertile and well-watered, abounding in minerals.

Now, the greedy encomenderos rule the region and grow rich off its soil.

"Leonora de las Casas Tlazohtzin to see Martín Cortés," I state firmly.

"The marquess is not home," the footman informs me in a tone that leaves me in no doubt that I am not welcome.

"When is he expected to return?"

"Return from where?"

"From . . . wherever he has gone."

"He hasn't gone anywhere."

The conversation is so absurd, I begin to wonder if I'm still asleep in the coach, trapped in some bizarre dream, or if the loss of tonalli is affecting my senses. "If the marquess has not gone anywhere, how is he not home?"

"Perhaps I should have said that he is not receiving visitors at present," the footman amends.

"Let me be clear on which Martín I am here to see," I say. "I'm here to see the elder Martín Cortés."

"He is not at home right now," the footman says.

I exhale. "If that is your way of saying—"

"He is truly not at home, lady. He is out for the day."

"Well then, will you tell the marquess that the viceregent of New Spain needs to speak with him."

He promptly leaves and returns a moment later, only to reiterate, "The marquess is not receiving visitors."

"Did you tell him who it was?"

"Indeed, your name was mentioned, lady," he assures. "It did not sway him. If I may be so bold, your name seems to have had an adverse effect. I'm sorry, but he will not see you."

"Am I permitted to wait inside for the elder Martín or am I to spend the day on your doorstep like a squatting vagrant?"

"I am under strict orders not to admit any visitors, lady."

"You seem a loyal servant."

He proudly inclines his head.

"Tell me, where do you think your loyalty lies? Are you loyal to a conqueror's son or to Viceroy Jerónimo, who rules New Spain for the king? No one does anything in this territory without official orders and permission directly from the king, or from his viceroy. You must ask yourself: would King Carlos enjoy your orders were he present in person? I think he would not be pleased if he learned the viceregent of New Spain had come all the way here to not be permitted an audience."

The man quivers for a moment, then gestures to the door, a slight note of panic filling his voice. "You may enter, lady."

I nod gracefully and wander inside the fortress-like palace. I linger in the courtyard patio before a statue which catches my eye. It's so out of place I turn swiftly in its direction. It appears to be a figure of a seated male form. It's carved in the round, like most Nahua sculptures were before the Fall. I find it odd that a work of Indigenous craftsmanship would be so prominently displayed in the palace of Cortés, an open symbol of the Tlahuica identity, encouraging adherence to paganism, which the Spaniards have certainly spent decades suppressing.

Why didn't they destroy this? I wonder, brushing my fingers along its rough edges.

The Spaniards erased every physical trace of Nahua culture, leaving little if no record of the past. This statue most likely occupied a safe position and survived destruction, for it's strangely untouched, merely weathered by time. Despite its tarnish, it holds an air of power to it that even the most exceptional paintings in the viceroy's gallery fail to achieve.

"I thought I heard a racket." Martín appears at my side. "What are you doing here, Leonora?" he asks, his eyes shifting about furtively.

"I *knew* it. Your footman said you weren't home."

"Yet you insisted."

"I insisted," I reply, a smirk curling my lips.

"I'm glad to see you, but it's not a good time. We're not receiving visitors."

Martín looks tired. He's older than I originally thought he was, at least more so than King Felipe. He's grown a scruff, so unlike his usual clean-shaven court appearance. It ages him in my eyes, closer to a man near thirty. His blond hair falls sleek and straight, and long, as if he's had no time to get it cut. It seems he couldn't care less. Maybe he doesn't.

He sees me eyeing him curiously.

"It's called a beard, Leonora," he says.

"Is that what it is? It looks like a wild animal."

"I know, I know. It suits me. I guess I have that animalistic magnetism people can't resist."

I quirk an eyebrow. "Animalistic magnetism?"

"Would you know," he says, "that on my way here, I was stopped by three ladies, all of whom said the same thing. What can I say? I have that effect. I can't help it."

"And what did you tell them?"

"I told them I get better with age. Like wine."

"More like cheese," I quip.

"I hope you understand it's not your fault you find me irresistible."

"Gracias, Martín. I feel better about myself already. I'll try to curb my lust for you." Looking at the statue, I ask, "Is this someone's idea of a sick joke? Because I don't think it's funny."

"That's Ozomatzin, a tlahtoani of Cuauhnahuac," Martín explains. "One of the most powerful kings of his time. They say he was a sorcerer."

"A sorcerer?"

Martín shrugs in response.

He must have been a great warrior. His hair is tied with tassels. "What is it doing here?" I ask.

"It was uncovered in the ruins," Martín says. "I guess someone buried it to keep it safe. Who knows how long it languished in obscurity."

It certainly looks old, but that doesn't answer my question. "Yes, but why does it still exist?"

"Why do you think? For the same reason this palace exists at all. It sends a message."

Why, of course, it does. Placing a Nahua statue in the shadow of a Christian residence lets everyone know, loud and clear, who continues to dominate over the remnants of Indigenous culture. Lest they forget who the masters are.

This man was a king, a great king, so I go down on one knee, touch a finger to the earth, then to my lips. When I rise, I lift my head to see someone on the other side of the courtyard, regarding me with a formidable scowl.

"Lady Leonora, your visit comes at a most inopportune time."

Don Martín Cortés y Zúñiga, marquess of the Valley of Oaxaca, is not what I expected.

I expected him to be a child. Instead, he's a young man, fairish, tall and angular, with features that would have most Christian ladies praising God for His goodness, while his elder half-brother Martín is faintly shorter, heavier framed.

I expected the palace of the richest man in New Spain to be grander, for there to be more pomp and show. Long introductions and elegant speeches. But Don Martín is brusque. Rude. He looks at me like I'm vermin, a rat carrying a plague to his beloved home.

Though he lacks political power in the colony, he wears an invisible crown. There's no question that he thinks himself superior to everyone gathered around him, a regular court of the blue bloods of New Spain, looking upon him as their natural leader. Such is the magic of his heavy name. Cortés the conqueror's second-born son is a pampered darling of privilege.

But, anyway, it hardly matters what I think of the marquess, or what he thinks of me. It's not as if we will have to deal together. It's not *him* I came to see.

"Did you inform Lady Leonora I'm not receiving visitors today?"

"Yes, I followed your instructions," Martín replies.

"It was made abundantly clear, Don Martín. I don't wish to intrude upon your valuable time," I say with my most humble voice. "If I may be permitted, I should like to speak to my stepmother. I've not seen her since—"

"What else? I'm in a great hurry on some urgent business," the marquess says.

"Only this."

"Very well. Make certain that Lady Leonora sees her stepmother and her visit comes to an end." He says this to Martín, who nods.

"Gracias, mi señor," I say.

The marquess leaves, and Martín sighs. "It's too early in the day to be *that* cynical. Why are you really here, Leonora?"

CHAPTER 16

La Monja

Viceroy Jerónimo believes Don Martín is a dangerous enemy because he inherited his father's title. Yes, he's a rich encomendero, but I don't think he's a threat. Even if the arrogant Don Martín attempted to be considered the foremost Spaniard in New Spain instead of the Crown's appointed viceroy—he's not the true heir.

The *true* heir of Cortés is entitled to the marquessate, an estate which covers a vast stretch of land across the valley—including Cuernavaca—properties, and an army.

"I need fighting men," I tell Martín.

"Ah, so that's why you've come," he says, leading a stroll, hands locked behind his back.

"The Chichimeca know battle, and they know the desert, but we don't have the numbers to match the enemy army."

"That is a favor only my brother can grant."

"Don Martín can do nothing for me," I say. "You and I both know that." He would never agree to send his army to the north. I wouldn't have wasted my time for a moment with him.

"He's the marquess," Martín reminds.

"Yes, he is. But he shouldn't be—"

"Lower your voice," Martín warns in a whisper as his eyes dart around. "Someone will hear."

"Good. Someone ought to listen. Let them hear. Let them know that Don Martín Cortés y Zúñiga is not the *true* heir of Hernán Cortés whose titles he bears and whose lands he possesses. He is just like me, pretending to be something he is not."

"Be *quiet*, Leonora," Martín responds, his gaze nervously traveling. He smiles and nods down the hall at passersby. "Do you understand what you're asking me to do?" he says under his breath. "You're asking me to challenge my brother's marquessal title."

"I understand exactly what I'm asking. I'm asking you to help us."

He swallows, seemingly taken aback by my boldness. "What you ask for is simply not possible," he says after clearing his throat. "Even if it was my wish, I could never be the marquess. I have enemies in Viceroyal Palace."

"Jerónimo is not a threat to you."

"Well, no, not at the moment. That's because my brother is the marquess. He's the one who rightfully owns Viceroyal Palace. But if things changed, if I took his place . . . then it would be different. Besides, it's not just your brother."

"Then who? King Felipe?" I ask. "He doesn't know it was you who impersonated him. No one knows. I've told no one."

"This is not my fight, Leonora. And if you were smarter, you wouldn't make it yours either."

"I suppose this is the part where I give you an inspiring speech about what's right and persuade you to risk your life for the greater good," I say bitterly. "Truth is, this shouldn't be anyone's fight. What are you even doing here, Martín?"

"Here?"

"Here. This place. What are you doing among the Spaniards? Hiding?"

"No."

"Then what?"

"I'm an advisor to the marquess."

"Why? I thought you wanted nothing to do with this life. You wanted freedom."

He stops walking and faces me. "Where else was I going to go?" he snaps. "What else *could* I do? Do you think I want to be here, Leonora? I had a life. I loved a man, then he died, and everything changed. I can think of a million places in the world where I would rather be than in this palace."

I tilt my head slightly to the side, looking at him intently. "Why don't you say his name? Why don't you say it, Martín? Nezahualpilli. His name was Nezahualpilli."

"Leonora. Don't go there," he cautions.

I'm already there.

"What, you have forgotten? He didn't simply die. He was *killed* . . . there is a huge difference," I say. "Neza was taken from us by Ichcatzin." Martín's eyes gleam with moisture, and my voice softens. "We both lost him. We *all* lost him. I miss him too."

Martín pushes out a defeated sigh. Battling yourself is tougher than any fight with a sword.

"I understand, Martín," I say. "The pain. More than you know. I lost . . ." My words trail off. "I've lost people I've loved."

"I don't want to feel like this anymore," he mutters, his hands tightened into fists, as if he hates just admitting that much. "Nothing is the same. I'm angry all the time, and I can't see an end to it. I wish I could make it stop. When will it stop?"

"I don't know," I say truthfully.

"What am I supposed to do with all this emptiness?"

I press my lips in a thin line. "I think there comes a point at which things start to get better, and you begin to even forget the bad you endured. Sure, it'd be nice to know the exact day that brighter times will begin to appear, but perhaps . . . the simple knowledge that such a day exists can be enough."

He's quiet, and as we resume our walking exploration of the palace, I add, "We can only honor the dead by not allowing the same agony that befell them to afflict others and to dedicate ourselves to the cause for which they gave their life. What would Neza say to you now, Martín? What do you think he would want you to do?"

"It is difficult enough to find comfort and direction in the life that I'm seeking. The last thing I want is to fight a fight that has absolutely nothing to do with me. I refuse to fight in the place of a person that is not here anymore. I just want to move on."

"It's too early in the day to be *that* cynical," I throw back at him. "Even King Felipe will fight with us."

That seems to get a reaction out of him. "Why would he do that?"

"How should I know? I can't read his mind."

Martín stares at me, giving me a look that says he doesn't believe my ignorance for one moment. "Pantera didn't ask?"

"I wasn't interested."

"You can't think of any reason? Any reason at all?"

With an air of indifference, I say, "One day he will be King of Spain. He wants to start proving himself a capable leader of men."

"He told you that?"

"Not so much in those words, but yes."

"And you believed him?" He laughs mirthlessly. "*You* of all people? Leonora . . . Leonora . . ." He looks at the sky with a sigh before turning his gaze back to me. "Please tell me you didn't."

"Didn't what?"

"Lie with him."

I snort. "I most certainly did *not*."

"Tell me the truth."

"That *is* the truth! I would never be in his arms."

"Why not?" he asks, serious. "Is that so preposterous? Let's look at the facts. Felipe is handsome, rich, and powerful. Oh, and he is the king's son. Am I missing anything?"

Now it's my turn to laugh. "Do you even know me at all?" I shake my head, amused and outraged all at once. "How do you know he's handsome?"

"I've seen his portrait," Martín replies quickly.

"You're a terrific liar, Martín, but there aren't any portraits of Felipe in Mexico. It's how you were able to fool everyone in the palace into believing you were him, remember?" As I say this, it occurs to me that Martín impersonated Felipe far too well, knowing details of his life that aren't recorded. I can think of only one reason for this. "You know him personally, don't you?"

"Yes," he admits. "I was his page in Spain, a position my father secured for me when I was a boy. We grew up together. I know him like no one else, Leonora. Even at night the bed didn't separate us. Felipe is more Christian than the pope and hates anyone who isn't. He has no esteem for any nation other than Spain. He consorts only with Spaniards. He would *never* help the Northmen. Whatever he's told you, it's all lies."

Did Martín love him? I wonder. What happened in Spain that drove them apart? Was it duty, religion, ambition? Or something more personal, more wounding? Is that why he's an enemy?

I don't know whom or what to believe. On one hand, Felipe has often displayed a character that borders on the ridiculous—silly, impulsive, and even foolish at times. He's prone to bouts of whimsy and seems to lack the seriousness that his position demands. I've seen him make light of situations that require gravity, and his penchant for indulgence has sometimes made me question his judgment.

On the other hand, he's on his way to becoming the most powerful man in the Western world.

It's this duality that confounds me—the contrast between the man who can be so frivolous and the one who is set to shape the future of nations.

"Look, Martín," I say, tired and resigned. "It doesn't matter. I don't care about Felipe. You can sit back and say, 'This isn't my fight, let the Chichimeca fight their war.' This is your war too. Shed your indifference and take up this cause now. This is a war against these lands. And you, and I, we were born here. Act like it and get to work. I need your help. I can't do it alone. I . . . don't have my powers."

"I'm sorry, Leonora. You've come all this way for nothing."

"Will you at least consider it?"

He sighs, his face full of conflict. "There's really not a thing I can do."

I want to scream, to shake him, to make him see what's so painfully obvious to me. He has more power than he realizes, more influence than he's willing to admit. But he's too scared to claim any of it.

As much as I wish I could force his hand, I know this is a choice he has to make on his own. When the time comes—if it ever does—I hope he'll stand with us.

Stop. Breathe. Calm yourself, Leonora.

I'm talking to myself in the courtyard, pacing—six, seven paces, no, that's not right; I try not to shuffle around. It feels like I'm being watched.

The next time I glance up, a figure framed in a white and brown habit is in front of me.

"Leonora?"

Nonplussed for an instant, I realize who it is.

"Vicereine Carlota?" I stutter. "A nun. You?"

I simply can't conceive a world in which Carlota de Sepúlveda y Olivares is a nun. Her mouth is marred by lines around her small lips. Her hair, once her crowning glory, is concealed under her habit, and her face is gaunt, her figure gangly.

But it's her eyes that haunt me the most. Carlota once had a gaze that could unsettle the bravest of men. Now she seems to be withering away.

"God called me, and I've taken holy vows," she says dutifully. "What are you doing here?"

"I came to ask a favor of the marquess," I tell her.

"What would you ask of him?"

"It doesn't matter. My request was denied."

"It must be important for you to come all this way."

"Yes, it is." I barely know what to say. "I'm sorry, I'm having a hard time believing you're a nun now. Aren't you supposed to be spying on Don Martín for Jerónimo?"

She meekly lowers her gaze before returning it to mine. "How is he? Jerónimo."

"Alive. But he's been imprisoned," I say, "and he seems to think King Felipe is a demon sent to destroy Mexico."

Vicereine Carlota says nothing; her face gives no sign of life, no indication of the impact of my words. "I will pray for him."

"That's it?"

"There's nothing more powerful than prayer," she says, her expression still impassive.

"He's your son. Don't you care that he's in prison?"

"I don't wish to be late for Mass. Go with God, Leonora." With that, she turns around and walks away.

"Wait," I say to her back, then rush after her. She stops and faces me, chin raised.

"You have nothing to say? Is religious life all you think about now? Have you forgotten Jerónimo since becoming a bride of Christ?"

Her silence is so out of character it's unsettling.

"If you're so holy now, can you explain why your God allowed this?" I go on. "Can you?"

Her voice comes in a soft whisper. "The Lord works in mysterious ways."

I scoff, shaking my head. "You know, I used to be much afraid of you. You never gave me any reason to like you. But even though I despised you, at least you had my respect. You're a fighter." I look her up and down. "You *were*. Now, you're just . . . ordinary. Invisible."

At that, Vicereine Carlota takes one slow step closer to me. Her countenance remains unchanged, yet she exudes a quiet fury that's somehow more alarming than violent rage.

"Leonora," she says, "we women are any number of things, as and when the need arises. Wouldn't you agree?" She smiles crookedly. "Before I left Viceroyal Palace, I said to Jerónimo, 'This viceroyalty is beset with wolves. You are the viceroy of New Spain, and you must be respected and feared by these wolves. How do you instill terror in their hearts? You become a stronger, more powerful wolf.'"

"What are you saying?"

"Success requires intelligence and audacity . . . qualities which the marquess tragically did not inherit along with his father's name and title. Don Martín seems to have been affected by some kind of poison."

"A poison?"

"He can't seem to make up his mind," she says bitterly. "At one moment, he schemes with the sons of the first conquerors, and at the next tries to curry favor with the Audiencia."

I frown. "You mean the encomenderos?"

"Yes. They chatter so much everyone knows about it. They are leeches, arguing that the Crown owes them a living. They hate the New Laws. They receive some assistance from the treasury, but they claim it does not suffice to support them. Their family fortunes are threatened. They see Jerónimo as their enemy—and they're right. Hernán Cortés and his men accomplished the most audacious conquest. But something—I can't say whether it's spirit or vision—has been lost over these thirty years. Maybe the conquerors' sons lack conviction. After all, they are rebelling to merely preserve inherited wealth. Whatever the reasons . . . they are revolting, and the Audiencia allows harsh punishments—torture, imprisonment, even death for those found guilty of plotting against the king's authority in New Spain."

I smirk. "So you *are* a spy."

"I am a nun." Vicereine Carlota nods penitently, but a calculating gleam lights in her eyes. "By God's grace."

If there's one thing I know, God and Vicereine Carlota are generally of the same mind. Their will is always done.

CHAPTER 17

El Desierto

The unwillingness of Martín to help leaves my mood sullen and despairing. In La Gran Chichimeca—the vast stretch of desert between the majestic Sierra Madre mountains—Inspector Corona threatens fighting and death. And if the Chichimeca don't hold them off, then nothing will prevent Inspector Corona from attacking the mine, plundering the silver, and bringing about the utter ruin of the Chichimeca. If I do nothing, Jerónimo hangs for stealing the King's Fifth, I fail Eréndira, people die, whatever Ichcatzin is plotting will likely bring more death, and the battle I'm fighting with myself will have been for absolutely nothing.

I refuse to let that happen.

I can go no farther this day, however. My legs feel like lumps moving through mud, so heavy they are with weariness. I seek an inn for the night where I wash, eat, rest. At dawn, I purchase a horse.

It takes me about a week to voyage to Zacatecas. At least, I think it does. I count the number of times Tonatiuh rises, but I can't be sure anymore. I have to ask for directions and am pointed down the path northwest, which is unspectacular, winding through some small towns and dry shrublands. The plains are vast and relatively flat, always framed by the distant mountains. Nothing grows here except for the yucca trees and prickly pears.

For the most part, I avoid the main road expanding across the desolate countryside as I hope not to attract attention. I'm not wearing my mask, and I don't want to have to explain myself to other travelers, soldiers, bandidos, or King Felipe, should I have the misfortune of meeting him.

Leaning forward, I pat my horse's neck. His coat is warm, damp with sweat. We're both tired. His head bobs up and down with each step while mine lolls from side to side. When the trail meets a pool of clear, cold water, I slow down, so he can drink and catch his breath. I take a moment to look around, trying to orient myself. I'm only familiar with the general area in which La Condesa is situated; I don't know the precise location of the Chichimeca gathering spot.

I gather the reins and straighten in the saddle. After crossing the featureless land, I come upon the province of New Galicia, a kingdom of the viceroyalty of New Spain. The first signs of the mining town of Zacatecas rise from the ground, set among hills rich with silver veins hidden deep within.

A peculiar greenish rock catches my eye, its crest shaped like the brilliant feathers of a quetzal, standing tall above the other hills like a watchful guardian. At its base, an army camp bustles with movement as warriors set up defenses, dig trenches, move quivers, carts, and barrels, construct ladders, and fortify the hillside in anticipation of battle.

"Who are you?" a warrior asks me as I approach.

Who am I?

Who . . . am I?

Bone-weary, every muscle aching from days in the saddle, I have barely enough strength to say, "I don't know."

The last thing I feel before I slip out of awareness are his arms stopping my fall.

Darkness, then, blinking, a figure comes into view. My vision clears, and I recognize the face peering down at me with concern.

"Tezca," I say breathlessly. My surroundings come into focus; I'm lying on a mat inside a tent. "What happened?"

"You collapsed. You shouldn't have come, Leonora. Without your tonalli, you could've—" he groans, twists his face away.

"I want what you want," I tell him. "To put an end to this. Together we can do that."

"You're a fool, you know that?"

"I don't want to be at war with you," I mutter.

My eyes feel heavy. I close them and take a breath. When I open them, Princess Nelli steps inside the tent with a man following behind her. A warrior, tall and powerfully built, garbed in armor that presumably befits his rank.

He looks at me and asks, "Is this the Godslayer?"

"Supposedly," Nelli says.

"She is," Tezca tells her.

"My name is Francisco Tenamaxtli," he says, approaching me.

"I know who you are," I reply. "You're the leader of the Caxcanes." Another Chichimeca tribe.

"Can you fight?" he asks, face dour, no time for the courtesies warriors love to exchange.

I've heard tales of his prowess. If the stories are true, Tenamaxtli led an uprising that started a brutal war in Mixtón—a hill here in Zacatecas that served as a Caxcan stronghold many years ago. Nelli's father, Pedro de Alvarado, assisted in putting down the revolt, but he was met by Tenamaxtli, and crushed to death when his horse fell on him.

In the end, Mixtón fell to the Spaniards, and Tenamaxtli was captured. They say he became a Christian, and the red wooden cross he bears tells me he now serves the Nailed Christ, though I don't know if his conversion was by choice or force. A warrior so legendary, lost in time. I thought he was dead.

"I can," I say finally, but as I feel the cold pommel of my sword beside me, I know I may not wield it as I have before.

139

"Your reputation precedes you. You're our best hope for avoiding a war we can't win," Tenamaxtli tells me.

"Best hope?" If that's true, then we're all doomed.

"You are Pantera. You are a sorceress. You defeated the Obsidian Butterfly," he says.

"You are Tenamaxtli. You are a war chief. You led a legendary rebellion."

He grimaces. "And lost."

"You waver?" I ask. "This is not the resolve of a warrior."

"I have considered it, again and again. Even God can't find a way through this."

"God has no place here." More energized, Nelli says, "We *can* win. We know where the battle will take place. We use the desert to our advantage."

"A time of miracles, to be sure," Tenamaxtli says.

I sit on a rock by the campfire, leaning on my sword, watching Tezca spar with Tenamaxtli in the firelight. Both of them move with the fluidity of seasoned warriors, both skilled enough that they shouldn't need practice, but in Tezca's movements, I catch tiny moments of hesitation. As he lunges and parries, his sword seems a split second behind. Each time, he has to adjust his grip or shift his stance mid-strike, trying to make up for the sword's delay.

It's subtle, but I can see it. Tezca is fighting against his weapon as much as he's fighting Tenamaxtli.

Nelli appears beside me, offering a cup of pulque. I shake my head, and she takes a seat on the rock next to mine. I stay quiet, my focus still on the duel.

"Nothing happened," Nelli says.

"What?"

She takes a slow sip of her pulque, then brushes her long red hair away from her eyes. Her gaze follows Tezca as he deflects a blow. "Between us," she says, nodding toward Tezca.

I stiffen, feeling a prickling tension along my spine. "I didn't ask."

She gives me a sidelong look. "You didn't have to. I can see it plain on your face."

"Tezca is free to bed who he pleases."

I didn't ask because I didn't want to know the answer, and now she's thrown it at my face. "It was only a night," Nelli says. "Nothing more."

I swallow the knot lodged in my throat. "Nothing?"

She drinks the last of her pulque and sets it down by her feet. "I suppose it was something. But fleeting. Like smoke." She looks at me, and I see a glimpse of honesty in her eyes. "He's more yours than mine. Maybe more than he realizes."

She stands, leaving me in a silence that feels like an open wound. The weight of her words presses down, and something inside me snaps. I rush to my feet and stumble into the shadows, retching into the bushes. When the spasms pass, I lean back and draw in a shaky breath, only to see Tezca approaching.

"Are you all right?" he asks.

I sit up straighter and suck in my breath. We've barely spoken; every time we try, it feels strained—mostly because he keeps asking questions I can't answer honestly. *What happened? Where is your tonalli? Are you all right?* I can sense the rift between us growing even more expansive, and it all seems so confusing as my body dwindles.

"Stop asking," I say, my throat raw and scratchy. "I don't want to keep lying to you."

"Then don't. Why can't you trust me? When did I lose your trust? What did I do?" More questions I can't answer. "There's no reason you have to face this alone. I'm here. I will protect you always."

"Tezca." My shoulders sag. Staring at him, I search for the right words. "It's not something from which you can protect me."

He presses his lips together, his eyes full of determination. *What would he do right now,* I wonder, *if I confessed everything?* For a moment, I contemplate it. But being truthful about my tonalli loss, why my power is growing, my real father—it would only lead to the revelation of his divine birth. Xochiquetzal warned me against this. And who knows a man better than his own mother?

I can't tell him what's really on my mind, so instead, I settle on something else.

"You're fighting your blade," I say.

He frowns, thrown off by the sudden change. "What?"

"Your thrusts are strong, but they lack precision."

He raises an eyebrow, giving me a look that's both amused and annoyed. "Do they now? I've never had any complaints about my thrusts." My cheeks warm, and it's not from the campfire. I do my best to look unfazed, but Tezca's grin tells me I'm failing miserably. "Oh, I'd love to know," he says, teasing. "How should I be thrusting, Leonora?"

My cheeks burn hotter. That's *so* not what I meant, but the way he's looking at me makes it impossible not to go there. Nelli's words float back to me—something happened between them. I didn't dare ask for the details. But now . . . I can't help but wonder what it might be like to be on the receiving end of that strength. Would his . . . precision match the confidence behind that smirk?

The thought lingers longer than I'd like. Just the mere idea is enough to make my heartbeat quicken. Before I can stop myself, I'm lost in the imagined sensation of having his attention fully turned on me.

Tezca leans in a little closer. "Well?" he murmurs. "You seemed so confident a moment ago."

I clear my throat, searching for words to bring us back to safer ground. "You're pushing too hard," I manage, though I instantly regret my choice. "You're adjusting your grip like you're compensating for the sword's size rather than letting it move with you. A warrior of your caliber should be better at handling his weapon."

He bites his lip, trying to sort out what just came flying out of my mouth. I don't blame him. I'm still trying to sort it out. My words are practically wrapped up in a golden ribbon, begging for him to turn them right back on me.

"So it's the *handling* of my weapon that's the problem? Not its size?"

Nine Hells, my face is on fire. Tezca looked upset a moment ago, probably about me critiquing his technique, but that irritation is gone. Now his gaze suggests we're no longer talking about swordplay at all.

He steps closer, clearly enjoying every bit of my flustered reaction. "Are you saying I should be more . . . gentle?"

"I'm saying you should *focus*," I reply, my heartbeat racing at his suggestive tone. "Precision isn't about going soft—it's about knowing exactly where you're aiming."

Tezca chuckles, his eyes intense and playful. "Oh, I know *exactly* where I'm aiming. I don't miss . . ." he murmurs, his voice low enough to make my skin tingle. "It sounds like you've been paying *very* close attention to how I wield my weapon. I'd hate to disappoint. Maybe I should take notes. Or better yet . . . maybe you could demonstrate? I'm more than willing to perfect my skills."

My mouth goes dry. I swallow and take a deep breath. "There's a delay. Your sword is resisting. Like it's waiting for something. A name, maybe," I say. "It will give it power."

Tezca pulls his sword free. The weapon gleams in the jumping firelight. "This," he tosses it in the air, then catches it, "is what gives it power. Not a name."

"Your sword obeys you now because you wield it, but a named blade becomes more than just a tool. It remembers, it listens, it starts to anticipate the hand that holds it. A true warrior doesn't just wield a weapon—they forge a bond with it. And that bond begins with a name. You *know* I'm right."

He looks at his sword, thinking. "What should I name it?"

"Well, it's long and slender," I say. "There are scratches all up and down the blade." Slights, dents, dust, imperfections. "They look almost like tiny scales."

"Yellow-Beard," Tezca decides.

"Yellow-Beard?"

"You find them here in the desert," he says. "They're quite fast, and like all vipers, quite venomous."

I look at him and wonder what he thinks of this. Of me. Wishing we could be somewhere alone, just the two of us, where a thousand things don't pull at us.

"Tezca. I . . . want to explain something. Felipe—"

"You don't owe me anything, Leonora," he says. "You aren't my woman, nor I your man."

I wanted it to be different. I still do. My desire for things to be other than they are is like a vise closing in on me. This is awful. This is terrible. I have to pick up my sword. I need to be in fighting shape. I have to be a good warrior. I have to be who I have worked so hard to become.

But that identity is not available to me as my sickness continues. Without it, who am I, exactly? Who is dying? Who is living? It all seems so complicated. My sense of being someone in the world is greatly threatened.

"You know where it is, don't you? Your tonalli." Tezca searches my eyes for answers. "You wouldn't be here if you didn't. You'd be somewhere off looking for it."

I lower my head, nod, and turn away. I can't meet his gaze. I can barely utter words.

"Where?" he asks. "Is it far?"

"It's safe."

"You're shaking. Come on, I'll get you warm." He begins to take off his armor, shoulder pads, belt, and bracers.

"What are you doing?" The question is barely audible through the chattering of my teeth.

How easy it would be to sink into him, pillow my head on his chest, our arms entwined. I can almost feel his skin, so warm, so unbelievably warm.

"I'm not trying to seduce you, Leonora."

"I'll deplete you."

"You won't."

"It can't be avoided," I say angrily. "You know how this works. It's why you're always tired. It's why everyone is intoxicated by you. They're the moth. You're the flame. You're the light they're drawn to. The star that burns brighter, not the one that falls; the one others make wishes on to the gods."

He sighs. "I'm always tired because there's battle every day. I don't sleep much. I don't know peace. I have not known peace a single day in my life."

"No," I counter. "You're tired because you freely and wantonly share yourself with everyone, and when there is a problem with your tonalli, sooner or later it reflects on your body." I should know that better than anyone.

He folds his arms across his chest. "So I waste my tonalli, according to you?"

"It's always been your problem."

"I have *another* problem?"

"That and repressed anger."

"Nine Hells, now I have repressed anger too?"

"A sorcerer uses their tonalli wisely. You squander it. Even gods—" I quickly stop myself from going any further.

"Even gods what?"

"Need blood to sustain them," I remedy. "Considering your recklessness, you've been lucky. You're healthy. I wouldn't take that for granted."

"I *hate* the way you presume you know me," he says harshly.

"No, you don't. You hate that what I presume is true. You forget, Tezcacoatzin," I say, "I see you as you are."

For a moment, Tezca looks as though he will lose it completely. "It's no wonder I'm always tired. You exhaust me, do you know that? I've never known anyone who tired me out as much as you do."

145

He leaves me with the sound of fire crackling, the flames dying, dying, dying away. I hug my shoulders.

It's going to be a cold night.

Much later, my eyes open at the sound of Tezca writhing in his sleep beside me.

"Tezca?"

I hasten to wake him, giving him a violent shake. His eyes are tightly shut, racing back and forth beneath his lids.

"Tezca. Wake up." I snap my fingers in his face. He seems lost in some sort of trance. "Wake up!"

In a panic, I do the only thing I can think of. I press my lips to his, taking his tonalli, and almost immediately feel it leaving his body. This dream will be over soon, one way or the other.

Come on. Come on. Wake up.

I let the kiss linger, and then he sits up so quickly that he gasps. He barely seems to recognize me. I stare at him. This face. His face. I know every inch, every pore, but I don't know what goes on in his mind. He looks confused and frightened for a few seconds.

"What did you do?" he says, wide-eyed.

"I—nothing."

He looks down at his hands and sees them trembling. "Nothing?" he says, trying to clinch his fingers together in an effort to stop it.

"You were dreaming, and I couldn't wake you."

"So you kissed me?"

"Without tonalli, you don't dream," I explain. "I wasn't going to drain you completely."

His panting breaths echo between us. "Go back to sleep." Even his voice is different. Raspier. Weaker.

"Did something happen?" I ask.

He grunts, rubbing his face.

"Tezca?"

"I'm fine." He sighs and closes his eyes like he wishes that was true. He wipes the sweat off his forehead. "It's the same every time."

"The same? The same nightmare?"

"Yes." His head is hung. "Always the same."

"What was it about?" I ask, unsure if I want to know the answer. "If you tell me, you won't dream it again."

"It feels real. It feels like a memory." He shakes his head as if to clear it and focus on something else. "It wasn't real," he says, trying to convince himself more than anyone else.

His eyes betray a haunting pain. Tezca's tonalli is the most fervent I've ever encountered. Yet, there are moments when I sense pockets of cold within him, like a gaping wound hidden beneath layers of warmth. Where does it come from?

It was the Precious Flower Xochiquetzal who said Tezca has lived many lives, and it's best to keep those memories dormant—for within them lies the knowledge of his sorcery—power that could reshape worlds, for better or worse.

Quetzalcoatl told me about Tollan, the once great city of the ancient Toltecs, men and women of knowledge who preceded the Nahuas, and how Tezca—as a powerful sorcerer—aided his father Tezcatlipoca in destroying the city.

It may or may not have been swallowed by a great flood.

It may or may not have been attacked by the Chichimeca.

It may or may not have been destroyed by a war between Quetzalcoatl and Tezcatlipoca.

No one is sure what is true; no two people can ever agree on what happened to the lost civilization of Tollan.

If Tezca's memories are locked away, how can I help him? What is he holding on to? What else is there? Is he remembering?

"Is that why you haven't been sleeping?" I ask.

"You need to stop worrying about me and start worrying about yourself."

"What does that mean?"

"It means what it means."

I roll my eyes. "Here we go."

"Where are we going?"

"Nine Hells, why are we fighting about this, Tezca?"

"Do we know how to do anything else?"

"Yes," I say forcefully. It's my turn to convince myself. "Of course. I told you I don't want to be at war with you. I meant it."

He lets out a tired chuckle. "Without war, you and I? We're not warriors," he says. "I am just a man, and you are just a woman. We can only obey our true nature."

How can he obey his true nature if he is unaware of it?

"You think that's true?" I ask, my voice small. "That we can't escape who we are?"

"Don't you? It's a punishment from the gods."

"I thought you didn't believe in the gods."

"That's why they punish me," he says. "Because I don't believe in them."

"Do you not believe that Quetzalcoatl carries the Fifth Sun, and that Tezcatlipoca would see it destroyed?"

"I believe," he says, "you are ruining the moment."

"What moment?"

"I'm being charming. Obviously. Now let me sleep."

"What if you have another nightmare?"

"Guess you'll have to kiss me again."

I give him a look.

"I'm sorry. I don't make the rules," he jokes, but uneasiness crosses his face. It passes quickly.

Tezca rolls onto his side. I lick my lips, the taste of him still lingering. His tonalli hums through me, warm and familiar. The headache I haven't been able to get rid of for days is instantly gone. I have no pain. Somehow, it's easier to breathe. It's as if this fog lifted—a veil—like mist over the fields when the sun breaks through, and you can see clearly again.

"What is it about war that makes us so emotional?" I say into the night.

"Knowing every second could be our last," Tezca whispers.

In a moment, I'm asleep. I sleep deeply and soundly.

CHAPTER 18

La Mina

A mounted Spaniard arrives bright and early, protected by a suit of finely wrought steel and iron. His face, like mine, is concealed beneath a helmet, and a guard of no more than twenty men accompanies him.

"Pantera." His voice is muffled beneath his helmet. I didn't think he'd come.

Tezca is in no mood for nonsense. "What is he doing here?"

Felipe lifts his helmet's visor to say, "I've come to offer my sword and carry it against Inspector Corona."

"Why?" Tezca asks.

"I'm Christ's servant, and if Inspector Corona wins, then Christ is defeated. I will do all I can for my master."

"Your master has no business here," Nelli tells him.

"He wants to fight. Let him fight," Tezca says.

While we prepare for battle, Felipe begs the Christian God to send a host of his brightest angels to protect us against the snares of the Devil and lead us in a victorious war.

"Michael, the great warrior, is with us!" he shouts. "We can't lose. Michael and his flaming sword are with us!"

"Oh, make it stop," Nelli grumbles.

A good battle speech stiffens the back, gets the blood flowing, tightens your grip on your weapon. This one is like sitting in Mass during the dreadful homily. Men yawning, having trouble holding their heads. At least Felipe keeps it short.

"A multitude of arrows could not finish Sebastian!" he goes on. "The Romans tried to kill him, but his faith was so deep! Our strength will be the same!"

"Who is Sebastian?" Nelli asks.

"Saint Sebastian is a patron of archers and soldiers," Tenamaxtli explains.

"Great," Nelli jeers. "We have angels and saints."

Felipe glances around at our warriors, puzzled. "Where are your horses? Do you not ride into battle?" he asks me.

"It is not our way," I say.

"But how can you hope to face an enemy on equal footing without the advantage of cavalry? Do you plan to outrun them?"

Some of our warriors snicker.

Nelli sneaks up behind Felipe's horse and gives it a little spook. She grins as Felipe calms the animal. "We only need to outrun their wits . . . Your Majesty."

Next to me, Tezca pulls in a sharp breath. "This is foolish. You need your vital force."

"You've seen me fight without it," I tell him.

"I'm completely aware of your fearlessness in the face of danger."

"Then why are we having this conversation? I have my sword. I'm good."

I stretch my neck, tilting my head back at the sky, letting Tonatiuh do his divine work. A hot wind blows past us, and our long braids whip against our backs. Tezca was right. Our life is combat. We feel most alive in the thick of battle. It's our element. It's who we are.

"Did you sleep well?" I ask. "No nightmares?"

He ignores the question. "Will you kill me if I ask you to be careful?"

"Will *you?*"

He looks away, grinning.

"What? Is that such a ridiculous question? I have news for you—you're not invincible, Tezca. And some of us might want you around after all of this."

Above, a tawny owl screeches, adding to my dread. You don't see birds of darkness flying during the day. They also don't spend much time in deserts either.

It's an omen of death, but whose?

We're a strange army fighting a strange war. Natives with Spanish allies against Spaniards with native allies. Then again, it's happened before. If not for the alliance between Cortés and enemies of the Mexica—the Nahuas of Tlaxcala, the Totonacs of Cempoala—Mexico-Tenochtitlan wouldn't have fallen to the conquistadors. Cortés had an army of some hundred thousand Indigenous warriors fighting for him. He couldn't have done it on his own.

History repeats itself today in that respect.

The first group, led by Felipe, is the Spanish guard; he has soldiers, horses, churchmen, angels, and saints. The second is the Chichimeca component: the Caxcanes assembled under their warlord Tenamaxtli, and the Red Sparrows under the command of Nelli. Third, the Tlahuica allies, headed by Tezca.

Nelli sends fifty of her best archers to produce a shower of arrows in different ambush sites in the hope that they can inflict considerable damage before the enemy reaches the mine.

"A welcome party," Nelli calls it. She makes it sound so simple.

"This is not a wise plan," I tell her. "We already have lesser numbers, and by splitting our army you leave us open to defeat. We don't have a true sense of what we're dealing with."

Despite the danger of her divided army being attacked and overrun, she is confident we will be reunited to confront Inspector Corona.

She is wrong. And my instinct is right, for two scouts arrive with news, their horses' manes tossing in the wind.

"What is it? What did you see?" Nelli asks.

The Spaniard's intimidating force took care of the surprise attacks with deadly efficiency, they're on the move, and there's little doubt they intend to penetrate the mine and strike the entrance at the base of the mountain. One of the scouts remarks that there are enough enemy soldiers to keep us fighting for two or three days.

Nelli is furious at the news and the many casualties suffered, but she swallows her bitter disappointment. Her people need her leadership to survive this defeat.

"The battle will be finished in one day," she arrogantly replies. Her warriors are dead, but she has no time to think about them. Nothing separates Inspector Corona from us now.

Felipe's priests offer blessings and sprinkle shields and weapons with holy water, promising the owners an immediate trip to paradise for all eternity should they perish in battle.

What the men need is fire in their spirit, not holy water.

"You have your god and we have ours," Tezca says, unsheathing Yellow-Beard. "I do not care if you are Christian or pagan, as long as your blades sing a song of victory today."

The men like what they hear.

"Axcan ahzo nehhuatl ahnozo tehhuatl!" Tenamaxtli exclaims. *It's me or you now.* "Quin ihcuac nomiquiz auh momiquiz!" *Until my death, or yours.*

That starts the cheering, and Felipe seizes the advantage. "Unleash Hell! We show them no mercy! God is with us!"

I know Felipe only says this to rouse the men. He doesn't mean it. Mercy is an important quality for Christians. A tenet of the Christian faith. God himself showed mercy when he sacrificed his son on the cross to pay the price for the sin of men. Felipe does as his God commands.

I wear my mask, a cowl helmet with a mesh that's easy to see out of, padded armor, belt, skirt, and sandals laced to my knees. I don't wear my robe, for the desert heat takes its toll. The Sword of Integrity hangs on my back. It's easier to draw over the shoulder than from the hip, and this way, the first stroke can be a downward slash.

That's the general idea.

But when the depth of the enemy army is exposed in full, stretching across the desert like a mirage of death, I stiffen like a rigid wooden doll. My mind tells me it's an excellent idea to run, but my body is rooted to the spot by incapacitating fear.

I've gone to battle, I've faced demons, but no one, not even the bravest among us, is so fearless as to be unimpressed by such a formidable sight. The priests are probably soiling themselves in their robes.

Tezca doesn't take his eyes off the enemy. I see the sheer focus of his concentration, how his grip tightens around Yellow-Beard's hilt.

"Together?" he asks.

I nod. "Together."

Inspector Corona's army advances at a steady pace.

Huitzilopochtli help us, I pray, looking down at the hummingbird on my sword hand. *Warrior, help us all, for I do not think we can win.*

The desert is a hostile place where most life struggles to survive, especially in the dry season, but today—today the desert is an ally.

Nelli scoops up a handful of sand. She holds it up in the air and opens her hand, letting the sand slip through her fingers and back to the earth.

"Loose!" Tenamaxtli shouts.

In perfect unison, archers release their deadly obsidian-tipped arrows. A blanket of arrows, searching for their targets. Lest they expose their bodies, Inspector Corona's army swiftly hoists their shields above their heads, linking them in a protective canopy to repel the barrage. But instead, a stillness settles, and the Spaniards, thinking no arrow found its mark, charge forward.

That's their first mistake.

Chichimeca don't miss.

In the distance, a rumble sounds. Slow to come, hesitant, gradual, then building, a long, low rumble beyond the hills.

Looking at each other in bewilderment, the Spaniards jerk their collective heads upward, searching the skies for a sign of attack but seeing only Tonatiuh winking back at them.

The arrows weren't aimed at the enemy lines. Where they bore down, I cannot guess, but the night before, the Chichimeca were hard at work, filling barrels with sand. When those barrels start rolling down the dunes, raising a storm of sand, it strikes the enemy army like the powerful wing of a gigantic bird. In one moment, the eyes and mouths of the Spaniards are filled with debris. Altogether, choking and coughing, trying to avoid the cloud of dust, the Spanish ranks are disrupted.

Their army is thrown into disarray. The sight holds me in thrall until Tezca shrieks his battle cry and thrusts Yellow-Beard in the air.

Tenamaxtli shouts, "Charge!"

Then Felipe, "Forward!"

"Find me Inspector Corona!" Nelli roars out. "The first warrior to take him will be richly rewarded!"

Felipe's guard shuffles unevenly, but the Chichimeca, on foot and more disciplined, retain their formation. As one, they move ahead.

Running, I rip my sword free. The dust has not yet fully settled, and my first Spaniard goes down with a cracked skull before he can even make a move. I hit him with my hilt, breaking his nose and teeth. Sweat pours from beneath my mask, the Sword of Integrity slips in my sweaty hands, and weariness makes my limbs numb, but it is a gloriously hot day with not a single cloud in the sky. I'm good and warm. I battle on.

Another Spanish soldier quickly comes at me. I bring my sword hammering down but then stumble with a cry, knocked to the side by a wounded horse. My legs are pinned. I try to free them, pushing weakly at the animal. My nose stings from a pungent, bestial odor like that of a slaughterhouse.

Blood and shit. Those are the smells of battle.

My opponent is upon me. I desperately fend him off, swinging my sword wildly, but before he can land a blow, his head is chopped off.

"Leonora. Can you hear me? It's me. Martín."

"Martín?" I try to blink away the blood from my eyes. "Are you really here?"

He tugs me free, dragging me by the shoulders. He then slits the horse's throat so that it might not endure any further pain. I turn away, anger and sorrow churning inside me. The horse was an innocent in all of this, a loyal creature that had no part in our conflict. Why must such pure, blameless beings be dragged into our brutal struggles, paying the price for battles they neither understand nor chose?

"Can you walk?" Martín asks, threading an arm around my waist.

I give an unsure nod. No bones are broken, but putting pressure on my legs pains me. "What made you change your mind?"

"Vicereine Carlota," he says.

"Vicereine Carlota?"

"Go."

"What about you?"

"I'm not alone." He winks at me, then he spins, slashing at the legs of a soldier who serves to swing at his head.

Martín has brought an army from Cuernavaca with him. His men fiercely throw themselves into the fray, coming at the Spaniards and surrounding them on every side. Tezca is shouting commands, beheading two as he does. Nelli whistles sharply and warriors fall in behind her. She marches on, sword pointed forward, nimble on her feet. For a tall and large man, Tenamaxtli possesses surprising speed; he bears no sign of defeat. The stories of him are true. He's a creature of bloodshed, swinging and hacking through many.

The enemy falters at this onslaught. Those who are able, run and scream, and those who fall are crushed.

The Spaniards have nowhere to go.

Chichimeca arrows find every flaw in the enemy's armor, and the Spaniards, who make their best attempts to bury their fine Toledan blades in the heart of every Northman, turn and run, shouting to go back to the presidio.

Tezca is screaming incoherently. "They're getting away!"

"Stop them!" Nelli orders.

Felipe cheers himself hoarse. "Inspector Corona is defeated! We won! We won! Praise God!"

His men celebrate victory, laughing and hugging one another.

"What are you so happy about?" I ask Felipe. "We won nothing."

"They're gone, aren't they? We've won."

King Felipe is a Knight of the Spanish Order of the Golden Fleece, whose Grand Master is his father. But he doesn't understand battle.

Tezca and I exchange looks with each other. We are warriors. And warriors know that in war, you can't let the enemy make the next decision. It's only when you attack that you win. We merely defended ourselves. We did not carry slaughter to the enemy.

"Did anyone see Inspector Corona?" Nelli asks.

"He's not among the dead or wounded," Tenamaxtli says.

"We have nothing more to fear from him," Felipe insists. "He's retreated. There's nothing we can do about it. It's over." He gazes over the field blanketed with fallen warriors. "Let us see to our dead and wounded."

"*You* can't," I say.

"What?"

"There's nothing *you* can do about it."

Felipe stares at me, his eyes wrinkled shrewdly. "If you make an assault on the presidio it will turn bad fast and even someone with your particular skillset, Pantera, will be—"

Martín cuts in. "You don't want to finish that sentence. Trust me."

"—*vulnerable.*"

"Vulnerable?" I parrot.

"It was nice knowing you," Martín says with a chuckle.

"It's Your Majesty to you," Felipe snaps.

Martín lifts his hands. "As you command."

"Say it. Use the words."

Martín makes a theatrical bow. "Your Majesty."

"If you two are done with your pissing match, we might have time to win this battle," Nelli grumbles.

With a shake of his head, Tenamaxtli says, "Corona has more men at the presidio. We could have overwhelmed them before, but now . . ."

"They're easier to defeat on open ground, but we can beat them," Nelli says.

No one is willing to throw everything into battle for fear of losing everything. So we wait. We wait like hounds for table scraps. The battle is less than an hour old, yet now it pauses. We're forced to wait for Corona to make his assault.

"Cowards," Nelli says. "They're skulking in their presidio because they don't dare come out to face us." She takes a few paces forward. "Am I talking to myself? They're *afraid*."

Some warriors take up the shout. "They're afraid!"

Martín scoffs. "*We're* afraid."

"If no one protects the mine," I say, "we leave it exposed."

Tenamaxtli nods. "This is what Corona came for."

"Then we must get to him before that happens," says Nelli.

"No one must do or say anything rash," Tezca advises.

"There's no time!" Nelli shouts. "It has to be now! This is the moment to attack and keep the battle alive. It has to end. Not tomorrow or the next day. Today. It ends with Corona's surrender."

"And if he doesn't give you that?" I ask her.

"Then he'll give me his life."

I think it's a mistake, but we go, chanting that the enemy is afraid.

CHAPTER 19

El Presidio

Less than half a day's march, we come upon Inspector Corona's presidio. It's a square fortress of stone walls with a scattering of buildings and a courtyard inside, positioned strategically on a rocky outcrop that rises above the sand. It holds tremendous advantages for its defenders, and conversely, presents an attacker with immense obstacles.

But, to our amazement, at the easternmost wall, we discover the fort's double-gated entrance is wide open.

"It's a trap," Martín says.

I agree but do not say so.

"Do you hear anything?" I ask Tezca.

"Footsteps inside," he says. "Faint. Hiding."

"What the hell are they doing in there?" Martín asks.

"Praying, probably," says Nelli.

"We can't dislodge Corona from there by ourselves," Tenamaxtli concludes. "It's suicide. The open gate is clearly an invitation to lure us into an ambush."

Most of our Chichimeca warriors stayed behind to protect the mine. Neither he nor Tezca wish to expend their men against Inspector Corona's presidio.

Nelli dwells on a battle plan, unable to decide what course of action to pursue. Her intent is to leave Corona isolated upon his rock, cut off his supplies, and starve him out. I find the plan wanting; that could take weeks, perhaps months.

What are they waiting for?

Nelli is aloof with her warriors, proud of her rank, and woe to the person who doesn't do exactly as they're told, but to her credit, she stresses safety above all else.

"Look alive. Be smart. I don't want to lose a single one of you. Is that understood?" Heads bob. "Good. We can get through this together."

All agree to further wait until she can come to a decision.

All except one boy.

Oh, to be young and fearless. It's a magnificent thing.

Nahua boys are warriors from birth. The boy is a shield-bearer. His duty is to carry equipment, weaponry and clothes, but above all, learn, so he can fulfill his purpose to die gloriously in battle. He has been to war three times and hasn't reached the rank of a tlamani, a warrior who has taken a captive, and desperately seeks to prove himself. It's obvious for all to see, for the tuft of hair on the back of his head has grown long. If the boy doesn't take a captor, he will be called cuexpalchicacpol, a shameful distinction, and will never achieve fighting fame. This is something any warrior can understand and relate to. Only Shorn Ones have taken more than six captives.

The boy makes his way toward the entrance. He advances no more than a few steps when the whistle of arrows rents the air, falling on us like a hammer. We scramble for cover, and the boy turns back at a run, throwing up his arms with a scream. An arrow goes through his gullet. He dies instantly with little noise.

Anger gives Nelli fresh courage. "Charge!" she roars in a murderous rage.

The order should have been to fall back, but it's too late to hide now.

As we race inside the presidio, arrows pursue us. Warriors fall.

Again, and again. The volley has wounded more; they're bleeding, but all are sure they can continue to fight.

A woman yells for help. An arrow shaft protrudes from her chest. Nelli.

Avoiding the slaughter, we round the corner and take cover inside the church.

"Is she still alive?"

"What are her chances?"

"Do something!"

Tenamaxtli rushes to crouch beside Nelli, putting his hands on her wound to stop the blood from flowing out of her. "Can you heal her?" he asks Tezca.

Tezca breaks a shaft sticking out from his shoulder. "I don't know. Her heartbeat is faint."

"I don't want to die in a Christian church," says Nelli, coughing blood. "Please."

"Try," Tenamaxtli urges Tezca. "Save her! You have to save the princess!"

Tezca nods. He picks Nelli up in his arms, and she grimaces with pain. "Leave me alone with her," he says, carefully resting her on the nearest bench.

"She has lost a lot of blood," I'm quick to say. "And you are injured yourself."

"I can handle it," Tezca says, not even bothering to look at the deep gash on his upper arm.

"You can heal from terrible wounds," I say, "but others—I've seen it take a lot out of you. Are you sure this hasn't passed beyond your skill?"

"I said I can handle it."

My heart is beating faster than a hummingbird's wings. "We can't afford to lose any more warriors if we intend to make it out of here with our breaths."

"Then *stop*," he says between clenched teeth. "Stop arguing for once in your life and give me space so I can focus."

I nod. I take the blow. I have nothing more to say.

"What do we do?" Martín says, his face grim.

"I'll go," I say. "After Corona."

"You'll do *what*?" Tezca asks.

"I can handle it." I throw his own words back at him, and if I sound bitter it's because I am.

"No, *no*," Nelli weakly says. "He'll see you coming."

"If the gods will it," I say.

"You don't stand a chance on your own. Do nothing, Pantera," she commands.

"That's all I've been doing! Nothing. I'm tired of doing nothing. Making myself small to make you feel bigger. Look around. This is what you've led us to. I'm done taking orders from you."

"Don't let her go," she moans to Tezca.

Tezca shakes his head, trying to find his thoughts as if in a battle with himself. His jaw tightens, all of him tightens.

"*Stop* her."

"I can't!" Tezca says with an irritated edge to his voice. "I can't stop her. No one can."

If it were his choice, Tezca would probably lock me somewhere safe and keep me there, but it's not. He looks at me and nods.

I don't rightly know what I will do once I step outside. All I know is that I need to do something. Tezca understands that.

"I'll go with you," says Martín.

"I go alone. Enough blood has been shed today."

"This is madness! You can't go out there alone," Tenamaxtli says.

"I'm the Godslayer," I say. "I can."

When I'm feeling hopeless and helpless, when I want someone to pity me, to say, "I understand what ails you," I call upon the Plumed Serpent because I know my father hears my weeping. But those

162

moments pass quickly when the Panther reasserts her rightful place inside me. Even though I have no tonalli to shift, she's always with me. A tree is still a tree without leaves. I can't lose my nagual. The Panther is who I am. Quetzalcoatl told me so.

Somewhere deep inside, buried under layers of fear, I find her. She keeps me alive. She keeps me fighting. Sometimes, in my weakest moments, I'm my strongest.

So I let loose. I set the Panther free. Free to bring harm.

In the courtyard, the rain of arrows has stopped. Other than corpses sprawled on the ground, there's no sign that there was a battle here just a moment ago.

"Rosendo!" I shout defiantly. "Come out and face me!"

What would his countrymen say? That Rosendo Corona, Inspector General of New Spain, hid in a fort like a feeble coward? How shameful would it be to leave battle conquered more by his own cowardice than by a girl in a mask? He can't live with that. He will face me like a man, and he will die with his honor intact.

"I know you're here. Stop cowering in the shadows. I'm alone. Come and show your face. I'm waiting!"

From his hiding place, Inspector Corona emerges. He stops a few feet before me, staring, thin-lipped, his expression cruel and hostile.

Too bad looks can't kill.

"Who are you?" he asks.

"You know who I am."

His upper lip twitches, nostrils expanding. "Pantera."

I open my arms to present myself.

"What do you want?"

"Your surrender."

A scowl comes over his face, lips taut. "And if I don't?"

"Then you must be certain you can win a fight against me, Inspector," I say. "I understand it would be distressing for your men to see you defeated and dead. But not to worry. It will all be over fast. Now, I'm sorry, but I haven't much time. What is your decision?"

He sighs disgustedly and puts on his most threatening countenance. "You presume too much, girl. Don't worry about my death, but instead worry about your own."

"You yield?"

"It's too late for that, I'm afraid."

"You should be," I say, "afraid."

"Make one foolish move and my men will strike. Regardless of what happens to me, you will never make it out of here alive, and neither will your friends. You're outnumbered. None of you will escape."

Any one of us is worth ten of him. "I'm disappointed, Inspector. Wait until I tell Viceroy Jerónimo that the commander of the Spanish army is such a gutless bastard."

Inspector Corona reins in his temper with effort. "Why should Viceroy Jerónimo believe anything a criminal would say?"

"He should not believe a criminal," I say, "but he should believe his sister." I remove my helmet and fling it at his feet.

He smiles, but his jaw juts forward, his muscles clenched. "Lady Leonora. It *is* you after all."

"Your fate is upon you, Inspector. Bear it like a man."

Inspector Corona draws his sword in a two-handed grip. He watches me, determined, no fear in his eyes. He's probably seen and fought more battles than I have, but those fights have been against mortal men, and he knows, from the fabulous stories, that my blade is not of this world, and once I set it on you, you can't escape.

"If that's your choice," I say, pulling the Sword of Integrity from her scabbard, then I turn fast, very fast, and whip her in a quick sweep that catches the hollow at his throat.

"It's done."

I hurl the severed head at the ground. It hits dully and rolls along, eyes still wide, dirt and leaves sticking to the neck.

Nelli, now completely healed, comes out of the church. She looks at the head, the nose, ears, bearded chin. "Who is that?"

"Inspector Corona . . . the man you struck a deal with," I say.

Nelli glances at Tenamaxtli beside her, then back at me. "That's not the man I struck a deal with."

"What are you talking about?"

"I've never seen this man before," Nelli says.

I hold the head up for her to get a better look. "Are you certain?"

"It's not him, I'm telling you."

I take a step back, my mind whirling with confusion.

"Leonora," Martín calls.

I turn around and look at him, and what immediately becomes clear is that I have been blind to what deep down I knew to be true. Yet, I could feel it there, urging me.

Certainly, Inspector Corona was an enemy, but the *real* enemy is a superb liar, whom I believed I kept distracted—but all this time, he was distracting *me*.

I sigh. "We left him behind with the silver."

"He could be anywhere by now," says Martín. "We'll never find him."

"I wouldn't be so sure," I say. "He's the Crown Prince."

"So?"

"So . . ." I say, "he always travels in a coach with the curtains drawn."

CHAPTER 20

El Anticristo

Somewhere down the King's Highway, a traveling coach comes to a jarring halt. Its curtains, drawn tightly closed, make it impossible to see anyone inside, which is precisely the intended purpose. He doesn't want to be seen.

An angry voice comes from within. "What's the problem, driver? Why are we stopping?" Felipe has scarcely gotten the words out of his mouth when I pull open the door at his elbow. I climb in first, followed by Martín.

Felipe shoots up from his seat. "Lady Leonora, what are you—?" The last shade of color drains from his pasty face. "Martín. What do you want?"

"Sit down and be quiet," I say as Martín and I slip onto the bench across from Felipe.

The coach suddenly shudders into motion, hooves clip-clopping on the dirt road.

Refusing to be daunted, Felipe narrows his eyes and raises his chin. "What is this?"

"You've been busy, Your Majesty," I say. "Where's the silver?"

"What silver?"

"You had it all planned, didn't you? Inspector Corona. Fray Anonasi."

He chortles. "You think I killed Fray Anonasi?"

"Don't be ridiculous," I say. "No one thinks that. I know you didn't kill him. You wouldn't dare murder a man of God. That would stain your purity and connection to your Nailed Christ." I pause, pursing my mouth in thought. "Don Ruy, on the other hand, would do anything for his master, wouldn't he? I notice he's nowhere to be seen. Where is your faithful dog, Your Majesty?"

"I must have misplaced him," Felipe says with a pretend innocence, "but have no fear, he is sure to turn up sooner or later."

He grins, a gloating grin. He's arrogant. He thinks he's won the endgame. The thing is, though, now that I truly see him, the game isn't really over, is it?

I grin back, all teeth, then pull my dagger and hold it under his chin. He doesn't flinch; he wills himself to smile as if I made a joke. "You're the witch," he says, eyeing the hummingbird on my right hand. "I should've guessed it before now. Your voice sounds different, but the description fits."

"My gods will be pleased with your blood."

"Pagan," he spits in disgust. "You state it openly. You will hang for this, you heathen devil-worshipper. God will show you who is the true king."

I push the dagger deeper. Martín tries to lower my arm. "Put it down."

"He has to die."

"No, he doesn't. Put it down."

"Get out of my way, Martín. Let me do this."

"Christ, you're obsessed with killing. Give me that," he says, seizing my wrist and knife.

"Whose side are you on, Martín?" Felipe asks.

Martín sits back, regarding Felipe with a stony stare. "You will keep your Fifth and return what you stole. You will then leave for Spain and never return."

Felipe laughs at that. "Or what?"

"Or you can leave with nothing."

"What will you do? Kill me?"

"I don't need to kill you," says Martín. "Look at me closely. Don't you remember me, old friend?"

Felipe's nonchalant façade evaporates. His lip twitches, accompanied by a guttural snarl. "Indeed. I recognize the Judas who betrayed me and the false friend whose only loyalty is to himself. You're a pretender, Martín. A poser. All I see is a fraud in fine clothes. You also need a haircut. You look like a heathen with that ungodly length."

"You always did want what you can't have, Felipe. Remember when we were boys? You looked upon a forbidden fruit with desire—pestered and pestered to have it, even after I warned you that the bitterness wouldn't suit your taste. You took one bite and said you didn't want any more. You made me eat the seeds. After all this time, you haven't changed. One bit. You knew there was something better to be had in these lands . . . if only you could get your hands on it."

Felipe's jaw is so tight the veins in his neck bulge.

"Does he know about us?" Martín asks.

"Who?"

"I wonder what the king would do if he knew." There is a world of threat in his voice.

That gives Felipe pause, just for a moment, until he adds, "I'm the Crown Prince. The king cares little for who I share my bed with—and my body."

Martín reaches up to stroke his cheek. "I couldn't bear to see you scandalized by the wagging tongues of malicious courtiers."

"*Don't* touch me." Felipe bats his hand away. "Who do you think will believe you? I'm the king's son. You are a bastard. You are nothing."

"I am the marquess of the Valley of Oaxaca."

My eyebrows raise in surprise. He is?

A condescending little chuckle from Felipe. "Don Martín is the marquess."

"I am a don now," Martín says. "My brother wasn't as perfect as my father believed. Like you, he had . . . his appetites. He was involved in a conspiracy with the encomenderos who aspired to take New Spain for themselves and crown my brother as king. He has been sent to Spain for trial. The marquessate has been bestowed upon me. The order came from Castilla."

"It was *you*, wasn't it?" Felipe hisses. "You impersonated me!"

"It wasn't easy," Martín says, "and it wasn't personal."

"Funny, it feels pretty fucking personal to me," Felipe snarls. "Did you like it?"

"Did I like what?"

Felipe waves a hand in the air with a flourish. "Bearing the weight of my name. Everyone knows you've always hungered for power. Poor little Martíncito. Raised among the nobility of Spain, yet no land or wealth to call your own. No path to follow but the soldier's life. You're a never be," he mutters, amused. "You'll *never* be anything more than the bastard of Cortés, you'll *never* be with me, and you'll *never* be me."

Martín spits in his face.

"Don't listen to this worm. It's not worth it," I tell him. "He's just trying to get under your skin."

"You don't want me as an enemy, Martín," says Felipe, wiping the spit. "Do *not* give me cause."

"Now can I kill him?" I ask.

Martín pulls himself together. "No, no . . ."

"I'll tell you who hasn't changed," says Felipe. "*You* haven't changed. I know you too well."

"You knew me a long time ago."

"People don't change," Felipe says.

Martín bangs the side of the coach shouting for the coachman to stop, which he does, pulling on the reins. When he speaks next, his voice is gentle, but it is like a fist to Felipe's heart. "I would have given my life for you. But I was a boy and stupid. I *have* changed."

Once it stops moving, Martín and I hop out of the coach. Felipe doesn't stay inside for long. As soon as he emerges from the shadows of his transport, he realizes his coachman has been replaced by Tezca, and Nelli, Tenamaxtli, and other warriors are waiting for him.

Nelli has her bow raised and ready, an arrow on the string. Slowly, she lowers the bow. She is satisfied. Her true aim has been reached. "Take him," she orders. Her men instantly comply, grasping Felipe as he tries to escape.

"Unhand me at once!" Felipe commands. "Where is Inspector Corona? I demand to speak to him."

That raises a great laugh among the men.

"I'm afraid he is unavailable at the moment, Your Majesty," Tenamaxtli says, gesturing at his spear, whose point carries the inspector's hacked head.

More boisterous laughter.

Felipe pales. "Savages! You cannot do this. I am the king's son! The king will hear of this!"

Nelli nods to her men, who tighten their grip on him, dragging him back to the coach. They shove him inside, and the door is slammed shut. Nelli secures it herself, tying a thick cord across the latch to ensure he can't escape. Leaning close to the small window, she says, "Give King Carlos our fondest regards."

"You'll regret this." The coach rolls forward, and Felipe's voice is swallowed by the growing distance.

Martín walks beside me. His face is tense as he watches the coach disappear.

"Don't worry," I say, patting his shoulder. "They won't harm him. He'll be fine."

"Who says I'm worried? I'm not worried," he says defensively. "Actually, I'm starving." He looks around at the others, trying to steer the conversation away from Felipe. "Does anyone want something to eat? Or maybe a massage? A bath, perhaps?"

"Why are you looking at *me*?" I ask.

"You're covered in blood, and the smell . . ." He leans in and sniffs. "You must get the smell off."

"I could use a scrub." I manage a smile. "And you could use a haircut . . . Martíncito."

It has been a brutal day, with hundreds of warriors joining Tonatiuh in paradise. It takes the exhausted army the rest of the night and the whole of the following day to gather the slain. So many were killed that it's impossible to return the fallen warriors to their homes to be cremated with honor. Instead, wood for pyres has to be collected from as far away as the forests of the Sierra Madre, and every wagon and cart, every horse and mule, has to bring it back.

There should be great lamentation at the funerals, but to die in battle is a tremendous honor. There is weeping, but there is also pride and joy. Life is a strange dream, and only in death does one become truly awake.

"I think he still cares for you," I say to Martín, observing the pyres burning.

"What?"

"Felipe. He told me he had only loved once. I think he was referring to you. He seemed troubled."

"You confuse desire with love, Leonora." Martín shakes his head. "You need a heart to love. Felipe has the emotional depth of an avocado. We were very young," he says, remembering, "and it doesn't matter."

We are quiet, paying our respects to the dead.

"There's something you must know," Martín says after a while, "about Vicereine Carlota."

I look at him. "What about her?"

"She succumbed to her illness." Surprise must show on my face

171

because Martín frowns. "She didn't tell you? She had been suffering for quite some time from terrible chest pains. Sometimes she could hardly breathe. I thought you knew."

There was nothing wrong with her that I could see. She wasn't particularly fervent; she spoke modestly and kept her words short, but I thought her mild countenance had more to do with her newfound holy profession than anything else.

"Did she suffer?" I ask.

"She's at peace now," Martín says. "She was buried in the Franciscan monastery."

"Tell me."

"Her spirit was strong until the end. You should know," he says, "it was she who warned that a plot existed against Viceroy Jerónimo and the Crown. A number of nuns gave testimony. The Audiencia acted swiftly and arrested the encomenderos, including the bishop. He was supposed to go to Rome to obtain the pope's blessing for my brother's dominion over New Spain. They summoned my brother under the pretense that a ship had arrived from Spain carrying a letter from the king, a letter that was supposed to deal with the renewal of the encomiendas. My brother went to the Audiencia and was arrested on the spot by the authorities. Vicereine Carlota died shortly after. I think," he says softly, "she was holding on."

Aside from her religious affairs, Vicereine Carlota also had personal interests in protecting Jerónimo. She wasn't going to let anyone—surely not Don Martín—threaten her son's position if that was the last thing she did.

"Are you all right?" Martín asks.

"She wasn't my mother," I say.

She wasn't my anything. But that she was dying when I saw her, wasting away from some illness and masterminding to the end—makes my throat swell.

I know she didn't do it for me, but I still thank her silently and offer a prayer as the pyres of the fallen warriors blaze up and burn down, billowing black smoke into the night sky. Were it not for her, Martín and his army would not have come, the Spaniards would not have retreated, and we would surely have lost the battle.

"What will happen to your brother?" I ask.

"I don't know," Martín says. "He will have to justify his conduct."

"You are the marquess now . . ."

In her doing, Vicereine Carlota thought she was shielding Jerónimo from Don Martín's scheme against him.

This was the final trick up her sleeve.

But had Vicereine Carlota known that the bastard Martín is, as it happens, not a bastard, and that the marquessate would pass to him in Don Martín's absence, she never would have tilted the scales in his favor. Not to Martín, who is older and experienced, certainly more in an advantageous position to effectively challenge Jerónimo's viceregal rule.

"I didn't ask for this, Leonora," Martín says. "This wasn't my ambition. You know it's not what I wanted for myself."

"I know."

Tezca comes to my side, and Martín clears his throat.

There's no friendship between them, but there is mutual respect—trust, recognition, perhaps even gratitude—albeit a wary one. Martín stood by Neza, risked his life to impersonate Felipe for La Justicia. He has been an ally, and he was an ally today. We all wanted the same thing. But now that Martín is the marquess, his domain is Tezca's homeland.

Martín's lips twist into the semblance of a smile. "I must go. There is much to do in Cuernavaca."

"Much joy and favor to you, Don Martín," says Tezca. His words are pleasant, but the look he gives him is less inviting.

Martín lowers his gaze for a moment before looking back at Tezca. "Know that I am not my father's son and that you are always welcome at my court and my side."

"Thank you, my lord, for the kind invitation. I should not like being chased from my home," Tezca says, "again."

The condemnation in his voice is unmistakable, and I can tell by the way Martín's shoulders slump that he realizes it too.

"Be well, Leonora." With a nod, Martín takes his leave.

"Was that necessary?" I ask.

"Yes," Tezca answers.

"Martín is not an enemy."

"*Yet.* Cortés took this land for his own and Malintzin betrayed her own people. How far does the apple fall from the tree?"

"Rather, her own people betrayed *her*," I counter. "Malintzin was sold into slavery as a child by her mother. Whatever she did, she was a survivor, not a traitor."

"And Martín? What about him?"

"Are you Tezcatlipoca?" I ask. "Are you your father? Or do you have your own life?"

"That's different."

"Is it?" I say. "Martín is not his parents any more than you are. We are not our parents. We don't have to be. We are a part of them, but we are ourselves. Not you, him, Nelli, I, or anyone has to live in their shadow or carry the burden of their choices."

Tezca looks angry for a moment, but then he seems to accept that there is truth to my words. "You're right. I'm sorry," he mutters.

"Me too," I say. "I'm sorry I gave you such a hard time about Nelli."

"I wasn't trying to make you jealous," he says.

"I wasn't jealous. I was scared," I admit.

"Scared?"

"Nelli was in bad shape," I say. "You pushed yourself so far for her, Tezca. Healing her—I thought you wouldn't make it. I can't go through that again. I just . . . I can't."

He nods slowly. "I understand." He reaches out, his fingers brushing mine. "Come with me."

"Go with you where?"

"I don't know. On a journey. Just the two of us."

174

I feel a stirring inside me, the idea of being with him. But even as the thought tempts me, reality pulls me back. There's still a lot to resolve with him, plenty of pieces to put together. We'll get there. "You know I can't," I say. "I must return to my tonalli. Will I see you again?"

"If the gods will it," he says, "and if not in this life, then in the next."

"I *knew* it. You *do* believe in the gods."

"Does it matter?"

"There are gods in Tamoanchan. Were you not there with the Precious Flower? We faced the Tzitzimime. And you're a sorcerer. Ometeotl is the source of our tonalli. Your father is a god. How can it not matter? How can you not believe?"

"Do I believe that they exist?" Tezca asks, his tone flat. "Or do I believe they watch over us? That they hear our prayers? Receive our sacrifices? They are very different things." He chuckles in his odd, humorless way. "I have very little reason to believe in the gods. I told you before, they're not gods any more than we are."

"No," I say. "That's not true."

"No?" he challenges. "Let's see. Can you do things others can't?"

"Yes," I say, wishing I could speak a different answer. "But it's not that simple."

"Can you feel another's pain?"

"Yes."

"Can you feel their love?"

I swallow. "Yes."

"Can you look into the eyes of a man and see him for what he truly is?"

Letting out a long breath, I nod. "Yes."

"What are these abilities but those of a god?"

"But we grow old and die," I argue. "Gods are immortal."

"And the words that will be written about us? The songs they will sing? The stories they will tell? Will those not be immortalized for all time?"

175

"I'm not a goddess," I say stubbornly. "I'm *not*."

"And I'm not a fool," he says. "You summoned a Nagual army and defeated the Obsidian Butterfly. In fact, you *are*, a goddess, in every sense of the word. Whether you admit it to yourself or not, you know it inside."

"Nine Hells," I grumble.

"What, you don't like it? Am I beginning to sound like you?"

He's speaking the truth, but his glib tongue bothers me, and the rush of annoyance that spikes through me—I hate that, too. Perhaps what bothers me the most is that Tezca is my mirror, showing me the parts of myself I don't want to face. What I'm afraid of becoming. Just the same, I'm his reflection, mirroring his fears and weaknesses.

I remember our first encounters. Gods, how I hated him. He was insufferable, having no trouble at all seeing past my mask.

It's hard to look in the mirror.

Fighting my pride, I push the realization to the back of my mind—but as I prepare to depart from Zacatecas, I am reminded once again of what I am.

Nelli says to me, "My people owe you a great debt, as do I. I look forward to doing battle by your side again, Godslayer."

"Not too soon I hope, princess," I say.

CHAPTER 21

La Traición

The Audiencia, and the rest of the capital, soon learn that the Mother Country is in dire economic trouble. The never-ending warfare between the Habsburg and Valois families, Carlos V and his great nemesis Francis, the French king, have weakened Spain so badly that the royal treasury is exhausted, to the point that the Crown is begging for loans.

To repay these massive war loans, Felipe intended to rely on the flow of silver in New Spain. Since he's not yet the king and has no authority, he planned for Inspector Corona to take the fall for his actions.

Observing Felipe, his travels in a splendid coach, swathed in sumptuous fabrics, covered with the finest ornaments and dazzling jewels, no one would have imagined that Spain teeters on bankruptcy.

Indeed, we all wear masks; his glittered more than mine.

I don't fault Felipe for what we are all made by nature to do. That is, survive.

The Habsburg Empire is one of the most powerful nations in the world. If his plan succeeded, Western Europe would escape financial ruin before anyone was the wiser. If it failed, he would inherit from his father an unsustainable economic system comprised of debilitating debt and deficits.

It was a meticulous plan, maybe even close to a perfect plan, carried out with caution and precision by a prudent king.

Unfortunately, he didn't plan for me.

Those who thought they had gotten rid of the child viceroy are furious when Jerónimo is released from prison and returns to the palace. The captive Northmen are freed. Don Bartolo, a powerful don, a good and decent man who stood by Jerónimo in his worst days, is tasked with conducting investigations and punishing the Spaniards in New Galicia responsible for disobeying the New Laws. New Galicia is an independent province of New Spain, managing all the northern mainland provinces of the viceroyalty; still, they are subject to the Audiencia of Mexico.

"Well? What does it say?" I ask, anxious.

Jerónimo reads the letter he unfolds carelessly. "King Felipe has boarded a ship bound for Spain with Don Ruy."

"Good," I say. "Very good."

"Yes, Praise Him." Setting the letter back on his desk, he looks up to heaven. "Merciful Father, I faithfully called upon your name for deliverance. My enemies were strong, but you were stronger. Thank you, Lord, for your perfect purpose and will." He shuts his eyes and crosses himself. "Felipe will have to work very hard to get Spain's financial problems under control. Should I be worried about what this means for the viceroyalty?"

"Of course you should be worried," I say. "You made yourself an enemy to the king of Spain. But who will intercede for all of us if not you, brother? You must reveal yourself as a beacon of light."

He raises a brow. "A beacon?"

"Should darkness surround us."

He nods, coming to the same conclusion. "One might have expected that King Felipe—being dedicated and persistent and the heir of Europe's wealthiest and largest empire would have succeeded in his aims. But his endeavors were doomed to failure." He grins at me, turning to his desk to pick up a roll of parchment. "I believe this is for you."

A thrill goes through me. I eagerly take the parchment from his hand, breaking the seal and unfurling it to read its contents. I scan over the ink scribbled therein, expecting his promise delivered, but as I read further down, my mood turns from elation to confusion to finally outrage. "What is this?" I say, holding up the scroll.

"Our agreement," he replies. "There's a horse and cart outside with all the provisions you asked for. It's all in there."

I breathe, my mind filling with anger and disbelief. "It's not *all* in there. We agreed I'd be done after this."

"Ah, yes. I'm afraid I've changed my mind," he says, neatly folding his hands upon his stomach. "You are needed here, Leonora. This is your home. If the new marquess challenges me, and I have more than a shrewd suspicion he will, you will be required to provide the necessary security measures."

"Security measures?" I stare back at him, dumbstruck.

"As Minister of Defense. I have not been able to fill the position. I realize this is no ordinary job, but then again, you are no ordinary woman. The Crown will not forget what we have done. We need to take precautions to protect ourselves. Mother has gone to join God in Heaven. Mother always worried that you would be a negative influence on me, but she's not here anymore, and you're all the family I have left. Now more than ever, I need advisors I can trust."

"An advisor or a bodyguard?"

"You will still be acting regent, of course."

"We had a deal," I seethe.

"You will have carta blanca—your own private quarters, horses and weapons, soldiers to command, generous pay. Everything will be available in your hands. Anything you want."

The sweet words fall from his mouth, stark in contrast with my rioting emotions. I'd be his to own, to control. He knew how

179

important this was to me, he knew how much I wanted to be free. To stop hiding. Stop running away. Start running forward.

"That's not what you promised me!" I rage. "You promised me my freedom."

"Freedom?" He scoffs. "What a preposterous idea, Leonora. Pantera is much too valuable to retire. You are simply the best. The best swordswoman. The best negotiator. You know the common tongue and the language of the natives. You know the land in ways that an outsider cannot."

"What I am is a sorceress," I say out of spite.

Jerónimo makes the sign of the cross to protect himself from the evil of my heathen words. "I know what you are. There is simply no one alive like Pantera. I may not be particularly fond of your methods, but you would never betray me or conspire against me. I can't say the same of anyone else. In my position, you learn quickly who you can trust and who you need to keep an eye on."

I stare at him for a long moment, cursing his existence. "After everything I've done for you. Without me, you'd be rotting in prison. You'd be wet and starving, forgotten in that godforsaken dungeon, with no way of getting out."

"Indeed, and I'm very grateful," Jerónimo says in an even tone. "You've been there for me many times. I don't deny it. That's exactly what I'm saying, Leonora. I need you. And you need me. I've always helped you, haven't I?" I chuckle at this, and he sorely asks, "Have I not? When you fell in battle, when the creatures came, when Captain Nabarres accused you of being Pantera, when Inspector Corona tried you before the Audiencia . . . *I* was there. I was there because I'm your brother. I'm with you. Always."

There's that word again. Always.

Jerónimo's perfect recall of the times he has come to my aid does nothing to thwart my anger. If anything, it makes me resent him more. "You only help yourself," I tell him.

"Why does everything have to be an argument with you? Don't

make it ugly. I don't want to fight." He shakes his head in frustration. "I wish you wouldn't react this way. It's very counterproductive."

Since he seems to like the word so much, I say with a fresh burst of defiance, "I *always* react with hostility when I'm betrayed. If you think you can imprison me in this palace against my will, you are more foolish than I thought."

"Take care of your words, sister. You're in my power. I can make life very easy for you," he says, "or not."

"I have destroyed greater powers than yours, excelencia."

With a calming breath, he reins back his scowl. "I won't make you do anything you don't want. You're angry. You need time to let it all sink in. Maybe in a day or two when you've calmed down, you'll come back, and we can talk. Things will be different this time. You'll see."

Damn him, I swear beneath my breath. *Damn him to Mictlan.* I hope Jerónimo makes the four-year journey fraught with trials. I hope that Xolotl the dog does not come to his aid. And I hope that, when at last, he reaches Chicunamictlan, the ninth hell, and comes face to face with the Lord and Lady of Death, he finds not eternal rest but extinction.

A gray horse saddled for me waits outside the palace walls as Jerónimo said. He's harnessed to a cart filled with vegetables and fruits, seeds to grow, various ointments and tinctures for rash relief, other medicinal remedies for fevers and headaches, as well as special cloths to cover the lesions.

The horse neighs when he sees me, and I caress his neck, blowing carefully into his nostrils to make his acquaintance. He neighs again, and with a raise of his tail, lets fall a great pile of manure.

"It's nice to meet you too," I tell him.

"I didn't know horses had a sense of humor," Tomás says into the crook of his arm to keep the stench from carrying.

"They do horse around."

He pulls a face as if embarrassed by my quip.

"No? I thought it was good."

He pastes on a smile. "Are you leaving?"

I nod, gripping the saddle horn. "I heard you have a new master. Don Bartolo is a good man. He'll be nice to you."

"I don't want you to go, but I'm sure you have things to do," he says. "Have you got everything?"

I look at the cart, see how full it is. Almost everything.

"When will you be back?" he asks. "*Will* you . . . be back?"

"Do me a favor, Tomás."

"Keep my ears open? Look at them; I couldn't close them even if I wanted to."

"I was going to say try to stay out of trouble."

He snorts. "Where's the fun in that?"

CHAPTER 22

El Aire

Despite all the impediments, the numerous difficulties, the false turns, the sometimes-profound feelings of resignation in my efforts to return to Tozi, despite all this, my task has been completed.

I have hope.

For an experienced traveler who knows the way, the journey from the capital takes a day or two. That is, in good weather.

Should Tlaloc pour showers from his first jug, it could take a week, but if he empties his fourth jug, the water will bring destruction, and the trip will be an impossible undertaking. Of Tlaloc's four jugs, only the first is beneficial. But it is the dry season, and Tonatiuh scorches the earth.

Either the rains come, or they don't; there is too much water or not enough.

If the Precious Flower was telling the truth, the lesser gods are weakening, barely sustaining our Fifth Sun.

They had great power once, but that power is fading, replaced by the Christian God and the power of the Holy Ghost.

Even Tezca says the gods have fled. Their presence is now something of the past. This saddens me.

I swallow a breath of air and begin the journey through the trees.

To the east, Popocatepetl and Iztaccihuatl make a most wonderful snowy landscape, the two volcanos sleeping next to each other.

My horse pulls the cart, and I am on my feet, holding his rope. I'm too tired to ride him. We are strange companions, this body and me.

I'm afraid, but not of wild animals, because although I know little, I *know* this forest. Every barren tree, every hollow. I've known it all my life. This forest is a second part of me, as familiar as the back of my hand. I have been away from it, but I always come back.

Yet somehow, nothing looks familiar.

I remember the path, but these woods—they can't ever be tamed. You can't grab hold of this land. It grabs hold of you.

I can't forget.

I can't let go.

Stay awake, Leonora. Stay awake.

My head sags down onto my chest. I will have to find somewhere to camp for the night—or is it day? I try to gauge the hours passing but I lose count. Though the trees bear more thorns than leaves, their limbs tangle thickly above me. There are only shadows, no shred of sky. Green life pokes here and there: scraggly grasses, gnarled saplings.

No sign of chaneques so far. I seek evidence of them: small footprints in the dirt, distant voices, giggling. But it's as if the horse and I are the only ones who move here.

My horse veers off the trail suddenly, snorting and whining.

"What is it? What do you hear?" My breath mists, hanging like an apparition. Every time I open my mouth, I lose valuable heat.

A branch snaps and I know, whatever it is, it isn't afraid of me.

With a shrill cry, an eagle swoops into sight and perches itself on a stump in front of me.

An eagle . . . at night?

The bird has long, broad wings and a deep golden-brown plumage. A powerful raptor. A true master of the sky.

My horse neighs loudly and rears up, pawing at the air. I grasp the reins and bring him down, but he barely settles, even when I rub his long neck. "Woah. You're safe," I whisper. "You're safe."

In truth, I'm not so sure.

"Who are you?" I ask. Eagle or Nagual, it must be one or the other. My horse didn't spook it. I'm a foot away from the creature, and it sits motionless as though it does not breathe. Its piercing yellow eyes stare into mine, unblinking, probing, studying.

"Who *are* you?" I ask again.

"Leonora."

I spin to face the source of a voice. "Amalia?"

"You've come back! Thank God!" Amalia throws her arms around my neck, embracing me with all her strength.

"How did you know I was—?" The answer dawns on me before I can finish the question.

Amalia answers, "Zyanya. She said you were near."

I look around. "Did you see the eagle?"

"What eagle?"

"It was just here," I say. "I saw it. It was looking right into my eyes. I don't know if it was an eagle or a sorcerer."

She frowns. "Does it matter?"

"Does it matter that one can rip my eyes out while the other can make it rain fire and then rip my eyes out?"

"Oh, how I've missed you," she says with a chuckle, tapping my cheeks. "I'm sure it was just a bird."

Whoops, cries, and yodels meet my arrival at Tozi. In the soft glow of moonlight, the forest is bathed in shades of blue and silver, and the round huts glow with the color of aged amber.

The chaneques are singing, beating on drums, dancing one behind the other, going round in circles. The music is ritualistic, reserved for the night. The rhythm of the drums and the patterns of their dance create a barrier of positivity, ensuring that the night remains safe and harmonious.

"Welcome back, Pantera," Itzmin exclaims.

"It's good to be back, my friend." I uncover the cart, filled to the brim with goods. "I've brought provisions. There's plenty for all."

Amalia inspects the medicine. "This will help with the symptoms." She hastily carries the supplies inside one of the huts, then pops her head out to say, "Don't come in. Even with these medicines, there's no cure, only relief. If you come in, you might carry it out with you—or worse, catch it yourself." Without waiting for a reply, she pulls her head back in.

"Princess," I say, coming to Eréndira's side.

"Fool," she grouses. "She doesn't sleep. She doesn't rest. She's the only one who seems immune to the sickness."

"Amalia is strong," I tell her. I glance at the tree line. "Have you been scouting the forest?"

"Every night. Why?"

"I saw an eagle."

"An eagle?"

"Nahualli."

"Are you certain?"

"It's night," I say.

Eréndira considers my reasoning. She knows eagles don't hunt at night.

"I've never come across another sorcerer."

"No," I say, "not around these parts. But there's no mistaking what I saw. It was a Nagual."

"What do you think it was doing here?"

"I don't know," I say. "It was an older Nagual, and female, or at least that's what I could tell from its size. It felt like she knew who I was."

Amalia comes out of the hut, and Eréndira asks, "How does it look in there? How are they?"

"It's hard to say until the last scabs have fallen off," Amalia says, choosing her words with care. "Some have made it through. Others haven't been as fortunate. The medicine will take effect soon. It should ease pain and start to slow fevers."

Eréndira breathes a sigh of intense relief. "Good," she says. "That is good."

The chaneques continue dancing, and I'm enthusiastically pulled into the circle. The dance has become frantic now, lighter on the feet, loose, and it's taking place outside Zyanya's hut. I have to stoop through the short door, though I can stand erect in the center. Inside, Zyanya is propping long pieces of bamboo against the wall.

"You made it," Zyanya says to me.

"I did," I say, "and I'll be needing my tonalli back."

"No," is her reply, putting up another bamboo pole.

"No?"

"Tonalli decides," she says. "Tonalli knows best."

I shake my head in confusion. "You always say that, but what does that even mean?" She presses her ear against a bamboo. "Zyanya."

"I'm trying to protect you. You are only making it harder for me."

"Protect me?" I echo, incredulous. "You're eleven years old, Zyanya. I don't need you to protect me. You need me to protect *you*."

"How many times do I have to tell you? I'm a chaneque. I'm a protector of the natural world and everything in it. We help the forest stay alive and balanced, and we guard it with our lives. I was born and raised in the forest, and I would do anything to ensure its survival."

"Survival?" I frown. "What is it you think you're protecting me from?"

"The air," she says.

"The air?"

"It's rotten. Do you not smell it? It's a putrid, smokey smell."

"I don't smell anything. You're not making any sense, Zyanya. I can't live without tonalli. You know that."

She looks down at the collection of tonalli-infused amulets dangling from her belt. "I've been dreaming a lot about jaguars. A sacred animal of great power and ferocity. They are the keepers of wisdom and balance the ecosystem. If they don't exist, the forest enters into disharmony. If we protect the jaguar, we protect the forest, and at the same time humanity."

I have to shake my head again. "I don't understand."

"My dreams are not for you to understand."

"Zyanya, please," I say. "I just want myself back."

"I know you do." She nods. "Gods and goddesses don't tend to die easily. You're the daughter of Quetzalcoatl. If you were merely mortal, you wouldn't have lived this long without tonalli."

I shake my head, feeling helpless. "Am I supposed to just sit around without my tonalli?"

"For now?" She nods. "Yes."

Sleep comes, but it's fitful. I toss and turn, shivering from a cold that seeps from within me. Even by the warmth of the hearth, no position feels comfortable, nothing brings relief. I ache from the constant shifting, and my eyes burn, desperate for the release that sleep should bring but never does. Every sound jolts me, my heart pounding as if I've been startled from a nightmare—except you don't dream without tonalli, so there is only a void of nothingness, which somehow feels worse than being awake.

When morning breaks, I'm more tired than when I lay down. But at least Tonatiuh shines offering his warm light. I make my way to the hut where Eréndira's people are staying. It's pretty much the only place around here that can fit more than a few people at once. Chaneque huts are quite small, but they built this one for a chaneque who was exceptionally tall. From what I've heard, he was already towering over six feet by the time he became a chaneque, practically a giant among them.

They called him Tlayolotl, or "Heart of the Mountain." These days, Tlayolotl has moved on to another village, but the hut still stands. It's become something like a community center.

Even though this is the largest hut in the camp, still, it's crowded with around fifteen to twenty people lying on straw mats, each one fighting off the pox. Some lie pale and sweaty, while others are caught in feverish dreams. The air inside is thick, smelling of earth, herbs, and sickness. Sunlight streams through small windows high up, but the far corners stay in deep shadow. In the center, a small fire crackles, sending wisps of smoke toward an opening in the ceiling.

Amalia doesn't notice me at first, wiping the brow of a young woman. A few of Eréndira's people who seem to have recovered, along with some chaneques, help by changing damp cloths and giving sips of water.

When Amalia finally notices me standing in the doorway, her face flushes with outrage.

"Leonora, you cannot be here!" she hisses. She rushes over as if to push me back but stops, afraid to touch me and risk spreading the disease. "*Leave.* If you catch the pox—" Her words falter, as if she can't bear to finish the thought.

The hut is quiet; the harsh breathing has eased, and the feverish sheen on their skin is fading, replaced by a hint of color in their cheeks. One of them stirs, opening tired eyes. "I had to see how they were doing," I say. "I wasn't sure if I was too late."

"You've seen them. They are improving. Now, for the love of God, will you leave?" Amalia pleads.

I linger for a moment, glancing around, a small hope rekindling. Then I give her a faint nod and do as she asks.

This early, the forest hums with birds greeting the dawn, creatures stirring from their nighttime hunts.

Tonatiuh gently lights my path ahead, casting golden beams through the canopy as the forest awakens around me. As I head to the river, I keep my ears sharp for piercing calls, whistling, or screeching.

What was a Nagual doing here? In this remote stretch of the forest, no less?

And, more importantly, who was she?

*

Amalia finds me lingering by the riverbank after bathing. "I'm sorry I made you leave," she says softly. "I was only trying to protect you."

"There seems to be a lot of that going around."

She lowers herself to sit beside me. We're silent, gazing at the gentle flow of the water.

"Amalia?"

"Hmm?"

"Are you happy here?"

"I'm not . . . unhappy."

"Given a choice," I say, "would you go back to the city?"

"Why do you always ask me that?" Silence, then, "You still don't understand, do you? You think that because I'm a Spanish countess, I must want to live in a palace, wear fine frocks the livelong day, eat as many pastries as I want, attend lavish parties, and compete for the heart of some unfortunate suitor who doesn't know any better."

"I didn't say that."

"That is what you *think*," she says, meeting my glance with hard eyes. "Isn't it? Like Eréndira. Like everyone else. I can't possibly want this life for myself. How? How can I want this? A woman like me can't live here. I must be mad!" Her words come out in a chaotic rush, all in one breath, like she fears she might not get them all out if she pauses.

"It might surprise you to learn that I have found purpose here," she goes on. "Do you know how many times I questioned my purpose, Leonora? When I was sick and bedridden because the pustules on my feet made it impossible to walk? How many times I lay there, begging God to take my life? I couldn't bear it anymore! I did not understand. Do you have any idea?"

"What kept you from turning against your God?"

Her eyes soften as she touches the beaded cross at her neck. "No Christian can grow without first having their faith tested. I now have a clear understanding that each day is full of opportunities to make use of my purpose. It's not to wed, bed, and breed. It's to be *useful*.

I was never taught to be useful. All my mother wanted me to be was a suckling cow. A cow with udders for my children to clamp on to."

"Your mother loved you, Amalia."

She stares at me, and I think she will erupt into a fit of blistering anger, but instead she smiles wanly. "No. She worshipped me," she says, "and that is not the same thing as love."

"Don't you worship God because you love him?" I ask.

"I worship God because He is God. He is the creator of the world."

Amalia believes in the Christian God because that is what she was taught. The same way her mother taught her to sew and spin and weave. If she's found purpose in the forest, then it must be, she thinks, the work her Nailed Christ intends for her. After all, she believes she wouldn't know how to help the sick if she hadn't suffered illness herself.

For a long time, I, too, wondered what my purpose was—or if I even had one. What the gods wanted for me. I still don't know for sure.

"Eréndira told me that there are five lakes in the valley," Amalia says.

"Yes," I say, wondering at the change in topic. Xaltocan and Zumpango to the north; Xochimilco and Chalco in the south, and Texcoco in the center, where the Tenochca established their altepetl Mexico-Tenochtitlan.

Amalia continues, "She said there are five lakes, but there's only one body of water. I think, just like the lake, your gods have many faces, many names, many aspects. And just like my God; I have Jesus Christ, the Virgin Mary, the Holy Spirit, and all the angels and apostles and saints to whom I offer prayers. They are not so different, your gods and mine." She smiles as though this satisfies her in some way.

"I can see that you care for her," I say. "Eréndira."

"Gah! You see too much. We should go. I'm getting hungry."

"Your cheeks are pink," I tease.

"My cheeks are always pink. What is that godawful smell?" she says, her voice nasal. She's pinched her nose shut against some horrible stench.

I chuckle. "You don't have to change the subject, Amalia. I'll stop now."

"Oh," she moans, nearly retching. "It's bad. You don't smell that?"

"Smell what?" I say, still laughing.

"The air," she says. "It's rotten. Do you not smell it? It's a putrid, smokey smell."

I stop laughing. Amalia is not trying to change the subject, nor offering me an explanation. She's confirming a dream.

Then it hits me. It's not the kind of smell you miss.

Smoke.

Zyanya.

The village.

CHAPTER 23

El Sueño

Without my tonalli, my senses aren't as sharp. It takes longer for these things to reach me, to feel the danger. My first thought is that it might just be the cooking fires of the village, some roast being prepared. But it's a foolish thought, for as a gust of air moves through the trees, a second smell permeates my senses—one I'm all too familiar with—and I *know* that isn't cooking smoke.

The smell is horrid and punishing. The heaviest rain cannot wash this away. This is carnage.

Tozi is engulfed in chaos.

All the huts are on fire. Chaneques lie dead all around or badly burned. I'm not unused to death, but this is a slaughter I've never seen. Inside the huts, the screaming is a great wail. I don't know which is worse, the sight, the smell, or the sound. I'm frozen with uncomprehending horror. This was not a fight. This was a bloodbath of innocents. It happened abruptly, without warning.

"Leonora, help me!" Amalia's voice stirs me into motion again.

Itzmin hurtles out of a burning hut, and Amalia throws handfuls of dirt to smother the flames, covering her face as best she can. "Come on! Help me!" Itzmin is frantically flailing, crying in pain. Amalia shouts for him to stop moving and tackles him to the ground, rolling him around in the dirt. "Stop this!" she yells to me. "You can stop this!"

My tonalli. Zyanya.

The gray smoke stings my eyes. I blink, trying to see through the cloud of ash. I search for movement, flashes of white hair showing in the night. *Which way is Zyanya's hut? Is it still standing? Godsdammit, where is it?* One by one, the huts are collapsing, becoming tinder.

I pull at Amalia's wrist. A hut will collapse on her. "Get away, Amalia!" If she hears me, she ignores it and jerks her wrist out of my grasp.

Eréndira douses the flames with moss from the forest floor. Itzmin is no longer on fire, and Eréndira turns to the aid of others. I fall to my knees beside him. "Who did this? Who?"

Itzmin drags in a shallow breath with difficulty, trying to lift himself, but he collapses back down.

"*Who* did this?" I demand again, my voice trembling with barely restrained wrath. Itzmin's eyes open, glazed with pain, but he doesn't answer. His flesh continues to smolder. The pain will never cease if he survives.

"You fought bravely, warrior. Go to Tonatiuh." I unsheathe my dagger and sink it into his neck.

"No!" Amalia cries. "You were supposed to help him!"

"I *did* help him. You want to be useful? End their suffering," I say harshly.

Another hut bursts apart. The force of the blast sends us hurling backward uncontrollably through the air. I crash into a tree, landing heavily on my back.

A silence descends, which is worse than the screams. My mind blurs, thick and suffocating, like the smoke around me. I groan at the pain shooting down my spine, coughing blood, my ears ringing. Shaking my head, I see something.

Someone.

A woman I don't recognize.

Two males follow closely behind her in the full panoply of battle, one a hulking presence devoid of a neck, the other a runt of a man with a sprout of gray hair like a feather. She wears no armor, the woman, as though her valor is enough. Her arms and ankles gleam with gold bracelets, and her black hair flows from beneath a plumed headdress with an eagle on its crest. There's no feeling in her eyes, only a callous, almost frightening, detachment that reflects in her still face, a face that betrays no remorse. What kind of mind is this? What kind of mind attacks a village of children?

"My master thanks you for your great sacrifice." Her voice is disturbingly soothing, given the destruction that surrounds her. "Rest and rejoice," she says, strolling among the dead and dying. "For you shall all be rewarded, honored in the kingdom of Tonatiuh."

I hear the angry roar to my side as Eréndira takes up a run, but she is tossed aside with a blast of tonalli from the woman's hand. Amalia, who rushes to her aid, is also sent soaring to the other side of the forest.

Nahualli, I say in the back of my mind. She's the eagle I saw; I am sure of it.

I might not have my tonalli, but I know how to deflect a sorcerer's attack. I crawl toward my sword, clawing at the ground, and I've just about gripped its hilt when the hulking man thumps his sandalled foot down on my hand. I cry out in grinding agony. He barks a laugh as he presses harder, forcing me to open my palm. I look up at him, grinning through my bloody teeth, not even trying to jerk my wrist free. I want the pain. Pain is useful. Pain keeps me alive. His brows pull together as he locks eyes with me, but his confusion doesn't last long. A whirling spear flies through the smoke, and my attacker glances back to see it heading in his direction, just in time to shift into a snake and slither away.

The figure who threw the spear steps into view, and I smile.

Chipahua. He's a sight to behold—confident, commanding. His presence ripples through the smoke.

The snake Nagual rattles its tail and lunges, trying to sink its deadly fangs into Chipahua's flesh. With a swift kick, Chipahua brings his spear up from the ground and back into his hand. He certainly isn't afraid of creatures that teem in Snake Mountain, isn't afraid of anything, except perhaps dying of old age or an unremarkable death.

Chipahua stabs forward, but so fast is the snake's movement, even for its large size, that he narrowly misses its head. The snake coils and prepares to strike again. Pulling back, Chipahua tosses his spear aside and quickly reaches for the dagger secured to his leg, tipped with a shard of obsidian. Judging by the stern look on his face, Chipahua set out this day intending to kill a man, and that intention leads him to wait for the snake to snap again, and this time he manages to stab it in the side of its belly. A hiss of pain escapes the snake as it writhes away and shifts back to human form.

The second male, the gray-haired man, promptly shifts into a wolf and pounces on Chipahua's back, biting his shoulder. As he battles the wolf, a roar comes out of the darkness, a roar so full of power that it makes the air snap and stops the flames. Then the bellow of a bear, the growl of a wildcat, the call of a howler—the loudest animals in the forest—but only one beast, the most dreaded monstrosity, a water-dwelling predator the gods created to collect souls. The ground shakes with his every darting step.

The ahuizotl leaps from the trees. All wet, he shakes his rubbery black hide and his fur spikes, then he takes a defensive position next to where Amalia lies scraped and bloodied. He bares his teeth with a menacing snarl, orange eyes glowing, and the claw at the end of his tail clenches the air, ready to strike at anything that comes near. The snake and wolf Naguals, who were fearless a moment before, now back away cautiously.

"Rayo," Amalia coughs out. "You came." She smiles as the ahuizotl prods her with his snout.

With a sudden, powerful lunge, Rayo's clawed tail snaps through the air. The snake is too slow—Rayo's claw rakes across its scales with a sickening crack. It slithers away, wounded. The wolf Nagual moves in, hackles raised. But Rayo is faster; his tail lashes out again, this time catching the wolf across the muzzle, sending it yelping backward with a deep, bloody gash. The wolf howls in agony and bolts into the underbrush.

Rayo watches the wolf disappear, chest heaving. He turns back to Amalia, and she looks up at him, a pained but grateful smile on her face. "Rayo," she whispers, her voice hoarse. "You saved me."

The ahuizotl nuzzles her, his earlier ferocity replaced with a tenderness that seems almost out of place for such a fearsome creature.

"Enough," the eagle Nagual sneers. She holds up her hand, and beside her, a mist gathers, floating in the air. Zyanya tumbles through it headfirst. She lands with a thud and a cry of pain as the opening closes.

"Zyanya," I croak. I try to push at the ground, but my arms only twitch. I rise only a few inches before dropping back. Gritting my teeth, I try again and manage to drag myself up.

"I couldn't . . ." she moans. "I couldn't stop—"

I blink at her, trying to focus my gaze. She looks weakened in a way I've never seen before.

"Your tonalli," the woman says to me, "or the chaneque's head."

Zyanya coughs, managing to explain in a strained whisper. "It's a protection spell. I'm the only one who can undo it."

"Undo it," I say, forcing the words through my heavy breaths. "Give it to her."

"You will die," Zyanya says. Her voice breaks on the last word.

"If you don't give it to her, *you* will die," I say. "I won't let that happen."

The eagle Nagual sighs, bored with our struggle. "One of you decides," she says, "or I'll decide for you."

"Tonalli decides," I murmur, repeating the words Zyanya taught me.

She smiles faintly, almost like she's surprised and glad that I actually listened to her.

"It's all right, Zyanya." I nod, feeling the tightness in my throat.

Her smile wavers, a tear slipping down her cheek. With a trembling breath, she places her hand on the obsidian amulet at her belt, fingers steady but reluctant, and says, "Tonalli knows best."

She closes her eyes as she gathers the last of her strength. From the obsidian amulet on her belt comes a chaotic wisp of tonalli shaped like a panther. It rushes back into me all at once, bringing me to my knees as it enters the crown of my head.

Warmth. Glorious warmth.

My tonalli chose *me*.

My feet connected to the earth, I slowly begin to pull tonalli from the ground. My breathing becomes shallower as the heat consumes my body, pulsing warmer and warmer. Tiny rocks and debris begin hovering around me as I draw tonalli into my palms, up my arms, my blood and bones. Almost immediately, the fires hiss, losing strength, as though Quetzalcoatl inhaled a great breath for a shout. They wither until finally nothing is left of Tozi except a terribly burnt landscape of dwellings and charred corpses.

I'm fully powered and fully angry.

"That was a mistake," the woman says.

Before I can launch my attack, she disappears into the mist, taking Zyanya with her.

"They didn't deserve to die," Amalia says in a soft, numb voice. She's bleeding from different cuts, covered with soot and sweat, and her clothing is singed. Rayo left her side after Amalia expressed her gratitude with the promise of dinner.

Eréndira staggers alongside her, nursing an arm, but she seems relatively unhurt. "Dry your tears, Amalia. We can't do a thing for the dead. They're dead," she says.

Amalia makes the sign of the cross, then bends over and heaves all over her feet. The more she looks around the village, the more she retches. She wipes her mouth with the back of her hand. "How can you be so cold?"

"I'm not cold," says Eréndira. "These bodies are cold. They don't care about us. We're meaningless."

"They died! Your people died!" Amalia says in outrage. "Don't you care?"

"I do," Eréndira says, "but not like a Christian. Not like you."

"You weren't here. None of us were here to protect them."

"You can't blame yourself, Amalia," Eréndira says. "It's a great burden. Put it aside."

Amalia angrily looks up at me. "Are you going to say something? Or are you just going to stand there and pretend nothing happened?"

I sigh. "You're right. They didn't deserve to die." My hand on her shoulder offers little comfort. "Everyone dies, Amalia," I say, "but for us, to die in battle is the greatest honor."

"So I should be happy—as you certainly seem to be? What is the matter with you? This was murder!"

"Amalia—" I want to tell her I'm not happy, but she storms off in a fury. "Where are you going?"

"Just leave me the Hell alone!"

She doesn't understand. She will probably never understand, but at least she doesn't condemn my beliefs like Jerónimo does. To her, I'm unmoved; in truth, I'm vibrating with rage. At the moment, all I want to do is kill. I want to fight, to taste blood and take life. And I want, more than anything else, to be the worst nightmare the enemy has ever seen. I want revenge. I can smell their fear, their trembling, waiting for me to come.

It's quiet for a while as we move through the wreckage and search the bodies, looking for survivors. There are none.

"Who were they?" Eréndira asks.

"Nahualli," Chipahua says, "sorcerers of Ichcatzin." Blood runs down his neck and arm from the bite mark on his shoulder, but he doesn't seem to notice. He looks more disgusted that they fled than in pain.

I close my eyes. I'm thinking of Zyanya and her dream about jaguars. She said she was trying to protect me. "They took Zyanya," I say, opening my eyes.

"They will have taken her to Snake Mountain," Chipahua says.

"To Snake Mountain then," I say.

"I'm sure you've heard already," Chipahua says. "Ichcatzin is in possession of a powerful weapon."

I nod, the warning already familiar.

"That's why I'm here. To warn you about Ichcatzin's sorcerers. But my arrival was too late. He has them performing sacrifices. They believe the more blood they spill, the closer they come to bridging the Fifth Sun and the Thirteen Heavens. They claim the gods speak to them, promising their return."

"I *knew* it," Eréndira says. "I knew Ichcatzin had a plan. What is this weapon, lord? Have you seen it?"

Chipahua shakes his head. "Not with my own eyes, but he repeats these words to any and all who will listen. He says that if he performs a ritual, then the gods will come," he explains, "and then he'll unleash them on the Christians."

"Gods walking the earth?" I ask, knowing it is possible although that seems unlikely. "Do you believe that, lord?"

"I'm an old man," Chipahua says. "In all my years, I have never seen the teteoh. Ichcatzin has long sought to bring them back to Mexico, and now he says he has the means. I don't know whether it will work. Or whether I'll even live to see it happen. I honor the past. I honor my ancestors. But it's been more than thirty years since the Fall. People have forgotten the gods. Neza knew it too. He tried to do things differently. And he paid with his life."

"So what do you think will happen?" Eréndira asks.

"I don't know what this is," Chipahua replies. "But whatever Ichcatzin is bringing forth, we can't allow it to reach full power."

Part 3: Toxcatl

Dryness

CHAPTER 24

El Usurpador

I hear the shuffle of sandals and bare feet before I reach Coatepec.

The heavy tread of hundreds moving through the city, the young and old, the sick and well, all invoking the gods to show themselves. It does not seem they will receive a favorable answer this day, and certainly not by such simple means. Divine power is unreliable. That's the best I can say for the gods, that their ways are beyond understanding.

Tonatiuh continues his journey across the morning sky. Babies wail. The old moan. Men shriek the names of the gods, and women cajole children with promises of a better life. I judge them all to be of the same mind, speaking the same thing, united in the same spirit, intent on the same purpose. Every face I pass is the same, filled with desperation.

Neza would have hated to see his people suffering. It would have hurt him deeply. It was a tragedy for Snake Mountain that he should die in the full flush of his manhood, as he proved himself a good and caring king.

And now I'm to see about a usurping tyrant on the throne. I'm eager to avenge the loss of every chaneque with the blood of all who dealt the slaughter.

Alone, cloaked by my robe, I blend into the crowd cramming the streets to see their tlahtoani at the top of the teocalli, where the veil between worlds—the Nine Hells, the Fifth Sun, and the Thirteen Heavens—is at its thinnest. They halt before the steep staircase, and I'm grateful. The climb is exhausting; you have to stoop and carefully sidestep your way, which is threatened by the slippery limestone.

We wait. It seems we wait for hours. From time to time, I swivel my head, checking my surroundings and listening to the subtlest sounds.

It was here where Neza welcomed me into La Justicia, and it was here where we battled the Tzitzimime. My last time in Snake Mountain, it was xopan, the wet season, and the forest stirred with green life. But now that Tlaloc holds back the rains, the magnificent ahuehuetl growing out of the temple has shed its foliage. The tree is deteriorating like the teocalli; some limbs are dead, and its tonalli is not the warm and strong force it once was. It is cold and uninviting.

"The forest is clear of its game. The trees bear no nuts. The lake is empty of its fish. Our families go hungry!" a man rages. "And the all-sustaining god of rain, wherever Tlaloc is," he says, his eyes on the sky, "does nothing!"

A few among the crowd agree, crying their displeasure. The heat, the parching land, the diminished flow of the springs, the dying vegetation, the withdrawal of the lake. There's no explanation for the dryness save that some offense has been committed. Why is it that Tlaloc has not defeated the dryness? Sons have been sacrificed. Food has been laid before the teocalli. Prayers have been made. In what way, are the people not sustaining him?

Some call out that the land is cursed, and so it would seem, for certainly, the valley puckers into a wasteland. But there is more afoot in Snake Mountain than just the drought.

At last, a shape appears atop the pyramid in a haze of tobacco smoke, which reveals itself to be a man dressed like a god. A cape of skulls and bones drapes over his shoulders, gold bands wrap around his forearms, shells and turquoises drip from his neck, and bells cover his ankles above obsidian sandals. Hardly any area of his body escapes extravagance. No one watching can deny the magnificence of his headdress adorned with yellow plumes. He carries a spear that rivals all spears, in a serpent atlatl, and after a while, lifts it to silence the crowd. With the spear held up, the crowd falls to a standstill of absolute attentiveness.

"My people," Ichcatzin says. "Your tongues are heavy with words. Your family is my family. It is through you all that I am reigning. The ears of the teteoh are wider than mine. And they have heard you. I shall let the gods speak to us!"

Ichcatzin points his spear toward the crowd. It wavers as if throbbing with unimaginable power. For a moment, I think the spear is the weapon Chipahua spoke of, and maybe the gods have come to Coatepec after all, and maybe I am to fall to my knees now, for the teteoh are present. The thought brings me a surge of joy. I want to believe so badly.

But nothing of the sort. No gods come, just four warriors.

Each is dressed as a Tezcatlipoca, sons of Ometeotl, four manifestations of one god: the Red Tezcatlipoca, Xipe Totec; the Blue Tezcatlipoca, Huitzilopochtli; the White Tezcatlipoca, Quetzalcoatl; and the one that men fear the most, the Black Tezcatlipoca. The Tezcatlipocas preside over the west, south, east, and north, respectively, and each of the warriors stand facing outward, back-to-back, looking toward the four directions.

Two of them, I recognize. The Naguals. The wolf. The snake.

"Soon, very soon," the four warriors say in unison, "our power will be unleashed. Mexico will be restored. We will restore the land as it was in the old days before the Christians tainted its perfection. The Nailed Christ will be broken!"

The wolf Nagual impersonates the yellow-painted Huitzilopochtli while the snake Nagual the green-plumed Tlaloc. Together Tlaloc and

Huitzilopochtli encompass the natural and social universe of the Nahuas. Together they represent life and death. Tlaloc marks the time of rains; Huitzilopochtli scorches the earth with sun and war in the dry season.

The god-impersonators walk toward two fire bowls. With a curl of their wrists, the flames begin to dance, and suddenly, they lash forward in two streams of fire, flying over the heads of the astonished crowd before whipping around to return to the bowls.

I scoff, shaking my head underneath my hooded cloak. *This* is what Eréndira feared? *This* is what Chipahua warned me about?

I don't know what I expected. Arrogance, certainly, and it is there in abundance. But a performance?

Fire? *Please.* It's the simplest form of tonalli control because fire already burns with the fervor of tonalli, as do all warm things. Had these sorcerers conjured a blizzard, frozen the lake solid, or made the ahuehuetl tree sprout ice, I would have been far more impressed.

Indeed, sorcery is bestowed upon us by the teteoh, and these Naguals seem far more advanced in tonalli control than am I, but they're not gods; they're not even Nagual Masters. Still, I have to accept that these men are warriors who have already been on the battlefield—they wear the decorated armor to prove it—and they are enemies. They will be dealt with accordingly, and viciously.

A frenzy breaks out among those gathered, especially those whose heads felt the warmth of the flames. Ichcatzin waits for the roar to diminish.

"You have witnessed the presence of the teteoh," Ichcatzin says, "and soon, very soon, you will see their power. I once sowed a seed. I watered it. I watched it grow, and with careful hands, I pruned it. It is now fully grown."

Ichcatzin is no harbinger of the gods at all, merely an illusion.

"A problem shared is a problem solved," he continues. "Allow me to share mine. For the teteoh to show themselves, they require a place, one that is befitting of them. The gods need us if they are to come."

The crowd shouts that they will help, and Ichcatzin beams approval at them.

"You must go to Mexico," he says. "Bring your weapons, for we shall meet enemies along the way. But when Tlaloc defeats the dryness, we shall summon the gods. Together. You and I!"

Above, an eagle soars, circling a few times. Then, it descends and folds its great wings to take the shape of a warrior. A woman. She takes Ichcatzin's side and whispers into his ear, "She is here."

Ichcatzin turns his attention to the crowd. "Go now, my people. See to your families, then go to Mexico. We are to see our gods in all their brilliance!"

The crowd obediently goes. The eagle Nagual takes flight, and Ichcatzin descends from the pyramid, his obsidian sandals expertly moving down the steps.

He flashes a wide smile, approaching me. "Pantera."

He is a king, but I do not bow. Lowering my hood, I look squarely into his face with defiant eyes. "Where is she?" My voice is no less stern.

"Who?" he asks innocently.

"The girl," I say. "Zyanya."

"Ah, yes. The chaneque. Follow me."

Ichcatzin's palace is a wonder to behold. It's a labyrinth of splendid halls and rooms with minimal furniture, most of which are reserved for his concubines. It belonged to Neza, and his tonalli still lingering makes that evident. I walk behind Ichcatzin into his great dining hall, a privilege, for there are not many who have the honor of watching a tlahtoani eat. Inside, it is musty and dark, lit only by torches that burn quietly.

Zyanya sits before a low wooden table laden with vegetable mixes, sweet potatoes and artichokes, avocados, tortillas, and roasted turkey that looks almost exotic after months of hardly seeing any game in the forest.

Ichcatzin beckons me to sit, and I take Zyanya's side. "Are you unharmed?"

She nods, but it's a slow, hesitant movement. She gives Ichcatzin a cold look. "Can I go now?"

On the opposite side of the table, Ichcatzin relaxes on soft cushions and helps himself to some turkey. "Is the food not to your liking?" he says, sucking on a bone. "I can have something else prepared."

"Kill me or leave me be," Zyanya says bitterly.

"Kill you? Dear child, I have no wish to kill you." Ichcatzin smirks. "In fact, you may go. Unless you wish to stay, that is. Don't you want to hear the good news?"

"I heard what you said. The gods are coming," Zyanya mutters, her voice small but bold.

"Rejoice, my child, rejoice!" Ichcatzin says exuberantly. "We have much reason to lift our praise, for we have been lost sheep, and our shepherd will soon return to us. It's a true and perfect joy. Would you walk away from such a prospect? The need is great, and the provision of the teteoh will be more than adequate. This is why we respond with our worship. Take heart: we will be liberated from this thorn bush and led to green pastures. The teteoh are coming. Do you understand? Do you have any idea what it means, child? All my life, I have been a servant of the gods. And all my life," he says, "I have been devoted to one thing. Bringing them back."

"Is that why you killed Neza?" I ask him.

Ichcatzin shifts his head toward me. "To change the world, you must remain unwavering in your purpose," he says. "Neza tried to protect our people. We were safe in Snake Mountain, for a while, but still the enemy exists, and they know where we are. In the end, what did my brother truly achieve? Nothing! There is only one way that leads to victory—the way of the teteoh. I have prayed. I have begged them to come and lend their terror to the slaughter of our enemies."

He wets his throat with another gulp of pulque, then continues,

"I was a boy when the Spaniards came. I don't remember my parents, but I do remember the Templo Mayor, the grandeur and magnificence that was Mexico-Tenochtitlan. One night, I had a dream. I dreamt of the place in the misty sky, where the Flowering Tree rises. It was green and so wonderful, the paradise of the west, the birthplace of the goddess of beauty, the abode of the gods, and ever since that dream, Pantera, all I've wanted is to make Mexico great again."

I won't disagree—Tamoanchan is a beautiful heaven. But he's wrong about the teteoh. The gods of creation are forbidden to interfere in matters of this world, and so all his efforts will come to nothing.

For a moment, Ichcatzin says nothing. "Being a priest, I almost achieved my dream," he says, breaking the silence, "but Neza started asking questions."

"What questions?" I ask.

"The same questions that plagued our father Nezahualcoyotl." Ichcatzin waves a hand grandly. "Who are we? Where do we come from? What is the meaning of life? Is it to be found in the gods? Nature? Or in man and his ability to create beauty here in the Fifth Sun?" He scoffs at that. "Neza was more interested in stargazing than he was in ensuring the safety of his people. I let him send Snake Mountain into political and religious decline. I was weak. I loved my brother too much."

I despise the sadness in his voice because I know he isn't lying. The grief in his words is painfully real.

"Our lives were neither easy nor peaceful. In our early years, it was often remarked that Neza and I were alike as two sheaves of wheat. We were anything but. He loved spending time with the scholars, always curious, always driven by a strong moral compass. He knew who he was from the start. He didn't have to search for it. Not like me. I admired him. I wanted that same certainty. But that admiration weakened me. It wasn't until Tezcatlipoca showed me my own flaws that I understood how truly weak I was. You can't escape his judgment or the future he has planned for you."

I shake my head, refusing to let him justify his betrayal. "So you murdered your own brother because you admired him? Or because you were a shadow in his light?"

"Nothing worth gaining comes without sacrifice, Pantera. Did the Christian God not sacrifice his only son on a stake?" He pauses to see if I will deny it. I don't. "Love *is* sacrifice," he says. "It asks that we do the hard thing. That's what it means to follow Tezcatlipoca. It was not enough to be high priest. It was not enough to turn Snake Mountain against its king. No—the gods demand *true* sacrifice. I gave my brother a warrior's death. I gave him an honorable death. It's what he would have wanted."

"I saw you that night of the battle. There was no honor in what you did. Yours was the work of a butcher."

Ichcatzin stares at me wearily. "The gods needed Neza's death, for he was the one I loved the most, and I had to bring myself to do it. And now I will summon the gods, and I won't fail. If it means killing all twelve of my brothers, I'll do it. Push them into a whirlpool and send them to Tlalocan."

"You're holding on to a dream that will never come to pass. You will never rule like Neza did," I say with a fire in my throat.

"What do you know about anything? In a hundred years," Ichcatzin says, "they will not remember his name. They will remember *I* gave Mexico back to its people."

I sneer at that. "You deceive them with magic tricks. What I saw today wasn't even close to the best I've seen from Naguals younger than me."

Ichcatzin sighs. "Are you a child, Pantera? Must I spoon-feed you everything or use smaller words to explain? The teteoh are not here, how clear can that be? But, to summon them I need believers, and to attract believers, I need to offer a little hope."

"You offer false promises. You offer deception and coercion. Your undue influence enslaves them."

"Your sword . . ." Ichcatzin says, fixing his eyes on the scabbard at my back. "Its power is certainly a great thing. It has served you well hasn't it, daughter of Quetzalcoatl?"

I grimace, tightly gripping the strap slung over my shoulder. "Who told you that?"

With a mirthless smile, Ichcatzin unfastens his cloak of skulls. He reaches down into his mantle and pulls a chain containing a medallion around his neck. At first glance it looks ordinary; there are many obsidian stones near Popocatepetl, especially after its eruption. But this, upon a closer viewing, is jet black. Pure obsidian.

My mind screams in denial. *It can't be. It can't.*

"No," I say, shaking my head. "That's not . . . possible."

"Possible?" Ichcatzin parrots. "What does your pathetic little mind know what's possible, Pantera?"

A chill runs down my spine. My ears throb, drowning out everything but the roaring terror that threatens to consume me.

The last time I saw the Dark Mirror, Tezca had ripped it from my throat. The ship caught fire under our feet, and the medallion went down with it. So far as I was concerned, it was lost to the sea, gone forever. But now, somehow, it's here, hanging from Ichcatzin's neck.

Shadows stretch and writhe around him. The air in the room seems to warp around the stone, distorting reality like heat waves rising off scorching sand. I can't help but flinch as the torches flicker. The room feels suddenly oppressive, as though the medallion is pulling all the light into its core. Nine Hells, this *can't* be happening.

"Don't look at it," I warn Zyanya, but the medallion pulses with god tonalli, and she does the opposite. "Zyanya, *don't.*"

She sits transfixed, unable to tear her gaze away from that allure of power. The Dark Mirror has ensnared her, and I can see the awe in her eyes as she fights against its pull.

Ichcatzin's laughter is like a knife scraping across glass.

Desperation fuels my next move.

I stand and draw the Sword of Integrity. The blade glows, slicing through the dimness and casting a verdant green light about the room.

Ichcatzin is a precise man. His movements are guarded, controlled. But he can't help but flinch as the intense glow of the sword washes over him. He shifts uneasily and straightens. There's a flicker in his eyes—fear, perhaps, or grudging respect. Cautiously he tugs the medallion back into the fold of his mantle. The Dark Mirror disappears like a serpent slithering into its lair.

"Are you all right?" I ask Zyanya as I sheathe my sword, its green glow fading.

She blinks rapidly, breaking free from her trance. "You looked at it," she says, her voice trembling slightly.

"It doesn't affect me."

A knowing grin from Ichcatzin. "Is that what you think? Do you believe yourself immune to the Dark Mirror's power?" He chuckles as he speaks. "Silly me, thinking you had reached the pinnacle of foolishness. You've surpassed it."

My jaw tightens. Tezca told me the Dark Mirror corrupts everyone who wears it, but he thought I somehow endured Tezcatlipoca's gaze.

I didn't realize at the time just how dangerous the mirror truly was.

And what I didn't consider, is that Tezcatlipoca had already used his Dark Mirror to corrupt Quetzalcoatl, turning the Toltec king into something wicked.

Every Nahua knows the story of Quetzalcoatl's fall, how he was tricked into exile, with a promise to return one day. Quetzalcoatl admitted this truth, and he still laments his downfall.

He didn't warn me about the mirror's power, but even Quetzalcoatl could not withstand the power of the Dark Mirror.

Why would I believe I could escape its influence?

I'm quiet, thinking this, and Ichcatzin gives me a bored look. He motions for me to sit down. I do, but not without first unslinging my scabbard and placing it on the table in front of me. Just in case.

"You wore the medallion not too long ago, yes?" Ichcatzin asks.

"Nican Nicah gave it to me," I say, even though he more than likely already knows. Perhaps I didn't wear it long enough to be affected by it?

A smile plays on Ichcatzin's lips. "And who do you think gave it to him? Do you *really* believe, Pantera," he says, "that the Dark Mirror would be so readily available that a white man just happened to chance upon it? No! It took me years to find it and even longer to wait for that imbecile's demise, only to lose the mirror again. But fate has its own rhythm—the ebb and flow of the world, what can I say? It takes time to do the work of the teteoh. I was chosen. I am the one who has done what I was chosen for. They provide for me. They protect me. Now, no one can stop me."

He watches me, daring me to challenge him. The power in his voice, the absolute conviction in his eyes—he believes this is his destiny. And maybe he's right. Maybe it is. Maybe he was meant to take this path. But what he doesn't know is that if this is truly his fate, then mine is to make sure it leads straight to his end.

CHAPTER 25

El Temor

Ichcatzin thought himself so clever. He used the Dark Mirror to corrupt Nican Nicah, Don Joaquín, the Spanish viceroy, and waited for his inevitable doom.

Questions flit around in my mind. The more I think, the worse they become. Did Father know he had the Dark Mirror? What did he see in its reflection? Did Tezcatlipoca whisper in his ear? Would I have taken up the Mask of Pantera had I not worn the medallion? Would I have met Tezca? How much of what I did then and who I am today is because of the Dark Mirror's influence?

Everything that's happened—is the Dark Mirror, and consequently Ichcatzin, to blame? Was this Tezcatlipoca's plan all along?

I never asked, nor did I wonder, how Father came by the medallion. I didn't know what it was for one thing. I didn't know what it could do for another. The night it came into my possession, Father lay on his deathbed, delirious with fever. He made me promise I would never take it off. He was the only father I'd ever known, and as long as his Nailed Christ gave him breath, he loved me as he did my mother, so I made my vow gladly, saying goodbye with tears in my eyes. After he went, I kept the medallion close to my heart, and I felt it pulse with Father's tonalli.

At least, I thought it was Father's tonalli.

How little I knew in those days. How only very little more do I know today. There was so much I didn't know about Don Joaquín, my mother Tlazohtzin, or my place in the world. I used to think there were no Naguals in the valley, nothing but whispered rumors. Tezca proved me wrong. And now Ichcatzin is aided by sorcerers, all far more experienced than I am. How flush with unawareness I was, wholly unhampered and unfettered in my ignorance.

The Dark Mirror stole Nican Nicah's life from him. Had Tezca not taken the medallion, it would have done the same to me.

"Leonora." Amalia's voice brings me out of my thoughts.

"What?"

"Well?"

"Well what?"

"Did you see it? Did you see the weapon?"

I nod.

"What is it?" Eréndira asks anxiously.

"The Dark Mirror," I tell them.

Chipahua lowers his head, then looks up. "The Dark Mirror is a myth," he says crossly. "Even if it did exist, it's not been seen or heard of since the fall of the Toltecs."

"I assure you, lord," I say, "the Dark Mirror is no myth."

Chipahua remains stoic, his expression a bland mask that betrays nothing.

"You're certain?" Eréndira asks with an unsettled edge to her voice.

"Yes. I wore it not too long ago."

"Lies," Chipahua grunts. "It's not possible."

"You're looking at a chaneque, a witch, and a sorceress." Amalia points at Zyanya, Eréndira, and me respectively. "We left impossible behind a long time ago."

"I've no reason to lie, lord," I say.

"It's true," Zyanya says. "I've seen it. I've seen it with my own eyes."

"Wait—slow down. You're talking too fast." Amalia struggles to keep up with Nahuatl. "Dark Mirror. What does that even mean?"

"It means," I say in Spanish, "that Ichcatzin plans to summon Tezcatlipoca."

Chipahua and Eréndira exchange knowing glances, their faces grim. Amalia frowns. "Who?"

The Dark Lord is a many-faced god, and so he has many names and titles.

Black Tezcatlipoca. Smoking Mirror. He By Whom We Live. The First Sun. Trickster god. God of night and darkness. Giver and taker of life. Bringer of fortune and misfortune. God of the north. God of sorcery. God of justice and judgment. Patron of kings, warriors, and thieves. Sorcerer. Shapeshifter. Jaguar. Weasel.

In the beginning, there was only Mother and Father Ometeotl and their four sons, Xipe Totec, the eldest, Tezcatlipoca, Quetzalcoatl, and Huitzilopochtli, the youngest. Nothing else existed except the ocean, which was home to the sea monster Cipactli, a caiman creature of limitless appetite. Every joint of the beast bore a mouth, and as long as Cipactli devoured everything the gods created, there could be no life, so Tezcatlipoca sacrificed his left foot to Cipactli to make the earth from its craggy green body. He asks the same of us in return, to act with courage and sacrifice if you seek his favor.

Chipahua says, "Ichcatzin is Tezcatlipoca's ixiptla."

"Impersonator?" Amalia translates.

"Incarnation," Zyanya corrects. "An ixiptla is considered to be the god in person."

"For what purpose?" Amalia asks.

I lift a brow. "Is it not obvious?"

"Ichcatzin wears the insignia of a god," Zyanya explains, "who in turn needs the ixiptla, a physical embodiment, in order to be present. They both need each other. In every sense that matters, the ixiptla is a god. And their powers can be accessed through their clothing, weapons, jewelry . . . armor. Every god has an object that represents their abilities. Quetzalcoatl has his wind jewel, Tezcatlipoca his mirror . . ."

Amalia is looking pale, drawn. "Will Tezcatlipoca come?"

"I don't believe it," I say, "but Ichcatzin will try to do the rites nonetheless, and he will kill many in his attempt. He threatens the very peace we've fought so hard to preserve and for which Neza gave his life."

"Let him," Eréndira says brashly. "He will not find us unprepared."

"He must be stopped before he commits worse slaughter," Chipahua says.

"I agree," I say, "but not me. Not now. I don't know how to fight the Dark Mirror. None of us do."

"We go after him," Eréndira suggests. "We know where he is. We march straight into the palace, find Ichcatzin, and cut off his head. We cut off his servants' heads, his wives' heads, and the heads of every last person who fights for him. Then my grief will be sated."

"Ichcatzin is too shrewd to be caught so easily," says Chipahua. "His men are his walls. They sleep with him, bathe with him, eat with him, shit with him."

"He'll know we're coming, thanks to the Dark Mirror. He probably already knows what we'll do. There is no way the five of us can win in enemy territory."

"Summon an army," Chipahua tells me.

He means a Nagual army. But it's complicated. I've only done it once, and by accident. I'm not so certain I can do it again. "It's not that simple, lord."

"It was not a request. You have a duty as a warrior."

"We can't resolve a threat we don't understand, lord," I say. "Besides, all sorcery has limits. My power is no different."

Chipahua's nostrils flare as he moves his spear to his other hand. "I have fought many battles," he says. "I have known great warriors. I've never seen anything like what you did on the battlefield the night the Tzitzimime came."

217

"You think too highly of my abilities, lord," I say.

"You think too little of them, Godslayer."

The chuckle Amalia lets out is a cynical one. "Let me guess. You'll do nothing, like you always do. That's what you did in Tozi. Nothing."

"Is that what you think?" I ask miserably. "The village was in flames, Amalia. What did you want me to do?"

Amalia clenches her teeth. "Oh, I don't know. How about—*anything?* You just stood there. Is that the justice I can expect from the great hero of the people?" Her voice is hoarse, broken. "Is it, Pantera?"

"Stem your anger, Amalia. It is misdirected," Zyanya says.

Amalia shakes her head as if to throw off his words. "What good are your powers if you're not going to use them, Leonora?"

Her words are poison darts, and I don't have a good answer that makes sense even to me. Sorcery doesn't exist for our whims. Quetzalcoatl, disguised as Master Toto, repeated this over and over. Everyone who wants to follow the Nagual Path must rid themselves of this fixation. Before, I would become so angry with Tezca. He has all of this power, and for what? If he wasn't going to use it, why did the gods supply it? I called him a hypocrite. He said I wouldn't understand, and that was the truth. I was weak in mind. I didn't understand that Tezca feared his power. Perhaps, I, too, fear mine.

I feel the knot in my throat grow bigger. "Amalia, you're the smartest person I know. But you're wrong. You think sorcery solves everything. It certainly helps, like knowing how to write, or how to wield a sword, but it doesn't solve everything. You don't seem to realize what we're dealing with. Tezcatlipoca is all-powerful, all-knowing, and all-seeing. He is impossible to deceive. No lie can outwit him. There is no way to escape him. Do you think I can defeat the god of sorcery?" I feel a chill snake down my spine as I ask the question. "Don't shrug, Amalia. Answer me. Do you think any of us stand a chance against the Black God?"

Complete silence, except for their erratic breathing and racing hearts.

"If not the Godslayer," Eréndira says softly, "then who?"

"Only one comes to mind," I say.

His son.

CHAPTER 26

La Idea

"Tezca is the only one who understands the mirror's power," I say.

I don't tell them why this is so, and thankfully, they don't ask. I watch them, gauging their reactions. No one says anything for what seems a very long minute, absorbed in their thoughts, putting pieces together in their heads.

Finally, Chipahua says, "Where is Lord Tezca?"

"I don't know," I reply. "We battled together in La Gran Chichimeca, and then we parted ways."

"So what *do* we do?" Eréndira asks.

"We know his plans. Ichcatzin will go to the city," I say, "and there he will perform the rites. He will use the mirror to summon Tezcatlipoca and purge the land of all Christians."

"*I'm* a Christian." Amalia touches her cross. "Jerónimo is a Christian. Many natives are Christians."

Eréndira gives Amalia a brief look. She seems conflicted; the Purépecha princess wants nothing more than to see the Christians gone, but maybe, just maybe, there is something else she wants more.

I nod. "We go south," I say. "We warn the viceroy. We assemble. We prepare."

"Go to Mexico?" Chipahua stiffly asks.

I answer his question with another question. "How many people live in Snake Mountain?"

"A few thousand," Chipahua says.

"It seems to me we need all the help we can get, lord," I tell him. "I can fight fifty warriors, maybe even a hundred, but not the thousand peoples who will be readying to march."

Eréndira folds her arms. "They are commoners, not warriors."

"True," I say. "This is no warband going to battle but a multitude of ordinary people. Mothers, fathers, children. Farmers and merchants and fishermen. I for one am not looking forward to the slaughter—and neither should you. These are Neza's people. I will do my part. I will deal with Ichcatzin," I say, hiding my fear that I can't beat him and three more experienced sorcerers alone. We have little time to act, and little hope.

Amalia bites her lips. "We're going to the Spaniards? What makes you think Jerónimo will help?"

"He won't," I say. "At least not at first. And not willingly."

"But?"

"But he will eventually."

Chipahua takes a step forward, and I notice how tired he looks. His sunken eyes are heavy with worry. "We go south."

"South then," Eréndira repeats gloomily.

We march through the forest in the dead of night. Amalia, Eréndira, Zyanya, Chipahua and five of his Mexica warriors who resented being forced to carry out slaughter for Neza's murderer. Among them is Miguel, Señor Alonso's son.

He's leaner than I remember, his jaw firmer, his gut trimmer. But more than that, there is something new about him, a surety in how he carries himself. His movements are precise. His steps deliberate. His tonalli warm. That's something that happens when you become a warrior. It also brings new confidence. His eyes, though, are still that of a youth rather than a man. They are his best feature, sweet, kind eyes.

"How are you, warrior?" I ask him.

"Good and ready," he replies, "to do battle with you, Godslayer." He touches his sword as he says this. The blade is light, strong, has a durable edge, and is effective for thrusting or cutting.

It's the distinct forgery of a Toledan blade, and as I look at the other warriors, I see a contradiction. Steel in place of obsidian, iron attached to spears, and shields with metal spikes protruding from the center. Some of them wear a kind of light mail banded with leather, designed with the heat of the land in mind. Another warrior carries a gunpowder weapon I've not seen around these parts. I have heard it's slow to load, and firing one involves a complicated process.

They're all straddling two worlds, the old and the new, and yet we cannot seem to find a place in either. They must maintain traditions to sustain themselves, and they must also embrace the new for the very same reason.

On this dry night, my head is in turmoil. I'm angry about the chaneques, haunted by their cries. I am guilt-ridden, for the eagle Nagual made a slaughter because of me. She wanted my tonalli. If Zyanya had not protected it, she might have succeeded.

Then there is Jerónimo. A boy for whom I've fought and killed. I've saved his life, and how has he rewarded me? Nothing but lies and betrayal. Everything I've done—it's not enough. Even when he showed concern about my sickness, it was for his own selfish reasons. He cares about how he can use me. And now I must go to his side again.

And what of Tezca? What of us? What would he do if his father came? Does Ichcatzin know where we are? Do his sorcerers? Do the gods? I look up, half expecting a nod from the Thirteen Heavens, but there is only the twisting canopy of trees and the Owl Witch watching the skies.

"Ichcatzin has been playing a long game," I say to Chipahua, walking next to him. "Always thinking several moves ahead, years in the distance."

"The only thing Ichcatzin understands is power," Chipahua says. "He believes he rules because he was chosen, but if this weapon exists, then it's the mirror that has carried him to power. And if he doesn't achieve his objective, he loses what he cares about most—his standing. He will be remembered as the ixiptla who was not worthy of Tezcatlipoca."

"He fears defeat."

"Indeed."

"I fear it too, lord," I say. "Don't you?"

"I fear not seeing my children again," he answers. "I can barely remember what my youngest looks like anymore."

"I understand, lord," I say, nodding, "the desire to see the people you care about again."

A gloom overcomes Chipahua. The look in his eyes is desolate. I have never seen him like this before, not even when Neza died. I've seen Chipahua angry, raging, annoyed, amused, and it's not very often—but this is something new.

"You seem sad, lord."

"War is a sad thing, Godslayer."

My forehead creases. "I thought you enjoyed war."

"I'm good at killing."

"Exceptional, I would say."

He exhales. "I'm not eager to kill, not like I used to be. The battle rage? The screaming joy? I don't have it anymore. Maybe I'm getting old."

"Maybe. But that only means your tonalli is stronger, lord."

We fall silent for a moment, our march steady.

"Ichcatzin told me Neza kept company with the wise men," I say. "Is that true?"

A look of haunting misery alters the line of his lips.

"They're all dead now," Chipahua says. "And soon Ichcatzin will join them."

"So it's true?" I ask.

"Neza was more complicated than what he appeared on the surface. He was a deep thinker. His prominence in certain circles and ideas often got him into trouble."

"What ideas?"

"The same ideas that gave birth to La Justicia."

"Rebellion?"

"Liberty," Chipahua replies.

"Liberty," I ask with some doubt, "from the viceroyalty?"

He offers a half smile, almost a grimace. "From Spain."

The idea is so bold it startles me. I stop walking, forcing him to halt. I meet his gaze and quietly ask, "Independence?"

"I can't say when his thoughts turned toward liberation," Chipahua says wistfully, "but his nature was inquisitive. Neza never accepted conventional thought, not even Nahua belief. If he didn't agree with something, he questioned it; he was denounced for his rejection of human sacrifice. He challenged others to do the same. To engage, to think differently, to march in another direction, not just for justice but for the future."

I've come to know Neza in death more than I did in life. I suppose it's a curious phenomenon; in death, the truth about oneself is usually revealed. The stories shared by loved ones, the reflections, the echoes of one's legacy. Though we may have never known them, we are our ancestors, and Neza undeniably carried his father, the sage poet-king within him.

I've only now begun to understand the depths of Neza's wisdom, the significance of his contributions with La Justicia, the intricacies of his thoughts. He wasn't just willing to ask the hard questions, but he was devoted to seeking the answers. Neza understood change, the way the great Nahua philosophers understood that the world is always in motion with teotl, the ever-dynamic, vivifying, self-generating, and self-regenerating power that sustains all life. And if this sacred energy is inside all of us, in all existing things, if trees, rivers, and mountains are always becoming, always in the process of renovation, if we live in the Fifth Sun, the sun of movement, how can we not do the same?

But to seek independence from Spain. Is such a thing even possible? Such a conspiracy would have all our heads. The scholars teach that the world is slippery, and it is in the nepantla that true transformation occurs. The nepantla forces you to change your beliefs and perspectives. And in this in-between, there can be a new world, a better one. Amid all this slipperiness, Neza resisted, of course, but he also adapted, for he knew that his people wouldn't thrive for long if he didn't.

Behind me, Miguel opens an ear of corn to reveal swollen, gray kernels. He strips a couple. He offers to share with Amalia, and with a sniff, she bites in, but then Miguel calls it a delicacy, and the two warriors at his side start laughing.

Amalia stops chewing. "This isn't really corn, is it?"

Miguel flashes a toothy grin. "No."

"It's raven's shit," the warrior to his right says.

"It's cuitlacochin," Miguel says. "It's the fungus that grows on corns. It tastes better than it looks." Amalia gives Miguel a little grin as she continues chewing.

One of the men quickens his pace until he matches mine. He tells me his name. "Notoca Yaotl."

"I am Pantera."

"I know who you are. Everyone does. They say you defeated the Obsidian Butterfly and her army of skeleton women," he says, "I wasn't there that night, when the Tzitzimime came. I should've been, but I've never fought the teteoh. With you on our side, we just might win."

"The Obsidian Butterfly was a lesser goddess," I say, my tone clipped. "Tezcatlipoca is a creator god."

Yaotl's brows pull together before he steps back to join the others.

To my side, Zyanya says, "Optimistic much?"

"They shouldn't place their hope in me," I respond. "I'm not their savior."

I pause suddenly, and so do the others behind me.

"What is it?" Zyanya asks.

A wind blows around us, lifting my hair. It breathes through the trees, rattling the branches, fluttering leaves.

"Where did this wind come from?" Miguel says, and the other warriors shake their heads to show they have no answer.

"You go on. I'll find you," I say to Amalia, turning away.

"What? No, no, Leonora." She chuckles nervously. "I don't know how to get to the capital."

"Just keep going."

"But I've only made the journey once."

Above, Eréndira screeches, her great wings soaring in the night.

"She knows the way," I say, then surrender to the urge that's been thrumming within me since my tonalli returned. I shift into my nagual and take off in the direction of the wind.

It's blowing from the west.

It's never comfortable, going from human to beast. There was once a time when the pain was incapacitating. I anticipated the agony of the Panther ripping her way out of my body, and I tensed. I fought the torture of my spine reforming, my jaw distending and narrowing, teeth popping out where none had been, my ears lengthening and reorienting, fur bursting through my skin. The harder I held on, the more it hurt. Finally, I surrendered, the Panther was free, and the most intense happiness came. It consumes you, and then it becomes you. You forget about everything, the past, the future. There is no fear or anxiety. My entire being is alive.

I hiss. *Hello, old friend.* The smells grow clearer. The air tastes crisper. The wind slices across my muzzle as I skulk through the underbrush. The dawn is still faint, not strong enough to pierce the trees, but I'm a night hunter, and my eyes are adapted for the darkness. I move boldly. All I can hear are my paws touching the earth. It's so quiet I begin to think the place is deserted, but after only a moment, I know that isn't true. It's not the sound of my own paws.

I crouch and stare, tail twitching. A dog-like creature stands a few feet away, looking at me, one-eyed and hideously hairless. It takes my nagual mind a second, but I finally recognize the animal.

I shift back to human form. "I *knew* it was you. What are you doing here?"

A flurry of dry leaves swirls around the creature, fast and impossible to follow, until the curtain of leaves falls away, revealing Quetzalcoatl.

"Father," I begin.

"War is coming," Quetzalcoatl says. He sounds weary, resigned.

"War is always coming," I say aloofly. "Will he succeed?" I ask after a moment. "Ichcatzin."

"Will he succeed? Yes, that seems to be the question, doesn't it? You may have your answer now," Quetzalcoatl says, "but knowing won't make a difference."

"Meaning?"

"The future doesn't change because you see it. You only see it."

"So what *will* make a difference?"

"Only Ometeotl knows."

A single leaf falls from a tree above, floating between us. I watch it sway into my hand.

"Can you feel it?" Quetzalcoatl asks.

I frown, staring at the leaf. "I feel . . ."

"Yes . . . you've been feeling it for months."

I can't deny it, and it's not just the dryness, although that's undeniable. I feel something else too, something in my mind struggling against me. I recognize the feeling, this weight that sits on my chest, forcing me to take deep breaths. Fear grips me. It's not death that scares me; death seems almost comforting right now. There are worse things than dying—like watching countless others suffer, feeling their pain, and facing overwhelming emotions like resentment, terror, loneliness, and despair. Death feels like a release compared to this. If

227

Tezcatlipoca showed me my reflection, what would I see? Who would I be?

I'm jolted from my thoughts when Quetzalcoatl speaks again, and I rapidly rearrange my features, hoping my worries aren't written all over my face. But Quetzalcoatl is a god. I cannot hide from him.

"Your biggest enemy is not Ichcatzin."

"I know," I murmur. "The teteoh—"

"The gods are near and far," he says, "far and near. Look." He points at the sky, which is slowly becoming brighter as Tonatiuh renews himself. "They are within sight of your eyes but out of reach. They come closer, and they go away. They die, and they are born again. You can always find them, though you may not see them, for the gods are near and far, Tecuani, they are far and near."

How I used to hate his riddles. I understand now he speaks the Sacred Speech, the elegant and elaborate style of Nahua nobles, approaching meaning obliquely and through metaphors. I do tire of his complex manner of speaking. I cluck my tongue. "Why must you speak in confusion?"

Nothing he says is intended to be clear. Why say "water" when one can say, "she of the jade skirt"? I shouldn't be surprised that Quetzalcoatl yields his secrets to me very elusively. I should be grateful. I can speak the Sacred Speech, after all. Though I don't always understand it.

"Why must you hide from yourself?" Quetzalcoatl counters.

"I'm not hiding," I say angrily. "I am what I am. I am the Godslayer. Is that what you've come to tell me?"

"You are a seeker, Tecuani. You always seek the truth," he says. "But the answers, you chase them in strange ways."

After a long hesitation, I say, "I don't know that I can do all that is asked of me." There it is—the weak thought languishing between my ears. "I know that is not how a warrior is supposed to think."

Quetzalcoatl's gaze intensifies. "Then make war," he says forcefully. "I was once like you. I, too, doubted myself at every turn."

"You were deceived by the mirror. Tezcatlipoca showed you your reflection."

"Do you remember how you faced yourself on Popocatepetl?"

"Do I remember it?" I say. "Yes. It is with me constantly."

"We don't wrestle against flesh and blood but against ourselves. You've hidden well, but you must put down the mask. Accept responsibility for your actions, but don't judge yourself. Become the Panther, stalk yourself, and hunt the fears inside you."

"You're not helping." I lower my head, a deep frustration taking me over, but then I lift my face and spill it all in one go. "Ichcatzin's sorcerers . . . their power outmatches mine. I can't fight them. There's much left to learn. I need you. I need to finish my training."

"What is it you think you need to learn?"

"Everything." The word exits my mouth in a rush. "I need to master tonalli control. I can't even lift a rock."

That seems to bother him. "You don't master tonalli control."

"I master myself. Yes, *I know*." The Nagualist arts teach us to fight inside, not outside.

"If you already know, then why are you asking me?"

"You know what I mean," I say, my voice nearly shouting. "I can't command another's tonalli. I can't part water. I can't vanish at will."

"I have taught you everything I can teach you since you were a small girl. Your training has engaged you in a war to win within. The only mystery left is whether you will resign yourself to your fate." His voice sounds distant now as he begins to drift away.

"Wait. Where are you going?"

"Your fate is set, Tecuani. You cannot escape it."

He shifts into his nagual, a feathered serpent of green and blue, and slithers away.

Fate, I conclude, is a bitch.

CHAPTER 27

El Destino

Your fate is set. I go in greater confusion than I was before.

They call me the Godslayer, and they speak of me as if they understand my power, with such earnestness and confidence in my abilities. They trust me, not knowing I'm riddled with struggles. I can't escape that gnawing sense of failure. The night has nearly passed when I return to the others. Just ahead, the small town of Ixhuatepec begins to emerge in the pale glow of dawn, and beyond it, I can hear the gentle lap of water. The island is near.

My face is bleak, not that anyone notices. All seem too preoccupied with their own anxieties to pay any attention to mine. Eréndira and Chipahua keep checking their swords, Miguel and the other warriors fidget with their armor, Zyanya keeps scratching behind her pointy ears, and Amalia is not so much consumed with nervous tension as she is with curiosity.

"What's it like?" she asks me. "Does it hurt?"

"Does what hurt?"

"When you change into a jaguar."

"Sometimes," I say, "if I'm sore."

"Where does your clothing go?"

I look at her for a moment, and then she laughs.

230

"I'm sorry," she says. "I know I have been salty with you of late."

"Salty?"

At least she isn't afraid. Then again, why would she be? How can you be afraid of something you don't believe in? Amalia has her Nailed Christ, and though she has no fight training, she's astonishingly calculating and knows how to survive, and those skills will be in need, for soon we will be throwing ourselves into battle.

"Listen," I begin, turning my attention to the group. "There's much of which to be afraid. The stakes are too high, the compromises required too great. I know I have not been who you've needed me to be." I find myself speaking easily, saying words that I did not prepare but know are right to say. "I'm a solitary creature. Jaguars don't pack together. We live on our own. The same goes for hunting. I rely on no one for survival."

"You're not going after Ichcatzin alone," Amalia says.

"I don't intend to. I need you. I need *all* of you." I glance at Eréndira, Chipahua, Zyanya, Amalia, and Miguel, then turn to the other warriors—four of them. "I don't know you, but if I live to be a hundred, I shall remember your faces as I see them now. It would be a joy to fight by your side." I unsheathe my dagger and cut my fingertip, not too deep, enough for a few drops of blood to fall. The teteoh—they thirst for blood, not for the fluid itself but the tonalli it carries, which is the most powerful.

The warriors, one by one, prick themselves in the tongue, ear, thigh, and arm.

"We are brothers now," I say, "bonded by the blood we've spilled and the blood we will spill in battle, and should we die fighting, then we will be brothers in the House of the Sun. So shall we put a stop to a madman or what?"

All give their confirmation.

There's a strange thing that occurs. I've seen it in battle, which is that the fear of others can steady you in such a way that whatever worry possesses you transforms into strength.

231

No matter their character or training, every man has their limit, even Chipahua, even Eréndira, even Tezca, even me.

Fear spreads, but so does courage.

"This is where we part ways," I say to them as we walk across the island's Tepeyac causeway. Tonatiuh's light has fully risen now, casting golden rays across the lake.

"Get word to the barrios," I continue. "Warn them of what's coming and prepare them for action. The governors are Mexica, and there are many who would fight in the memory of Sin Rostro, the tlahtoani of Coatepec, and if not for Neza, then for you, my lord." I look at Chipahua. "If they will not fight, advise them how to stay safe and where to seek sanctuary until we are finished with the enemy. You will find rest in Los Tres Pablos."

"Rest?" Miguel scoffs.

I grin and give his shoulder a pat. "And good pulque in El Burro Blanco. It's the best pulquería on the island." Given a task, any task, most people will forget their fears—and if not, the pulque will help.

Amalia folds her arms. "And what will I be doing?"

"You're coming with me," I tell her.

I'm learning. I can be the quiet in the storm.

But as Amalia and I make our entry into the Plaza Mayor, the tumultuous buzz of Mexico City assaults my head with an almost physical force, and my calm disintegrates faster than crusted snow before an avalanche.

A great tent is erected in the middle of the plaza, filled with all manner of diversion: singers, dancers, contortionists, and balancing acts. On one side of the tent, a long table on a raised platform is reserved for courtiers of high rank. Jerónimo is there, dons and doñas too, laughing, drinking their wine. It's maddening. Why should we help them? I grow angrier with every laugh. I have to slap my hands to my ears.

I can see Amalia's mouth moving, but I only hear voices upon voices upon voices, each one on top of the other, until there are no words anymore, just a riotous roar filling my head. I want to scream to make it stop.

It's happening again. I'm losing control.

"Don't—don't come near me," I say in a panic. My voice is almost the roar of a jaguar.

Amalia flinches, stepping backward.

"I don't want to hurt you. I don't want to hurt anyone."

My heart pounds like a drum, and I shake my head, trying to block out the music, the laughter, the shouting—all merging into a nightmarish din. An enormous pressure builds in my chest, suffocating me.

Amalia's voice is a distant echo, lost in the chaos. "Leonora, breathe! Stay with me!"

A curious crowd quickly gathers.

"What is happening to her?" someone asks.

"Stay back!" I growl, feeling my fangs press against my lip.

Every instinct is screaming at me to let go, to release the Panther. I clench my fists, digging my nails into my palms, trying to anchor myself to anything human that's left. But the more I fight it, the more it pushes back.

All around me a rattling starts, tables, chairs, the grass, fruits on carts. Nearby horses whinny. The tent flaps begin to flutter as if caught in a storm.

Amalia wraps her arms around me. "It's going to be all right. Come on," she urges, guiding me away from the growing crowd and into the cathedral to the rear of the tent.

As we step inside, she leads me to a secluded bench in a corner.

"Focus on me," Amalia says. "Easy now." She steadies me. "Breathe. That's it. Now another breath. Good. You're breathing. Open your eyes." I didn't realize I'd shut them, but at her bidding, I notice my whole face is scrunched up. I inhale and exhale. The pressure in my mind seems to ease. "Just breathe. I'm going to let go now," she says, but she's still looking at me like I might pose a danger, like she might fear me. "There you go. Feeling better now?"

I nod, but my jaw is clamped shut.

She pushes a strand of hair from my forehead. "You're burning up. What was that, Leonora?"

"Zyanya said my power is growing."

"Growing? Why?"

"I don't know," I say, but I think about the world having balance. If my power is increasing, is it rising to meet another's?

CHAPTER 28

El Cordero

"More wine, excelencia?" asks Tomás, peering over Jerónimo's shoulder.

My lips curve as I glance at Tomás underneath my cloak. Jerónimo nods and hands him his cup. As the wine reaches the rim and Tomás moves off to serve someone else, Jerónimo's focus turns to the stage, where a contortionist is attempting to make his way out of an impossible angle, and momentarily, his eyes flicker in my direction. He pauses and frowns, slowly lowering his cup, as if he isn't quite sure what he's seeing. After dabbing a napkin at the corners of his mouth, he then turns to Don Bartolo seated beside him and says, "I must visit the privy now." His voice is a whisper, but it reaches me. Wordlessly, Don Bartolo nods.

Jerónimo stands from the table and levels his gaze at me before striding toward the rear of the tent. I steel myself for the ordeal as I follow him to a discreet entrance and into a smaller tent fashioned for such private tasks.

"I'll be, if it isn't the Legendary Pantera," he says pleasantly. Amalia slips in behind me, and he stares at her with mixed disbelief and aversion. "Lady Amalia."

"Jerónimo—Dios mío, how you've aged. How long has it been since we last saw each other?" From the irritated look on Jerónimo's face, not long enough. "You seem surprised to see me."

235

Jerónimo smiles, as if little Amalia does surprises him. "Indeed," he says politely. "You've come on a grand day. We have been blessed with the arrival of Fray Simon, the new Minister of Evangelization, and Don Juan de Alvarado, who will serve council as Minister of Intelligence."

"What happened to Don Cino?" Amalia asks.

I worried that eliminating him might bring a more perverse successor. This Don Juan de Alvarado—what will he bring? Opportunity or threat?

"Tragically," I say, "he was found dead in a brothel."

"He was a powerful man," Jerónimo says. "I'm sure more than one wanted him dead. How are things with you, countess?"

"Oh, don't pretend like you give a care all of a sudden," Amalia snidely remarks. "We both know you do not . . . excelencia."

"You've always been treated fairly in court."

Amalia snorts her contempt. "Fairly?"

"It's a good thing for you that I'm in fine spirits," Jerónimo says. "I knew you'd be back, Leonora. I assume you've thought about my offer and decided to reconsider."

"I have not reconsidered," I say.

"Ah." He clears his throat. "Then why are you here? What is it you need this time?"

I scoff. "What?"

"You always want something. What is it now?"

To save your pathetic life. Again.

Gods help me, Jerónimo is not going to make this easy. Amalia tenderly touches my arm. I am fighting the urge to scream, and she knows it. I give a patient sigh. "You were right," I say. "You need my help, and we need yours."

"I am listening."

"We must ally to defeat the enemy that marches from the mountains."

Jerónimo's brows draw together as he looks at Amalia, then back at me. "I don't understand. There is peace with La Justicia."

"Not La Justicia," I say. "An enemy far greater than any I've ever faced."

"What enemy?"

"The gods."

"The . . . gods," Jerónimo echoes. His nostrils flare at the force of the breath he exhales. "Leonora."

Amalia interrupts, "You don't believe her. I understand. It sounds like nonsense, doesn't it? I didn't believe it at first either. But then I remembered my friends are an ahuizotl, a jaguar, and a lechuza. Perhaps we should all be examining what we think we know."

Jerónimo is silent as he tries to grapple with the concept of mythical creatures and gods. It isn't comfortable having your beliefs shattered.

"You were there when the demon creatures came," I remind. "You can't deny the existence of such powers."

"Certainly, I cannot. There are forces of darkness in this world, human and otherwise, that have harmful and destructive intentions. My *belief* is that there is only one God. The true God."

"What about the Father, the Son, and the Holy Ghost? That makes three gods," I argue, even though I already know the Christian God has multiple personalities.

"They are one spirit," Jerónimo replies. "Satan is very real and very strong, but no one and nothing is more powerful than God."

"Don Bartolo needs your presence at the table," I say, hearing his chair scrape on the platform as he pushes it back and stands. He excuses himself and walks in haste.

Jerónimo gapes at me in confusion. "What?"

"The food is ready," I say simply.

"How do you—?"

Don Bartolo enters through a slit in the tent. "Excelencia. The food—"

"I know, I know. I'm coming."

"Viceregent, it's good to see you," Don Bartolo says, glancing at me. "And you, countess."

"Please don't call me that," Amalia tells him.

Don Bartolo lowers his head graciously. "Shall I have the cooks serve?"

Jerónimo nods and turns toward me. "We'll continue this conversation after I've eaten."

"Wait. Jerónimo," I say before he exits the tent.

He faces me. "Yes?"

I shake my head. "Never mind."

Courtiers eat while musicians play. The luncheon goes on forever, until one of the twenty courses of meat leaves guests retching and others voiding themselves. It's a mystery; no one knows what dish caused the disaster, and Jerónimo is outraged that he has to spend the rest of the day in bed. His face is purple from violent exertion, and he sits limply, sweating profusely, his throat raw with pain. He asks God to end this punishment, though He is perfectly just, and restore his health again.

I don't think his Nailed Christ had a hand in the preparation of the food. Perhaps he did for all I know. But I do think it poetic justice that it should turn their stomachs—just as they turn mine.

"*You* did this." Jerónimo glares at me. "You wanted reprisal. I didn't honor our agreement, so you poisoned the food."

"Jerónimo," I say tiredly, "you can't blame me for every little thing that goes wrong. If I wanted to harm you, I wouldn't do so with food."

"Then why didn't you stop me? I knew it—I saw it in your eyes then, and I see it now—you *wanted* me to eat. You knew I would fall sick."

"Maybe you ate too much, too fast."

He shakes his head as I say this, refusing to accept the possibility. "Look at me! I was poisoned!"

"If you'd been poisoned, you'd be frothing at the mouth," Amalia points out.

Jerónimo huffs and crosses his arms angrily. "Doña Manuela complained about a funny smell," he blabbers. "She is with child, and her senses are heightened."

"Yes, there was a particular smell, but I thought it was the normal stink of the privy," I say innocently. "You should get some rest. You need your strength for what is to come."

We leave. Amalia asks if I knew the food was bad. I tell her I had absolutely no idea the lamb was rotten. She does not believe my professed ignorance.

The following morning, Jerónimo is heavy-eyed from a sleepless night of vomiting, but he never misses prayer. He rises to his feet, gritting his teeth, and forges inside the private chapel in his bedchamber.

After prayer, he summons Don Bartolo, and Amalia and I watch him break his fast with a meal of soup and vegetables. Don Bartolo is pale, still a little queasy from the day before.

"Pan—" Tomás says, walking behind him. "I mean," he clears his throat, "Lady Leonora. You've returned."

I give him a stiff smile. "Tomás. How are you?"

He straightens, hands nervously clasped together. "Better now, my lady, knowing you're back."

"How may I be of service?" Don Bartolo asks.

"I bring news of an enemy," I say without delay. "He is approaching Mexico, and we are ill-prepared for him."

Don Bartolo blanches.

Jerónimo picks up his bowl, slurps the last bit of soup, then smacks his lips appreciatively. "Yesterday, I was sick," he says grandly. "Today, I am purged. God is good."

Don Bartolo crosses himself. "Praise Him."

Jerónimo leans back in his chair and juts out his chin. "Indeed. Praise Him. I needed to be purged for God's power and glory to shine through me." He laughs. "Sometimes, it takes a lot, doesn't it?

Christ will protect the capital," he says, looking at me. "Christ will protect you too if you humble yourself before Him. If you renounce your pagan gods and are baptized, then we will have victory over the enemy."

I've been baptized twice in the Christian church. I cannot possibly be baptized a third time.

It takes everything in me to keep myself from strangling this fool. "We don't have time for nonsense—"

"Nonsense?" Jerónimo balks. "God is not nonsense!"

"Are you willing to die, Jerónimo?" My next question burns into him. "Are you ready to die?" He hangs on my words. "The enemy is coming for our blood—*your* blood. He's a formidable opponent who has been patiently waiting for years to strike. He's in control of an army and a weapon not of this world. With it, he has unimaginable, destructive power," I add, trying to remember everything Tezca told me about the Dark Mirror. It isn't very much at all, "and it scares me, in all certainty scares me, that I have seen it with my own eyes. He must be stopped, and none of us can do it alone. It's a matter of certainty that the days of peace here are numbered. Soon the city will be under siege. We need to mount a defense and prepare to fight."

I must sound and look as desperate as I feel, for the room goes completely quiet.

"I would not be here if there was any other way," I say.

"Excelencia, if I may?" Don Bartolo looks at Jerónimo, and he nods for him to speak. "Perhaps we should put aside our differences now and come together. If this enemy wishes us destroyed, it behooves us to defend ourselves."

Jerónimo's shoulders sag. "I just want fucking peace," he finally says with a world-weary sigh. "If what you say is true, how are we to defeat this evil?"

"Together," says a deep voice that is a distance away, a voice that can't be heard by those around me, a voice I recognize.

I hurriedly step out onto Jerónimo's private balcony overlooking the plaza. Here, standing before the palace's main entrance, Tezca looks up at me and nods.

CHAPTER 29

El Espejo

"Tezca," I say as he comes inside the room. I try not to sound too delighted and fight my desire to put my arms around him. "What are you doing here?"

"Who are you? Do I know you?" Jerónimo asks him. "You seem familiar, and yet I cannot place you."

"My name is Tezcacoatzin," he says, coming to attention before the viceroy, "but here I'm known as Andrés de Ayeta."

"Ayeta." Jerónimo beams. "A Christian?"

"I'm baptized," says Tezca.

"*Lieutenant* Ayeta," I amend. "He fought in the Long War under Captain Nabarres."

"A military man?" Jerónimo asks.

"Yes."

"A good man," Jerónimo concludes. "And what has brought you to us, Lieutenant?"

"He knows about the threat," I answer, imagining his reason is the same as mine.

Tezca nods. "The Dark Mirror. The longer the enemy has it, the more dangerous it will be to him—and to all of us."

242

Jerónimo stands and begins pacing the room. "How do we destroy this weapon?"

"The Dark Mirror is made of obsidian," Tezca explains.

"So we crush it," Jerónimo says.

Tezca chuckles as if the notion is absurd. "It's not ordinary obsidian. The Dark Mirror is not something that can be shattered into pieces. It was not created by man, and there is no fire or force that can destroy it."

There is doubt in Jerónimo's face, thoughts racing through his mind. After several moments, he sends for the rest of his advisors, the two new ministers, both concerned about battle but confident that Viceroyal Palace can resist any attack.

They're wrong.

Viceroyal Palace was not built as a fortress. It was strategically positioned, yes, but its stone walls are vulnerable, as I remind them of the siege by La Justicia not too long ago. The quakes did extensive damage and further weakened the palace, and so I tell them, "We can't run, and we can't hide."

"We have to find somewhere to fight," Tezca says. "We choose the battlefield to make sure it guarantees the greatest possible advantage."

"How many men do we have?" I ask.

Jerónimo sighs wearily, his eyes tired and troubled.

"Jerónimo?"

"I don't *know*," he says, vexed. "I'm short of a Minister of Defense, aren't I?" He looks at me pointedly, reminding me of his proposal that I fill the position. "If Captain Nabarres remained, we would have an idea. But I don't know the enlisted men. I just don't know."

The men of the council stir uneasily. The Franciscan friar, Simón, the oldest of them, coughs. He can barely walk but seems to have the support of the Audiencia for he was elected by them. "Excelencia, the city must be protected," he says, his gnarled hands trembling slightly.

"It will take time to gather a force, but we must do everything possible," Don Bartolo says, looking at the map spread out on the table. "There are roughly fourteen blocks." He points to a square-shaped area on the map. The streets that compose la traza begin to extend outward from the center of the Plaza Mayor, including the barrios, each separated by causeways. Most of the canals crossing the capital have been dried out to be replaced by streets, but one can still reach the palace by boat. The largest canal, the Acequia Real, runs along the sound end of the plaza. "We send messengers to gather our soldiers," Don Bartolo continues, "and to anyone else who can help stop this threat. I'll give an update when I have numbers."

"Our allies are working on spreading the word," I say. My voice is bleak, and I wish I could offer more assurance. I don't know what to say. I don't doubt that Tezca, Chipahua, Eréndira, or any of the warriors can fight against the best of Ichcatzin's army, but I'm helpless to know what to do if Tezcatlipoca comes.

Juan de Alvarado, recently appointed Minister of Intelligence, is sober. "I'm beginning to believe these lands are cursed, suffering the rage of God. The island is too big for us to defend. We're surrounded."

"Indeed, we are surrounded by *water*," Tezca says. "The lake forms a moat around the island. The causeways were built as roadways, but also systems of defense. We raise the bridges. Here," he says, pointing to the map. "Here and here. It won't stop them, but we slow them down."

"Then what, Lieutenant?" asks Jerónimo.

"Then," he says, "we inflict serious harm."

Amalia, who's been quiet thus far, speaks up. "Let me be the first to point out the obvious," she says. "Don't you think they expect us to raise the bridges? They'll have thought about that, to be sure. So we shouldn't do that."

Jerónimo stares at her coldly. "Are you suggesting we roll out the welcome mat and make them feel at home?"

Amalia gives him a biting look. "I'm suggesting we wait. If we move first, we expose our strategy."

"We don't *have* a strategy," I tell her.

"And that's why we should wait," she says again.

"Wait for what?" I ask.

"For the enemy to make a mistake," Amalia replies. Frowns of confusion spread over the men's faces. "I always play black in chess," she explains, "so I have a disadvantage. White attacks, but black can play offense, and my defensive skills are quite good. If white plays too aggressively, black can take advantage of those positional weaknesses. There is more sloppiness when playing white. You assume you're going to win."

The men around the table blink with bewilderment.

"We *want* to win," I say to her.

"They will make a mistake," Amalia says resolutely.

Jerónimo's face is a mask of despair. "How can you be so sure?"

"I just told you. Because they *think* they're going to win. White moves first, but white also makes the first mistake. No one ever has won a chess game without their opponent making some kind of mistake."

"One has to wonder about resting the fate of New Spain on a game," Jerónimo argues.

"It's for our Minister of Defense to decide," I say.

"The position remains vacant," Don Bartolo reminds.

"Yes, which is why I propose Lady Amalia be made Minister of Defense."

There's a ringing silence, and Amalia gapes at me.

"Leonora," Jerónimo says in warning, his face set with anger. I've forced his hand now, even though he was the one who dealt it.

Don Juan laughs cynically. "Preposterous," he spits, disgust coating his words. "The men would never follow a woman to combat."

"They won't have to," I say. "Best to leave the fighting to the fighters, and the strategy to the strategists. Of all of us standing around this table, Lady Amalia is the sharpest. I have no doubt she can prepare a defense more than adequately. That is, if she accepts the nomination."

Amalia gives an unsure nod. "I will do my best."

Jerónimo, Don Bartolo, and Friar Simón look doubtful but voice no complaints; Tezca, who is standing beside me, tilts his head at me in agreement, so it falls to Don Juan to bicker again. "I am opposed."

"Gracias, Don Juan. Your disagreement has been heard," Jerónimo assures.

"Since Captain Nabarres has left us, God rest his soul," I make the sign of the cross, "I further propose Lieutenant Ayeta be promoted for the seat of Captain General of New Spain."

Tezca stares at me, his eyes intense. He has this way of looking at you. It devours you.

If mad before, now Don Juan is overcome with fury. "This man is not a Spaniard. We don't know him. He could be anyone. What are his qualifications for such a rank? What type of education, training, or military experience does he have that is relevant to this position?"

"Put a sword in my hand," Tezca says, "and I'll show you."

"Excelencia, this is beyond outrageous," Don Juan argues. "The king will not be pleased. You can't allow an Indian—"

Jerónimo holds up a hand to silence him.

From the look he turns on Jerónimo, it's clear that Don Juan finds him infuriating. His eyes—they are an irreverent grey; he has a hook nose that resembles an eagle's beak, and his cheekbones jut out of his face above a spade-shaped beard. He's more than unhappy; he's furiously, adamantly, resentful. No native has ever had a seat in the Audiencia.

Jerónimo glances at me. "What about you?"

"What about me?" I ask.

"What will you do?"

"I'm the viceregent. I know my place, and it's most certainly not in the battlefield," I say with a honeyed voice. "I will shelter with the women, children, and elderly, of course."

Jerónimo's gaze on mine is grave, unblinking, as he realizes this means Pantera will fight. I know what he wants of me. This is how he gets it. He drums his fingers on the table, weighing his decision. "Very well," he finally says. "Captain Ayeta will mobilize and lead our men." He then looks at Amalia. "What does our Minister of Defense suggest we do?"

Amalia smirks. "I'm glad you asked. I will need my board and pieces."

At once, a servant appears with a wooden box and lays out a chess board with intricately carved pieces. Amalia studies the board in front of her, her face a mask of concentration. It's like she has no sense of her surroundings, only the different patterns and combinations, imagining the possibilities.

She moves her white pawn two squares forward. "This is a good move, but if black responds directly, white loses control of the center."

Don Juan fumes. He makes no reply, except to grunt.

"In the game, proper positioning is vital to winning, and that starts at the center," she says, giving the men a serious look to match her even more serious tone.

She picks up her king and plunks it down on the map.

"All roads lead to Rome." She gauges our reactions but sees none. "No? It's a phrase that means—" She shakes her head. "Never mind. My point is, if we control the center, then the battle is in our hands. The men can coordinate and support each other as a united force. If we have the center before the enemy, Ichcatzin will either sacrifice his men, or he'll be forced to make a bad move trying to obtain it. Now, just exactly how do we do that? Well, I suppose I ought to tell you." A smug grin. "La Plaza Mayor is an important position for the defense of the city." Amalia looks down at the map again. "Is Tepeyac the only causeway to the north?"

Don Bartolo points on the map. "And the causeway to Tenayuca."

Amalia considers this for a moment. "It's too far. The Tepeyac causeway is the easiest path to Snake Mountain. We close off all the entranceways to the causeways that give access to the island, except that one." There is pride on Amalia's face as she begins moving pieces so fast and in so many directions, I can barely decipher what is happening. "They will find themselves being led into the plaza. The blunder will soon be committed, then we checkmate the enemy king."

How many will die first? I wonder.

CHAPTER 30

Los Nobles

All the warriors gather in San Juan Moyotlan, the mosquito-infested barrio where the canals and streets end in marshes. The barrio is untouched by the Spaniards, save for its Nahua name, which after the Fall was changed to the name of a Christian saint, and the shrines the friars have built on the temple in the main square. The community is home to Mexica, along with some poor criollos, and mestizos.

The governing officials—better known as the Diegos—along with other prominent figures, come together at the tecpan, the Indigenous government house. The news of war is met with apprehension and puts everyone in an unsettled state of mind.

"You are vital in this fight, my lords," Eréndira is saying. "Everyone counts in this war."

"Ours is a peaceful district, princess," says Diego de San Francisco, the governor of San Juan Tenochtitlan. "It's my wish to remain so."

Seated to his right, the governor of Santiago Tlatelolco, Diego de Mendoza, says, "I agree. War is not the path I would have my people tread."

Both Diegos speak Spanish and soberly. They're clad in rich mantles, with headdresses ornamented with the green, red, and blue plumes of the quetzal, together with precious stones.

"There's truth in what you say, my lords," Eréndira responds. "Why should you have to fight? You're nobility and lead good lives. But there's no wealth that can procure the luxury of choice when it comes to survival. There's imminent danger with a false tlahtoani out of control that none can ignore. He slaughtered my people, my kin, while they lay sick in their beds. He has killed children, the defenseless. He will not hesitate to destroy those who stand in his way."

The men look sick at these words. They seemed quick to dismiss Eréndira at first, but now their eyes meet hers with concern.

"We regret your loss, princess," says Diego de Mendoza. "Alas, we want no part in your war."

"Then, and I mean only to offer advice," Eréndira says, "flee. While you still can."

"We are merchants, farmers, and artisans. We do not carry weapons. Ours are made out of faith," Diego de San Francisco says, "which is the word of God."

Chipahua shifts the conversation to Nahuatl. "Has it been that long, my lords? Or have you simply forgotten?" His eyes settle on Diego de San Francisco. "Your name—your *real* name—is Tehuetzquititzin. You are Mexica. You are a grandson of Tizoc, and you are wearing tilmahtli," he says, looking at his distinctive cloak. "On your coat of arms, you have the prickly pear growing out of a stone in the middle of a lake, and you have the eagle. You are a warrior, Don Diego." Chipahua turns his head to the left, then to the right. "We all are. And ours is a noble calling, for we shall gladly die on the battlefield. We do not cower in the dark, my lords."

Diego de San Francisco runs a hand along his beardless chin, staring at him with disbelief. "How do you know who I am?"

Chipahua smiles vaguely. "As my cousin told me, knowing whom you deal with is a smart thing," he says. "My cousin was a clever man. You may have heard of him. His name was Nezahualpilli."

The Diegos look at each other before shifting in their seats.

"Yes, we have all heard of your cousin's achievements," says Diego de San Francisco. "From what we are told, he is a good king."

"He was," Chipahua says, "until he was murdered by the enemy. His own brother. His own flesh and blood. What do you think he'll do to you given the chance?"

Diego de San Francisco makes a face, a wry grimace. "You have said your words, and our ears have not been shut against them," he says sharply. "But now it's time you take your leaves."

"Mis señores," says Tezca, returning the conversation to Spanish. "I understand you're afraid."

Diego de Mendoza gives Tezca a stern glare. "Why should we be afraid? This is not our war, and so far, no one has threatened our lives."

Yet. How long will that peace last? A day, a week, a month? They were once persecuted as pagans. Now they will be hunted as Christians.

Tezca shakes his head. "It's not war you fear, my lords. You're afraid of what happens after, and I do not blame you. Most of you have grown up as subjects of the Crown, baptized members of the Church. This is all you've ever known. But some of you," he says, "retain memories of life before the Fall. Some of you remember what it was like to experience the nepantla, one foot in one world, one foot in another, and be forced to assimilate this new reality."

Complete silence. Diego de San Francisco regards Tezca curiously. "Who are you?"

"I'm of no importance to you, my lord," Tezca says. "But this," he looks at me, "is Leonora de las Casas Tlazohtzin, Viceregent of New Spain."

"What are you doing?" I mutter under my breath, as the men murmur among themselves, *la virreina.*

Diego de San Francisco stands and bows without delay. All the men rise with him. "You have our apologies, Your Excellency," he says. "The runners did not bring news of your arrival. We sincerely beg your pardon."

All eyes are on me now. I clear my throat. "You have no forgiveness to seek, my lords. Your atonement is not necessary, only your help to defeat the enemy. We can survive this."

"How?" Diego de Mendoza asks.

I look at Tezca as I say, "Together." I return my gaze to the men. "We ask the people of San Juan Tenochtitlan and all the barrios under the district, and we ask Santiago Tlatelolco to stand with us against the enemy that threatens the island. What say you, lords? Will you stand with us?"

Silence, then Diego de San Francisco says, "Tell us what to do."

I give Amalia a brief glance. "Raise all the bridges," I tell them, "except yours." I say this to Diego de Mendoza. His is the causeway which leads to Snake Mountain.

The teteoh, they're always hungry, and the nobility, who have the divine right to rule, are no less ravenous. We dine like royalty that night. A huge feast is prepared; fowls, turkeys, pheasants, partridges, geese, venison, peccary, and other birds and beasts no commoner can afford. There are barrels of pulque and frothy sweet chocolate, as well as chocolate flavored with chili peppers. There are tamales stuffed with plums, pineapple, and guava; with game meat such as deer, maize cakes with a cross pressed into their crusts, and a variety of salsas made with different kinds of tomatoes and chiles, red chiles, hot green chiles, yellow chiles, broad chiles, thin chiles. Indeed, we eat well and drink even better.

I drain my cup and follow Tezca to the barrels.

"Your tonalli has returned," he says.

"Yes, it has. Why did you do that?" I ask, handing him my empty cup. "Why did you tell them who I was?"

"For the same reason you made me captain general."

"You know it's not who I wish to be, or to stand for."

"It worked, did it not? The Diegos are Mexica, but they are loyal to the Crown. They weren't going to help us otherwise."

"You can't say for sure they wouldn't have. Eréndira and Chipahua were bringing forward strong arguments in our favor."

"And yet," Tezca says, "you didn't even have to *make* an argument. What pleasure are you enjoying this night, Your Excellency?"

"What?"

"Pulque or chocolate?"

"Chocolate. And don't call me that."

He fills my cup from the chocolate barrel, and I take it as Tezca fills his own. I have a sip of the spicy drink, then say, "Are you going to tell me?"

"Tell you what?" he says, bringing his cup to his lips.

"How you knew about Ichcatzin. And don't say you heard it somewhere."

His head turns to where the Franciscan priests are seated like small statues; motionless, expressionless, their souls perhaps in heaven for a moment. They are a sad, tired-looking bunch, and Tezca says they could use a drink, but many priests fear the sinful effects of consuming pulque and chocolate, claiming that it provokes a blaze of passion and scandals in the monasteries. "I suppose it's considered incompatible with a life of abstinence," he says with a dry chuckle.

I roll my eyes. "Why won't you just tell me?"

"Because you're not going to like what I say."

I already don't like what he's saying. "What kind of answer is that?"

"The only one I can give you at this time," he says, then goes his own way.

Amalia joins me at the barrels. "What's going on?"

My shoulders slouch a little. "I don't know. Tezca is hiding something from me."

She dunks her cup into the chocolate barrel, throws her head back, and slurps it down all at once.

"Do you have to drink so noisily?"

She lets out an even noisier breath of satisfaction and wipes a drip from her chin. "You know, they say chocolate excites the senses, makes you feel like you're falling in love."

"It's like I don't even know him," I snap. "He blows hot one moment, cold the next. I'm not so sure of the man I will face at any time. He always knows more than he says. How does he expect me to trust him?"

She laughs for some reason. "Oh, Leonora."

"What?"

"Here's an idea. Why don't you two act like adults and go have sex or something?"

"*What?* No. This isn't—" I shake my head. "If Tezca knows something we don't, then he needs to share it with us."

"Sure," she says, and gives me a pat on the shoulder before heading back to the table with another full cup of chocolate.

I brood in my seat, nursing my drink, unable to shake the glumness I've sunk into.

"What do you think he's doing right now?" Eréndira asks. "Ichcatzin."

"Right now?" I say. "He's thinking about us."

"He's thinking about *you*," Amalia says. "You're the only one who can stop him."

"What if you're wrong?" I ask her. "What if he doesn't make a mistake?"

Her pale brows wrinkle as she thinks about this. "If you apply pressure to anything, even a rock, eventually it cracks. The man is going around thinking he's a god. That belief will drive him to push things to the limit, and he will snap. After all, he's only human."

"If he doesn't?" I insist.

"If he doesn't," Amalia says, "then tell him he's made a mistake. Something he can't prove or disprove, something that gets under his skin and starts to make him worry a little."

"Ichcatzin has been planning this for years," I say, "and he has the

Dark Mirror. It's the eye of Tezcatlipoca. It shows him the past, the future, everything."

"It shows him what he wants to see," says Tezca, approaching the table. "That's why it corrupts the wearer. Whatever Ichcatzin sees in the mirror, it leads him on a path to wickedness. And, eventually, death. Ichcatzin does whatever the mirror tells him, and the mirror does whatever Tezcatlipoca tells it."

"So we wait for the mirror to corrupt him?" asks Amalia.

"Because he hasn't been already?" Eréndira says. "How do you know so much about the Dark Mirror, Lord Tezca?" she asks, and my lips thin, waiting for him to answer the question, though I already know the answer. They don't know he's Tezcatlipoca's son.

Tezca holds Eréndira's gaze, his expression guarded. "I saw what it did to Nican Nicah," he says, then he shifts his focus to me.

I know that's true, but I also know it's not the whole truth.

"Leonora's father?" Amalia asks.

Tezca nods. "He wore the medallion. Not for long, but long enough. It consumed him. The Dark Mirror doesn't just give power; it takes. It demands a price, one no mortal should ever have to pay."

My stomach twists. Don Joaquín was a good man. He didn't deserve this, to be tricked by Ichcatzin, corrupted by the mirror.

"Did you wear it yourself?" I ask Tezca. "Is that what you won't tell me?"

Tezca looks at me for a long moment, either coming up with a response or trying to decide whether to reply or not. At last, he says, "No."

"Then how did you know Ichcatzin had the Dark Mirror?" I press further. I hate that he's hiding things from me. "How do you always seem to know things before anyone else?"

"Why don't you ask me what you really want to know, Leonora? I can tell you're holding back, and I see it burning you up. Why don't you ask me if I'm working with Ichcatzin?"

Is he? Does he want to summon his father? Maybe he believes that by bringing Tezcatlipoca into the Fifth Sun, he can fix something in his past. And that would mean he might be willing to do anything— even work with a man like Ichcatzin.

No. That can't be. Tezca has always fought with us, *for us*. He wouldn't align himself with the man responsible for Neza's death.

"That's not what I was thinking," I say.

"Then what?"

"I think," I say, "you know more than you're saying. You're not being truthful."

A humorless laugh escapes him, and he looks away. "There is no truth. Just perception."

I snort. "Is that true? That there's no truth? Because that statement sounds like it's claiming a truth."

Eréndira groans. "Gods, just hump already."

"That's what *I* said," Amalia says with a chuckle.

CHAPTER 31

El Deseo

At dawn, when Tonatiuh has only begun to brighten the east, I run through the forest of Chapultepec, sometimes as a woman, sometimes as a jaguar. My paws are a blur, eating up the ground. I'm running too fast to smell anything, but then a warm wind blows freshly, and with it comes the teasing smell of sweat, blood, and breath, as intoxicating as eating teonanacatl mushrooms. On the south side of the hill, I come to one of the springs that feed the aqueducts to the city, to quench my thirst, hush my mind, and give my feet rest. There, I find Tezca in the water. His was the scent I followed.

Bathing there, the water is up to his waist. He smiles when he sees me, and his eyes give this suggestive glance.

"Why are you looking at me like that?"

"Like what?"

"Like your sword needs its sheath."

He chuckles and wades through the water, already so shallow from the dryness that if he stands straight, it will reach no higher than his knees.

"You seem tense," he says, scooping water over his shoulders. "Am I making you nervous?"

His smile is unrepentantly wicked. I remember how much I hated

257

his smugness in the beginning, his mock cordiality, that permanently plastered smirk, his Christian name, his voice, his entire existence. Desiring him was the work of the Devil himself.

My leg jiggles. "Not at all."

"Are you sure?" he says, his tone curling over my senses, warm and inviting. "Your heart is racing. Thump, thump," he muffles the sound, "thump, thump."

It thuds all the faster.

I glare at him with utter disdain. "What kind of game are you playing?"

"I'm not playing any kind of game." He angles his head. "What are you so afraid of?"

I fight to keep my face blank and breathing normal. "I'm not afraid."

"You *do* know I can tell you're lying now? Your hands are sweaty. Your blood is quickening. And your skin . . ." he says, sniffing the air. "Fear is pouring out of you. It's the smell of someone who wants to survive."

"Is there something you *don't* know?" I regret the question as soon as I utter it.

"There's plenty I don't know. To start, I don't know why you're here."

"I was running."

He gives me that expression that suggests I should save my breath. "You still don't trust me, do you?"

I waver, and he sees it. How do I answer that? How *can* I answer when I'm not exactly the paragon of trust myself? I suppose I've established my hypocrisy.

"No," I admit.

I expect reproach, maybe even outrage, but to my shock, Tezca says, "That's because you're a smart woman, and you know better." He exhales as if finally resigning himself to the fact that there's nothing he can do. "I don't blame you, Leonora. I wouldn't trust me either.

Let's face it, I blow hot one moment, cold the next. No one is so sure of the man they will face at any time. I always know more than I say."

I sigh. He heard me talking to Amalia.

I realize this is how the teteoh are—fickle, and changeable, and suspicious, for all that we may try to understand them. So I suppose that is Tezca's nature too. The Christians say that's why our gods are evil, because they're hellish beings out to exploit man through sin. This is not a comforting thought, but I'm left to trust that Tezca has his reasons, like I have mine.

"I'm sorry," I say, "about last night."

"There are things I don't tell you, not because I don't want to, but because I don't understand them."

"Maybe I can help you." My heart beats a little faster, hoping he might let me in.

He shakes his head, a sad smile forming on his lips. "Remember the beach in Acapulco? You believed I was a wizard because I deflected your tonalli attack. And I told you I wasn't. Then when I healed your leg, you asked me what I was. I told you I didn't know because no one had ever asked me that before. Because I didn't have an answer. I wasn't lying. This . . . it's not that simple. I don't have the answers you want from me, Leonora."

We look at each other, just look for a moment.

"Where does that leave us?" I ask quietly.

"On the same ship we were on when we met," he says. "Just two people sharing space, staring at one another."

"What are we going to do about it?"

"We could fight," he says. "We do that so well."

I shrug. "I didn't bring my sword."

"You don't need one. You could disarm me," he says, raking a hand through his long, wet hair, "if you felt the urge."

My mouth goes unreasonably dry. I clear my throat. "I thought you said you weren't playing a game."

"Well, if you insist on casting me as a villain, I suppose I ought to prove myself thoroughly debauched."

"Tezca."

"Leonora."

"Really?"

"Really."

"This is stupid."

"Indeed. Are you joining me," he says, "or am I to wash alone?"

"I already washed." Another lie. Another lie he can smell.

He lazily dips his head in the water. He then comes up with a mouthful and spurts it back out. "Here's what I will do," he says. "I'm going to close my eyes and count to ten, and when I open them, you will either join me, or I will finish my bath in peace."

"Fair enough. I'll leave you to your privacy."

He shuts his eyes. "One . . . two."

I kind of laugh.

"Six."

"Six? You're not even—" I huff. "Doesn't matter. I'm walking away now."

"Eight."

I swear under my breath. This is misery, torment. Torture that frightens me more than swords.

"Having second thoughts?"

My pulse is in my throat. "No."

"Nine."

Gods be damned. I'm only fooling myself and Tezca knows it. I throw off my clothes and go naked to him. The cool water is a relief against my skin. I have turned molten, red-hot with desire.

"Ten," he says, opening his eyes. "What took you so long?" He reaches for my face, caressing my lips with his thumb. I can't fight my yearning any longer.

"You know me. I like to make an entrance."

"Well," he mutters, "it's about damn time."

He claims my mouth then, putting a stop to such tremendous vulnerability. There's a hunger here, an intensity that's as wild as the forest around us. I let my fingers roam through his wet hair, over the dips and curves of his arms, his broad chest. He bites down on my bottom lip, and I brush my tongue to taste blood. I laugh a little. It's not so different from a duel, and I do enjoy a good fight.

We wade toward the shore. My body answers instinctively, skin rippling as fur erupts. I circle him, letting my tail tantalize his legs. Grinning, Tezca gives himself to his nagual. My claws brush against his flank, light and teasing, and he responds by swiping back, leaving just a hint of a mark. The game is aggressive, primal, a dance of challenge and invitation.

When I'm ready to accept him, I lower my body, allowing him to approach. Our bodies meet with a force that would be brutal if it weren't so exhilarating. There's no gentleness here, no holding back. His growl vibrates through me, and I match it. We are not just a man and woman, nor even jaguar and jaguar. We are nature itself.

We shift back and continue to battle, for control, for air, crashing into each other, making the forest floor our battlefield as he hurls me there, kissing me, entering me, the feel of him, our hearts, our tonalli, together creating a joyous enchantment.

Warriors, lovers—there's no difference in this moment. We warriors make love like we battle, for we love to fight, and we fight for love, and it's perhaps that same madness that inspired the poets of old Mexico to write their greatest words about love and war.

How I missed his lips, his touch. I'm floating. The world exists no longer. There is only him.

My Tezca. My love.

After, we lie on the earth, resting. Tezca is stroking my hair, a satisfied grin on his face that tells me he missed me just as much. I'm just about to fall asleep, but then he breathes my name.

"Hmm?" I say, my head swimming.

"What is bothering you?"

"Bothering me?" I roll to my side and place my head on his chest. "Nothing is bothering me. This is perfect."

He looks down at me. "You run when something is bothering you."

"What are you talking about?" I say, frowning. "I run all the time."

"Something is always bothering you then. What is it this time?"

I release a breath and sit up, my arms on my knees. "I don't want to fight this war," I admit. "I don't want to kill Neza's people. I don't want to defend the Spaniards. I don't want any part of it."

"What do you want?"

"I want—" *No, I won't say it.*

"Go on."

There's a long pause. "I want the gods to come," I say finally. "I want Ichcatzin's Mexico. I want the Christians gone." I look at Tezca over my shoulder. "Is it what you want?"

He sits up. "We can't fight for the past, Leonora. We must look to the future. Things can never be what they once were."

"But if Ichcatzin succeeds, perhaps they will," I say. "Have you thought about what you will do?"

"If he wins?"

"If Tezcatlipoca comes," I say. "If your father comes."

He exhales and rubs a hand over his mouth.

"You must have thought about it at least a little bit . . ."

"I've thought about it," he says, gazing at the water.

"And?"

"And . . . I envy him."

"Tezcatlipoca?"

"Ichcatzin. He lives for himself," Tezca answers. "He killed Neza, not for the good of his people, but for himself. It must be nice to only think about yourself. I don't want to sit on the throne, and I don't care for Tezcatlipoca, but I envy Ichcatzin all the same." He grimaces. "Our responsibility is to others. Our lives are subordinated to duty. We're fighting to protect the Christians, and I want none of it. Of course, I want none of it! But," he says, "what I think—what we want—it doesn't matter. Chipahua should be King of Snake Mountain. We owe it to Neza to make him king, and if we defeat Ichcatzin, Chipahua will rule. If Ichcatzin wins, Neza loses. La Justicia loses. Everything we've done . . . all our efforts will have been for nothing."

"But the teteoh—"

"The gods," he groans. "The fucking gods. They are not here, and perhaps that is not such a bad thing." *The gods are far and near.* I recall Quetzalcoatl's words. What did he mean by that? "Don't you see? They envy us."

"What are you saying? We should recant and become Christians?"

"I'm saying we take control of our own fate. We become our own gods."

"And what is it you want?" I ask.

"It doesn't matter."

"It does to me."

He shrugs. "Land."

"What else?"

"Water."

I pause, waiting for more. "Is that it?"

"To die a warrior's death," he says. "I'm a simple man."

"Don't you want a family?"

He smiles, but it doesn't last long. "I don't see how that's possible in the world we live in."

"But in another world," I press, "if you could have it all?"

He shakes his head solemnly. "I don't know."

I wrap my arms around my chest, feeling suddenly cold. "What about Cuauhnahuac?" I ask through the thickness in my throat.

"What about it?"

"Martín's palace stands on Tlahuica land. I was there," I say, "in Cortés's castle."

"You mean *Don* Martín."

"Does this not anger you?"

"What do you think? Of course it angers me," he says tartly. "My ancestors died for Cuauhnahuac. It's my home. I do not wish to see it ravaged by war. There is peace. For now."

"For now?"

"Our stolen lands will be returned to us," Tezca says. "We will rise again. Perhaps not while I live. Perhaps three hundred years from now. But someday."

His words make me think about Neza, his vision that Mexico be free of Spanish rule.

"Yes," I say. "Perhaps one day."

CHAPTER 32

La Calma

The days are dreadfully hot.

They are also odd.

There's a strange calm in San Juan Moyotlan. A slow, at times even boring, lull that almost makes me think for a moment that things might be normal. Whatever version of normal exists these days anyway. But, I know, no matter how tranquil the world may seem, the calm times never last.

In the middle of the night, Tezca tosses awake, jolting me out of sleep.

"Another nightmare?"

My hands go to soothe him. His chest is wet, drenched in sweat.

He slides an arm under my head and clutches me to his side, tucking me under his chin. He tenses as he holds me, as if I am the only thing between him and falling off the edge of a cliff, and I can feel it in every line of his body.

"What was it about?" I ask softly.

His grip tightens.

When was the last time he had a decent sleep? What he needs is more than sleep though; what he needs is to rest his mind.

What aren't you telling me, Tezca? The question is on the tip of my tongue, but I don't ask. It was there and gone, leaving only a faint shadow of doubt that I don't have the courage to pursue, instinct telling me that maybe the answer isn't something I really want to know.

What is terrifying you so?

The Christian priests preach of "holiness"—that it's not something only saints can achieve. One can find holiness in daily tasks. I suppose there is truth to that. Every moment is precious, for it can be our last, and so every moment is holy. Maybe this will be the last time I will ever lie with Tezca. Maybe this will be the last time we will ever fill our bellies to our heart's content and drink pulque until we fall asleep in our drunkenness. Eventually, everything has to be done for the final time.

In the morning, I'm at the edge of the marsh, watching the ducks float in the water. I hear the slithering of a snake somewhere in the distance, the whir of a damselfly's wings, the murmuring of the grass. The stillness feels abnormally threatening, like something terrible is preparing to descend and rip it all apart. I lift my hand to the water, my palm down, concentrating. I tug gently at an unseen thread, as if I'm reeling in a catch, but I draw tonalli rather than bending the water to my will. I try harder. My hand quivers. Nothing. The ducks quack. It's almost like they're entertained.

"Pantera."

I grumble.

Zyanya asks, "You *are* Pantera?"

"I suppose."

"Are you certain? Because a lot of people need you to be."

She stands beside me, wearing a straw hat that hides her pointed ears. We look at the water for a long while, as if fearing we might forget how it looks. The silence hangs in the calm between us.

At last, Zyanya speaks. "You are anxious."

"Aren't *you*?"

"Ichcatzin walks a path of imbalance. Sooner or later, he will slip," she says. "All things inevitably fall apart. The sages understand the toltecayotl, the art of living wisely. In the slippery earth, the middle-ness is necessary."

"Nepantla," I say in understanding.

She nods.

"I don't know how to live a well-middled life," I confess.

"Yes, you do," Zyanya assures. "You're not the same woman I met on the battlefield. Even now, you're experiencing nepantla."

I turn my head toward her. "How so?"

"You have love for him," she tells me.

I look away, returning my gaze to the ducks. "What does love have to do with anything?"

"There is nepantla, when two people love each other. Your identity transitions into that of a friend, a partner, a lover. Two becoming one and yet remaining two, here is the middle. Here is the nepantla. Losing your individuality or the togetherness, well," she says, "then it does not work."

Her words are like a breeze blowing past me. How can someone so young hold so much wisdom? Zyanya understands more than most, more than I likely ever will, about our world which is constantly in motion.

"You're the only one who sees me as I am," I tell her. "You know what troubles me. You know who my real father is. You understand my tonalli, better than I do. I value your guidance, and I also hope I can be a good listener, if you need an ear. We can talk about anything . . ."

"Do you mean about my village being burned down?"

I drop my head in shame. "I know it was my fault."

"Did you burn it down?"

"No."

"Then it's not your fault."

"They came for me, Zyanya. They came for my tonalli."

"It was my fault."

I stare at her. "Did you know it would happen?"

A sigh gusts from her lips, heavy and bitter. "I knew *something* would happen. I didn't know what."

"Your dream?"

She nods. "It was . . . warning me. I couldn't see it clearly, not until it was too late." Her jaw tightens, a muscle in her cheek twitching as she speaks. "If you think tonalli is confusing, try interpreting dreams. I thought—" Her voice breaks slightly. "I thought I had to protect them from *you*. That your power was growing, and you would lose control, drawing something dangerous. If I hadn't focused on that—if I hadn't been so damn sure that was the reason—they would still be alive . . . When I became a chaneque, it was Itzmin who invited me to Tozi."

"Zyanya," I whisper, reaching for her hand. "You couldn't have known."

"I *should* know," she snaps, pulling her hand away. "I was entrusted with this sight. It's my responsibility. I saw enough. I felt enough. They all died because of me. Because I misread the signs. Some chaneque I am. Protector of life—and yet I couldn't save anyone. I'm sorry, Pantera."

It was difficult to be without my tonalli for so long. Knowing now that there was no reason for it, that it was all based on a misinterpretation, stings deeply. But seeing Zyanya burdened with such guilt cuts even deeper.

I reach for her again, feeling her anguish as if it were my own. "The blame lies with those who brought destruction, not with you. *None* of this is on you."

A tear slips down her cheek, and she brushes it away quickly. "Why are you so forgiving?"

"Because I know what it feels like to make a mistake. To focus on the wrong threat. To blame yourself for it," I admit. "Because I care about you. And because I understand what you were trying to do. The eagle Nagual would've taken my tonalli if you hadn't protected it. She's a more powerful sorceress than I am. And what then? If my tonalli didn't leave me so easily, you wouldn't have needed to keep it safe. How can I protect it, Zyanya? How do I know if someone has stolen it? Can you feel it when it happens?"

She stares into the distance, lost in memories of a village and a people she can never bring back, and I know it will take more than words to heal this wound. "Tonalli has its mysteries, that even the wisest don't fully understand. But the wise respect tonalli lore. You must stop connecting tonalli to power, thinking of it as a weapon rather than a tool. That much has always been clear to those of us who have studied tonalli."

Tonatiuh sways in a slow dance with the shimmering waters of the marsh. Zyanya smiles when a duck dips its head into the water, then flaps its wings to shake the water.

"I would like to be a duck," Zyanya declares casually, "without any care in the world."

"That's how it seems, doesn't it? It's almost magical how they move about. On the surface they appear calm and serene as they glide smoothly across the water, but the fish," I say, pointing at a bubble breaking the water's surface as a fish gulps an unwary fly, "the fish can see what's happening underneath, two flippers furiously thrashing away. The fish can see it."

Zyanya's lips tremble, and her eyes glisten. "Just promise me one thing," she says, her voice stuck in her throat.

"What's that?"

"Promise me you'll make them suffer."

"What if I can't?" I ask under my breath. "I'm a sorceress, and I can't even make a little splash. How can I defeat Ichcatzin if I have no tonalli control?"

"Tonalli control has nothing to do with controlling tonalli," Zyanya says. "I know you're afraid, Pantera. You have the key to the door, but you have not yet opened it." A hot wind blows across the marsh, stirring the grasses, as if Quetzalcoatl agrees with Zyanya's words. "Why do you think they follow you?"

"Because they're fools," is my hateful reply.

"Because you're in the middle. It's what I've been saying. You are Leonora and you are Pantera. You are of two worlds, neither here nor there. You are one of us, you are one of them. You are made of the Fifth Sun, and you are made of the Thirteen Heavens. You have the ability to bring worlds together. *That* is why they follow you."

I hesitate, then releasing a deep sigh, say, "I promise I will try."

CHAPTER 33

El Presagio

Back in Mexico City, council is organizing, planning, strengthening fortifications. It's not easy to predict from where Ichcatzin's attack will come, but we know his position in Snake Mountain, and we know his purpose. We don't have enough troops to effectively defend multiple positions, the southern and western causeways leading into the mainland, nor can we risk Ichcatzin circling the island, flanking us instead. By raising all the bridges except the northern causeway, we have some control. Ichcatzin gets to choose the time of the strike, but we get to choose the battlefield, and the plaza is the most advantageous ground for a defense. So Amalia's plan is a good one, though it's not without its weaknesses. The plaza is a flat open space with little cover. I would've preferred high ground.

"That's why we're making them cross to us," Amalia reminds council. "They already know they have the numbers and brute force enough to win the battle. They will take the path of least resistance."

Don Bartolo licks his dry lips. "And if they don't? If they surround us?"

"Then we'll be corpses," I say.

Jerónimo's disturbed gaze shoots to me. "For the love of God, Leonora, must you make it sound so sordid?"

271

"We will be pretty corpses," I quip.

"What do we do now?" Jerónimo asks.

"We continue to wait," I say.

It's a strange dynamic, to wait to be attacked.

Try as I might, I can't sleep that night. There is a series of happenings that unfold.

First, the chachalacas gather in the trees and scream to each other like a mob of men arguing.

Second, a Spanish lady gives birth, and she haunts the night with her screaming.

Third, a red streak crosses the sky. A wisp of light extends from the horizon's edge to the highest heaven and is covered in fire sparks, giving the impression that it's a bloodied blade. Cries of terror can be heard from every corner of the palace, and people pour out of every door to look at the strange phenomenon that is blazing in the east.

Jerónimo comes rushing out to the courtyard. "Stand aside."

"Did I not say that these lands were accursed?" Don Juan mutters. "It's a red flag of evil."

"It's Toledan steel," says Don Bartolo, "the blade that has come to slay the dry season."

"And a great star shot from the sky, flaming like a torch . . ." Fray Simón hums. "It's a harbinger," he concludes, "sent by God to announce a cleansing by fire for the wicked."

"You are alarmed needlessly. I have read about this," Amalia says. "It's a celestial object wandering too close to the earth."

"It's a red star of doom!" exclaims one frenzied lady. "The imminent end of the world!"

More fearful cries and wild screams from those gathered.

"It's an assurance of victory," I say, speaking loudly over them, "a sign we will win this war with fire and sword." I don't really believe it, but that is what I'm claiming to thwart off the turmoil.

As if suddenly having the same thought, Jerónimo says, "Yes, yes.

What better weapon than God's conquering sword? We are equipped!" he shouts, smiling broadly. "We will overcome this evil with His strength! Look," he says, pointing at the torching glow tearing through the heavens. "The one true God has spoken. He will protect us. Now, let us go back inside."

Jerónimo speaks fiercely, with authority, and nothing more is said as he goes back inside the palace, lords and ladies in their night garments about him, worried and wondering. But in private, Jerónimo asks me, "Is it an omen?"

Yes, but I dare not admit as much. Already Jerónimo is like a candle burnt to its end.

"I miss Mother," he wails. "She is gone, so she can't protect me, the dons have never accepted me, the Christians can barely stand me, the pagans want to kill me, and Don Martín sits in Cuernavaca like a great snare waiting to noose my neck. Is there no one who doesn't want me dead?"

If Vicereine Carlota were here, she would make him see sense. "Jerónimo, control yourself. We can't have the palace falling apart. You are the viceroy of New Spain."

"Precisely," he says. "I've made too many enemies. I'm tired, Leonora. Much too tired."

"You must show strength, Jerónimo. Be strong for them, and for *yourself*."

He sighs sorrowfully.

"I will have the servants draw you a bath," I say.

"I don't need a bath."

"You always feel better after a bath. The salts will soothe you."

Shoulders slumping, he cradles his forehead in his hand for a moment then finally nods.

As I make for the door, he says, "I'm sorry."

"What?"

"I didn't give you what you asked for. Your freedom. I was selfish. The truth is, I can't imagine my life without you in it."

273

My brows furrow in disbelief.

"I mean it," he says. "Even when we clash, when our views are at odds and our beliefs diverge, at the end of the day, you're my sister. I'd be lost without you."

I'm shocked silent.

"I'll fetch the servants." I don't know what else to say.

All the while, the crimson light bleeds in the sky.

It means blood, fire, war, and death.

It was Doña Manuela who gave birth in the night and whose cries haunted me. Twins, they were, and stillborn. It causes quite a stir and many cross themselves in dread. To the Christians, two babes in the same womb can only mean that the father is Satan himself, so they are a curse, an abomination.

I've not known twins in my nineteen years, but they are depicted in the codices as heroes and monster slayers. Xolotl, the psychopomp, who symbolizes Quetzalcoatl's shadow, is the patron of twins.

Doña Manuela demands a baptism for her unborn babes, for how else will they be saved but with water to open God's arms? Fray Simón declines the request since, he says, the sacraments of the Holy Church are meant for the living, and the only thing that can be done is entrust them to the mercy of God.

"What will happen to her?" I ask.

"Doña Manuela? She will become a bride of Christ," Jerónimo replies.

"A nun?"

"What else can she do?" says Jerónimo. "She's a widow. She has no children. She can't recover her dowry."

"So she's inevitably doomed to waste away like some old toad?"

"Committing your life to God is not a waste," Jerónimo snaps. "The best thing for Doña Manuela would be for her to marry far away. That or join the nunnery."

Amalia doesn't forget she is a childless widow herself and scoffs.

"My mother would have sooner drunk her own blood than send me to the cloisters."

Time passes. Still, no attack comes. Still, the unnatural red light lingers, leaving a dreadful red mark on the snowy crests of Popo and Izta.

The palace is plunged in commotion. All of court is plagued with fear of the future, and so they enthusiastically engage in pleasures. All begin leading lives that are completely novel. Women who were once thought to be virtuous now reveal themselves to be wanton, and men bearing respected names show themselves to be scoundrels; even children are seen running around, disrupting the hallways, dodging their parents.

Soon, Church is swarming with sinners. I've never seen the lines for confession go so long, but now, all are going to the priests to confess everything and anything. There seems to be such a rush to confession that if one forgets to confess anything, no matter how small, that later comes to mind, they must go back and confess again.

The priests are sick of hearing great mischief all day. It becomes such a problem that Jerónimo is forced to loosen the bridle of guilt. He's the first to stop going to confession because God takes pleasure in seeing His children happy, and so it's not a sin to delight in the desires of our hearts. His words help lift countless consciences—and dresses.

In the morning, as I enter the council chamber, several servants exit. Jerónimo is there, seated behind papers upon papers piled on the long table.

"What's going on?" I ask.

"Ah, Leonora," Jerónimo says, briefly looking up, "the festival of Corpus Christi is upon us."

"The festival of who?"

His focus settles on a parchment as he writes a few notes.

"Jerónimo."

He looks up. "We shall have a great feast to celebrate the blood and body of Christ."

Christians. They balk at bloody pagan customs, yet they eat and drink their god. True, the host is nothing more than a breadcrumb, but they still believe that some ghostly essence of the Nailed Christ's body is somehow in it.

"This is no time for feasts. The enemy—"

"The enemy," he says brashly, "is *nowhere* to be seen. Where is this foe that threatens us? The scouts report the horizons clear. I'm beginning to wonder if we are waiting for an attack that will not happen."

I fold my arms. "You think the enemy has suddenly abandoned his ambition? Is that your reasoning, Jerónimo?"

"I don't know . . . perhaps they accepted defeat. Whatever the reason, it matters not. Have you been outside today? The clouds are thickening."

"So?"

"So the forest is not easily traveled."

"To *you*," I say. "You're thinking like a Spaniard. It's the dry season. Even if it wasn't, do you think rain will put an end to their marching? It's your duty to protect and defend the city."

His chest puffs, indignant. "I need no lecturing on my duty. I'm the viceroy," he says, "and my will is ordained by God. The feast will proceed as planned."

My anger rises. "I will give no such order. Viceroy or no viceroy, I'm the viceregent. I alone possess the authority to make such decisions. And I denounce this one."

Jerónimo scowls. "Mind your words, good sister."

"They are true."

"And yet you should rue them. You do *not* rule. You are my steward."

"Steward? My duty is to the people, not to your whims."

How quickly his warmth faded. How swiftly the walls between us have risen again.

"The Audiencia believes me a pagan sympathizer," he says, "and that my leadership will cost us everything."

I groan. "We will deal with the Audiencia, but this is not the time to be celebrating or joining in any festivities. The enemy will be upon us any moment now."

"We can't have the palace falling apart. Isn't that what you said? Wasn't it also *you* who said I must show strength?"

"Jerónimo, listen to me—"

"No, *you* listen. The enemy is not out there. The enemy is within these walls. I must tread carefully now. More so than ever. I can't afford a misstep and incite further chaos. I will not have them see me with terror upon my face. Whoever fears, at least I must seem brave."

I force myself to say what I must. "I will protect you."

"How?" He narrows his eyes. "How will you protect me?"

I don't have an answer, so I say nothing.

CHAPTER 34

La Fiesta

Amalia studies the battle plan spread on the table before us, revising it again and again. She shifts pieces around, rooks, pawns, small objects. She corrects a bean, pushing it further away from the rest of the pieces.

"Who's that?" I ask.

"You," she says.

"Why am I a bean?"

"I don't have enough chess pieces." She moves the bean again. "We should meet Ichcatzin as he comes south."

"No. We can't hold the city *and* fight the enemy," I tell her.

"But you're Pantera."

"And Pantera is not a fool," I say. "I can't be in two places at once."

"If we intercept Ichcatzin's forces rather than try to beat them in the city," Amalia presses, "we might be able to keep them from even reaching the island."

"We don't have a numeric advantage."

"We have *you*."

"Don't patronize me, Amalia. The place of battle is chosen. This was *your* plan."

She's not wrong though. Battles are won before they even begin.

If we could somehow subdue Ichcatzin, the larger threat would be no more, but to attack with insufficient forces would be foolish; our fighting men are as good as dead.

"All this talk of battle tires me. You do what you need to do, Leonora. Make your decision, and live with it. Just like the last time."

The last time. In Tozi. I bite down my frustration. Is my fear of making another mistake clouding my judgment?

It's a time of waiting. Waiting for news. We are certainly not idle.

Tezca circles me, his steps sure. We're deep in Chapultepec, the thick forest muffling the sound of our sparring. As he lunges forward, our weapons meet, and startled birds scatter from the trees. His blows are steady, precise, making me move faster and think on my feet.

"Slow down," I say, catching his blade with a quick parry. My arms are burning just keeping up with him.

His eyes narrow. "What was it you said? That I had a thrusting problem?"

"That's clearly not the case anymore, is it?" I shoot back, barely blocking his next strike. "You named your sword. You're welcome."

Tezca twirls Yellow-Beard, and it hums as it cuts through the air. "And you're holding back. Why? You're not going to hurt me."

"I'm tired, Tezca," I say with a sigh, lowering my sword.

"Rest then."

It's a deeper kind of tired. I'm anxious. I'm on edge. We all are. It feels like the tension will snap.

"I hate it," I say. "The waiting."

"I know." He nods and sheathes Yellow-Beard before stepping closer. He places his hand under my chin, lifting my gaze to meet his. "No one expects you to carry this fight alone." He slides his arms around me, pulling me close. For a second, everything fades. His embrace is warm as I rest my head against his chest, feeling the strength in him, the resolve that never seems to waver. Just knowing that he's here, that he stands by my side through all of it, brings me comfort. But it's not enough.

Every day, I practice tonalli control with Zyanya. She has me talking to mushrooms, hugging trees, collecting morning dew. Today, I'm crouched in the dirt, following a line of black ants, each one with a leaf above their bodies.

"This is stupid," I remark. "How is watching ants supposed to help me defeat Ichcatzin?"

"It's not," Zyanya says with a straight face. "But at least you're focusing, which is more than you usually do."

"Great," I mutter unenthusiastically. I glance back down at the ants. They march in a single line. One path. One objective. There's something oddly hypnotic about their movements. They are determined, like I should be.

I raise a hand, just slightly, willing them to move. For a second, I think it's working—the ants pause, a few of them seeming to change direction. But as soon as I feel a faint pulse, it slips away.

I grumble. "This is a complete waste of time."

"You're forcing the connection," Zyanya says. "You have to let it come to you."

"What does that even mean? I try every single day, and nothing changes."

"Now *that* is a complete waste of time. You can't do the same thing every day and expect a different result."

I grumble again.

"Nothing grows from desperation, Pantera. Tonalli lives in balance, like everything in nature. You'll never master tonalli control with doubt and impatience clouding your mind."

How in the Nine Hells am I supposed to stay calm and grounded knowing what's coming? How is anyone?

I look back at the line of ants moving with such certainty. Maybe there's a lesson there.

"Why do they even call it tonalli control if it has nothing to do with control?"

"Look at the ants." Zyanya points, annoyed.

"I *am* looking," I say, thoroughly unimpressed.

They're just . . . being.

It's so hard when every part of me is screaming for action, for progress, for proof that I'm not failing.

Each night, the Owl Witch scouts the skies for enemy sightings, and we know much of what is happening on the island because of her.

"Anything?" I ask as she lands on my balcony.

Eréndira shifts to her human form. "Nothing."

I sigh. "What is he waiting for?"

"I don't know," Eréndira says, "but I'm getting too old for this."

My eyes squint as I look at her. "How old *are* you exactly, princess?"

"How old do you think?"

"I don't know. I heard stories about you from thirty years ago . . . but you don't look much older than I am."

"What stories?"

"You were about seventeen when the Spanish invaded your lands," I say, remembering Inés. She spoke of the princess with great admiration and respect, dwelling on her fierceness and refusal to submit to the conquistadors. "You killed a soldier, caught his horse, learned how to ride it, and led a war against the Spaniards."

Eréndira lifts a curious brow. "Then what happened?"

"You tell me," I say, shrugging. "You fled on your horse and were never seen again."

"Did I?" That sly smirk on her face.

Her response confuses me. One of the stories of the Owl Witch tells of a woman who made a pact with the Lord of Mictlan for shapeshifting magic. As for the tales of the Purépecha princess, all agree she was never seen again.

Before I can ask, Eréndira chuckles.

"What's so funny?"

"Irony," she replies. "Eagles and owls have always been bitter enemies. A natural rivalry, sure, but still. Eagles are asleep at night, and we can freely hunt without competition."

"What are you saying?" I ask.

"The eagle Nagual," she says, "the blood she spilled demands justice."

"Justice or revenge?"

"What's the difference?"

I search her face, seeing the pain and fury that have shaped her into the woman she is now. I know I can't sway her. "What do you want me to do?"

"Absolutely nothing. When the time comes, stay out of my way," she says. "It's the only way I'll find peace."

I nod. "I understand."

June arrives, and with it, the feast of Corpus Christi to honor the body of the Holy Ghost. Every wall, window, and balcony is adorned with tapestries, wreaths, and lanterns. There is not one Christian household that doesn't celebrate. Even the less pious take part in the merriment. Despite my griping, at midday, the church bells begin to toll, and a procession departs from the cathedral, accompanied by musicians and dancers. Jerónimo is exuberant, of course, even though I advised him not to have the fiesta. But God, he said, was more important than anything else.

I keep watch from one of the balconies facing the plaza, my thoughts on Ichcatzin. Standing there, I strain my ears to hear more clearly—anything out of the ordinary, anything to indicate the enemy's presence—but the clatter enveloping me is as unsettling as it is uninterrupted.

In the sky, the will of the gods shifts back and forth like a game, here a gray cloud, here a bolt of lightning. The petals and herbs scattered on the streets are pungent, traveling easily in the sticky air.

And the masters of the croak, the frogs, sing their loudest notes, as frogs do when they mate, particularly in wet conditions.

But no rain comes. And no foe.

As the procession goes on, the noise spreads all throughout la traza, even in the barrios, until I can no longer focus on any one sound. I start to feel faint and leave my post. Moving through the palace, I curse under my breath when I find Tomás pressed outside a door, looking through a peephole, tongue hanging out the side of his mouth.

I fist a handful of his shirt and yank him around a corner. "Niño, you have to stop eavesdropping."

"What? I wasn't!" he cries in defense.

I give him a glowering look. "What if I had been someone else? Any number of guards could walk down the hallway. You can't put yourself at risk. I'm not always going to be around to protect you. Do you understand?"

He grunts in defiance. "I don't need you to protect me."

"What is this *incessant* need to snoop?" I ask.

"Look at me. I can't help it!" he pouts, cupping his protruding ears, only partially covered by scruffy brown hair. His expression softens, and his lips crack into a serpentine grin. "Do you want to know what they were talking about in there?"

"No."

"Not even a little? It's interesting."

I stretch my hearing to listen past the walls. ". . . criollos, mestizos, indios in the Audiencia, can you believe this circus?" Don Juan is saying. "What's next? Are we to bow to them? They're useful yes, but as servants, not equals. They're getting too comfortable, too bold."

I glance back at Tomás, wondering if he heard the same.

"Told you it was interesting," he says.

This isn't just palace gossip. It's scheming to maintain control.

I have the wild urge to find Tezca. The past few days, he's been away gathering Spanish soldiers and readying them for battle. I put

283

forward his promotion to captain general. Did I also unknowingly put him in danger? I shake my head out of its imaginings. Tezca is in no more peril than anyone else. He can take care of himself. I have nothing to worry about.

"Why are you spying on Don Juan?" I ask Tomás.

"Why do you think? He's Minister of Intelligence," he says, "and a wealthy encomendero."

"So?"

"So . . . I think it's important to know who's who around here. Don't *you?*" Tomás says. "The Alvarado brothers are avid card players, and Don Juan is not a graceful loser."

A deep crease mars my forehead. "Alvarado brothers? As in . . . *Pedro* de Alvarado?"

Cortés's comrade. Nelli's father. The Tlaxcalan princess stood strong in her hatred for him.

"Pedro, Jorge, Gonzalo, Gómez." Tomás makes a smug face. "Don Juan is the youngest. He runs a betting business. Illegal, of course."

"How in the Nine Hells do you know all that?" I regret the question immediately. Tomás has scarcely opened his mouth before I speak again. "You know what? No. I'm not going to do this."

"But I—"

"I don't *care*. Stop it. Don't put fresh ideas into my head. There are more important matters that need my attention. Go. Now."

"But—"

"Now."

Try as I might, my mind races. If not so renowned as his more famous brother Pedro, is Don Juan as perverse?

The endless doings of the feast of Corpus Christi continue at night. Jerónimo invites his court to dinner, just as their Christian God did during his last supper with the disciples.

"Tezca will return soon," Amalia assures me as we make our way to the reception hall. "You have nothing to worry about."

"Nothing to worry about?" I retort. "Should Ichcatzin decide to attack us this moment, how are we to defend ourselves with no army and the Christians frolicking in the streets? We are not ready."

When we stroll inside the reception hall, my heart stills. Tezca is there, outfitted in Spanish attire, surrounded by a concourse of ladies who seem much pleased to be in his company. I'm not such a fool as to greet him with adoration, so I gracefully go to his side and clear my throat. "Captain."

Tezca turns his attention to me and lowers his head respectfully. "Virreina. Good evening," he says, giving me a knowing smile.

"Pardon my interruption. Your presence is required outside. This is a concern of safety. Come immediately."

Tezca promptly excuses himself and follows me out of the reception hall, then into an empty storage room.

"Leonora," he says, shutting the door behind him, "if you wanted me alone in a closet, you only needed to say so."

I ignore his flirty manner. "We might have a problem. I have heard rumblings of discontent. Don Juan didn't take your promotion lightly. We must be careful with him."

"The only problem I see," he says, his gentle fingers spanning the width of my jaw, "is you're wearing too many clothes."

"He's Pedro de Alvarado's brother. Nelli's uncle. Did you know?" Tezca gives me a pointed look. "Of course, you knew. Why didn't you say anything?"

His stare grazes my lips. "I will say . . . I missed you." He speaks in a near whisper.

"Stop it." I tug at the drawstring of his shirt, and it gaps a bit at the neck. "You look like a Spaniard."

"So do you."

"I have appearances to keep."

"So do I." He scrubs a hand over his mouth. "What is this? You lure me into a dimly lit room, undress me, and expect me to do nothing?"

"Tezca."

He smirks and leans down. His lips are close. So close. His nearness, his tonalli, his breath, is sending me into a daze.

"I need to run," I say. "Clear my head."

"Where do you feel it?"

"Where do I feel what?"

"The hunt. The chase. Running through the woods." he whispers, bending to my ear. "The excitement. Where do you feel it?" He lifts my dress, and I let out a gasp. "Here?"

I'm about to kiss him when the raucous, hair-raising screech of a lechuza pierces the air.

CHAPTER 35

La Neblina

The lechuza screams again, a sound that might have just sent every honest rat scurrying back into their holes, staring with twitching whiskers and beady eyes.

Tezca and I tear apart from each other. In dread, we rush to where Chipahua stands watch from one of the balconies facing the Plaza Mayor. Amalia is already there, her attention on the Owl Witch soaring silently through the night sky.

"What is it?" Tezca asks.

"Trouble," says Chipahua.

The Owl Witch circles above us. For the first time, I see her red eyes, like two drops of blood. She lands on the balcony, and with a fold of her great wings, shifts back to human.

"What news?" I ask impatiently.

"Ichcatzin's sorcerers," Eréndira replies.

"Where?" I peer down into the plaza. Many are still celebrating the festivities: some singing and dancing, some strolling about, chatting in groups here and there.

"See the bridge?" Eréndira points to an overpass crosswalk festooned on both sides with red, orange, and purple-blossomed dahlias crossing the main canal. "They're here. I saw them pass."

"Where?" Amalia strains her eyes. "Some of us don't have owl vision."

"The scouts haven't reported any sightings," I say, looking at the canoes traveling along the water.

Eréndira points again. "There. Look."

Streams of people are coming and going, it's difficult to focus my gaze. I shapeshift my eyes like I'm on a hunt, and my sight sharpens to night vision. It's then that I see them blending in with the crowd. Three figures, in their war livery, standing together in front of the palace. The one in the middle, the eagle Nagual, curves her lips into a harsh grin as she looks up at us.

"That's them?" Tezca asks.

I nod. "That's them."

Amalia fiddles with the cross around her neck. "What do you think they want?"

"I will find out," I say.

"What? No," Amalia says. "You can't go down there alone. There are three of them. Who knows how many there are? It could be a trap. It's too dangerous. I'm not watching you die."

"It'll be a battle of words," Tezca says. "There's always a battle of words first."

The eagle Nagual stands like a warrior at a lull in battle, cool and merciless. She's slender and long-legged, with her sword slung across her shoulders, and crowned with a mass of dark hair underneath a feathered helmet.

I stand a few paces before her.

She chortles, her eyes traveling down my dress and back up to my face. "Is that you, Pantera? I hardly recognize you."

"Where's Ichcatzin?"

"Lord Ichcatzin has left it to me to swat you away while he summons the teteoh to remove the smell of the Christian filth from Mexico. My name," she says, "is Iztla, and you must flee this earth before the thread of your fate unravels."

I'm angry. She slaughtered the chaneques. We are past negotiating. I want to make her suffer.

"My name," I reply, "is Tecuani, and I'm the sorceress who sent the Obsidian Butterfly back to her abyss."

I'm boasting, of course, and if it unsettles her, she shows little sign of it.

"How you mewl like a newborn kitty," Iztla says derisively. "You have an hour to come and grovel before me, Godslayer," she says, "and if you don't, everyone and everything you know will die." She turns and walks away, and the two other Naguals follow, leaving me with the unsuspecting passersby of the plaza.

I enter the palace just as Amalia and Jerónimo are coming down the principal stairway.

"What happened?" Amalia asks. "Did you win the battle of words?"

"No," I say, "but if we defeat Ichcatzin, the war is won."

"You saw him?" Amalia asks.

"No. He's somewhere," I say, "out there."

Jerónimo draws his eyebrows together. "So we will fight?"

I nod. "Sound the alarm."

The waiting is over.

Amalia calls after me as I turn away, and I face her. "When you're out there—"

"I know. I'll look out for Eréndira. Don't worry."

"I was going to say be careful." She clears her throat. "But yes," she says, "that too."

Tezca is in my bedchamber, fastening his greaves. They're crafted out of bark. He's wearing little protection, only a neckpiece with shoulder pads, giving the illusion of armor. His forearms are wrapped in guards. A loincloth kept in place by a belt inlaid with obsidian stones drapes from his hips. Sandals made from woven leather strap up his calves. He looks more like a Tlahuica lord than he does the captain general of New Spain.

"Now that is more like you," I say, smiling my appreciation.

I lay out my war gear and ask him to help me arm.

My mask comes over my face so that the enemy doesn't see a woman, but a killer with two black shadows for eyes. I strap my belt and heft the Sword of Integrity.

"You look like a goddess of war," Tezca says behind me. He sweeps my braid aside, and his lips find my shoulder, the back of my neck.

"Stop your teasing."

He slides his arms around my waist and brings me close. "You tease me all the time. With a smile. A look. Your scent. When you walk into a room."

I have to stop myself from pushing him against the wall now.

"We can't do this," I say breathlessly.

"Yes, we can." The softness of his lips on my ear does nothing to strengthen my resolve. I want him, want every glorious part of him.

"Battle is on our doorstep," I say. "I can't abandon my duty just because I love you."

That makes him pull his face away. "What?"

"You didn't hear me?"

His hands find my belt, and he slowly turns me to face him. "You love me?"

I grin. "I do."

He moves his fingers to my lips, caressing them. "Say it again."

I rest a hand on his warm chest, my smile beaming at him now. His heart is racing. So is mine. "Nimitztlazohtla."

Tezca tips his head down and brings his forehead to mine, his mouth parting in a small sigh. "The other day," he says, "you asked me what I would want if I could have anything. I said I didn't know. I lied. I do know."

I meet his gaze. "What do you see?" I ask. "When you close your eyes, what do you see years from now?"

"I see my daughter."

"Your daughter?"

290

"*Our* daughter," he corrects, a tender smile touching his lips. "She'd be loved, and she would live in peace, without the fear that strangled my youth. She'd have her father's strength, and courage, like her mother. She'd be a great beauty. Her name would be Miahuaxihuitl, and she'd be a queen."

A queen? No, more than that. She'd be a goddess.

"Queen of where?"

"Mexico-Tenochtitlan."

"But Mexico-Tenochtitlan is gone," I say, "and neither you nor I are pipiltin."

"You asked me what I see."

Moving away, he runs his hands through his dark hair, bound in a tight knot, but now he undoes it. It falls long and straight, the vigor and potency of his tonalli woven in its growth.

"What are you doing?"

He draws my dagger from my belt, swipes his hair all to one side, and in one quick motion, shears it at the shoulder.

My smile wilts. Whatever it was I was expecting him to do, it was not *that*. "What have you done?" I say in a horrified voice. "The danger has not passed. Your tonalli . . . you could die—"

"*Stop.* Stop moving your lips. You're ruining the moment," he says, "and I need this moment." After sliding my dagger back into my belt, he ties the lock of hair into a knot and hands it to me. "I'd trade all the certainty for uncertainty with you. This is my oath to you in this world. My blood is yours. My strength is yours. My life is yours."

My hands tremble holding his powerful, tonalli-charged hair. This is why men go to war; what warriors fantasize about; why they take the heads of enemies. It's to capture their tonalli and increase their own, as well as their reputation. What songs they would sing, what poems they would recite, what great fame the victorious hero would attain for capturing and subduing such a formidable enemy. His sons, and their sons, and the sons of their sons, all guaranteed immortal glory.

My duties, my loved ones—they all flit into my mind for an instant, but they're gone quickly, together with the words that come unbidden to my tongue. "I take your oath, your heat, your vitality." I use my dagger to slice open my palm. Tezca holds it and smears my blood across his bottom lip. "In the joining of our blood," I say, "so too are our lives bound one to another."

"May it be so," Tezca says, his touch healing my palm, "until our lives shall be done."

The kiss he gives me then isn't about love. It's not even about lust. It's a merging between the deepest part of him and the deepest part of me, so that something greater than both of us can exist.

By my estimations, there are at least fifteen bells in various wooden scaffolds in the cathedral. Each one is made of a different material and size and is hung so that the slightest pull produces a different sound. Some welcome distinguished visitors, others call worshipers to prayers. Sometimes they toll for christenings and weddings, and other times they announce holy days. The bellringers do their special work; they are divided into day and night shifts, required to toll the hours. An honorable and distinguished profession.

I have always hated the damned bells. Tonight, I hate them even more. My least favorite bell clangs in a defeating tumult. It contains large amounts of precious metals, which give to it tones of distressing quality. They are the deep, harsh tones of war. I'm told the ringer is stone deaf, whether from the repeated clatter or birth I cannot say, but he yanks on the rope with experienced precision.

In a matter of a few minutes, the plaza is empty, the bell ceases its alarm, and an eerie silence settles. Tezca takes his position at the head of the Spanish troops, while Chipahua and Eréndira join Miguel and the rest of the Mexica warriors. I shoulder my way through the soldiers until I reach the front. Don Juan gives me a scowling glare as I take Jerónimo's side. Who he sees is not Leonora but Pantera, though it's clear he has strong disgust for us both.

Metzli bathes the streets with her full silvery glow, lovely and romantic, but the moon's light is greatly trounced when, from the east, a sinister black fog starts to roll in, unlike anything I've ever before seen.

"What in God's name?" Jerónimo whispers.

My mind gathers a single word: sorcery.

"It's an enchanted fog, is it?" Even *he* knows that.

"It's just a fog," I say. "Nothing more."

The first to emerge from the spreading fog is Iztla, then the other two Naguals, the snake and the wolf, their arms held out, collectively conjuring the fog.

Behind them, their army marches.

"There's no end to them," a Spaniard wails. "They'll overwhelm us!"

"Let us not despair, soldier. We can't lose faith and certainly not in God," Jerónimo says firmly, but as I lower my eyes to my side, I see his quivering fingertips, the way he squeezes his rosary more tightly, and the moment when he quietly whispers, "God helps us."

I don't think he can.

This is no warband coming to fight. Most appear to be macehualtin: merchants and traders, hunters and feather workers, potters and carpenters. They keep spilling out of the black fog, skilled warriors and Ichcatzin's sorcerers leading the way, while those who've never seen a fight take cover behind those who have. Whether farmers or craftsmen, the old ways see that every Nahua male receives basic military training from a young age.

War is a sad thing. Chipahua spoke this truth. It's even sadder this night. Whatever the outcome of this conflict, there will be no winners. How can there be? This is the worst kind of war any person has to fight: against their own.

I watch them come now and know the soldier is right.

"Yes," I say, "they'll overwhelm us."

I wish I could say something brighter, but I'm gripped by an enemy

I don't wish to kill and helpless to know what to do if Ichcatzin summons the gods.

"What choice do we have?" Jerónimo asks.

"None," is my answer.

CHAPTER 36

La Lluvia

The people of Snake Mountain come slowly, not rushing into the slaughter. Their best warriors are in the front rank, shields locked, thick spears, blades shining. Still there is no sign of Ichcatzin; it seems this massacre will be left to the common people and his sorcerers alone.

We knew we were outnumbered, and this isn't the first time the odds are stacked against us, but what we lack in numbers, we make up for in appearance.

Eréndira is a striking sight in red and blue paint, her long black hair billowing out behind her. Chipahua wears his yellow tlahuiztli, the distinctive war suit of a cuachic, a Shorn One. It's battered and seems to have been through hard times, like the man who wears it. The sides of his head are shaved, but a single braid hangs down the middle, decorated with a red ribbon and, like Eréndira, his face is painted red on one side and blue on the other. The pamitl of a Shorn One—a tall and colorful banner—is easily recognizable. It's fastened to his back, so it does not hinder him in battle. The suit pairs with his shield, which is the same shade of yellow. It does little to offer protection against injury, but it does mark his high status and success in combat. It's the first time I've seen him wear the suit, perhaps because it means more to his own people than it does to the Spaniards.

As the black fog dissipates, the enemy ranks halt, all stopping as though by a single command.

"To arms." Don Juan holds on to the reins of his horse and with his other hand frees his sword from its scabbard. "To arms!"

"You hold no authority here," I tell him. "Stand down."

"Nor does a lawless sinner hold authority over me," he seethes. "I only follow orders from God, and you risk His wrath . . . Pantera."

"Be warned," I say, "any man who doesn't stand down risks *my* wrath."

Tezca laughs. "I would do as she says."

Don Juan grudgingly obliges.

Tezca gives Don Juan a pat on the shoulder. "Good choice."

No one moves unless the order is given. None except for Chipahua who steps forward.

"This isn't part of the plan," Jerónimo says. "What is he doing?"

I stroke Tezca's lock of hair dangling from my neck, tied in a knot on a leather strap. "Giving us a choice," I say, tucking the necklace under my armor.

"You know me," Chipahua tells the people of Snake Mountain. "I'm your brother." His voice is calm, but it has a sharp edge that cuts like an obsidian knife. "I'm not your enemy. Ichcatzin is your enemy. He murdered Neza. He rules over you with tyranny. He wants to destroy you. He wants to destroy everything Neza built. Surrender yourself lest you die for naught."

Chipahua is different these days, like he has something on his mind. There must be, for it is unlike him to reason things out. He knows what Neza wanted, and what he would want if he were standing with us here tonight. His purpose was not only to create a bridge between all Indigenous peoples, unite the past and present regardless of previous enmities, but also to make a way for the future. His heart has ceased to beat, but he's still among us. Great as Neza was in life, in death, he is greater.

I contemplate what Zyanya said the other day about nepantla. I realize now, hearing Chipahua speak, that the only way we resolve this war is by meeting in the middle. Alas, we are afraid of the middle ground. Of the Mexico we might become, of opening ourselves to an unknown. And no one wants to face their fears, least of all me. More importantly, we're afraid of losing what we already have. There's too much at stake, a journey we don't want to make, even when we know there is more to this.

"Surrender?" Iztla tilts her head, amused. "What manner of cuachic are you?"

"One who is weary of death," Chipahua says.

"Then step forward, warrior," Iztla says. "Let me help you on your way to Tonatiuh. I hear him calling your name!"

"It will be no easy feat," Chipahua retorts. "Put your best warrior against me. If I win, you retreat."

"And if *I* win?"

"One of us must die," Chipahua says, tossing away his shield. "The gods will decide."

Iztla's face brims with arrogance. "You have little chance of winning against me."

"He'd have to be mad to try," Jerónimo murmurs under his breath.

"He'd have to be brilliant to succeed," I say.

I feel suddenly cold. Chipahua is both brave and a singular warrior, a legend amongst other tribes. To die in combat is the only way a warrior should die, but I fear he still has much to do to go to Tonatiuh today.

"I promise you a swift death," says Chipahua. "It's more than you deserve."

"Very well. I agree to your proposal," Iztla says, "but you are not fated to fight this battle. It's not you he wants." Her eyes flick over to me. "It's *her*."

At that, multiple heads jerk toward me, but before anyone can offer resistance, I nod and step forth.

"Yes," Iztla says triumphantly. "Come, Godslayer. Let us discover the fate of our struggle. We shall see who earns entrance to the House of the Sun."

In the shield wall, Miguel begins chanting, so softly it's hardly more than lips moving. Another warrior joins in, then all of them together. They always chant before battle, and it strengthens our spirits. The hymn speaks of a terror, a maker of war, a lord of battles, a stirrer of strife. It tells of the Hummingbird of the South holding his serpent spear, headdress of heron and quetzal feather, and bracelets upon his arms. It was him who made the sun rise. He guided the Mexica to where they would build Tenochtitlan. An eagle would be perched upon a nopal cactus while devouring a snake.

To him we pray.
All hail, all hail our god of war.
Hail Huitzilopochtli.

The Christians have their prayers too, and I'm sure they say them. Tonight, however, the hymn of Huitzilopochtli is heard all around the heart of the city, where thirty years ago, the white invaders razed the Templo Mayor. The sound is so full it reverberates off the stone walls of the cathedral like the heartbeat of Huitzilopochtli himself, for it was constructed from his demolished temple. It echoes against Viceroyal Palace, whose stones of red tezontle and white chiluca were pilfered from the rubble of Emperor Moctezuma's palace. The Plaza Mayor is, then, connected to the old gods, in both presence and spirit, in both past and present.

Behind my mask, my eyes glaze. I shed a tear for the thousands who bled at this site. My mother Tlazohtzin is with me. I honor the valor of my ancestors. I don't know who they were, or where they stood, when they fought against the conquistadors, but I want to believe this hymn was chanted then. Even some of the people of Snake Mountain look as though they might join, but with one glare from Iztla, their teeth are clenched shut, so as not to sing. They look nervous. So am I.

Zyanya said I have the ability to bring worlds together. What if there's another world to discover? What if Neza was right and we can begin to work toward finding one?

When the chant ends, I take a breath and steady myself.

"I don't want this war," I say, looking at the sea of faces. "I know many of you. I fought alongside you in the Battle of Coatepec and against the Tzitzimime." My voice echoes across the plaza. "You don't have to do this. You think, if the gods come, then everything will be better. But this isn't the way to achieve your purpose." I swallow, thinking this is more difficult than wielding a blade. Peace is so much harder than war, especially when you're built for battle. "The gods have their own desires," I continue, "and those desires do not always equal our own. You risk unleashing a power this world can't contain."

The Sword of Integrity on my back has tasted more blood than the gods. I've always struggled to maintain integrity. Either my sword lights up at my touch, or it doesn't. I've fallen off the Nagual Path. I've been unworthy. Honor means integrity in what you do, and it will not let me slay Neza's people. Though integrity does nothing to protect against insidious harm, and integrity does little to quell anger. Neza is dead, Eréndira's people are dead, the chaneques are dead, and integrity doesn't stop me from wanting vengeance.

The silence is heavy, until one shield-bearer speaks up. "There isn't another way."

"We make one," I say firmly.

"How?" the warrior asks.

"I don't know," I say, "but we have to start somewhere, and we have to try. The decision you made tonight tells me we can do that. The Spaniards were celebrating their festival. You could've attacked while they were distracted, but you didn't. You can make a choice again. We can avoid bloodshed."

This isn't the promise I made to Zyanya—to make them suffer. "Give them hell," Amalia said before taking shelter, and if I think about what Ichcatzin and his sorcerers have done, the anger reemerges. But I sense a chance. One last chance to stop this.

"Avoid bloodshed?" Iztla spits out her revulsion. "We are servants of Huitzilopochtli," she says, "and our master likes blood. I do as he demands."

"Your master can't command the living," I say. "This is your choice and yours alone. It was your choice to commit the heinous slaughter of innocents. *You* killed those chaneques. *You* killed those sick people."

"This from the woman who slayed a goddess?" Iztla snorts. "It's sad, really. So much vital heat wasted. You have not the slightest clue what to do with it."

"You want my tonalli? Take it. You'll have to kill me first."

"Gladly."

Lips curling, Iztla charges toward me, but behind her, a shield hits the ground with a loud thud. To her utter disbelief, one by one, her warriors start to lower their shields. I smile beneath my mask, knowing they have made their choice. Their wall has almost come down when I hear the creak of a crossbow being drawn, and almost at the same time, an arrow shoots through the air. In a slow-moving blur, I see it fly from our own ranks. Before I or anyone else watching can end its course, it pierces the throat of one of Iztla's warriors. His hand reaches up, lips moving as if trying to say something, but he falls limply before he ever touches the wound. The entire incident takes but a moment to unfold, too quick for even Iztla to intervene.

"Send the heathens to hell!" Don Juan signals the Spanish soldiers to attack.

"No, *don't!*" I bellow.

"Kill them all!" Iztla orders. With a shudder, she shifts into her nagual and launches herself into flight.

Eréndira looks at me, and I nod. She moves past me in a blur, her body reshaping. In an instant, she's soaring, her white wings beating furiously as she rises to meet Iztla in the sky.

The Plaza Mayor erupts in chaos, but not the chaos of battle, rather the sort of confusing chaos where everyone is pitted against everyone, for nobody knows which enemy to fight. Many of the Spanish soldiers side with Don Bartolo against Iztla's army; some of them decide to throw themselves against the Spaniards, and others are left scrambling to know what to do as the plaza fills with the song of swords.

I wanted peace, but war is my fate.

My nerves are crushed by my nagual instinct. The Panther has taken over. I don't resist her, that savage side of me that disconnects from my humanity.

I draw my sword. I narrow my sight at Don Juan and his men, then bang the Sword of Integrity against my shield. The Panther longs for what she sees, wanting it for herself. Such longing fills me, such need that I growl with full rage, inviting death.

Jaguars are not aggressive by nature, but like all big cats, when they are, they're unforgiving. You don't escape a jaguar if it wants you. When a mail-coated Spaniard comes screaming, he instinctively swings his blade at me and, just as instinctively, I slam my shield into his helmet. The soldier groans as he collapses.

"Mind your back, warrior!" I shout to Miguel, just in time for him to ward off a killing strike. His face is covered in blood, but he shakes his head when I ask if he's been wounded.

A screech above pulls my gaze to the sky. Two predators engaged in a deadly dance. The perfect rivalry. The eagle rules the day, but the owl is the terror of the night.

A soldier charges at me, but even as I defend myself, I keep looking up. Iztla dives with astonishing speed, talons outstretched. Her beak snaps at Eréndira's neck, and a loud, piercing scream escapes her.

I'm seized by panic. I promised Eréndira I wouldn't get in the way, and I can't fly, but I can't watch her face Iztla alone. Then, too, Amalia will have my head if anything happens to Eréndira. I search the battlefield frantically, and my eyes land on a fallen spear. Dashing toward it, I grab it with a firm grip and steady myself, taking aim at the eagle Nagual. The battle above is a whirlwind of feathers, but I wait for the right moment. I have to. The eyesight of an eagle is extraordinary.

"Come on," I mutter. Just as I'm about to hurl the spear, a soldier grabs me from behind. I whirl, using the spear to knock him away. When I turn my gaze back to the sky, Eréndira and Iztla are gone—they're plummeting to the ground. I shove my way through the chaotic plaza, desperate to reach them.

I pick my way across the dead and fighting. Eréndira is standing with a hand pressed against the deep bite on her neck, while Iztla lies crumpled at her feet, missing an arm. One of her legs is broken, and her torn wing is splayed out beside her, feathers matted with dirt and blood. The sight chokes me. As I come closer, Iztla looks up at my mask with eyes full of hatred. Her remaining hand twitches, fingers curling weakly as if trying to channel her tonalli, but her power, her blood—it's quickly pooling around her.

There's no recovery from this. Even if she survives, Iztla will never fly or fight again.

"This . . ." Eréndira rasps, "this is for my people. For the chaneques. For the lives you took."

One last, ragged breath, then Iztla goes still.

Eréndira watches for a moment as if to ensure it's truly over.

"Your neck," I say.

"It's nothing. Let's finish this," she says.

Nodding, I move through the battlefield. Tezca is roaring orders one moment, hacking Yellow-Beard across a soldier's armored stomach the next, then shifting to race after the wolf Nagual. I don't watch. I know who is more equipped to kill. A one-on-one encounter between a jaguar and a wolf is no contest. It's not even a fight. Just a meal. The chase is the best part of the hunt. It makes victory taste so much better. The wolf Nagual won't stand a chance. It never did.

Beside me, Chipahua is howling an undulating war cry. He too wanted peace, but he too was forced into war. Few men are natural-born warriors, and a man like Chipahua is worth a dozen others. Anything standing in his path doesn't remain that way for long. His focus is on the snake Nagual as he waves his blade over his head in a way that leaves me amazed he doesn't harm himself in the process.

Don Juan runs his horse into two warriors, tramples one and takes the chest of the other with his sword. My eyes scarcely leave him, except to deal or dodge blows. Movement flickers to my right, and the Sword of Integrity's deadly edge sinks into a soldier's gut. Hissing impatiently, I release a blast of tonalli to create an opening through the sea of bodies. With the amulet of Tezca's hair, it's more than I intended, flinging many aside or bringing them to the ground.

I easily make my way toward Don Juan, power driving my path. My vision starts to blur as blood trickles down my mask, and I stop for a moment to slip it off and wipe it away. My hands come back wet but not with blood.

I jerk my head to the skies. A drop of water lands on my cheek. Then another on my forehead.

"It's raining . . ." I say in amazement. "It's raining!"

Tezca turns around to look at me. I shout at him, "Look! Tlaloc has defeated the dryness!"

So begins xopan, the wet season. Tezca laughs as he comes closer, and I let out a shout of joy, but the sentiment fades quickly enough, for suddenly, sickeningly, I know where Ichcatzin is.

"Toxcatl," I say in the merest whisper.

Tezca hears me. It takes him a moment to understand my meaning, but when he does, he says, "The festival."

As if to confirm our suspicions, in the distance, a flute begins to play.

CHAPTER 37

La Musica

We're under the rain, and the battlefield quickly becomes soaked. I stand there, chest heaving, feeling foolish. They could've attacked us while the unprepared Spaniards celebrated their Nailed Christ, but they didn't. Indeed, it was their choice, though not for the reasons I believed. I pathetically thought they showed goodwill.

It was not a mercy.

It was the plan.

Time is intertwined with the health of the earth. Rituals are used in the old ways to maintain or restore balance. And when these rituals take place is likewise important.

To the Spaniards, it's June. To the Nahuas, it's Tloxcatl, the fifth month of the solar calendar. Each is dedicated to a god. And the teteoh, they need their bloody libation.

The people have fed Huitzilopochtli with war over the dry season of tonalco; they have paid their debt, and now, with the start of xopan, Tlaloc has released the beneficial rains, and they have turned to another god.

Tezcatlipoca.

In Snake Mountain, Ichcatzin told the people, "When Tlaloc defeats the dryness, we shall summon the gods." I was listening, but I wasn't paying attention. I should have. It was a performance, in my view, nothing more than what someone in a position of power says to garner support and advance their own plans. Ichcatzin also said the gods require a place befitting of them to show their true presence. I can think of no other place than their temples, their sacred dwellings. They didn't fully survive the Fall, but Ichcatzin knew it was crucial that the ritual happen at the right time, just as the year 1 Flint is such a right time for big beginnings and endings.

I curse myself for my own foolishness, but none of that matters now. All that matters is stopping Ichcatzin.

I shift and run, following the music. My limbs are strong, my paws eating the ground in great bounds.

East of Viceroyal Palace lie the ruins of the Sacred Precinct. Once an impressive ceremonial center with the Templo Mayor towering above dozens of lofty temples, grand palaces, shrines, ballcourts, and halls for warriors, the area is now a crumbling enclosure. This was the religious hub of Mexica life. It's hard to imagine the site in its original splendor. Very little remains; what's left are vestiges of the city of Mexico-Tenochtitlan, exposed like a wound, a reminder of both the world that was and the life its destruction brought.

The Templo Mayor no longer stands some ninety feet in height; it's now merely a platform with fewer than twenty steps.

Ichcatzin is ascending this platform with regal grace. He pauses at each step to play a flute before breaking it to pieces. It honors Tezcatlipoca, for it was him who ended the silence of the world with music. Turning to the east, he lifts another flute, and turning to the west, north, and south, he does the same, each direction representing a child of Ometeotl.

Another step.

Another broken flute.

In the festival of Toxcatl, when the ixiptla reached the top of the god's shrine, priests would seize him, while one of them would use an obsidian knife to murder the ixiptla and take his heart out.

Without question, Ichcatzin is Tezcatlipoca's ixiptla.

However, he's not taking the stairway to his death.

As soon as I become human again, I waste no time and hurl the Sword of Integrity at him.

It hums in the air. It should've entered and sliced. He should've stumbled, should've collapsed. Instead, Ichcatzin turns and stops the blade with raised fingers before it can reach him. It shimmers with green light for a moment, then it ceases as he flings it aside. I stare, astonished.

Ichcatzin is not just a musician playing the flute.

He is not just wearing the Dark Mirror.

He is not just a substitute for Tezcatlipoca.

In essence, he *is* Tezcatlipoca.

"Daughter of Quetzalcoatl," he says as he turns around on the steps to face me, his voice a susurrus, like it's part of the rain. "Have you come to stop me?" He tilts his head to one side, like a curious hound. He knows. He knows what I will do.

How do you defeat someone who knows the past, present, and future? Ichcatzin knows my every thought, my every battle plan, my darkest fears.

"If you give me the mirror now," I say, slowly approaching the platform, "we can put this all behind us. The time will come when it will be too late for you to make a decision. You can still be in control."

He gives me a look of stubborn determination. "I *am* in control."

"You don't learn from your mistakes do you, lord?"

Tezca told me there's no truth, just perception. I fumed at the time, believing he was mad. I realize now what he meant. It doesn't matter what the truth is. What matters is what one believes.

"I have done everything right," Ichcatzin boasts, lazily coming down the steps. "I killed Neza. I sacrificed the one I loved the most."

"Yes, you killed him," I say, "but you were wrong. Tezcatlipoca tricked you."

"I was not wrong!" He hurls the words into the night, cutting through the rain.

"You're not a part of Tezcatlipoca's plans," I say. "You're just a pawn to him. Wearing the Dark Mirror doesn't make it yours. It doesn't make you *him*."

"You're irrelevant, daughter of Quetzalcoatl. It matters not what you say, or who your father is, or what silly little obstacles anyone tries to throw my way! I put them to rest, just as I did Neza. Just as I will do you."

"Oh, but it does matter. It matters," I say, "because your plan is flawed."

Ichcatzin takes several more angry steps down the platform. "Silence yourself!" he hisses, his features pinched. "I possess the Dark Mirror! I have completed the ritual! I will have everything I want!"

He unleashes a black fire wreathing his hands. I'm forced to counter the flames streaking toward me, my blast of tonalli meeting his own.

"Do you somehow believe that your sorcery is more powerful than mine?" Ichcatzin intensifies his spell as if to show me. I slide backward, barely blocking an attack that would otherwise obliterate me. "Do you think you can play games with *me*?" His voice booms with pleasure. It's no longer quite male, or even human. I watch him go from man to jaguar. His yellow eyes are a bright blur in the night. He roars. I bare my fangs. The Panther is ready for him. We lunge at each other, ripping at each other's fur, pawing at our snouts.

We shift back to human form, and he says, "Your power is pitiful, Pantera. Yet you persist?"

"You were wrong before," I say. "I've not come to stop you. I'm here to watch you fail."

"You've lost your entertainment value. The time has come to put an end to your miserable existence."

"You still don't understand, do you? Tezcatlipoca deceived Quetzalcoatl with the Dark Mirror."

"Yes, I defeated him. I showed him how weak and pathetic he was, and my brother fled the world in shame."

I chuckle, a soft floaty sound. "She said you would make a mistake. I didn't really believe her if I'm being honest. How could you possibly make a mistake having the Dark Mirror?"

"What nonsense is this?" he exclaims in disbelief.

I come closer, until we stand facing each other. "Every god has a symbol of power, an object that represents their abilities," I say, repeating Zyanya's words. *In every sense that matters, the ixiptla is a god,* she said, *and their powers can be accessed through their clothing, jewelry . . . weapons.* "Quetzalcoatl has his wind conch, Tezcatlipoca his mirror, Huitzilopochtli his scepter . . ."

"And?"

"And I have my sword." *Tonalli control has nothing to do with controlling tonalli.* I clutch a hand around Tezca's amulet and snap out the other, beckoning the Sword of Integrity. It takes off from the ground and plants itself securely into my grip. I swing it at Ichcatzin, slashing the rain instead. He's vanished in a black swirl of smoke.

As I look around to see where he went, he reappears behind me. Whirling, I raise my sword, but he disappears again. "Even with your sword, you make no difference," Ichcatzin taunts, showing himself at the top of the platform. "No one can stop me. Not even you, daughter of Quetzalcoatl. I have power beyond your miserable imagination."

"My father gave me this sword." I hold it up, admiring its lethal beauty, how it shimmers with the rain, green like the Plumed Serpent.

"I assure you, Pantera," Ichcatzin says, "there's nothing you can say that I don't already know." He taps the omniscient mirror hanging from his chest. "I see it all."

"Do you? Or do you only ever see what *he* wants you to see?"

Ichcatzin smiles, but his eyes maintain a trace of anger.

"For a long time, I was confused." We circle each other warily, moving around in a slow courtship of death. "I didn't understand why the Dark Mirror wouldn't affect me. But then you told me the

Dark Mirror affects everyone. And you're right, it does. It affects everyone . . . even gods. And I *finally* understand what that means.

"The only way Tezcatlipoca was able to defeat Quetzalcoatl is because he had the Dark Mirror. The only way *I* was able to defeat the Obsidian Butterfly is because I had my sword. Do you understand now? It wasn't because gods can only be slain by gods. That's where I was mistaken. The real reason is gods can only be defeated by their own weapons . . . or those of other gods. But Tezcatlipoca didn't tell you that, did he?

"The Dark Mirror showed you the future. You saw victory. You also saw defeat. You wouldn't have sent your sorceress to steal my tonalli otherwise. That's where *you* were mistaken. The future doesn't change because you see it. You only see it," I say, remembering when Quetzalcoatl told me this in the forest.

For a moment, Ichcatzin's expression is one of blank astonishment before fury replaces it.

"I suppose what happens from this moment on, no one, perhaps not even the Dark Mirror, can foresee. What do you say, Lord Ichcatzin? Will you raise a sword to me?" I don't fear for my life. If I'm to fall this night, what does it matter? I will die a warrior's glorious death, and that suits me well enough. "Do you dare find out what the mirror hid?"

Within Ichcatzin, something snaps. His face flushes, the veins on his temples become prominent, and his eyes fill with a madness. Focusing his ire, he puts out his hand and conjures a sparkling dark blade.

Our weapons meet.

Ichcatzin and I attack in a flurry of thrusts, furious slashes and sweeping arcs. The rain is no ally. We leap over ruined stone structures, drive one another against snake-carved walls. Back and forth we deal our blows with neither gaining much advantage. A stillness comes upon me, that odd battle calm where things move slowly, where I have all the time in the world, where I can see the fight two or three moves ahead. I've faced opponents who've wielded their weapon with skill and confidence, but dueling with Ichcatzin fills me with a crazed joy. With a turn of his hand, a sculptured snake comes alive, and as it slithers toward me, I hack it in two, just below its head. I advance, thrusting the Sword of Integrity—only to leap and flip over Ichcatzin's head when he strikes as if with multiple swords, not a single blade. As I land behind him, his form splits into identical versions of himself. All his replicated selves surround me now.

"Now what, daughter of Quetzalcoatl?" Ichcatzin says, his voice echoing around me, all his replicas speaking.

My flesh begins to glow red with burning vital heat coursing through my body.

"Now this."

A scream rips from my throat as I unleash the fiery force threatening to consume me. Ichcatzin and I separate with such intensity that his replicas merge back into him and the ground rattles, bringing down the already ruined site, shattering rocks to bits, pulling trees up by their roots. I come crashing down, face first. The edges of my vision blur. My head pounds with pain. Rolling to my side, I tug shards of stone from my belly, feeling blood drip. I push to my feet in a dizzying stupor.

The rain has ceased, and it's silent now. Fighting for breath and balance, I look up at the surrounding chaos I caused.

"So it's true then," a familiar voice says. "You're a goddess after all . . . daughter of Quetzalcoatl."

"Tezca," I rasp. How long has he been standing there?

I clutch my stomach to ease the loss of tonalli. "I will explain," I say, "but not now."

"My son," Ichcatzin says with open arms. He smiles his knowing grin. "Come. It's time you learn the truth."

Tezca clenches his jaw. "What truth?"

"Tell him, Pantera."

"Tell me *what?*"

"Tell him who he really is . . ."

"Ignore him," I say. "He is a mad man. He will say anything to avert his fate."

"Tell him," Ichcatzin says, "who his mother is."

"Tezca, I—" I take a step toward him, he takes a step back. "She . . . she made me promise."

Tezca remains quiet, but his eyes don't leave mine.

I hesitate. "Your mother," I say at last. "Xochiquetzal."

I can't bear the pained look he gives me.

"Finally," Ichcatzin says. "Now you know the truth, Tezcacoatzin. Spread it wide and far, my son. You are a god!" He laughs.

"Tezca," I utter defeatedly. I'm not sure what reaction I was expecting, but his silence is far worse. I look away, wishing I hadn't been forced to tell him the truth. But it's a foolish thought. I feared this day would come.

"Join me, my son," says Ichcatzin. "Together we will cleanse the valley of the Christian scourge and the teteoh will rise again. *We* will rise again."

"Tezca, please," I beg. "Don't listen to him. He is *not* Tezcatlipoca. We must take the Dark Mirror from him before he destroys everything."

"Enough," Ichcatzin seethes. "I am Tezcatlipoca! I am the First Sun, Lord of the Night, master of all that is hidden in the darkness. I am the god who eliminated the Toltecs and defeated Quetzalcoatl. And I am the god who will destroy the Christians!" He lifts his arms to lash out at me with a spell, but as he gathers the tonalli for his attack, he finds himself lacking power. I see him then as he truly is: a man wearing borrowed armor, his divinity a façade.

Behind Ichcatzin, someone steps on a rock. A white-haired figure stands on the top of the platform, arms outstretched, stealing Ichcatzin's tonalli.

"Zyanya, no!"

It's too late.

Her face is taut with strain. She trembles, looking down at one of the jade amulets dangling from her belt, fighting to control a power beyond her ability. It's tearing her apart from the inside.

"Zyanya!" I rush toward her, but the darkness within her forms a barrier of shadows that hurls me back, as if it's protecting its new vessel or punishing her for daring to contain it.

Her hands clench into fists, knuckles white as she fights with every ounce of her strength. "It's too much," she gasps, barely able to force the words out. "I . . . can't hold it."

"Let it go!" I yell desperately. "You have to let it go!"

The Black God's tonalli thrashes within her, tearing at the walls of its prison, seeking escape. Zyanya's yellow eyes roll back in her head, and with a wrenching cry, her grip on Tezcatlipoca's tonalli slips. It bursts free from her, wild, soaring in the night. The force of it sends a blast wave through the Sacred Precinct, and I barely manage to keep my footing as the ground shakes. The untethered tonalli hovers for a moment, a black, writhing mass. It twists and writhes like a living thing, searching, hungry for someone to attach itself to.

It finds Tezca.

"No!" I scream.

CHAPTER 38

El Adios

I stare at Tezca in disbelieving horror. The air chills, shadows coil about his shoulders, whispering in his ear, and his eyes blaze black as an immense power consumes him, like a poison entering his veins.

Zyanya made clear that an ixiptla is a god in every sense that matters. But as I look at Tezca now, as I sense his tonalli, I know—there's no consideration to be had, no forethought necessary.

He is a god.

He possesses the power of a creator god.

And he *remembers*.

Tezca begins to move through the wreckage, pausing here and there, looking up and to the sides, as if thinking of earlier times; a recapitulation of all his past lives—cycles of births, deaths, tragedies, joys. From the way his forehead creases, he'd rather not bring those memories to this life. Some memories can be a different type of prison.

I understand too late that this was Tezcatlipoca's ambition all along. Ichcatzin was a means to an end. While his role was certainly essential, he was a weak ixiptla, only human.

Tezcatlipoca is one of the four creator gods, but in his creation, he is the exemplar of deception, a lord of jaguars and sorcery, and a master of fate and fortune.

Dawn of Fate and Fire

Your fate is set, Tecuani. You cannot escape it.

Once again, Quetzalcoatl bewildered me with his Elegant Speech. No one—certainly not I—can escape Tezcatlipoca. Fate isn't some fickle mistress. Every child comes into the world with a destiny. You're either born on a good day or a bad day, which is then interpreted as favorable or disastrous, and humans have little control over the outcome of their lives. But greater than the day count are the powers and whims of Tezcatlipoca. I was born during the Nemontemi, the most unfortunate of days. My fate, my tonalli, is not to live a simple life of happiness. Mine is a life of battle. *He* deemed it so.

Tezcatlipoca wanted his son. His great plan has not only been revealed . . . it's also come to pass. Don Joaquín, Ichcatzin, Pantera, perhaps even my birth, everything—it's all led to this moment.

"Tezca . . ." I call softly. I don't know what to make of him. "I'm sorry. I should have told you the truth sooner. I didn't know what to do." My voice rises, and the words are a lament. "I didn't know what you would do. I'm so sorry." My chest feels impossibly heavy. "Tezca, look at me."

In his crushing silence, I realize that Tezcatlipoca has won.

I take a few steps closer toward Tezca and force myself to speak once more. "Just say something. Anything. *Please.*"

Finally, he turns around. He looks like the same Tezca he was just minutes ago, but there's a darkness behind his gaze that wasn't there before. I wait, hoping for any sign of the man I love. Just when I think he'll say something, his attention is pulled away.

Ichcatzin tries to make his escape. As the gods would have it, the steep staircase of the Templo Mayor was not designed purely with ascent in mind. Rather, with descent. The dismembered bodies of those sacrificed were flung down the stone steps, and these flowed with blood, bright red against the white stucco of the temple walls. So, as Ichcatzin furtively comes down the wet steps of the platform, he loses his footing. His fall makes me think of what Zyanya said about Ichcatzin walking a path of imbalance. Sooner or later, he'd slip. I don't know whether her words were prophetic, or if simply it was a coincidence that his feet should sweep from under him. But they do, and the man goes tumbling down.

Tezca turns toward Ichcatzin, and with a flick of his wrist, he summons the Dark Mirror into his hand. Then he snaps his neck.

I gape dumbly. "Tezca."

A black, narrow slit appears to his side as if he sliced open the air. It hovers, waiting to swallow him.

"Don't go," I plead.

Tezca glances around, one last look. Perhaps he sees the past, or perhaps he sees the future. His cold gaze then focuses on me. My cheeks are slick with tears. My lips quiver wordlessly. There are thousands of things I wish I could say.

Without averting his eyes, Tezca retreats into the opening and vanishes.

Quetzalcoatl and Xochiquetzal didn't say what would happen if Tezca came awake, if the day came when he remembered who he was, but still they warned me, and their words took root in my heart.

You will fear him.

I don't fear him. I fear what this power will do to him, what Tezcatlipoca has prepared for his son.

"I had to stop him," Zyanya says softly. "I knew no other way. Ichcatzin had the Dark Mirror, and there was no one else who—"

"I know." My fingers curl into a tight fist. It's true, there were other forces at work in this, forces beyond my perception and understanding. There was nothing I could've done to prevent such a thing from happening, no matter what. But it doesn't make it right, nor does it lessen my despair, and that tiny whisper of doubt in the far recesses of my head grows louder. *If we'd had more time . . . if I had prepared more . . . if I'd fought harder . . .*

"What will you do?" Zyanya asks.

"What I always do."

"Fight?"

"Keep going," I reply.

Darkness relinquishes its hold. To the east, Tonatiuh begins to peer his bright face over Popo and Izta, bathing the sky in a golden glow. If I close my eyes, I can imagine Xochiquetzal in Tamoanchan. In the quiet solitude of her home, she finds herself caught in the grip of fear. Her heart aches with the weight of a secret she's carried for thousands of years. Day after day, she gazes down into the Fifth Sun, her mind tormented by visions of what her son could become. And so, whether for love or concern, she kept him asleep, shielding him from a reality that might prove too harsh, praying that one day he will understand her intentions and forgive her for the chains that bound him.

Praying?

Praying to whom?

Does Xochiquetzal bend her knees and look up?

Who do the gods turn to for support when they are helpless?

The sounds of battle are replaced by the hum of flies, the cawing of carrion birds, and moaning—for help, water, mothers, even death. The landscape is desolate. Bodies, both friend and foe, alive and dead, lie scattered like disregarded chess pieces on a gory chessboard. I'm filled with misery, surveying the aftermath.

No sign of Don Juan. Jerónimo steps forward, barking orders at the Spanish soldiers to clear the wounded and dead. They obey, but they watch their backs, ready to draw their weapons at any moment. Our warriors remain close, just as alert. This is no truce. Without Ichcatzin and the eagle Nagual, the people of Snake Mountain disband and abandon the plaza.

Eréndira's cheekbone is badly bruised, and the bite on her neck continues to bleed. "Still standing?"

"It'll take more than a little nibble to put me down," she says. "Where's Tezca?"

"I don't know." An honest answer. The only one I can give. "What of the other Naguals?"

"Taken care of," says Chipahua, approaching us. Blood trickles from his eyebrow, tracing a path down his rugged face, and he seems to be limping. He looks weary, his limbs damp with sweat, gore, and rain, but like Eréndira, he refuses to yield to pain.

I let out a weary sigh. "Good. Ichcatzin too."

"What is to be now?" Chipahua hears Ichcatzin met his end and thinks this over.

I look at him, remembering that night we first crossed paths in the forest. I knew he was a Shorn One then, he's since become my friend, and now he will be a king.

"You're to be the tlahtoani of Snake Mountain, of course," I tell him.

Chipahua juts out his chin at me. "Why not you?"

"Me?" I say dismissively. "I'm not a man nor pipiltin, and I have not one drop of Neza's blood. It must be you. The nearest eligible successor."

"Neza and Ichcatzin come from a large family of brothers," Chipahua insists.

"They are not here. You are," Eréndira says. "The people have already survived this battle. The last thing they need is to enter a war of succession. They need somebody they can rally behind. You have a duty now."

Chipahua grouses. "I don't have a way with words."

"Perhaps," I say, "but the words of your predecessors will guide you, my lord." I kneel, put my fingers on the ground, and kiss them. Eréndira also prostrates herself. Then, Miguel, Zyanya, and other warriors bearing witness. We all fall into a reverent silence, honoring the new king before us.

"Long may your voice lead us, tlahtoani," Miguel says.

"Long may he speak," we echo back.

Chipahua's eyes show a glimmer of renewed resolve. He knows the expectations placed upon him and the responsibility. No man bears more responsibility than a king. The shoes he now stands in are not just any shoes; they're Neza's footsteps. His legacy looms large.

There will be a feast in Snake Mountain. A transfer of power from the departing tlahtoani to the succeeding one. Once Chipahua offers his royal blood from his pricked calves, arms, and earlobes, he will be dressed, seated, and carried in a litter to the temple-pyramid to participate in the ceremony of speeches. As the tlahtoani, he will accept the position with a lengthy speech, first expressing himself humbly then elaborately in the style of nobility declaring that he will bear the burden, he will reign.

Chipahua bids us to stand. We come to our feet, and I find myself wobbling. Miguel holds his hand out to help me. I take his offering. I'm wounded and tired. We're all wounded and tired.

"Warriors. Men of Snake Mountain," Chipahua says. "You have earned more honor for yourselves and your families. Nothing remains for us to do here. Let us go home."

We cheer. A moment of relief as the tension of battle begins to ease. We've earned this moment.

But then, my brother's scream pierces through the celebration. "Leonora!"

His voice reaches me in a long, stretched moment. My heart seizes with sudden, overwhelming panic.

I spin, my heart hammering. Jerónimo is running toward me. It happens so slowly, yet is somehow impossibly fast. He throws himself in front of me, shielding me with his body, then the sharp crack of a firearm splits the air.

"Jerónimo, no!" I cry out, dropping to my knees as he stumbles to the ground. I catch him before he falls, cradling him in my arms.

"Don Juan." Jerónimo sputters, blood bubbling from his lips.

I move his hand away from his chest to get a sense of the damage. Blood pours from the wound, and I press my hand against it, trying to stem the flow, but it's too much.

"How bad is it?" he croaks.

"I've seen worse," I say, forcing a smile that I don't feel. "Let's get you to the palace. You'll be fine."

My eyes dart around wildly. The scent of smoke guides me to its source—still curling from the musket's barrel. I see the weapon, and the man holding it.

Don Juan. Our eyes meet. I wear no mask.

Chipahua is quick to raise his spear. Our warriors follow without hesitation. They move into position as soldiers rush in, forming a protective wall around Don Juan.

It's crushing, unbearable. The bullet was meant for me, and yet it's Jerónimo lying in my place. I can't reconcile the cruel twist of fate that spared me but claimed another.

My hands tremble with intolerable rage, itching to claw him apart. Rage as I've never felt before.

Jerónimo's shallow breaths restrain me. "Leo," he says, faintly smiling. "It . . . it was my turn to save you."

"No." I vehemently shake my head, refusing to accept it. "I won't let you die. Come, you have to sit up. We'll get you sorted." My voice cracks, ending in a strangled sob because I know the truth—I can't save him. Nothing can help my brother now, except perhaps Tezca, and he made his choice. He left me. "Jerónimo." I rekindle my anger to hold back crying. Rage is my anchor. "Live, damn it. Don't let them win. Live!"

"I'm . . . scared," he says, gurgled. It's one of the worst sounds I've heard, like being submerged and drowned. "I don't want to die."

A single tear rolls down his face as I cup his cheek. He leans into my palm, and I push wet curls away from his face. If I could, I would take the pain for him. I would bear his suffering.

"Jerónimo, do you remember when you were little and saw shadows on the walls?" I say, holding his hand. "Do you remember being frightened and scurrying to my chamber? You would crawl into my bed and talk to me about monsters. Do you remember what I would

319

say? And do you remember how glad you were when you woke up and felt the sun peeking through the window, and all the horrid shadows weren't there anymore?"

He weeps, his teeth stained with blood, but he's stopped choking. "Everything will be better in the morning."

I struggle against the knot of emotions stuck in my throat. I press his hand against my lips and look up toward a rising Tonatiuh, awakening the valley from its slumber. I've battled gods. Popocatepetl. Great foes. The loss of my tonalli. This is far grimmer and more challenging than all of it. "Rest now," I say. "Everything will be better in the morning."

Jerónimo slowly raises his face to the sun, welcoming the warmth on his cheeks. He shuts his eyes to appreciate the sensation more, opens them, and looks at me. "I'm sorry," he says, "for everything." I nod and draw a cross of his own blood on his forehead.

Then my brother's eyes close again. And I know, it's for the last time. I can't hold back the tears anymore. They flow freely as I embrace him, clinging to his fading tonalli.

Full of fury, full of grief, full of aching, I push myself from the ground, wincing with every move I make.

I draw my sword and march forward. I don't get far before Eréndira stops me.

"What do you think you're doing?"

"Get out of my way, princess."

"Look around you. Another fight now will destroy us."

"*Move*, or I'll make you."

Over my shoulder, I see Don Juan slipping through the soldiers, heading toward the palace. His men follow close behind. They seal off the main doors, block the side entrances. Others fan out along the perimeter.

From where I stand, a helpless fury pounds in my chest. My grip hardens on my sword, but I don't move. I can't risk more lives for my rage.

I glance to either side of me. Chipahua still has his spear raised. Our warriors stand poised.

This isn't just *my* rage.

I lock eyes with Chipahua. His gaze is fierce as he says, "We will fight for Nican Nicah's son."

The warriors nod. There's no hesitation, only a shared purpose. They're willing to give up their lives for Jerónimo? This realization robs me of breath.

In the end, Jerónimo was defended by those whose beliefs he condemned and murdered by the same people who pledged loyalty to him. It's an irony so bitter, so senseless. It cuts deep.

"I'm sorry," Eréndira tells me. "I understand how you feel. But this isn't the time. Your brother is in no better place than with his God, and Chipahua is to be king. There is much to be done before that can happen. The wounded need our attention, and the dead must be prepared for their final rest." She glances back to where Jerónimo lies. "For his sacrifice, he deserves a proper burial."

Sacrifice. The word seizes my heart. Jerónimo sacrificed himself for me.

Eréndira is right; the dead must be honored, the wounded tended to, and the living led forward. I force myself to take a step back, to sheathe the Sword of Integrity.

I turn my attention to Chipahua and our warriors. "Our fight has ended. For now."

Chipahua nods, lowering his spear. He knows we will battle again. But now, we must honor those we've lost.

I turn back to Jerónimo's side, where Miguel and another are lifting him onto a stretcher of wooden poles and woven reeds. I swallow a sob as I watch them carry him away.

My brother is gone. Tezca is gone. I feel so alone.

"Amalia . . ." Eréndira says, and with rare timidity, stiffens, as if regretting speaking her name.

I sigh, shifting my gaze to Viceroyal Palace. "The viceroy is dead.

Don Juan and his supporters have seized the palace for themselves. Amalia is a Christian. She's safe. *We're* not."

Eréndira purses her lips, not convinced. "Is she really? Don Juan hates Amalia."

"Amalia knows how to survive. That's what *we* need to do now. You're injured, and the sun is rising," I say, noting she can't take flight. "What do you want to do, princess?"

"I don't know," she says with a shrug.

"You don't?"

"I don't *know*." Her voice is exasperated.

She knows. But she needs a reason. Any reason other than what her heart is telling her. "We will never hear the end of it if we leave Amalia behind."

"Yes. She's utterly insufferable," she harrumphs.

"There'd be much quarreling."

She reddens and mumbles, "I suppose . . . I should stay. Just to make sure she's safe. Merely to keep the peace and avoid her ceaseless squabbling."

"Of course."

"Good," Eréndira approves.

She takes her leave. Chipahua leans on his spear as he hobbles toward me.

"Your loss saddens me," he says. "I know what it is to love and lose a sibling. Neza was more my brother than my cousin." There's a quiet grief in his eyes, a pain that resonates with my own. "A great deal has been asked of me this day, but whatever small help I can give, it's yours."

"Thank you, lord."

"I suspect you will not be joining us in Snake Mountain."

I shake my head. "I will stay for the burial," I say, "then there is something that requires my attention."

"Ah, something . . . Lord Tezca, I presume?"

"You are very perceptive, lord."

322

He gives my amulet of Tezca's hair a glance, before settling his gaze on mine. "I am old. Not blind."

I allow myself the barest of smiles. "You will make a fine king."

"There is a great task ahead of us," he says, moving his spear to his other hand, a new position for support. "Do you understand my meaning?"

I nod.

"I don't know what awaits, but it will be trying. It may take a year. It may take two hundred years. I will need skilled warriors and competent strategists by my side, and if the gods will it, we will find ourselves in a world without Spain. At least," he adds, "those of us who are willing to fight for it."

"I'm on your side, Lord King," I say, but my thought is, *what if Tezca isn't on ours?*

Part 4: Teotleco

Return of the Gods

CHAPTER 39

La Limpieza

Peace is harder than war, and peace following war is even more difficult.

It's October. The last day of Ochpaniztli, the month of brooms. The festival honors the goddess of carnal acts. Her weapon, her object of power, is a broom. In the old ways, there is much sweeping and dusting: houses, roads, courtyards. The flesh, too; everyone bathes, the bathhouses are cleaned, as are other waterways, the ditches, the streams, the springs. Even the gods sweep—Quetzalcoatl blows his breath upon the earth's surface. Christian priests and friars likewise sweep their churches and friaries, around the altars of their favorite saints. Although they value cleanliness, they have a suspicion that the practice retains its pagan meaning. They're not wrong.

During this season, everything is blooming.

In Cuernavaca, the land is a lush paradise. The bougainvilleas are everywhere, adorning walls, trellises, and gardens, climbing or spilling over in cascades of violet. Vicereine Carlota would gush about the goodness of the weather. In her letters to Jerónimo, she wrote that Cuernavaca was a place of leisure, a heaven of peace and calm. King Carlos bequeathed thirty cities to Cortés, including Cuernavaca. It's no wonder he built his palace here.

In Cuernavaca, in this palace, everything around me serves as a reminder of Tezca's presence—or *absence*. It's the simplest of things, a word, a scent, a tree, a flood of emotions awakens. The air itself seems to whisper his name.

I've not seen or heard from him since he vanished in a haze of smoke. *Where are you, Tezca?*

The last time I visited Cuernavaca, I found it unusual that a Nahua sculpture of some Tlahuica king was so conspicuously displayed in the Palace of Cortés.

Martín said it sends a message to the lower castes—a message of power intended to instill fear. I study it again, now. The statue is some two feet in height and made of andesite, a kind of volcanic rock. It's also in remarkable condition, even after being buried and dug up, which makes me wonder if Ozomatzin, the sorcerer of Cuernavaca, somehow preserved it magically.

At the statue's base, something catches my eye—a few grains of maize and some cacao beans carefully placed on a brightly colored cotton cloth. I tilt my head, intrigued.

"Where've you been? No one's seen you all day," Martín says, joining me in the courtyard inside the palace. Flowering shrubs line the edges, and a few tall trees provide patches of shade. In the center, there's a stone fountain, with the statue of Ozomatzin nestled beneath the shade of a tall jacaranda, its purple blooms cascading above me.

"I've been here," I reply, "thinking."

"It's been months, Leonora," Martín reminds me. "What makes you think he'll come?"

"The same way I know this was him a hundred years ago," I say, my eyes on the statue. "Cuernavaca is his home."

"Why are you so sure it's him?" Martín asks.

"He has offerings," I say. I rest my hand on the sculpture, the volcanic rock warm to the touch. Its tonalli carries an unmistakable heat. "He's a god, Martín. And he's his father's ixiptla. He can finally do what he's not been able to do before."

"What's that?"

"Reclaim his throne," I reply.

"Ah. So, you're here to ensure my safety then?" Martín asks. "Tezca would never harm me." His tone is firm, confident, then it falters. "Would he?"

My heart withers. I don't know the answer.

Where are you, I think, wishing there was some way Tezca could hear me. Maybe he does, and his choice is to ignore me.

"Right, well," Martín says uneasily. "Never mind that. Come." He motions with his head. "We have visitors."

We walk together through the palace, offering nods and smiles. Nods and smiles that aren't reciprocated, at least not toward me. Martín finds some acceptance here, as a don, a marquess and, most importantly, a man, whereas I am no longer a viceregent or much of a lady for that matter. I'm a title-less, unwed, openly pagan woman.

"Think they've figured out I'm not here to sip tea and curtsy?" I ask Martín.

"I think," Martín says with a wry grin, "that you're the most fascinating thing these people have seen in their dull lives."

I give him a half smile as we pass by the entrance gates. The footmen pull open the doors, and together Martín and I step out. The sounds of the city echo through the morning: horses trotting across the cobblestones, people milling toward the market, guards mounting horses, cooks slapping dough into tortillas. The trees are veiled in a silvery mist. It makes the area look mysterious, hostile even, like one of the previous suns before the teteoh created our fifth world. It feels far too cold for this time of year, especially in Cuernavaca, the land of eternal spring.

It takes me a moment to place the visitors. One flame-haired woman; the other, a tall, strongly built man, both combed, polished, dressed in the finest Spanish attire.

Without all the blood, the war paint, and the armor, they seem like entirely different people.

It's Princess Nelli and Francisco Tenamaxtli.

"Pantera," Nelli greets. "Or should I call you Godslayer?"

I risk a glance over my shoulder. "What are you doing here? And what are you wearing?"

Nelli touches her dress, fluffing the coils atop her head. "Playing the part, of course."

Tenamaxtli has his hair slicked back, revealing his broad forehead—something I don't think I've ever seen before. "We, too, seek to reclaim what is truly ours."

I trade an uneasy glance with Martín.

"I hope your journey wasn't too unkind," Martín says. "We have much to discuss, friends, but we mustn't speak out loud here, even in whispers." He raises his eyes to the balcony on the second level of the palace. A fraternity of friars stands watching under one of its arches. "Follow me."

Our footsteps echo through the hallways as Martín leads the way to his strategy room. It's ringed by two guards, who close the door behind the four of us as we enter.

Martín takes his place at the head of the long, polished table. There are no windows here—to keep decisions away from prying eyes—just walls decked with tapestries, and a few flickering candles, casting a soft glow that barely touches the corners.

We sit, and there's a faint knock on the door. "Come in. This is Ignacio," Martín says, indicating the man carrying a carafe of wine. He approaches the table in a gentle glide and goes round pouring our cups. "He's my most loyal servant. I would trust him with my life. We may speak freely in his presence."

"Very well." Nelli voices her thoughts. "We hear rumors in Zacatecas. How is my dear uncle Juan?"

I know which rumor they heard because it's the same rumor throughout New Spain, not only in Mexico but the kingdom to the north that Spain calls New Galicia. In hushed conversations, behind closed doors, within the folds of clandestine meetings, and in the hidden corners of the streets, the whispers for independence are gathering strength.

"Don Juan killed my brother," I tell her. "He justified the coup to King Carlos by claiming he had to save the colony from falling under the influence of natives and mestizos. He's since proclaimed himself viceroy. Every guard is Spanish-born and chosen for loyalty to him. The servants who've worked there since before my brother's viceroyalty have been replaced by his own people. His reach extends beyond the city walls too. People who speak against him vanish. Bodies wash up in canals . . . alleyways, made to look like common robberies. He has eliminated anyone who threatens his power. Your uncle," I add, "is dangerous."

Nelli laughs. "Fortunately, it runs in the family. Everyone says I am my father's daughter."

"We heard, too, about the Battle of the False God," Tenamaxtli says. "We resent not taking part in the war."

"I, like you, had no part in it," Martín says. "I'm being a poor host. First, we will eat and drink, and then we will discuss these rumors."

Martín signals to Ignacio, who leaves the room and returns shortly with a stream of servants carrying trays of food. Nelli and Tenamaxtli enjoy the tortilla cakes of cactus and escamoles, sweet corn tamales too, sipping on wine kept replenished by Ignacio. I eat very little, watching our guests.

Tenamaxtli's face is deeply lined and there is gray in his hair, but even so I reckon he's not yet forty. Few warlords have surrendered themselves, been imprisoned, and changed their faith to Christianity. Why is he here exactly? I can understand he wishes to keep his people safe, possibly even take back Nochistlan, his homeland in Zacatecas. He was beaten before in the war of Mixtón. Is this about retribution? Freedom? Survival?

Nelli leads, too. Although she is Tlaxcalan, like her noble mother before her, the Red Sparrows look to her for leadership. Maybe they follow her because she inherited her Spanish father's red hair. Or, maybe, because the Tlaxcalan, like the Chichimeca, steadfastly resisted being conquered by the Mexica. They were enemies, and the Tlaxcalan were so eager to exact revenge when the Spaniards arrived.

And so, for helping them bring down Tenochtitlan, the Tlaxcalan were given status, allowed to preserve their culture, and escape the pillaging and destruction that came after the Fall.

The Tlaxcalan provided no aid in Mixtón, but Nelli *did* fight against Inspector Corona's army in La Gran Chichimeca. Surely, she has enjoyed a certain privilege, being the daughter of a conquistador and a Tlaxcalan princess.

I don't know the reason for this alliance with the Red Sparrows. As far as I can tell, Nelli identifies as one of them.

Then there's me. I am no leader, only a warrior. Chipahua rules Snake Mountain, and I am here, in Cuernavaca, thinking about what must be done not just for my friends, but for all of Mexico and those to come.

Being a child of the Nemontemi, fated to die in battle, I was never one to look too far ahead into my life. I had no hope of anything for myself, or for the future.

Now, I yearn to escape the clutches of Spain, to make a home, to finally lay down the mask because there is no need for it.

I never knew I wanted such a thing, but ever since Chipahua spoke of Neza's vision, I can't imagine it any other way. It's not just a desire; it's necessary for our continued existence. The only way we live is by freeing ourselves from Spain.

If the Chichimeca were to fight with us, if all the Indigenous peoples of Mexico were to make a stand . . . why, wouldn't that be a great battle? There are more of us than there are of them. And if I summoned a Nagual army? If Tezca was on our side? He has the Dark Mirror, wherever he is, and possesses his father's tonalli. Who could stop us? The thought is both exhilarating and terrifying.

The servants troop out of the room. Martín waits until the last sandals have stopped scuffing across the floor, then says, "No one will overhear our conversation."

"Tell us about these damn rumors," Nelli says, her impatience finally getting the better of her. "Are they true? Are you planning a rebellion against my uncle?"

"Yes," I answer. "They're true. But it's not a rebellion. What La Justicia did, that's a rebellion. What *we* will do—it'll be different. Something better."

"What?" Nelli asks.

"I don't know what to call it yet because all previous efforts seeking to challenge the Crown's authority have failed," I say.

"So what is taking you so long? Aren't you the Godslayer? A sorceress? A warrior sworn to duty?"

"I have never avoided a fight, and you know it, princess," I say sourly.

"Then what is the delay?" Nelli asks irritably. "My sword arm is getting restless."

Tenamaxtli's brown eyes crease at the corners. "Your itching is nothing compared to the fire that burns in my bones all day long. Let us get on with it."

"Aren't you wearing a cross, Francisco?" I ask, tilting my head.

"Yes, I am a Christian." He fingers the wooden pendant. "Do you care which God I pray to?"

"No," I say, "but patience is one of your virtues, is it not?"

He smiles. "I said I was a Christian. I didn't say I was a *good* Christian. He can tell you that," he says, pointing upward. "I see you in the battlefield, Godslayer, strutting around like the Devil himself cannot touch you. I may have converted, but don't think I've forgotten what power looks like. I certainly know what *that* is." He points to the amulet dangling from my neck. "Whose tonalli have you claimed, hmm? Your hair is already at a formidable length, and you wear an enhancement. So," he says, leaning with a curious glint in his eye, "what's stopping you from tearing down the walls of Viceroyal Palace?"

"Tearing down walls is easy, Francisco," I say. "Leaving them standing—that's the challenge. If we're going to do this, and if we're to succeed, our victory can't be one built on ruin and bloodshed. We have to be smart. And I cannot be a lone sword. It will take all of us."

Nelli narrows her eyes at me. "You're avoiding the question. Whose tonalli is it?" She looks at the amulet, then chuckles knowingly. "Where is he?"

"Who?"

"You know exactly who."

I shift uneasily in my chair. She holds my gaze, daring me to deny what we both know—*Nine Hells*, what everyone knows. "I don't see how this is relevant right now," I say, my voice tight.

"No?" Nelli presses on. "Don't play coy, Godslayer. We both know Tezca is a great warrior. What we need to know," she says, "is where he stands."

"Nelli is right," Tenamaxtli says. "Tezca should be here. We can't afford uncertainty, not now. If he's abandoned you . . ."

"He hasn't abandoned me!" I shoot up from my seat, my fingers gripping the table so hard I feel them lengthening into claws. My voice echoes in the room, betraying more than I intended.

My heart pounds, fast and frantic. Fury edges my thoughts, a shadow that's been growing ever since . . . since Tezca left.

Their eyes are on me now, wary, as if they're seeing something in me they hadn't noticed before. Something new. Something dangerous. I don't care. Or at least, I tell myself I don't. I feel a twisted sense of satisfaction in their discomfort.

My necklace feels heavier than ever, constantly reminding me of the bond I share with Tezca, and the fact that he decided to leave. Why do I even bother wearing it still? It's more of a chain now than a symbol of connection. The moment he seized the Dark Mirror, he vanished. Like I didn't matter.

All this time has passed, and I still don't matter.

A part of me knows I'm not thinking clearly—that this anger isn't right, but it feels good, powerful, in a way that's almost intoxicating. The more I lean into it, the more it takes hold, latching itself on to my thoughts, my emotions.

It's a contradiction, feeling like I'm in control, and at the same time, losing it.

I retract my claws, noticing how they left marks on the table. "I don't need your doubts," I sneer. "What I need is your trust. If you can't give me that, then perhaps you should question where *you* stand. So, if there's even a shred of doubt in your mind, you'd better rid yourself of it now."

Martín clears his throat. He shifts awkwardly in his chair before speaking. "Right now, our focus must be on the task at hand. My brother participated in a conspiracy to proclaim himself viceroy. He was spared death and exiled to Madrid, but other accomplices were executed. The Audiencia hangs anyone who entertains thoughts of revolting. We must be careful when seeking new and old alliances to overthrow the Spaniards."

I take a deep breath. "We have friends in Viceroyal Palace who keep us informed," I say, thinking of Amalia, who stayed behind, and Eréndira who delivers her messages. "The time will come to fight; trust in the gods for that. Our war will come to a head."

"Very well," Nelli agrees, then turns to Tenamaxtli. "We have our own friends. We'll gather our people in the north."

"We keep our planning hidden. Tread lightly," I caution.

"I always do," Nelli responds with a sly smile.

CHAPTER 40

El Sueño

My mind is agitated all through the day and into the evening. I stir in bed, unable to sleep. I drape a robe over my nightgown and leave my bedchamber. I wind my way up the staircase, my bare feet silent, unlike the soft moans of pleasure floating from Martín's sleeping quarters.

He must have dismissed the footmen. I step inside his room, and Ignacio makes another sound, like a squeal, as he jerks away from Martín and buries himself beneath the covers.

With a groan, Martín throws his head back, more annoyed than he is embarrassed. "Hell, Leonora," he pants. "Can't you come at a more decent time or be announced like a normal person?"

"Did a war end so we could start another one?" I ask him. "Can we even win?"

Martín pulls a face. "Do you need an answer now or can I finish what I'm doing?"

"I will go," Ignacio mumbles, quickly gathering his clothes from the floor and departing.

Martín scowls in my direction. "Why should *I* be punished? It's not my fault no one warms your bed."

The anger—it's a flicker. It catches, and soon it's a flame, spreading like wildfire in a dry forest, consuming everything. I'm finding it harder and harder to contain.

"I'm sorry for interrupting your evening, *Don* Martín." I turn sharply toward the door.

"Leonora—wait." I pause and glance over my shoulder. "I'm sorry. That was spiteful. It's been a long day, and *clearly*, it's not over yet." He sits up, the sheets pooling around his waist. "What's on your mind?" He rests his head back on the pillow and pats the space next to him. "Come, tell me."

I ease onto his bed and curl into him, laying my head on his chest.

"You do realize I'm naked?" he asks.

"I've seen you naked."

"When?"

"When I found Neza in your closet."

"You did *not*."

"I did."

He groans. "You've *got* to quit this habit of barging into my room unannounced, woman."

Martín's humor is disarming. The fire within me dims, though it doesn't completely disappear.

"If I'd known I'd have an audience," Martín continues, "I might have chosen the balcony. The view is much better from there."

"A show for the friars," I tease back.

"And what a show it would be."

My laughter fades as I settle back against him. Silence envelops us for a moment. "When you think about Neza," I say, "what is it you remember?"

"That's easy," Martín says, his arm drawing me closer. "His love, his calming presence. Neza could make me feel safe in a way no one and nothing else could. It's also what I miss the most."

"Did you . . . bond?" I ask faintly.

"Yes, but he was never my mate. Not truly. How could he be? Neza had several wives."

"I know how painful it was for you to stay in Snake Mountain. It was the same for me in the capital," I admit.

"Because of your brother?"

I nod. "I told him I would protect him. Jerónimo feared for his life. He knew everyone was against him, and I said I would protect him. I didn't keep that promise."

"Don't blame yourself, Leonora," Martín says. "Believe me, it'll consume you. I know it's hard right now, but with time, it'll ease. I promise you that."

I wonder if his words are born of experience. "Do you miss your brother?"

"Every day," he replies. "We had nothing in common but blood, really. He was only a boy, and I'm double his age. There's a part of me that wishes I could have done more, that I could have convinced him not to entangle himself with the encomenderos. But I couldn't sway his ambition to become viceroy. At least I know he's still alive in Madrid, though I may never see him again. Maybe one day, when I am old."

"You're nearing thirty. You're already old," I tease.

He laughs. "I prefer seasoned."

I raise my head to look at his chin. "Is that what those are?" I ask, brushing my fingers through the gray specks in his faint beard. "Seasonings?"

He laughs again.

I'm quiet, listening to his heart. After a while, I ask the question that has been haunting me all day. "Was Nelli right? Has he abandoned me, Martín?"

His chest heaves with a deep sigh, my head moving with it.

"Don't lie to me. I know when you're lying."

"I—" he starts. "I don't think Tezca is the kind to leave unfinished

338

business." His words are careful, measured. "He can't have abandoned you."

He strokes my hair. I close my eyes, trying to feel some comfort. His words, instead of soothing me, are a trigger. *He* did *abandon you,* a voice says. It's my own, but it sounds stranger, colder.

"I should go," I say.

"Before you do," Martín says, "would you open a window? The air in here is so heavy."

I wave a hand to unlatch the window and push it open. The air stirs the curtains and flows over us, bringing the scent of flowers from the garden.

"Oh, I do enjoy your new abilities," Martín jests.

"They're not new," I say, standing from the bed. "I had the knowledge. I just didn't have the skill."

"So . . . *new* then?"

I roll my eyes. "Do you need anything else?"

"Yes. Next time," he says, "*don't* come in."

That gets a little grin out of me. As I head for the door, he says, "Leonora. Are you all right?"

I look at him across the room, my teeth pressed against each other. I feel a rope of tension pulling tighter around my chest.

"Ever since Mexico City, you've—"

I cut him off with a chirpy, "I'm fine."

"You *do* know I was kidding, right? You can always come in. Maybe just not when . . . you know."

"Sure," I say, the word empty.

I take my leave. My eyes beg for respite, fluttering shut as I descend the staircase, but snapping wide open when they trace a shadow in the courtyard.

I proceed tentatively into the area, my senses sharpened.

No guards, servants, or snooping friars. Only the statue of Ozomatzin gaping back at me in the moonlight.

My vision is much better suited for the night, so I exhale a breath of tonalli, sweeping through the courtyard. Torches extinguish one after the other. I silence the fountain's trickle.

All is hushed . . . then the torches rekindle themselves. My heart quickens. I stand still for a moment, watching, listening.

Still, nothing.

I retreat to my chamber. In bed, my eyes finally close. They open briefly, and the ceiling seems to transform before me.

I'm lying in a sprawling meadow, the ground beneath me blanketed with orange cempasúchiles.

Surprised, I quickly stand. I look around, blinded by the daylight. There are nothing but marigolds stretching away in all directions. The sky looks as if painted by a master artist; ribbons of orange and pink intermingle with deep purple and soft blue like celestial brushstrokes— colors that seem to belong to another world.

Is this a dream? One of the Thirteen Heavens?

I wiggle my toes, enjoying the tickle from the dew-kissed grass. I walk about and each step reveals a new scent. I'm in total solitude, but I'm not fearful.

This can't be real. I feel at peace.

"It's real."

CHAPTER 41

El Paraiso

My heart stops, then begins to pound violently.

Tezca faces me, draped in a celestial blue tilmahtli that shimmers and bathes him in an ethereal glow. His hair has grown to his shoulders, framing a face that is at once familiar and unsettlingly foreign.

There's something in his presence now that wasn't there before.

I don't see the Dark Mirror on him, but his tonalli has changed. He stands there, captivating and terrifying, burning with vital heat and yet cold, light and shadow all at once, mortal and divine.

He embodies divine duality, the contradictions that define the teteoh—their beauty and their wrath, their mercy and their vengeance.

Humans are like this, too. Everything under the Fifth Sun seeks balance. The problem is, I don't know which side of Tezca now prevails. I wonder if I've lost him entirely—if the man who stands before me is no longer the one I knew, but someone, *something* else.

"Tezca," I croak. "Where's the Dark Mirror?"

The glow around him seems to fade, as if the fabric of his cloak reacts to the question. "Seven months." His tone is frigid, steeped in bitterness. "Is that what you want to know?"

"No," I say. "I mean, it's not like that. I just . . . you've been gone for so long, and now you're here. I don't know . . . things aren't the same. *We're* not the same anymore."

He turns away, the light that surrounded him now dimmed to a mere flicker. "I never really left," he whispers, his words so faint they seem meant only for him, yet the breeze carries them to my sharp ears.

If he has the Dark Mirror, then he sees all—watching but not engaging, like the teteoh. I remember the words of my father. *The gods are near and far.* He pointed to the sky and said, *They are within sight of your eyes but out of reach. They come closer, and they go away. They die, and they are born again. You can always find them, though you may not see them.*

"I didn't want to leave you that night," he says, his back to me. "I'm sorry I couldn't be there for you after your brother's death."

"Why did you?" I need an answer that makes sense, something that will help me understand. "Tezca, look at me."

He turns around. "I didn't have a choice."

The air between us feels like the thinnest glass, ready to shatter with one wrong word. Still, I say, "You could've stayed . . . you made a vow to me, Tezca." I touch the amulet with his shorn hair, holding it as a reminder. "We are bound to one another. Was it a lie?"

"I didn't lie to you."

"I didn't lie to you either."

"Yes, you did, daughter of Quetzalcoatl," he says, his words like a whip. "You hid the truth of my mother."

"I . . ." I falter. "It's complicated. I was . . . afraid."

"Of me?"

"No!" I cry. "Of . . . of . . ."

"Did you think I would harm you if I remembered who I was?" he asks.

"What? No! Of course—"

"You don't need me for that. You do that quite well all on your own."

I open my mouth to answer, but the words die in my throat,

choked by the realization that he's right—my fear, my silence, has hurt us both.

My hand drops to my side, the amulet slipping from my fingers.

"Tezca, I—" Beneath his anger, I can see the pain that I've caused. "I was afraid of what the truth might do to us. To *you*. I'm so sorry I didn't trust you."

His expression softens, but it's fleeting.

My robe flutters gently in the breeze. The marigolds around us sway. I look around, taking in the strange, otherworldly beauty. "Tezca, what is this place? Is this Teteocan?"

"It's the safest place for the mirror," he answers, "and for you."

"Why bring me here? You didn't have to leave." I move toward him, the marigolds brushing against my ankles. "I would have fought for you, Tezca. I would have *fought*."

He comes closer, and just when I think he'll draw me against him, he stops. "And you would have lost," he says sharply. "The only way to control the darkness is to stay away."

"So, you thought you would figure this out on your own? What happened to 'together'?"

"I wasn't willing to risk losing you to the mirror."

"You're losing me now," I say, my voice breaking.

He nods. "I know," he whispers.

My heart clenches painfully. "I should've trusted you, Tezca. I made a mistake. I can't take it back. I don't know that we can ever go back, or if we should. We've both changed. But that doesn't mean we can't start over, find each other again . . . what we had. We don't have to be the same."

For a moment, he seems caught between the pull of his fears and the hope in my words.

"We've faced worse, haven't we?" I ask.

"No. This is worse."

"Don't push me away again."

"You don't understand," he says tiredly. "I am now bound by

something greater than us, greater than myself. I can't fight it. I can only protect you."

"Protect me from *what*?" I snap. "From Tezcatlipoca? From the darkness?"

"From me!"

Tezca's roar reverberates like the earth itself has split open. The meadow disappears, replaced by a sky strangled with fire and smoke. The ground quakes, and marvelous buildings made from gold, jade, and turquoise begin to collapse before my eyes. Destruction. Tragedy. So many people screaming. Men, women, and children flee in terror as their world falls apart. I try to help them, but they pass through me like ghosts.

Everyone is running except for one person—Tezca. His face is different, but I know it's him because his tonalli is always the same, in every life. He's just a boy. His hands are raised, bending nature to his will, summoning gusts of wind, fire, rain.

My heart aches as I watch him, a boy forced into a role that no one should ever have to fulfill. He was a tool, a weapon wielded by his father to bring ruin upon those who stood in his way.

This isn't the Tezca I know. It's a version of him from a past his mother never wanted him to see. And yet, here it is, laid bare before me. I thought Xochiquetzal feared him, but I understand now that her actions were driven by love—she was trying to protect her son.

"Stop," I beg. "Stop it, Tezca."

His voice pierces the chaos. "You need to see."

I'm forced to witness the fall of the Toltecs and their once-great city Tollan. As the final walls crumble, the vision shifts again, and I'm pulled deeper into his memories.

A young girl in a tower wails. Spiders. Scorpions. Cotton tunics stained with blood. Warriors clash. A quetzal-feathered headdress lies in a pool of red. The images assault me, one after another, too fast to grasp. I can't make sense of them, but the pain and grief is overwhelming, suffocating. I sink to my knees. I'm being swallowed by it all.

I cry for the boy Tezca was, and for the man who bears this burden. He might not have remembered, but the scars—those are never lost. His nightmares were echoes of a past haunting him.

I close my eyes and press my hands to my ears. "Stop it, Tezca!" I scream. "I can't take it anymore!"

The images begin to fade. I open my eyes and find myself back in the meadow with Tezca.

I breathe unevenly, my chest tight. "So much destruction."

Tezca watches me cry, and for a moment, I think he might offer some comfort, but he stays where he is. "That's who I am."

"No . . . you were just a boy." I stand and take a tentative step closer. "You were just a boy," I say again. "It wasn't your fault."

He shakes his head, as if my words can't penetrate his wall of guilt. "It doesn't change anything. I was the one who did it. It was still me."

"But you were forced into it," I argue. "Ichcatzin—he was a weak ixiptla. Your father knew that. That's why he needed you. Because you're strong. You are not a mere man. You are a god. You can make different choices."

I believe that, but I also believe Tezcatlipoca is the god of fate and destiny.

If this is Tezca's fate, how can he possibly outrun it?

Quetzalcoatl told me I can't escape my own fate. Still, I have to believe that the gods can't control our destinies.

My hand trembles as I place it on his arm. Tezca remains still. He doesn't lean in to my touch, doesn't acknowledge it in any way. I wait for some reaction—a shift in his expression—but there's nothing.

"Our fates—they may have brought us both here, but you can choose what happens next, despite everything," I tell him.

Tezca stares at me, torn, doubt and hope warring inside his eyes.

"That doesn't change what I did. I wield the power of a creator

345

god, and I can't bring back the lives I destroyed. I can't undo the past. I can't banish the darkness. I can't remove these memories. I can't—"

I tighten my grip on his arm, refusing to let him slip away into a dark place where he feels nothing can be mended. "No, it doesn't change what you did," I say. "You might not have been who the people needed you to be then. But you can be now. Yes, you have the power to destroy this world, but you can also save it. I'm not asking you to be a hero. Whatever the Black God is whispering in your ear, Tezcatlipoca is using you. He's using you now, just as he did then. He doesn't care what you want. He only cares what *he* wants.

"Don't you see? This has always been Tezcatlipoca and Quetzalcoatl's fight. It's not ours. We've only ever had one enemy. Not the Obsidian Butterfly. Not Ichcatzin. Spain. Even after Nabarres, Inspector Corona, King Felipe, Don Juan, it's always been *one* enemy.

"I know the mirror has shown you our plans for Mexico. It can be our future, but you have to let the Dark Mirror go. You are no longer that boy, Tezca, and you have something you didn't have two hundred years ago." I pause, letting my hand slide down to his, lacing our fingers. "Me."

His gaze drops, focusing on our intertwined hands. His touch is warm, familiar, a comfort I desperately cling to, but his hand dwarfs mine, reminding me how small it is compared to his. That's how I feel now. Small. Vulnerable. Scared. After a while, the warmth in his hand fades. I clasp his hand with both of mine, then I slide one up to his wrist to chase away the cold creeping there too.

"You have me," I insist. "And you have Cuauhnahuac—your home."

At that, his demeanor hardens, like I've touched on a hidden wound.

"Tlalnahuac," he says coldly.

"What?"

"Tlalnahuac fell to the Mexica in the year 8-Flint. It was them who renamed it Cuauhnahuac."

346

Year 8-Flint is . . . I convert the date in my head. *1396.*

I stare at him, incredulous. The Tlahuica were already conquered before the Spaniards came? This knowledge hits me like a cold slap in the face. If this is true, I don't know who—if anyone—is alive to remember it.

But Tezca does. He remembers because he was there.

"Tezca, come with me to the palace."

"You haven't gone anywhere. Only your mind has been here." He gazes into the distance, as if looking beyond this heavenly realm. "Dawn's breaking. I'll let you rest."

I realize time might move differently in this place, wherever we are. It feels like only moments have passed. Have I been asleep this entire time?

"I don't want to go. What I want," I say, "is to destroy the Dark Mirror."

His eyes finally meet mine, and I see sadness there, so profound it nearly drowns me. "You're smarter than that, Leonora. It cannot be destroyed."

I refuse to let go of his hand. "It *can*. We just don't know how yet."

He lets out a bitter laugh, as if mocking his own past naivety. "It's been seven months. Do you think I haven't tried everything?"

"Then we wash it away, bury it where no man or god can ever stumble upon it. We can find another way—together. Unless . . ." A chilling thought occurs. "You don't want to destroy it, do you?"

"I *can't*," he says, and it's so quiet, so forlorn.

Tezca brushes his thumb softly against my hand. The tenderness makes my heart swell. I want so much to pull him into my arms, to kiss him, and hold him close. He looks down at me, searching my features for any sign of doubt.

"I trust you to control your own fate," I say firmly. "I believe in you, Tezca. We've faced so much together. This is just another battle, but one we can win."

He closes his eyes, as if allowing himself to believe—if only for a moment—that this might be possible. Or maybe he's looking into the mirror. When he opens his eyes again, that fragile hope has vanished. "You saw . . . I've done terrible things."

"And you've also done *great* things. You've saved lives, protected those who couldn't protect themselves. You've brought light into this world, Tezca. I'm not afraid of you. I'm *not* leaving."

"This is my own battle to fight. You will have yours."

"What does that mean?" I ask, but I can already feel his hand beginning to fade. "What are you talking about? What did the mirror show you? Tell me. Tezca, tell me!"

I feel a cold, unsettling sensation—a pull, like the very essence of him is slipping away from me. "Tezca, wait!" I cry out, trying to hold on.

My vision distorts. The shadows are closing in.

"Goodbye, Leonora."

And then, there is only darkness, his voice the last echo connecting me to his world.

CHAPTER 42

El Linaje

I awaken with a sharp gasp. My eyes snap open, and I'm lying in my bed, golden light pouring through the curtains. Tonatiuh's warmth on my face, the gentle rustle of the breeze, the chirping of birds—they pull me back to the here and now.

I sit up, my head spinning, heart racing, trying to piece together what just happened. I reach for my amulet, then touch my dry cheeks. My eyes feel heavy, as if the tears I shed in that heavenly place have followed me into this world.

Tossing aside the covers, I slide into a black cotton dress with floral embroidery. My fingers work frantically, buttoning the top and lower skirt and braiding my hair with more speed than care. I barely pause to secure the belt that cinches my waist.

These days, I've abandoned the bodiced dresses with sweeping skirts, the lace gloves, petticoats, headdresses, and mantillas, and I certainly don't dress like a Spaniard anymore—a fact often repeated to me by Spaniards, priests and, most frequently, men. Always the men.

I make my way through the palace corridors, my woven sandals barely making a sound against the floors. When I reach Martín's room, I'm met by his usual footmen. Their eyes narrow as I approach; it's clear they're not pleased by my presence.

I square my shoulders. "I need to see Martín."

The guards exchange bored glances.

"Martín," I call out, raising my voice.

"Let her in," Martín says.

After a tense pause, one of the guards grudgingly steps aside and ushers me in.

Martín sits at a small table, nursing a glass of wine. The daylight streaming through the tall, arched windows highlights the sharp lines of his face, the blond in his hair. He looks up as I enter, setting aside a sheaf of papers.

The guard closes the door behind me, and Martín asks, "What's wrong?"

"Aside from the looming threat of another war? Or the reality that I'm the most despised person in Cuernavaca? Or the unsettling sense that something insidious seems to be festering within me? Or even the fact that Tezca is hidden away, being consumed by a power none of us comprehend?"

"I wouldn't say you're the most hated person in Cuernavaca. In the palace, perhaps."

"Thank you, Martín. That's reassuring."

He leans back in his chair, resting his hands on its arms. "What do you mean something is festering within you?"

I lower myself into the chair across from him, and Martín pours me a glass of wine. I take a sip, the taste too sharp for my liking. I've always preferred pulque, with its earthy warmth. Wine, by comparison, feels foreign, a drink for those with time to savor things.

I swirl the glass in my hand, wondering how I can explain this feeling that's been creeping, the gnawing sense that I'm losing control. I can't put it into words.

"I don't know," I admit finally. "Zyanya said my power is growing, and that's true. But there's something *else* that's growing too, and I can't seem to push it back. Every day it gets a little stronger."

350

I'm terrified—terrified that whatever this is, it's more powerful than I can handle.

"You're angry," Martín decides. "You have every reason to be in pain, Leonora. Losing a brother . . . it's not something you just get over."

I can't deny that Jerónimo's death has left a wound in me, one that hasn't even begun to heal. But it's not grief that's consuming me. It's something darker.

"I . . . saw him. Tezca."

"Where?"

"I'm not sure."

"And? What happened? Does he have the Dark Mirror?"

I nod. "He knows about the conspiracy."

"Shh!"

"Did you just shush me?"

Martín rubs a hand over his face. "It's not safe to talk here," he says, his voice wary.

I strain my ears. The only sounds are distant. "There's no one nearby, except for the guards."

"This place is crawling with spies. We can't risk being overheard."

He leads the way to the courtyard. We walk past the fountain, its water dripping softly.

Martín gestures for me to sit on a bench. Someone has recently placed a basket of cotton at Ozomatzin's feet, arranged with the maize and cacao beans.

"Tell me everything," Martín urges, sitting beside me.

I recount the vision, my voice quiet as I describe what I saw. "He was tormented, Martín," I say. "I tried to reach him, but the darkness . . . he's convinced he has to face this alone. The Dark Mirror's power . . . it can't fall to him to save us all. It *can't*."

"We'll bring him back," Martín says, placing a hand on my arm.

"How?" I ask. "I don't even know where he is."

His eyes shift to Ozomatzin. "Didn't you say that's him?"

I follow his gaze, looking at the statue.

"It must be connected to him somehow," Martín says. "His tonalli. There has to be a way."

"What way? He has the Dark Mirror," I remind him again, the dread returning. "He's hearing this now. It shows him everything."

"Not everything," Martín offers. "You said it shows him what Tezcatlipoca wants him to see. Isn't that how you defeated Ichcatzin?"

"Ichcatzin was a formidable enemy, but he was just a man. Men make mistakes. Tezca is a god with a creator god's power. And who knows what Tezcatlipoca shows him? We know nothing!"

Martín's attention shifts from me to the statue, as if seeking answers from the stone. The sunlight streams through the jacaranda's leaves, dappling his face with light and shadows.

"We might know more than we think," Martín insists. "Tezca is still human. We need to find a way to reach that part of him. The things that connect him to his humanity. Your amulet, the statue . . . I don't know . . . there must be more items in the palace discovered in the wreckage. This place used to be a site to collect tribute for its rulers."

"Tribute?" I ask, eyeing the gifts laid out before the statue. They're offerings?

"Yes. The people from here. They must know."

"Know *what*, Martín?" I say defeatedly. "Ozomatzin lived a hundred years ago."

"Are you just going to give up on him?"

I touch my amulet, running my fingers over the bundle of Tezca's hair. "No, I'm not just going to give up on him. But I can't save Tezca *and* protect the people *and* keep our conspiracy alive and relevant while also a secret."

Martín leans back on the bench, crossing his arms. "Well, I didn't say you have to do it all by yourself, did I? There might be records in the library that could be of value. One slight problem, though."

"Which is?"

"Well, the task of documenting events falls solely to friars and missionaries. The library is inside the friary," he explains. "So, only the friars have access."

"How is that helpful? I'm not a friar."

He smirks, amused. "If only you had a certain flair for pretending to be someone you're not."

"Why not you?"

"Let's be honest, I'm much better suited as the one who gets you *out* of trouble when things go wrong." He nods for me to follow him. "Come. Let's find you some robes."

Of all the things I've done, this is perhaps the most preposterous. I itch everywhere, wrapped in the coarse brown robes of a friar. The fabric is rough, the wide sleeves billow as I move, and the hood casts a deep shadow over my face.

My only company in the library are actual friars, who glide around like eerie phantoms in the faint light. I can't see their eyes, and they can't see mine; nevertheless, I feel them on me as I discreetly navigate the aisles.

I start sifting through each book, hoping to find something—anything—about Ozomatzin. Instead, I'm treated to tales about Christian saints, sins, and salvation, legal documents, and chronicles of the conquest.

I'm not surprised—the Spaniards were nothing if not meticulous in their destruction of everything not blessed by the Church.

As I'm flipping through a dusty tome filled with the dire warnings of eternal damnation, a friar approaches.

"Brother," he says, "is there anything I can help you find?"

What would a real friar say? I lower my voice to sound less like myself. "Thank you . . . Brother," I say, trying to look devout and absorbed in the book I'm holding. "I'm searching for some historical records."

"Historical records, you say? Hmm . . . we don't get many inquiries for those. Are you sure they're in our collection? We mostly keep holy texts here."

"Indeed," I say, my voice still deep. "I'm looking to deepen my faith, Brother, and I think the past—the past has much to teach us."

The friar tilts his head, almost as if trying to see through my hood. "I suppose there might be something in the back."

I try not to trip over my robe as he leads me to a corner of the library. He gestures to the shelves, stretching up to the ceiling. "This is where we keep the older records. I'd help you reach those, but . . . well, ever since Fray Pedro had a fall, we avoid the top shelves. Just be careful up there."

"Thank you." I wait until he's out of sight before allowing myself a small, relieved sigh.

My eyes drift to the top row of books, quickly realizing that what I'm looking for is likely out of reach, untouched by time and hands. I push up on my sandals, but it's no use—the top shelf is too high. I briefly consider the ladder. I can't risk drawing attention or repeating Fray Pedro's mishap.

I glance around, making sure I'm alone.

I extend my arm toward the highest shelf, calling to a book. It drifts effortlessly into my hand. I search its pages before guiding it back to its place. One by one, I summon more volumes, each floating down at my command. But as I lower another tome, it brushes against its neighbor. The second book wobbles, then tips forward.

The slight movement creates a ripple, and before I can react, a small cascade of books begins to tumble down. In a panic, I raise my other hand, stopping the falling volumes just before they touch the floor.

At the same time, a slip of paper flutters free. It spirals down like a feather caught in a gentle breeze, landing softly at my feet. I place the suspended books back onto the shelf, then pick up the folded paper. I mean to tuck it into a book without a second thought, but the texture makes me pause.

My breath catches—it's amatl.

The tree that gives birth to the parchment grows in the north, and the Spaniards call it evil paper because some pueblos believe it to have special power in their rituals. So of course, they banned its use. Yet, in the mountains, far from Cuernavaca, there are still places where amatl paper, and the craft of forming it, is kept alive by those who refuse to let go of the old ways.

Curiosity tingles as I carefully unfold the parchment. It reveals a family tree with glyphs in black and red ink, listing names and marriage alliances. Some of the branches are incomplete, but the tree is nearly ten generations deep, tracing the lineage from the founding rulers of Tenochtitlan to its last tlahtoani, Cuauhtemoc. His bloodline continues through his marriage to a daughter of Moctezuma II, who later wed one of Hernán Cortés's own daughters. The rest of the Cortés children aren't recorded.

I've never seen anything like this. It must've been painted by a tlahcuilo, an Indigenous scribe. Tlahcuilos are artists by birth.

As my fingers follow the lines, one name stands out: Ozomatzin, a king of Tlalnahuac. He had a daughter, a princess. She bore a son. I gasp softly as I trace the line to her child. That son would grow up to become Moctezuma, the *first* of his name.

My mind spins—Tezca, the grandfather of Moctezuma I? He was the fifth tlahtoani of Tenochtitlan, long before Moctezuma, second of his name, ascended to the throne.

I force myself to breathe, to be steady. There are too many eyes, too many ears. With trembling hands, I fold the paper inside my robe and make my way out before anyone notices.

"Any luck?" Martín asks me as I'm sliding into my nightgown. His tone betrays him; it suggests he already knows the answer.

"No," I mutter. "Tezca doesn't want to be found." I throw off my slippers and climb into bed. The cool sheets are a small comfort as I bring them up to my chest.

Martín's brow creases. "What are you doing?"

I sink further into the bed. "I'm tired."

He glances at the window. He points with his thumb and says, "The sun is still high."

With a flick of my wrist, I draw the curtains, and with a snap of my fingers, I light the candle by my bedside. "If I can't reach Tezca in the waking world," I say, "maybe he will visit me in my dreams."

Before I go to sleep, I take out the parchment of amatl paper hidden beneath my pillow, dip my quill into the inkwell, and add a new branch next to Leonor Cortés Moctezuma: *Martín Cortés I.*

There's no mention of Hernán Cortés, and I do not write his name; he doesn't belong here. There will be countless books about him.

Instead, I draw a line above Martín's name and inscribe another: *Malintzin.* I write her name with the reverence it deserves. Some may label her a traitor, but she was a woman who did all she could to survive.

It's *her* blood that runs through Martín's.

There. The tree feels more complete.

The ink dries quickly, but the truth will remain.

I'm not rewriting history; I'm revealing the pieces that have been buried by the very same people who've twisted the truth to suit their story, painting themselves as the victors, the civilizers, while we are reduced to the conquered, the forgotten.

The angry voice in my head hisses, *We will not be forgotten.*

Some battles are fought with pens.

CHAPTER 43

El Viejo

Tezca doesn't come. Instead, in the dead of night, the Owl Witch descends upon my balcony, white wings rustling like whispers of doom, red eyes gleaming in the moonlight.

I don't know who is more terrifying—the woman, or the bird.

I leap from the bed, flinging the doors open wide before I even reach the balcony. The cold night air rushes in, but the chill in my bones is something else entirely. "What is it?" I demand. "Is Amalia safe?"

Eréndira tilts her head, her form shifting. Her feathers give way to flesh, her beak becomes the sharp angles of her face. When she stands before me, fully human, her expression grave, I know—she doesn't bring good news. "As safe as one can be in the wolf's lair," she replies somberly.

"And Zyanya?" I press, fearing the answer.

"Chipahua sends word that all is well in Snake Mountain. His defenses are strong, and Zyanya is safe under his protection. The Spaniards will not come for them, but well, one can never be too sure."

"Good," I say. "Very good." A small measure of relief settles over me, but it doesn't last long. "What brings you to me?"

357

Eréndira pulls a letter from the folds of her cloak, the wax seal catching the candlelight as she hands it over. The seal—it's Amalia's mark. I quickly break it, unfurling the parchment. The cold dread in my stomach coils tighter with each line I read.

"Amalia writes that tensions are high," I say. "The people are on edge, whispers of rebellion growing louder." I pause, the next words bitter on my tongue. "She says Don Juan . . ." I pause, the name alone curdling my blood.

My mind sends me back to that moment—Jerónimo crumpling, the life draining from his eyes as he whispered his last words. The angry voices return, rousing something menacing inside me. They tell me that my hatred is justified, that it's the only thing holding me together. *Make him pay*, they hiss.

"He wants to *talk*," I spit the words out.

"I don't like it either," Eréndira says, "but Don Juan knows about the conspiracy. It's a matter of time before he moves against us. If he wants to talk, it means he's not ready to attack—at least not yet. We need to use this to our advantage."

"Why?" I ask.

"Because we're not ready either."

"*I'm* ready."

"No . . . you're ready for butchery. We need other weapons now—strategy, cunning, dialogue."

"This is evidently a trap," I argue. "He saw my face that night. He knows I'm Pantera. That's why he—" I can't bring myself to say it. "He's a depraved encomendero, a sadistic murderer, and in general, a cunt. Do you seriously believe Don Juan will negotiate in good faith?"

"No," she says, "but we need to buy ourselves time, and this might be our only chance. What's he going to do? You're more powerful than him." She pauses. "Than a hundred men. Than *all* of us."

I can feel it now, my tonalli strong, and the knowing that I could end Don Juan if I wanted to. The voices in my head battle for attention. They tell me this is the only way, that I must give in, that the only justice is one forged in blood. They lure me with the promise of control, of vengeance, of everything I've ever wanted—and more, reminding me of what I could be if I just let go. Tempting, dangerously so. The pull is strong, stronger than anything I've ever felt. I close my eyes, trying to shut them out. *Surrender*, they entice. *You have nothing left to lose. This is your path.*

"Leonora?"

I open my eyes. "Tell Amalia I'll come."

"Absolutely *not*," Martín tells me in the morning. The first light of dawn creeps into my chamber, pale and hesitant, as if it, too, fears what the day might bring. I haven't slept. My thoughts are too tangled, too restless.

I sit by the window, watching Tonatiuh climb the sky with a dull orange glow.

"Don Juan can't touch me," I say.

"Oh really?" He scoffs. "What on *earth* makes you think that? You're not untouchable, Leonora."

I smirk. "I'm not?"

He hesitates.

"Go on, say it," I challenge, leaning in just a little.

"You can stop arrows, but you can't stop bullets."

I narrow my eyes at him. The wound of Jerónimo's death is still raw, barely scabbed over, and Martín's careless words have just torn it wide open again. Let loose, the voices tempt. *Show him just how powerful you are.*

I rise from the chair, crossing the room slowly toward him. Martín takes a cautious step back. "Leonora . . ."

Martín has always seen me as strong, but he's never seen this side of me—the side that's ready to set everything ablaze if it brings me my vengeance. I know because *I've* never felt this part of myself so fiercely before. And right now, it's clawing its way to the surface, begging to be released.

359

"You have *no* idea what I'm capable of," I snarl.

A trace of regret passes through his blue eyes. He closes the distance between us, knowing that I won't hurt him. "You're right. I'm sorry, Leonora. I didn't mean—" He sighs. "I don't doubt your strength. But that's *exactly* why I worry. These past seven months have changed you. We joke, yes, but do you think I haven't noticed a difference? When I said I enjoyed your new abilities, I meant it. It's all fun and games, sure . . . until someone gets hurt. I don't want that to be you. You mean too much to me. If you're going to Mexico City, then I'm coming with you."

The voices insist that he's wrong, that I *am* invincible, that no one can stand against me. But Martín's genuine concern quiets them, if only a little.

He doesn't push me further, doesn't try to talk me down. Maybe he knows it's futile, or maybe he's finally beginning to understand just how far I'm willing to go.

"Very well," I say.

"No, Leonora, don't even—*wait*, what?"

"I'm agreeing."

He stares at me. "No argument?"

"No argument," I repeat.

"Why?" he asks, scarcely believing I'm yielding so easily.

"You know why," I tell him. "Because you're the true heir of Cortés. You hold more power than I ever will. Don Juan isn't afraid of me. He's afraid of *you*. You're the only one who can stop him without a single drop of blood being spilled, should you wish to claim your inheritance. You're already in the middle of it, whether you want to be or not. The only difference is whether you'll stand up and use that power for something more, or if you'll let it go to waste while Don Juan tightens his grip on everything you should rightfully control."

Martín groans, frustrated by the legacy he carries like a curse.

"And because," I add, "I will feel better having a friend there with me."

"If that's what you need," Martín says, "then it's what I'll do."

"I don't want you to do this for me. You will become an enemy of Don Juan when you reveal your identity to him, when everyone knows it was you who impersonated King Felipe. I wouldn't put you in that kind of danger. But there isn't another way without resorting to violence."

"Hell," he mutters. He blows a breath, running a hand through his blond hair. "What about Tezca?"

"He's gone," I say, "and that is his choice. We do this without him."

"We go together then."

As he turns to leave, the voices whisper words I don't wish to hear. *You're a goddess. You're powerful. You don't need him. You don't need anyone. You can handle Don Juan on your own.* The confidence they offer is a torment, flaring up like this.

The most unsettling part? I'm starting to like it.

I try to push away the voices in my head, especially the ones about Tezca. But as Martín and I prepare to leave, and I head toward the stairway, my gaze drifts to the courtyard below, and my thoughts betray me.

I pause beneath an archway. A man, bent with age, is discreetly placing an offering at Ozomatzin's feet. He must be the person who's been leaving the tributes.

Before I can think, I call out to him, "Señor!" He glances up, startled, and turns to walk away. "No, please! Wait!"

Who is he? What does he know? My eyes dart around, searching for who might be watching.

On second thought, I don't care who sees me.

I leap over the railing and soar into the air. Like always, I land on my feet.

The man is surprisingly swift for someone of his age. I'm faster.

The thrill of the chase awakens all my primal instincts, sharpening my focus.

I dash through the garden and see him slip through a hidden door in the courtyard wall—one I hadn't noticed before. The door begins to close before I reach it, but I hold it open with a flick of my wrist. I step inside into a narrow passageway with twists and turns, leading me deeper into the shadows. I can hear the old man's hurried footsteps echoing ahead.

The passage opens into a long corridor, presumably the servant quarters. I sniff the air, strain my ears. Among the many doors, I choose the one where his presence lingers the strongest.

As I open the door, the old man shoots up from his bed, making a move toward the window.

"Please, wait!"

He freezes, his hunched shoulders rising and falling with the effort of his breath.

"Why are you leaving offerings at the statue of Ozomatzin?" I ask, stepping closer. Up close, I can see the deep lines etched into his wizened face.

"I'm—I'm sorry."

"Don't apologize," I say in Nahuatl. "Do you know of Ozomatzin? His reign? Is there anything you can tell me about him?"

The man wavers. "You shouldn't be here, señorita."

"Please. I'm not going to tell anyone. I just want to understand."

He glances toward the door, as if weighing his options, then sighs deeply. "It's dangerous, what you're asking about."

"No one will hear of this," I assure.

He rubs his forehead, considering. "Ozomatzin was a great king, but his story is not one that many wish to remember."

"Why?"

"It's heavy with heartache." He gestures for me to sit on the edge of the narrow bed. He joins my side, his gaze distant as if he's reaching into the past. "The offerings you saw at his statue, they are not just tribute—they are attempts to appease him. There are others who leave them . . . they do so because they believe its where Ozomatzin's tonalli was laid to rest."

My heart races as I listen. "Why have these offerings continued after a hundred years?"

He looks at me for a long moment, as if assessing whether I should know. "Because, señorita, there are those who believe that the power of the old ways is not lost. That if Ozomatzin was truly a great sorcerer, then he can return, if one knows where to look and how to ask. And with the Spaniards ravaging these lands, some have begun to seek out that power once more."

A chill runs down my spine as I absorb his words. "Return?"

"He was not properly honored in death, and that has left his tonalli lingering, waiting. Those who know how to reach him believe he can be a guide, a protector—or a weapon."

Or all three? The answer forms in my mind.

"I read that he had a daughter," I say, recalling the family tree. "She gave birth to Moctezuma, first of his name."

"Yes. Miahuaxihuitl."

"What was her fate?"

"She was a beautiful princess—Mia," the old man shares. "And Ozomatzin a defensive father. He guarded her from suitors, espe-cially from Huitzilihuitl, the Mexica emperor. Some believe Ozomatzin had the gift of foresight and knew the emperor desired to wed the princess not only for her beauty but for the wealth of cotton grown in this land. So, Ozomatzin kept her locked away in the palace, shielded by powerful sorcery. The emperor sent emis-saries, gifts, and even warriors to claim her hand, but all were turned away."

I lean in, eager to know the rest of the story. "What happened?"

"He couldn't protect her. The threads of fate are not so easily severed. The princess became a queen of Tenochtitlan."

"So, she married the emperor?"

"Not willingly," the old man replies. "One night, the emperor's forces struck. They breached the palace walls, and they took Mia. The emperor brought her back to Tenochtitlan and made her his queen.

Ozomatzin waged war. The marriage was more than a union—it was a conquest sealed by blood."

I sit quietly with this knowledge.

This was the conquest of Tezca's people.

He told me these lands were once known as Tlalnahuac, before the Mexica conquered them.

That's why it angered him when I spoke of this. He didn't say why, but now I understand.

His land, his right to rule, and his daughter were taken by force.

The past suddenly feels closer, more personal.

"Ozomatzin was broken," the old man continues. "His power waned, crushed by the loss of his daughter. He never forgave himself for failing to protect her."

Mia's fate was sealed by forces beyond her father's control.

"Thank you for sharing this with me," I say and stand. I reach the door and turn around. "Perhaps they are right to believe—those who offer tribute to Ozomatzin. Perhaps . . . he will return one day."

"May your words reach the Thirteen Heavens."

"What is your name?"

"Hernando."

"Not your Christian name."

"Tezcamacatl."

I grin. "That is a good name."

It means "Hand of the Mirror."

CHAPTER 44

El Heredero

Martín and I come up through the south, crossing the causeway of Iztapalapa, and enter the barrios dedicated to farming on the chinampas and the raising of fish and birds.

The first thing we notice is that the wet season has brought its challenges. The humidity has attracted a swarm of pests, though mosquitoes don't seem like the worst worry. The lake's waters lap at the edges of the causeway, higher than usual. It's the rains; they've caused the water of the lake to rise.

Netzahualcoyotl, the sage poet-king of Texcoco, built a structure to separate the fresh and brackish waters of the lake. The dike protected the city from the flood waters, but after the Fall, Cortés ordered its destruction so his brigantines could sail.

More than thirty years later, the city has grown, but the Spaniards have not understood that Tenochtitlan was built according to a perfect design.

They still haven't learned. They don't care to.

My heart aches seeing how much the island has changed, even in the barrios, and because all my losses come together here in Mexico City—Inés, Jerónimo, Tezca, Señor Alonso, even the man I once believed was my father.

I remain vigilant as we ride into the Plaza Mayor, filled with vendors who've pitched their tents, their calls vying for the attention of passersby.

Martín stays close, one hand on his horse's reins, the other never straying far from his sword. The city feels tense, bracing itself against some unseen threat. Guards are positioned around the plaza and key intersections near the canals. They wear mail and leather and are well armed with long spears, blades, and shields strapped to their backs.

"Looks like Don Juan is expecting trouble," Martín says.

"We're already here," I say.

Martín chuckles.

As we pass through the crowd, I search faces—elderly merchants, young mothers herding children, lords and ladies hurrying on some business or other—for anything that might suggest loyalty to our cause.

Could these people be allies? How can I ask them to put their lives at risk? The wrong move could expose our plans to the wrong people.

You don't need their loyalty, the voices murmur sweetly. *You only need their obedience.*

The whispers know exactly where to strike, exactly how to weaken my resolve.

Why fight what you know to be true?

They snake around my weakest thoughts and emotions.

You've seen betrayal, felt the sting of loss. Why trust again when you could seize control?

With each passing moment, they grow more insistent, promising an end to the struggle if only I would surrender.

You could end it all. Take control.

"Leonora?" Martín says. I realize I've halted my horse without even noticing. He rides up beside me. "What's wrong?"

"Nothing." I shake my head, urging my horse forward.

We reach Viceroyal Palace as Tonatiuh dips below the horizon.

Don Juan's footmen stand rigid and alert at the entrance. We dismount from our horses, and they step forward to collect our swords. I expected as much. The man who takes the Sword of Integrity does so fearfully, as if he's afraid the blade might bite. I release it, and its full weight transfers to him, causing him to stagger under its heft.

I glance up at the palace for a moment, and my stomach sinks. I've returned here many times before, but this is the first time my brother isn't here to greet me.

As the guards lead us into the building, a heaviness grips my heart. Jerónimo didn't believe in tonalli, but I can sense him all the same. He lingers, in the walls, along the hallways, and especially in his beloved chapel. I can almost hear his laugh, see his shadow flit around the next bend.

Martín shares a glance with me, and I nod. I'm ready. I can tell he's nervous. In truth, so am I.

The dining hall is crowded. There are at least twenty men crammed around the table, including Don Juan, the Audiencia, and one woman—Amalia. Some of the men clutch their crosses as Martín and I enter; others just murmur to each other.

Don Juan stares at me like I'm a roach he can't wait to squash. It takes all of me not to leap across the room and make him regret that stare. *It would be so easy.* The hall blurs as my focus narrows on him, the temptation almost too sweet to resist. *No one would blame you,* the voices urge. *He deserves it, after everything he's done.* I instinctively feel for the Sword of Integrity's hilt, but she's not with me. *You don't need your sword,* they whisper. *Do it. Make him pay.*

Martín touches my wrist lightly. The warmth of his touch thaws the cold rage. I blink, forcing myself to breathe, to push down the violent impulses threatening to take over.

Tomás stands in a corner with a few other pages and servants. He looks at his feet but gives me a discreet glance and a subtle smile. I nod back, relieved he appears well, and finding a small comfort in this den of snakes.

"Leonora!" Amalia exclaims, pulling me into a tight embrace. "I'm so glad you came. It's good to see you."

"And you," I say, my eyes lingering on her dress. It's black, I note—the fabric rich, trimmed with lace at the cuffs and a high collar. It suits her nickname, "La Viuda." They dub her the widow for she is one, but the way she wears it reminds me more of a spider at the center of its web. I wonder if she missed this . . . if she enjoys this.

I glance at the window, taking in the fading light. Night approaches. Eréndira will soon find her perch somewhere, ears open to catch every word spoken here.

As we take our seats, it irritates me to see Amalia settle so comfortably at Don Juan's side, with Don Bartolo and Fray Simón flanking her.

The set-up feels like one of Amalia's chessboards, where each of us is positioned strategically. Don Juan and I are at opposite ends of the board, poised to avoid checkmate.

No one says anything. We just look at each other. The only interruption to the silence is the soft clink of glasses as Tomás and the other servants move around the table, filling our cups with water.

I know Amalia. I know how she thinks. She favors the black pieces in chess—always waiting for the opponent to show weakness. Is she playing the same game now, hoping for us to make a mistake? *Don't let her play you like a fool. Take control.*

I hold my tongue. I wonder if she still holds the position of Minister of Defense.

When she finally speaks, she provides confirmation. "As Minister of Defense," she begins, "it's my duty to assess all threats."

I catch the rapid beat of her heart, the slight tapping of her foot under the table. She's nervous. I tilt my head, narrowing my eyes at her. *You can't trust her. You can't trust anyone.*

She clears her throat. "The last war has left us in a bad way. We've lost too many souls. We don't wish to see another conflict. I've gathered you all here today to work toward a peaceful resolution."

Peace? The voices mock the very idea. *What peace?*

I clench my fists under the table. *How can they talk of peace when they've spilled so much blood? When all they've left you with is pain? Peace won't bring back Jerónimo.*

"We meet halfway," Amalia adds.

"That sounds messy," I say.

"The goal," Amalia says, "is to find common ground."

I smile thinly as I look at Don Juan. "We have nothing in common."

"Leonora," Amalia reprimands underneath her breath.

Don Juan hasn't blinked, nor has his gaze wavered. His eyes narrow as he says, "A peaceful resolution would certainly be in everyone's best interest."

Peaceful resolution or not, this is a game of power, and I intend to play it well.

"As it happens, I agree," I say smoothly. "Let's discuss our interests. Starting with yours—when will you start packing?"

A friar at the end of the table interrupts, "You are no longer the viceregent, and this isn't your home anymore."

I turn my head toward the man, his thin frame draped in a brown robe. A fringe of graying hair clings to his otherwise bald head, and a wiry beard juts from his chin. "And who are you?"

"A man of God doing God's work."

"What is your name, Man of God?" I ask.

"Friar Berto."

"Well, Friar Berto, I fear it is *you* who is trespassing. In fact, I'd say you are *all* trespassing."

A few of the men chortle at my boldness, while Amalia gives me a peeved look.

Don Juan raises a hand to quell whatever retort is brewing among the others. "And how, pray tell, could we possibly be trespassing?"

"Señores," I say, "as we all well know, Viceroyal Palace belongs to the heir of Cortés."

"Don Martín has been exiled to Madrid," Don Juan reminds me. "Besides, he's not of age to claim anything more than his underpants."

"Hmm, yes, that's true. But haven't you heard?" I say. "He is not the heir of Cortés. His rightful heir is here, actually, in the room with us, sitting right next to me. This man," I gesture, "is Martín Cortés the Elder. And you trespass on his land."

Whispers ripple through the hall. Don Juan is too cunning to react, but his smugness vanishes.

"The bastard of Hernán Cortés!" another man is quick to correct.

"There is proof of my claim," I add.

Don Juan scowls. "*What* proof?"

"Marquess?" I pass the question to Martín.

Martín exhales, bracing himself. Every pair of eyes around the table fixes on him. "My father had me legitimized by Pope Clement when I was five. I have the bull that says this is so."

"A bull is an official decree, granting him the legal status and recognition by both the Church and the Crown," I say facetiously. "Quite binding, wouldn't you agree?"

The friars squirm in their robes.

Don Juan clenches his jaw. "Papal decrees," he says, "can be . . . contested."

"By you?" I challenge.

An owl hoots in the distance. The sound goes unnoticed by all, but not by Martín, Amalia, and me. We know immediately—Eréndira is close.

Amalia's eyes dart between Martín and Don Juan. "Surely," she cuts in, "we can find a way forward that respects all parties involved."

"That is a *wonderful* idea, Amalia," I say with exaggerated enthusiasm. "Marquess, might you be seeking a new owner for Viceroyal Palace?"

"I am not selling," Martín replies firmly.

"Well, then," I say, "it seems we're back to my original question: when do you plan on packing?"

Don Juan runs his knuckles underneath his chin pensively. He takes a drink of his water. I reach for my own cup and watch him as I sip.

"Is there something on your mind, Don Juan?" I ask, placing the cup down.

"Are you threatening us?"

I raise my hands in mock surrender. "Do you feel threatened?"

"Let's not make this any harder than it has to be, Leonora," Amalia says.

I turn my attention to Amalia. "Countess, since you seem so committed to resolving differences, respecting ownership seems like a good place to start. Perhaps you can propose a solution to the fact that your friends are squatting in Don Martín's palace."

She looks at Don Juan, searching for support, but he remains stone-faced. Her gaze settles on Martín. "Perhaps there's a way to . . . share the space temporarily, until a more permanent arrangement can be made."

"I'm afraid that that's not going to work for me," Martín says. "Many of you knew my father. He took what he wanted without a shred of mercy for those who stood in his way." His gaze sweeps the table, lingering on each face. "I have no wish to emulate the man he was, nor do I seek to deprive these lands of their true owners. Yet, let there be no misunderstanding—I will not stand by while you lot revel in what rightfully belongs to me. The burden of my name has shackled me for far too long, dragging me through the mire of my father's sins. No longer, señores. Today, right now, I cast off the chains."

A smile creeps onto my face hearing him.

"I am Martín Cortés the Elder, Marquess of the Valley of Oaxaca," he declares. "I reclaim my name, my legacy, and all that comes with it. The good and the bad. I will not ask. I will not tolerate. I will not permit you to enjoy what's mine."

The men seem unsettled; no one speaks, no one denies the truth of his claim.

Amalia clears her throat. "We understand your position, Martín, but—"

"*Don* Martín," he corrects.

"Don Martín," she concedes. "We're trying to avoid conflict, not escalate it further."

Just as I'm about to speak, something catches my eye. Movement in the corner of the hall. I pause, my attention shifting as I squint to make out the man lurking just beyond the reach of the dim light.

It's Tezca.

I blink. An impossible sight before me. *He . . . came?*

"Tezca?" I ask in disbelief. "What are you—?"

My vision falters, everything hazy, and when I blink again, Tezca's figure wavers. Something's wrong.

I know it when a strange sensation begins to worm its way inside me, subtle at first—just dizziness, as though the room is tilting ever so slightly.

I grip the arms of my chair, steadying myself. My heart begins to race, a cold sweat breaking out across my skin.

"Leonora, are you all right?" I hear Martín ask, but his voice is distant and hollow, as if it's coming from the other end of a long tunnel.

My head spins. The walls of the room close in on me. The table seems to ripple like water, the men melting into nightmarish shapes.

Through the disorientation, I see the faintest glimmer of satisfaction in Don Juan's eyes.

The water . . .

In a panic, I try to stand, but my body refuses to respond. The room turns round and round faster, colors bleeding into one another, everything twisting.

"Amalia," I croak, "what have you done?"

"Nothing!" she cries. "I *swear*, nothing. He promised—you promised you wouldn't hurt her!"

I manage to drag myself upright, clutching the edge of the table. My legs barely hold me up. Before Martín can reach me, guards grab him by the shoulders. He shouts, trying to wrench free.

In a desperate attempt, I gather what little focus I have and direct tonalli to my palms. I thrust my hands forward, aiming for the guards restraining Martín, but my vision sways. Instead of striking them, my tonalli scatters chaotically around the hall.

Chairs topple over. Glasses shatter. Doors slam shut and then burst open again. The chandelier crashes onto the table, its flames igniting a tapestry with the portrait of King Carlos.

Some rush to put out the fire as I stumble to the floor. "Why?" I ask Amalia, my voice a broken whisper.

Tears stream down her face. She chokes out, "I thought . . . I thought I could protect you."

"You can't help anyone," Don Juan sneers. "Arrest the conspirators."

The guards close in on Amalia. Even though she struggles, they overpower her, forcing her arms behind her back.

I can't lift my arms, my head; whatever Don Juan slipped into my water has left me a prisoner in my own skin.

"Eréndira," I murmur, praying she can hear me, can do *something*.

"Don Juan stop this cruelty," Don Bartolo demands. "We are not brutes—we don't resort to these barbaric methods." Behind him, Tomás watches in a helpless rage. That makes two of us.

"Take your seat, Don Bartolo," Don Juan snaps. "You were perfectly content to sit and do nothing while the masked witch ran rampant through the city, spreading the work of the Devil."

Amalia's sobs grow louder. "This wasn't the plan! We were supposed to negotiate. Not . . . not this." She turns to me, her eyes filled with regret. "I'm sorry, Leonora! I'm so sorry!"

"I don't negotiate with terrorists," Don Juan says.

Fury bubbles up inside me, fierce and hot, but I'm powerless to act on it. The rage deepens when Don Juan crouches before me and brushes a strand of hair from my face.

My mind screams at the violation.

He curls the strand around his finger, tugging it gently. "Such a shame. All that power, trapped with nowhere to go," he says with callous satisfaction. "Don't worry, Pantera, the effect will pass. Can't have you perish quietly without a large audience. I must admit, I had no idea if it would work. The Indians—they do have marvelous plants, don't they?" He pulls a white flower with a purple center from his pocket, holding it up like a trophy. "What do they call it? Oh, the name escapes me, but it's fascinating, isn't it? See, it deadens the body. Best of all," he says, waving the leaf under his nose, "it cannot be noticed when it has been drunk."

All of me wants to claw at his face. The Panther roars within, fighting against the numbness, desperately trying to break free from the intoxication.

Don Juan stands and lets the strand of hair slip from his fingers. He motions to one of the guards. He steps forward to grab a fistful of my hair and yank my head back. The pain is sharp, but it's nothing compared to the terror that fills me now.

I'm pinned down by my own body, and I know *exactly* what's coming.

The guard tightens his grip on my hair. I can't hold back the gasp of agony.

"Do it," he orders.

"Please," I beg, my voice breaking. "Don't."

I feel the pull again, more brutal this time. At the same time, I hear him unsheathe a knife.

It's not my throat or my head he's after. That's not what fills me with dread.

No, he's going for something far more precious.

I can't fight it, can't run from this horror.

The sound of the knife slicing through my hair is a roar in my ears. My eyes cloud with tears. I can feel the weight of the loss, the gut-wrenching sensation of my power, my strength, my very identity being stripped away, strand by strand.

When it's done, the guard steps back. My head throbs. The room is in a crushing silence. I can't bear to look down, can't bear to see what has been taken from me, the pieces of myself lying on the cold floor, lifeless.

"Take them to the dungeons," Don Juan says. "They will await their execution as traitors."

The guards haul us away. My thoughts spiral into a frenzied chorus: *How did he know? Who told him? It had to be Amalia. Why would she do this? How could she turn on me?*

I feel a harsh shove, and I'm thrown into my cell. I collapse onto the floor, the misery so thick I can barely draw a breath.

She betrayed you, the voices say. *They all betray you in the end.*

Martín's voice reaches me from the cell beside mine. "Leonora. It's going to be okay. Can you hear me?"

Down the corridor, Amalia shouts, "I didn't do this, Leonora! I didn't! I swear! I told him nothing! I would never betray you!"

Liar, the voices sneer. *This is what happens when you trust. This is what you get.*

Alone, in the darkness, I let out a guttural wail.

CHAPTER 45

La Pérdida

It's so cold I can see my own breath clouding in front of me.

I blink, shivering. My body aches as I lie on the rough, stone floor of my cell.

There's no light, no window to greet Tonatiuh's rise, no warmth to chase away the chill. No hope. Everything dies here in this cursed place. The air is thick and musty. It makes the cold even harder to bear. I take shallow breaths, but there's no escaping the stench of shit. The walls themselves seem to exhale the stink, the recesses where chamber pots are emptied only adding to it.

I curl into myself, thinking about the last time I was in these dungeons. I was different then, determined. Jerónimo was here, and I was going to prove his innocence, make everything right. I remember the way he looked when I visited him; filthy, clothes in tatters, marinating in his own filth, his spirit shattered, as mine is now. My brother didn't believe I could do anything for him, and he was right to doubt. In the end, I couldn't.

I shut my eyes, but the darkness inside me is no different from the darkness around me. I tremble, not just from the cold but from the guilt. It gnaws at me, whispering in my ear: *It was your fault, you should've done more, been more.* I'm alone with my pain, my regrets, and the voices in my head that refuse to let me rest.

I can't remember ever feeling this small, this powerless. Even in all the moments when I was injured, dying, or stripped of my tonalli, I've never felt as hollow as I do now.

"Leonora," Martín calls. I can't see him through the stone walls, but his voice carries through the narrow recesses for chamber pots. "Are you there?"

"I'm here."

"Thank God. I don't know where they've taken Amalia. I can't hear anything. Can you?"

"No."

I steel myself, forcing my fingers to trace the evidence of what's been done to me. My hand drifts to my waist, where the weight of my long hair used to fall. Now, there's nothing. I whimper. Slowly, I move my fingers upward, weeping when they reach the jagged, uneven edges at my neck. I was too afraid to face it before, too terrified to see the full extent of what they've taken from me.

Martín hears me sob. "We will find a way out of this, Leonora."

"There's no way out," I cry.

"Remember," he says, "when you first came to Cuernavaca? And you said you needed my help because you didn't have your power? But remember you went to La Gran Chichimeca anyway and fought against Inspector Corona? You've faced worse than this. You survived because of your courage and your wits. You know how to fight without your tonalli. Think about everything you've accomplished. It wasn't your power that got you there. It was your resolve, your resilience, your heart. Those things haven't been taken from you—they're still with you."

The fog of anguish doesn't lift.

"We've come too far to let Don Juan win," Martín insists. "Leonora, focus on my voice. Don't let go."

After a long silence, I say, "I'm sorry I dragged you into this, Martín."

I only know the days pass by the pitiful meals the guards bring.

"Well, what have we here?" sneers the taller of two guards, a burly man with a scar running down his cheek. "A feast fit for a fallen witch."

The sight of the stale bread and boiled beans turns my stomach. The bread seems hard enough to break teeth, and the beans—if they can even be called that—float in a watery, murky broth.

"Don't be shy," jeers the second guard, a shorter, wiry man with a crooked grin. He shoves the tray closer with the toe of his muddy boot. "Eat up. Wouldn't want you to wither away before you face whatever Don Juan has planned for you next."

The tray scrapes across the stone, and the slop nearly spills over the edge of the bowl.

I pick up the bread and tear off a small piece. The guards trade amused glances.

"There you go," the shorter guard says, his lopsided grin widening.

I force the bread into my mouth, chewing slowly despite the way it grates against my teeth. It tastes as bad as it looks; it scratches the roof of my mouth, and I can almost feel it sitting like a rock in my stomach. The beans aren't any better—a tasteless mush that slides down my throat like a punishment.

"Is it true?" the taller guard asks, leaning against the wall with a smirk. "That your hair held some kind of magic?"

I keep my eyes down, focusing on getting through the meal, as disgusting as it is. This isn't nourishment—it's survival.

"Must be hard," he goes on. "Losing what made you special."

I swallow his words along with the last dry piece of bread.

I hunch over a bucket, my stomach twisting violently as I retch.

From the cell next to mine, Martín laughs.

I wipe the back of my hand across my mouth. The bitter taste of bile lingers on my tongue. "What's so funny?"

"I was thinking about the last time I was imprisoned, and you came to my rescue. You brought a shovel. A *shovel*!" He laughs again. "I really thought you were going to bury me alive. And *you* really thought I was going to dig my way out of here." He laughs louder, more manically. I wonder if he's lost his mind.

Martín gets ahold of himself, letting out a breath. "My point is . . ." he goes on. "You weren't as powerful then. You didn't have—what do you call it? Tonalli control? But you've always been resourceful, Leonora. Even in the worst situations."

That day seems like it belongs to another lifetime entirely. I didn't know any other way to save Martín back then. It wasn't power that drove me; it was determination, stubbornness, maybe even a bit of madness. I had anger and grit, and those two things carried me through battles that should've crushed me. I wasn't going to let Nabarres destroy Snake Mountain. I wasn't going to let the Tzitzimime bring an end to the world.

I lean my head back against the cold stone. "What does it matter?" I rasp.

"It matters," Martín says. "You always find a way. That's who you are."

A rat scurries past my feet, its tiny claws scraping against the stone. It pauses for a moment, sniffing the air, before darting into the shadows.

The iron bars of my cell door slide with a grating sound, pulling me upright from where I've been slumped against the wall.

I brace myself for the guards' routine mockery, but today, their footsteps are lighter.

When the door fully opens, it's not the guards who step in, but Tomás, carrying a tray.

"Tomás?" I say, my voice hoarse from disuse. "What are you doing here?"

A small smile tugs at his lips, though his furrowed brows betray his concern. "I thought you might enjoy a little company," he says, setting the tray down before me. "And maybe something better for your belly."

He shows me a meal that looks like it was prepared with care, unlike the scraps I've been surviving on. The scent hits me first, a warm savory aroma that makes my mouth water. There's a plate of roasted pork seasoned with herbs; a loaf of fresh bread; a bowl of sausage stew; and a platter of fruit—slices of fig, crisp apples, and grapes arranged around wedges of cheese. And then there's hot chocolate in a clay mug, tendrils of steam carrying the sweet and spicy scent of vanilla and cinnamon.

My eyes sting. I have to blink back tears. "You didn't have to do this," I murmur. I reach for the hot chocolate, cupping the mug in my hands. The first sip is an escape from the harshness of this place. I'm somewhere else, somewhere safer.

"I hoped it might remind you that you're not alone. You still have friends in the kitchen," Tomás says. He kneels beside the tray, looking around at the cracked, damp walls.

"I'm sorry this happened to you." He sighs, looking at my clipped hair. I must look as terrible as I feel. "So, what's the plan?"

I bite into the pork. After a moment, I swallow and look at Tomás. "Can you take some of this to Martín?"

He nods. "I'll be back to bring him food. But we haven't much time. There might be a way out of here. Amalia tried to escape during a guard change. They caught her before she could get far. But now, every time they change shifts, the ones assigned to this wing leave to her cell. They're keeping her under constant watch. There's a brief window where there's no one here—just until the next set of guards arrives. It's the only reason I was able to sneak in."

"Is Amalia all right?" Martín asks.

"I think so," Tomás says. "I don't know."

"And how long is this gap?"

"I don't know, *exactly*, but . . . well . . . that's part of why I came. To figure that out. The guards change shifts every time the church bells ring. The none-bell just rang."

"So that's midday," Martín murmurs. "The next would be at sunset, for the vespers."

"Yes," Tomás agrees. "We time it with the bell. It'll be easier at night."

"But if they're watching Amalia like hawks, how can she possibly join us?" Martín asks.

"She might not be able to," Tomás admits quietly. "Not immediately. But I've located the Sword of Integrity." He pauses to lean in closer. "I heard some of the other guards boasting about it. They were having some sort of competition to see who could carry it without swaying. Apparently, it became a game for them. They didn't dare keep it too far out of sight. Your sword—it's in the armory, near the eastern wall." He bites his thumbnail nervously. "Getting it back shouldn't be too difficult, but there's one tiny problem . . . I can't carry it. It's massive. How do you even wield it?"

As much as I want to be reunited with my sword, the enthusiasm dims. Even if the Sword of Integrity is enough to get us out of here, what then? There are too many unknowns.

I tear off a piece of bread and dip it in the stew. "Stay out of it, Tomás," I tell him. "You've risked enough."

He rolls his eyes. "Do you even know me? When have I *ever* stayed out of it?"

I slide the bread down onto the plate. "Look at what was done to me, Tomás," I say and pull the edges of my hair. "Don Juan doesn't know about tonalli. Someone told him. My guess is Amalia." My voice cracks on the last words.

"You're wrong," Tomás says. "You were compromised, Pantera. Don Juan has a spy in Cuernavaca."

Martín asks, "A spy? Who?"

Before Tomás can answer, footsteps echo down the hall. Tomás's head snaps toward the cell door, then back at me. He shoots to his feet. "Someone's coming. I'm sorry, I have to go."

My breath catches. "Tomás—"

Without wasting another second, he picks up the tray and slides the door as quickly and quietly as he can, the iron scraping against stone. Then he vanishes.

It isn't long before the door opens again. This time, Don Juan enters, his mouth and nose covered with a rag to shield himself from the stench. It conceals most of his face, but I can see his eyes squinted as if trying to block the foul air from seeping in.

"I don't enjoy this, Pantera," he begins, his voice muffled by the rag. "I'm not a cruel man." He lowers the rag, just enough for me to see the tight line of his mouth. "But you've left me no choice," he says, almost as if he's trying to convince himself. "You've been defiant, resistant, even when I've offered you a way out. If it's a matter of who survives, I'm going to make sure it's me. It's that simple."

I say nothing. He nods, as if he expected nothing less.

"May the Lord have mercy on your soul," he says, then he's gone.

"Leonora," Martín says from the adjacent cell, "don't let him break you."

He already has.

The door slides open with a sharp clamor, and I scramble backward. I quickly realize—it's not my door. But it's close. Too close.

"Where are you taking me?" Martín demands.

"Quiet, traitor!" one of the guards barks. "You'll find out soon enough."

I press myself against the bars, straining to see beyond the confines of my cell. "Martín? What's happening?"

The only response I receive is the crack of a whip, and Martín's muffled grunts of pain. The sound carves into me like a blade.

Weak. You're helpless. You can't save him. You can't even save yourself.

"No!" I cry out, slamming my fists against the bars, the iron biting into my skin. "Don't hurt him! Martín!"

He's paying for your failures. And there's nothing you can do.

"Stay strong, Leonora!" he shouts back. "No matter what happens. Stay strong!"

CHAPTER 46

El Grito

It takes five guards to haul me out of my cell. I wouldn't have resisted, but I'm flattered all the same. Their hands clamp down on my arms, and they yank me into the dimly lit corridor. I stumble, struggling to keep my footing as they drag me through the dungeons.

I'm led into the Plaza Mayor. Tonatiuh blazes down, and after so many days, perhaps weeks in the dark, the sudden assault of daylight blinds me. I squint, my eyes watering.

The plaza swarms with a restless crowd. On raised wooden platforms stand Martín and Amalia with nooses about their necks, their wrists bound behind them. My feet barely brush the ground as the guards force me toward a separate platform, made just for me, and my breaths come in rapid gasps, realizing my own fate.

They tie me to a stake, the ropes biting into my waist and chest. Torches are lit nearby, poised to set the wood piled high around me ablaze.

The crowd tosses hateful words at us, as if our deaths will bring peace or cleanse them of their sins.

Would they even care if they knew about the conspiracy, about what we've tried to do? It doesn't matter now. It'll all be over soon.

Amalia is muttering what I assume are prayers, clutching her cross.

Martín, on the other hand, keeps his head high, refusing to cower. We've fought so hard, sacrificed so much, and yet here we are.

The wood creaks beneath me as the guards tighten the ropes. I force myself to stay calm, to keep breathing.

Don Juan ascends the platform where Martín and Amalia are detained, positioning himself between them. The crowd quiets as Don Juan raises his hand.

"For too long," he begins, "terror has plagued our streets. These traitors," he says, gesturing toward Martín and Amalia, "have conspired against the Crown, against the very foundation of order and peace in our land. *She* is a deceiver and a manipulator, who worked her way into our trust only to betray us. And *he* is a usurper who attempted to undermine our rule and spread dissent. It ends here and now. This is the fate that awaits those who betray God, and the king."

The crowd responds with shouts of approval.

"And here," Don Juan continues, raising his hand in my direction, "we have the former viceregent of New Spain. But that was not her only role. I give you the *true* identity of the masked witch Pantera."

At that, a hush falls over the plaza.

I see the understanding dawn on some faces—people who once saw me as a symbol of resistance. There's shock, confusion, spreading through those who cheered my name. Some avert their eyes, unwilling to reconcile the figure they believed in with the one now bound before them. Others stare with brows furrowed, as if trying to comprehend how a sorceress, more myth than mortal, could've been captured so easily.

A few faces, though, harden. It's those faces I focus on. They give me strength.

"You see, even now, there are those among you who would follow this witch into Hell," Don Juan says. "Make no mistake—*this* is the true face of evil. A woman who hid behind a mask, sowing chaos and rebellion. Pantera's pagan practices have threatened our souls, and her crimes against the sanctity of our beliefs cannot go unpunished. They *won't*."

Some murmur their agreement, but it's weak, unsure.

"Leonora," Amalia whispers desperately. I don't look at her as she says, "Please, do something. I don't want to die."

I lean my head back against the stake, closing my eyes for a moment as I gently bang it against the wood. Her words sting. I'm furious with her, but I don't wish for her death.

Why not? the voices challenge.

She betrayed you.

And now she begs for mercy?

Why should you lift a finger to save her?

"She doesn't deserve this . . ." I argue with myself.

After everything she's done to you, this is exactly what she deserves.

Let her face the end she tried to bring upon you.

Don Juan paces the platform. "Let it be known," he says, "that treachery will always be met with the harshest of retributions. Remember this day. Today, we rid ourselves of this menace once and for all."

The crowd stirs, the initial shock lessening. Some shout curses, others chant for punishment. Another voice, however, cuts through the chaos, strong and clear.

"Pantera fought for the people!"

Eréndira. She stands among the crowd, fierce and formidable. Tomás is by her side. He smiles my way and nods.

"Pantera fought for us. For *all* of us," Eréndira exclaims.

Don Juan interrupts, "This is no time for lies and heresy. Do not let this devil woman poison your minds any further."

"It is not I who poisons them," Eréndira retorts. "She fought with La Justicia. She stood against the Tzitzimime. She protected our families. Pantera isn't the enemy—Don Juan is. Spain is."

"Touching," Don Juan says. "Light it up."

The guards hesitate for a moment, glancing at each other before lifting their torches. They approach the stake, and I'm overcome with panic.

"This isn't justice!" Eréndira bellows.

As fire begins to consume the wood, the heat pressing in, thick smoke begins to swirl around me. I cough, the harsh air burning my throat and lungs.

I close my eyes, wondering, is this how I seek entrance to the House of the Sun?

I've sent many to Tonatiuh, to the Third Heaven, where fallen warriors enjoy eternal glory hearing the beautiful sound of beating shields and accompanying the sun god on his journey. After four years, they return as hummingbirds or butterflies.

For a moment, I feel a strange joy—it has always been my desire to die with my sword in my hand.

But you don't have your sword, the voices remind. *And this wouldn't be a warrior's death. This would be defeat.*

I open my eyes.

The flames are climbing quickly, and so are the voices. *Fight,* they urge, more demanding than ever. *You're more than this. You've always been more.*

Amalia's cries and Martín's shouts echo, but they're drowned out by the voices inside my head.

You're the Godslayer, they say.

I'm a child of the Nemontemi, daughter of Quetzalcoatl, servant of the Nahualli Order, wielder of the Light of the Feathered Serpent.

By the Gods, I will not have the Spaniards sending my teyolia to anywhere other than the Third Heaven—where it belongs.

My fate is written in the fires of the sun. I have not fought all my life and defied death itself to be denied my rightful place among Tonatiuh.

This isn't how I go down. Not today. Not like this.

The flames are radiating a blistering heat. It should be unbearable, agonizing even.

Yet . . . it isn't.

Don Juan took my hair in a violent act of humiliation, ripping away a part of me, thinking he had stolen my power. I believed so, too. But as the flames crackle, I remember—my tonalli isn't bound to those strands. No, it runs through my veins. It thrums in my blood. And now, the flames are kindling the god tonalli within me, rousing what has always been there.

The fire feels like a living force, wild and untamed. It's the closest I've felt to Tonatiuh himself.

I raise my chin, welcoming him, his breath, his fury. I'm not afraid. I'm one with the flames, with Tonatiuh, for he himself was born of a sacrificial fire, and through his fiery birth, the Fifth Sun was brought into being.

Focusing inward, I feel the rush of god tonalli pulsing inside me. My hands are tied behind my back, but I open my palms toward the flames; I draw power from them, the sun, the earth, even from the people watching. Every breath, every heartbeat—it's all fuel. Indeed, my skin blisters, but the flames begin to weaken, their heat waning.

The crowd stares in disbelief, watching the fire's strength diminish. They feel it too. The flames are not consuming me. They're feeding me.

The Spaniards thought they were giving me a witch's end, but I'm being reborn in the flames that birthed the very sun.

The fire shrinks and sputters, the wood smoldering in its place. The ropes binding my wrists strain, the flames turning them brittle, and they snap. I flex my hands, feeling a rush of newfound power. The sky becomes blood red. The air is thick with the scent of smoke and scorched earth.

A strange calm blankets the plaza, the kind of stillness after a storm has passed.

The guards take a cautious step back. The crowd, too, is in a daze. Some drop to their knees, murmuring prayers. The ropes around my waist fall away as I come forward, burnt, liberated. Every step I take causes the guards to retreat further.

They fear you now, the voices say, triumphant.

The guards have their hands on their weapons, but none dare draw them.

Don Juan surveys the scene, noting the terror in his men and the stunned faces in the crowd.

End it. Show him what real fear feels like.

I walk forward, the voices shouting now to make him pay, my hands itching to strike.

Don Juan turns for his horse, casting a panicked glance over his shoulder. He thinks he's getting away. He thinks this is over.

Do it now! the voices demand. *Make him pay for Jerónimo. For every betrayal. Make him suffer like you did.*

"Leonora."

It's Martín.

"It's over," he says. "We're safe."

I halt, looking at him. The voices are screaming. *Don't listen to him. He doesn't understand. You need to do this.*

I turn my attention back to Don Juan. His foot is already in the stirrup. Before I realize it, I'm moving, ready to finish this, but just as I close the distance, a line of horses rears up in front of me, riderless, stomping and neighing. I stumble back, dodging hooves, but they thrash around me, kicking up dust.

Through the debris, I see Don Juan swinging himself onto his saddle. With a quick jerk of the reins, he's off, galloping away.

"No," I whisper harshly. But by the time I finally break through, Don Juan is gone.

Go after him, the voices insist. *You can still catch him. Don't let him escape.*

"Leonora," Martín calls again. Seeing him and Amalia on the platform, with nooses still around their necks, their faces pale, gives me pause.

I glance back at the horses, now calming. My mind wars against itself. *Go after him!* But I shake my head and instead walk toward Martín and Amalia. I undo their knots, ignoring the sting in my flesh.

Once freed, Martín takes my hands. His fingers gently touch the blisters that mar my palms. "You're hurt," he says.

"So are you," I tell him, smelling the blood on his back. "We'll mend."

"Leonora, how did you—?" Amalia mumbles, struggling to comprehend what she just witnessed.

Eréndira and Tomás are pushing themselves through the crowd, but before they can reach the front, a girl weaves her way forward. She can't be more than ten years old, her clothes threadbare and patched in places, her hair tangled in messy braids. Her small face is smudged with dirt, but her eyes are wide and bright, full of curiosity.

She stops right before me. "Are you really Pantera?" she asks, looking up at me on the platform.

I nod. "You don't have to be afraid of me."

Her eyes light up, and she smiles, showing a gap where a tooth used to be. "I'm not," she says. I grin back at her. She reminds me of Zyanya.

"Tlalli!" A woman rushes to grab the girl, pulling her close to her chest. "Don't run off like that," the mother, presumably, says, and glances up at me warily.

"Mamá, it's Pantera," Tlalli says.

The mother's grip tightens, acknowledging me with a jerk of her head. Tlalli gives me one last look before allowing herself to be led away.

I turn to face the crowd. "It's true," I say for all to hear. "I once fought with a mask, to protect myself, to protect those I care about, and because I am a mestiza woman. I hid, so I could be seen. But those days are behind me. I stand before you now unmasked."

I'm not one to make men feel that the impossible is possible and that victory is assured simply by following my lead.

How I wish Neza was here to make these people believe that we stand on the cusp of something extraordinary, to see the spark in his eyes as his vision finally begins to take shape. To have Chipahua, the Great Speaker, be the one to say the words I'm about to utter.

But it seems that fate has placed this on me, and so I must find the strength to speak, to lead, and to make this dream happen—for all of us.

"Who among you is tired of living under the yoke of tyranny and oppression?" My voice echoes through the plaza. "Who among you is tired of fearing for your lives? Who among you has had enough?"

The murmurs start low. I begin to see the anger in their eyes, the tension thickening, then a roar begins to rise, to swell with a collective fury.

"Then shout," I say. "Take that pain and rage, and let them hear you."

More and more voices join in. I glance at a wild-eyed Eréndira, and she is howling.

"Let us be liberated from Spain's grasp!" I go on. "Will you free yourselves? Will you reclaim your stolen lands? Will you be slaves of Don Juan, or will you be seeds of change?"

An uproar fills the plaza.

"Then join me," I say. "Join us. They don't tell us how we live or how we die. No one can give us freedom. We must take it. Who is with me?"

Fists rise in the air.

Eréndira goes to Amalia first. After ensuring her wellbeing, she comes to me. She unslings the Sword of Integrity strapped across her back.

"Pantera."

"Princess," I answer, bowing my head.

"I told you I'd find your sword," Tomás says. "Fine, I had a little help."

I take the scabbard and wrap my fingers around the hilt. "Did you hold her?"

391

Tomás shakes his head. "It's too heavy."

"Here," I say, offering the sword to him. She responds to my touch as I draw the blade fully, glowing a vibrant green.

Tomás stares at the blade as if he's never seen anything like it before, unsure whether to take it.

"Go on."

After a moment, he grips the hilt awkwardly with his left hand. The sword gleams with a fainter glow, and even though he hasn't had enough training, his hand hardly trembles.

However, he does give her a clumsy swing.

Tomás smiles a toothy grin. "I thought she'd be heavier."

"Careful," Eréndira says. "What if you break it?"

"Come now, it can't be destroyed . . . at least not by men." I reply. "Do you still want to be a knight, Tomás? Or do you want to be a warrior?"

"What's the difference?" Tomás asks, giving the sword another amateurish swipe.

I glance at Martín, inviting him to explain as someone who is both. "Well, isn't it obvious?" he says. "One is easier than the other." He smirks. "A knight of the glorious Order of Santiago bows to the king; he follows orders without question, marches in line with his shiny armor to fight for medals and honor. And a warrior—a warrior battles himself to do what must be done; he charges ahead because he fights for something greater than himself. And that's why knights wear capes, and warriors wear scars."

Tomás looks down at the Sword of Integrity in his hand, contemplating the choice. "I want to be a warrior."

Martín's eyes drift to Tomás's sword hand, noticing a scar tracing the back of it. "Seems like you already are."

With a sheepish grin, Tomás gives the blade back to me, and the light disappears as I sheathe her again.

"Thank you," I say, "for finding her—and for helping."

Amalia, who's been quiet so far, speaks up. "I'm so sorry. I never meant for this to happen. I didn't—Leonora, I swear." Tears well in her eyes, her breath coming in shallow, uneven gasps. "I didn't tell Don Juan anything. I never imagined . . . I only wanted to—" She touches her neck, as if remembering the feel of the noose around it. "Please, forgive me, Leonora."

"We know it wasn't you," Tomás tells her. "Don Juan has a spy in Cuernavaca."

Amalia sniffles. "Who?"

Tomás shrugs. "I don't know. He never said a name, but he said they were *very* close to the marquess."

Martín and I look at each other, the same person crossing our minds. Ignacio. It had to be.

Martín's face hardens. "I should've seen it coming," he mutters, jaw tight. "He's as good as dead."

"So, what happens now?" Eréndira asks.

"We continue to spread the word," I answer. "We assemble. We war on."

Eréndira's lips curl. "If you insist," she says, not bothering to hide her enthusiasm.

"I insist," I say. "Go to Lord Chipahua, and we will reconvene in Cuernavaca."

Eréndira nods, the glint in her eyes betraying her eagerness.

Amalia reaches for Eréndira's hand. The gesture leaves Eréndira nonplussed. I suspect she isn't a stranger to the closeness—in private, that is.

Eréndira's usual confidence falters. She tries to pull away, but Amalia tightens her grip, as if saying, *I don't care—I almost died.*

"I need to hear you say you forgive me, Leonora," Amalia says. "I did nothing wrong."

"If you did nothing wrong," I say, "why do you need my forgiveness, countess?"

She gives me a look of deep hurt. "I deserve that," she says. "I was stupid to think an agreement was possible, and because I was stupid, they did *that* to you." Her eyes linger on my shorn hair. "I wish I could take it back. I would've slit Don Juan's throat myself right then and there if I'd had the chance. No hesitation."

I'm quiet for a moment. "I heard you tried to escape."

"And failed."

"How did you do it?"

She pulls a hair pin from her disheveled updo, causing a tendril to slip free from her already untidy chignon. "My mother used to lock me in my room when I misbehaved. I've been picking locks since I could reach them." She turns the pin in her fingers, pensive. "I was on my way to find you, but I didn't know where they were keeping you, and well . . . I didn't get very far before they caught me."

I purse my lips in thought, looking at my hands, where the blisters have already begun to heal. "I understand why you did it," I murmur. "You had purpose here."

She shakes her head. "It's not what I wanted."

"What did you want?"

"The same thing I told you in the forest. The same thing I've always wanted," Amalia replies. "To be useful."

"Then go to Snake Mountain with Eréndira," I tell her. "Chipahua will know what to do."

Amalia frowns. "How do you know?"

"Because freedom from Spain was always Neza's vision. He created La Justicia not for resistance but for liberty. We're wasting time. Let's move," I say steadfastly.

"What about me?" asks Tomás, and I turn around to look at him. "What do you need me to do?"

"You've done enough," I say.

"I've proven myself," he snaps. "Tell me what to do, Pantera."

"Very well. Listen carefully. What I need from you is very important . . ."

Tomás raises his eyebrows, impatient to hear where this is going. "Uh huh?"

"Behave yourself," I finish.

Tomás harrumphs.

There's little I can say to sway him. Every time I've asked him to steer clear of danger, he's done the complete opposite—anticipating my needs, uncovering vital information, always one step ahead.

It was Tomás who first told me that Don Juan was Pedro de Alvarado's brother, and Nelli's uncle. Perhaps I would've discovered it eventually, but my mind was consumed with other matters at the time.

Tomás was right to plant that seed of suspicion, and I was wrong for not acting on it sooner. If I had, maybe Jerónimo would still be alive.

How do I protect someone who insists on standing in the storm with me?

Tomás is only a boy, and I've tried to keep him safe, but that's been the hardest battle. He's become a capable ally, and he's already a part of this, whether I like it or not. I can't ask him to step aside now.

Tomás has survived this long without me. All I can do now is trust in him.

"We need to send word to the conspirators in Zacatecas," I say. "Princess Nelli of the Red Sparrows and Francisco Tenamaxtli with the Caxcanes. They'll have heard of what happened here today but tell them to assemble their allies and bring them to Cuernavaca. Don Juan won't remain idle for long. We must rally everyone who's willing to fight."

It's a complex request, and frankly, I don't know what it entails. Still, Tomás meets my gaze resolutely and says, "Done."

"Leonora," Martín calls.

"And," I add, "keep us informed of the palace's happenings."

"Done," Tomás repeats.

"Leonora." Martín again.

"What?"

"We should get some rest."

"I'll rest when my work is done."

CHAPTER 47

El Lazo

Cuernavaca is cloaked in a serenity that almost feels comforting. The darkness of the night is like the constant companion in my head; lately, I rely on it, even thrive.

Yet now, it offers little solace. The journey has drained Martín and me—first, a canoe across the lake where I direct my tonalli to push us through the waters, then some twenty miles on foot. I'm accustomed to traveling long distances, though that doesn't mean I relish them. I'm miserable. Martín is miserable. I consider shifting and carrying my companion on my back, but he's no featherweight.

Through pure chance, we stumble upon a passing fruit cart, pulled by a pair of hulking men. Martín immediately haggles for a ride, and we settle in among avocados. The cart jostles us with every rut in the road, though I barely notice. All I can think about is Don Juan, the conspiracy, the war ahead. Doubt consumes me. I do not know if I made the right decision, rallying the people.

Martín grimaces beside me as the avocados press against the lash wounds on his back. I reach for his bloodied shirt.

"What are you doing?"

"Let me."

"Leonora."

"Shut up."

I carefully lift his shirt. My fingers lightly graze against the torn skin on his back, and an odd warmth spreads from my hand. I don't know where the sensation comes from, but it feels natural.

Martín flinches at first, but then he notices the change.

Slowly, the torn flesh begins to knit together, the angry redness fading into healthy skin. I can hardly believe what I'm seeing.

I stifle a sob, feeling his pain become my own, his suffering being absorbed into my own flesh. His wounds begin to close, but I feel the sting of every lash.

"Leonora. *Stop.* It's hurting you."

The warmth flowing from my hands grows stronger, and with it, the agony in my body deepens.

The last of the wounds close, leaving only smooth, freckled skin. My own pain slowly ebbs away, leaving me drained and trembling. I pull my hand back, gasping for breath.

Martín takes me in his arms. "Don't you *ever* put yourself through that again for me."

I nod weakly, still reeling from the experience. But even as I agree, I know that if it comes down to it, I'd do it all over again. For Martín, for those I care about, I would endure the pain.

When we finally reach the palace, the first words out of Martín's mouth as he approaches his guards are, "Where's Ignacio?"

"He has not been seen since you left, marquess," the guards report.

"Don't bother. He's already fled," I tell him.

"Treacherous rat," Martín grumbles. He turns on his heel and paces furiously. "He was right under my nose this whole time, and I didn't see it." He stops with a sharp exhale.

The guards glance at each other. "Shall we send out a search party, marquess?" one of them asks.

"No need. When he crawls out of whatever hole he's hiding in, I'll handle him myself."

The guards nod and retreat.

"He's not worth it," I say. "I'm sorry. I know he meant something to you."

Martín lets out a harsh breath. "It's not you who should be sorry, and it's not him I'm angry with. Look what they did to you because I trusted him." As I place a hand on his shoulder, he jerks away. "He knows everything, Leonora! Our movement, our plans. If he's gone to Don Juan—" He trails off, raking a hand through his hair. "Fuck!" He stands there, wrestling with himself. After a moment, he turns back to me, his voice quieter. "You should get some rest. Do you need anything?"

"No, thank you." I reconsider. "Yes. A knife."

Martín frowns. "Leonora . . . if you need to talk—"

"It's not what you think. Just get me a knife," I say, already turning toward my bedchamber. Inside, I stand in the quietness, with only the moon for company. Metztli is bright and at her fullest, a gentle beauty. I take a deep breath, but it does little to ease the tightness in my chest. Even though my skin no longer bears signs of a recent brush with fire, save for the dark smudges of soot and ash, it feels as though the smoke is trapped inside my lungs.

The last time I was this close to fire, the Old Palace burned after the earthquake. I remember the fear, the suffocating air, a tawny jaguar leaping through the flames.

It was the first time I saw him shift. I despise how my mind drags him back to my thoughts, how our past is so entwined that it's nearly impossible to think of anything without him making an appearance.

The voices whisper the truth: *He wasn't there when you needed him. He left you to face this alone.*

I flick my wrists and unleash my tonalli, sending a dresser hurtling across the room. It crashes into the wall with a loud thud.

I'm angry at myself, at Tezca, at the realization that this strength too, has been shaped, in part, by him. I can't untangle him from who I am, from who I'm becoming. I close my eyes, touching the amulet with his hair around my neck. He is within me, yet outside of me. He is here, yet absent. He is everywhere and nowhere.

He abandoned you, the voices say. *He could have saved you. But he chose not to.*

I curse my fate, and his.

The voices hiss in agreement. *You're stronger without him. You don't need him.*

And yet, I can't let go.

I open my eyes, and the room is a mess—shattered wood, splintered debris everywhere.

There's a soft knock at the door. "The knife you requested, señorita," a servant says, holding it out with both hands, and I take it. The edge is sharp, just what I need.

"Thank you," I say.

The servant retreats, and I sink into a chair at the small table beside my bed. I don't recognize the woman in the mirrored glass before me; it reflects a weary face, dark circles shadowing brown and green eyes, hair hanging unevenly, with some strands brushing her neck.

I pick up the knife from the table and raise it to my head.

I shear away what remains of my hair until it falls in a straight line just below my jaw. I smooth it aside, allowing short locks to swoop down from my forehead, framing my face with precision.

When I'm done cutting, angling, and shaping, I step back and face the mirror once more. Tears fall. It's not the hair that matters. That's not why I'm crying.

I'm met with a reflection that feels new, yet familiar. In the mirror no longer stands someone tethered to the past, weighed down by what was. In her place stands a new woman, one with purpose.

I take the shorn tresses to a hearth and burn them with copal.

"Christ, Leonora, did you not sleep at all?" Martín asks me the following day.

I'm hunched over a table in the strategy room, drawing up plans of the palace. It's a much smaller residence than Viceroyal Palace, fewer halls, rooms, and balconies, and the friary. Its design is simpler;

there are fewer corridors to defend, fewer entrances to guard, but that also means there are fewer places to retreat if we are overrun.

The Palace of Cortés is a stone stronghold, built to withstand a siege, though it's not impenetrable. The main gate is our first line of defense and the most vulnerable. I identify potential chokepoints, where narrow passages could be reinforced to slow any advancing forces. Because the courtyard is exposed, it'll need to be fortified with spiked barricades. Up on the terrace, I make notes to position the Chichimeca archers when they arrive.

I pause for a moment.

I don't know if Tomás was successful in reaching Nelli and Tenamaxtli, and I'm also no strategist; that is Amalia's expertise. But there's no time to dwell on uncertainties.

The Cuernavaca Conspiracy, and Martín's marquessate, with all the weight of his inheritance, are a threat. *When*—not *if*—Don Juan comes, we'll make our stand, and we'll make it count.

I scan the plans again, searching for weak points.

"It looks good," Martín tells me. I don't meet his eyes, but I know it's not the plans he's referring to, rather my new appearance. "Leonora, are you all right?"

"Stop asking me that." I swallow the lump in my throat. "We need to be prepared for Don Juan."

"I see. And exhausting yourself is going to stop him?" Martín asks. "Is that the course of action you intend to pursue?"

"If I sleep, he'll visit my dreams," I say. "Or maybe he won't. But either way, I'm not taking any chances."

"Who?"

I look at him pointedly, because he knows the answer. I don't even want to say his name. "Nelli was right. He abandoned me, and . . . I don't want to see him, Martín."

"Ah. So, you're planning to stay awake forever?"

"If you're not going to be helpful, then leave," I say, the words crueler than I intend. But I can't stop it—my mind is already on edge, and his concern is like a mirror holding up all the things I'm desperately trying to shove away: the fear, the doubt, the pressure.

"Leonora," Martín says softly, trying to soothe me, but it only stokes the fire inside me.

"What?" I bite out, glaring at him. "What is it now?"

He doesn't respond right away. Instead, he studies me, looking at my hair, searching my gaze for something, a way in. When at last he speaks, his words land like arrows. "You were almost burned alive."

My mind drags me to that moment—heat searing my skin, smoke choking my lungs, the desperate fight to stay alive.

"And you were whipped," I retort.

"Those two things aren't remotely the same. You healed me. Who healed *you*?"

"What do you want from me, Martín? Do you want me to lie down, fluff a pillow, take a nice little nap, and wait for Don Juan to come and finish what he started?"

"No," he says, his calm only infuriating me further. "I want you to let someone help you."

"I don't *need* your help. I don't need anyone. Just leave me alone."

"Leonora."

"Why can't you listen?"

Martín flinches as a sudden surge of tonalli bursts from me, toppling the candles from their stands. The plans spread on the table catch fire, the flames quickly curling them into blackened ruins. Martín rushes to douse the flames with a tapestry, knocking over a chair in his haste.

I stand there, my breath heavy, watching the fire consume my carefully laid strategy.

Nine Hells.

Martín meets my gaze across the table. I despise the pity I see in his eyes.

"Leonora, I know that a lot has happened to you, but you're pushing me away, and for what? Revenge? At what cost? You're not just fighting Don Juan anymore. You're fighting yourself. The Leonora I knew had fire, yes, but it was purposeful. Now . . . I see someone willing to burn everything down, including herself."

I take a step back, shaking my head. "You think I want this? To be like this? I'm doing what I have to do for all of us."

"No," he says, "but if you keep this up, Don Juan won't even have to defeat you. You'll destroy yourself long before he gets the chance." He glances at the ruined plans. A moment of anger, and they're gone. "If the horses hadn't blocked your path, what would you have done?" He comes around the table, his eyes never leaving mine. "What happens next time? What happens when you can't stop yourself?"

I sigh. I don't know. I don't know what I would've done.

"I'll redraw the plans," I say, then turn to leave.

"Where are you going?"

"I need to run."

I leave the strategy room behind, stomping down the corridor. I'm one wrong thought away from shattering, from letting the tears that burn behind my eyes fall.

I squeeze my hands into fists, digging my nails into my palms, grounding myself. I slip out of the palace, quickening my pace until I find a small grove of trees where Tonatiuh's light pours through the leaves in golden shafts.

This is where I stop, panting, the Panther clawing inside me for release.

The shift starts almost instinctively. My hands start elongating, claws emerging. Bones crack and reshape. Muscles twist. I drop to all fours, the change quickening as fur spreads across my skin, turning a rich black that gleams in the daylight.

It hurts. It always hurts. But the pain brings a giddy relief as the Panther takes control.

I'm not plagued by the voices in my nagual form. No more guilt, no more fury—just the primal urge to survive, to hunt, to dominate.

My senses sharpen, my body lowers into a sleek, powerful stance.

I feel the cool earth beneath my paws. The air smells richer, full of life and warmth, the scent of foliage, the distant musk of animals that I can almost taste.

I climb up a tree, my claws sinking into the bark. From there, I launch myself in the air. I am free. I land on my paws and shoot forward. The wind rushes past me. Nothing can touch me here. I am movement, I am strength. I push myself faster, needing to feel the speed, leave everything behind.

The Panther doesn't care about human worries, pain, or heartbreak.

And yet, even in this freedom, I know I can't stay like this forever. The pull of responsibility is strong, even now, tugging at the edges of my awareness, reminding me that no matter how far I run, I can't outrun who I am or what my duty is.

For now, I let myself get lost, if only for a little while longer. I leap over fallen logs, weave through the trees. I chase birds, feeling the rush of excitement as they fly out of reach. I run until the sun blazes high overhead and the earth feels like it's spinning beneath my feet, until there's nothing left but the pure, animal joy of the chase.

Eventually, I slow to a trot, then to a walk. My paws feel heavy, tingling all over. I climb a tree and find a wide branch, where I settle into its crook. My tail flicks lazily. Up here, I find the deep peace I can never grasp as a human, the kind of peace that comes from knowing I don't have to be anything other than what I am. There is no past to haunt me, no future to fear. Only now.

The peace is brief, however.

It's subtle at first—a shift in the wind, something in the air that doesn't belong. My ears twitch, and I catch the faintest scent. There's power here, old and familiar. My awareness tenses, alert.

I leap from the tree, landing silently. The trees seem to hum with a presence that feels too potent.

Tezca stands ahead, between two trees.

Even in my nagual form, without my human thoughts and emotions, somehow, my heart tightens at the sight of him.

The dwindling light casts long shadows around him. Or maybe they are coming *from* him.

I blink, trying to clear the image before me. It can't be him. This must be a trick of my mind, a delusion conjured by tiredness. I'm awake, aren't I? I blink again. Did I fall asleep?

As if hearing my thoughts, Tezca says, "Did you really think I'd be confined to your dreams?"

He doesn't speak to the Panther but to the woman beneath the fur and claws. Part of me wants to leap forward, to tear into him. The other part of me wants to know—*needs* to know—why he's here. Why now, after everything.

"You've always been more than what the human world could hold," he says. His gaze roams over me, as if he is savoring the sight of me like this, unleashed, wild, beyond the constraints of my human form.

He's taunting me, daring me to shift.

"You don't need to hide from me," he says. "You can't."

I circle him slowly. He lets me prowl, lets me look at him from every angle.

Tezca exhales. "I don't want to have to take your tonalli, Leonora. I'm asking you to show yourself—on your own terms. I just want to talk."

Would he really dare? I position myself directly in front of him and let out a low growl. The Panther is ready to pounce. But the woman, the one who still remembers the feel of his lips on mine, the one who loved him enough to bond with him, hesitates.

Tezca takes a step closer, the shadows seeming to part as he moves.

The shift ripples through me, muscles and bones realigning, fur pulling back into skin.

My feet touch the earth, and I stand before him, my chest heaving with anger. "Talk about *what*?" I seethe.

As the words leave my mouth, the voices return, furious and unbidden, shouting over one another. *He abandoned you. He'll leave again. He doesn't care about you.*

"Leonora . . ." he says, and this time, there's no challenge in his voice. It's quieter, as though seeing me like this pulls something deeper from him.

The sounds of my name on his lips almost breaks me. I want to stay angry. I *need* to. "What in the Nine Hells do you want? I have nothing to say to you."

"I had to see you."

"You have the Dark Mirror," I say, the bitterness sharp in my tone. "You can see me whenever you want."

"No. I needed to see you for myself." He takes another step toward me.

"Don't," I warn.

He ignores me, drawing nearer.

"I said *don't.*" I release a wave of tonalli that should have struck Tezca, as it does the trees behind him. Instead, the shadows quickly wrap around him like a shield. They form a barrier, impenetrable, absorbing the light and heat. My tonalli scatters the moment it touches the shadows.

With a shake of my head, I scoff and move toward him. When we're face to face, I raise my hand and slap him across the cheek. Hard.

Tezca's head jerks to the side with the force of the blow. Slowly, he turns back to face me. I expect to see rage in his eyes, but there is none, only a quiet acceptance, as if he expected the strike—perhaps even saw it in the mirror—and understands that this is what I need. And so, he lets it be.

"*Where* were you?"

He licks a trickle of blood from the corner of his mouth. "Never far."

"You were just going to let me die?"

"You were never in any real danger."

A cold, harsh laugh escapes me. "Is that so? I wish I'd known that when Don Juan was taking my hair!"

"You acquitted yourself very well. Exceptionally, I would say."

The more he speaks with such casual detachment, the more my hand trembles with the urge to slap him again.

"I could tell that you doubted yourself," Tezca says, "at first. And I would've stepped in if I thought you were going to be hurt."

"Look at me! I *was* fucking hurt!" I cry. "You let me suffer, let me believe I was alone—" My voice breaks.

He abandoned you.

Tezca's brown eyes soften, but it doesn't lessen my resentment. "Don Juan did nothing to dull your edge, Leonora. If anything, he made it sharper. It would've been an insult to you if I had intervened when you clearly did not need it. But you were never alone. I was with you, always."

He's lying, the voices hiss. *He was never there. He let you suffer because he didn't care.*

"With me?" I yank his amulet from my neck and toss it at his chest. "What good is your oath if you aren't there when I need you the most?"

He opens his mouth to speak, but I don't give him the chance. "He intoxicated me, took my hair, humiliated me. And all the while, you watched from your heavenly paradise. Why? Were you waiting for me to prove something to you?"

"For you to prove something to yourself," Tezca answers.

"I waited for you to come. I was sure you wouldn't let them hurt me," I whisper, the admission costing me more than any battle wound. "Do you know how I felt?"

"Yes," is all he says.

He watched while they tortured you.

"The mirror might've shown you," I say, "but you didn't feel my pain, did you? You didn't feel the fear, the agony I endured, the desperation of not being able to move while trying to hold on to something that was being ripped away from me."

"Yes, I did. We are bonded."

"Oh, *now* you remember?" I scoff. "You weren't there, Tezca. You were just some distant observer . . . watching me like cruel entertainment."

"No," he says, shaking his head sadly. "That's not what happened."

"That's what you made me feel!"

"Leonora, I . . ." he begins, then stops, searching for the right words. "It was never my intent to cause you pain. Do you think I don't want to kill Don Juan? Do you know how easy it would be for me to end him right now? How simple it would be to erase him from existence?"

"Why haven't you?" I demand.

"You know why."

I do, but the answer doesn't ease the ache in my heart. The Dark Mirror. It feeds on Tezca's anger. If he were to act on his rage, he would give in to the darkness, and the mirror would consume him. He would become something far worse than Don Juan.

"If I had acted in that moment, I wouldn't be standing here. And I couldn't—" He pauses, lowering his gaze. "I couldn't risk becoming something that would destroy you too."

I know what the mirror can do. I've seen its power, how it twists and consumes everything it touches. But it doesn't lessen the sting of his absence, the loneliness I felt in those dungeons.

It hurts so much because I love him.

Tezca stands there, so close yet so impossibly distant. Even as the anger rages, it's the love—Nine Hells, the love—that makes it unbearable.

"Has the mirror shown you what Don Juan will do?" I ask quietly. His throat bobs. "Yes."

"Then you know we need you in this fight. *I* need you."

Tezca's chuckle is an airy breath. "You don't need me, Leonora," he says, with both pride and a trace of sadness. "You're a goddess. You burn brighter than the sun."

"What does that matter if I'm to fight without you by my side?

What good is it to taste victory yet stand alone in the battlefield when it's all over? I don't need you because you're more powerful, Tezca. I can face what's coming without you. I just don't want to. I *want* you there with me. You can reclaim your home, and we can be free."

Tezca's shoulders slump slightly, and for the first time, he seems vulnerable, miserable. "I know I've failed you, and for that, I am angry. And I am sorry. But I can't be the man you want me to be."

My heart tightens, and I weep. "You already *are* that man. Beneath this—this mask you wear. Abandon this path, Tezca," I plead. "Leave the Dark Mirror behind. You don't have to be enslaved by its demands. We can find a way to end this, to move forward without Tezcatlipoca controlling you."

"I can't," he says through gritted teeth. "This isn't about your wishes or mine. It's about what must be done. We aren't the same people who made those vows."

"So our bond means nothing to you?"

"It's because it means *everything* to me that I stay away. I cannot be near you without the risk of losing myself, and in turn, losing you. The constraints I face are not of my choosing, and I'm bound by more than just my own will. You don't understand the sacrifices I've made—the things I've had to endure to keep everything in balance. I don't want to hurt you, Leonora. Understand that my fight is not against you. And accept it, once and for all."

I wipe my tears. "I don't. I don't accept it."

"Fine. Suffer needlessly, then."

"Great. Go on then. Sacrifice your life for us all. *Leave.*"

I don't mean it, but still he takes me at my word.

I storm into the palace so violently that courtiers eddy out of my way.

Martín doesn't bother to knock on my bedchamber door, and this time, I don't bother to mask what's tearing me apart.

I collapse into his arms, the sobs flowing. My hands clutch at his shirt, and I bury my face against his chest. My heart feels like it's being wrung dry, the pain of it leaving me breathless.

Martín embraces me without hesitation, pulling me close. His heartbeat is a steady rhythm beneath my ear. He rubs my back in slow, comforting circles, his touch light enough not to overwhelm me but firm enough to remind me that he's here, that he's not going anywhere.

Eventually, the sobs start to subside, leaving behind a dull, aching exhaustion. I rest my forehead against his chest, and after a while, pull back to meet his gaze. "I don't know how to win," I admit, my voice fragile.

Martín raises a hand tenderly to dry my cheeks.

I swallow a scratchy gulp. "I don't know if I made the right choice, rallying the people in Mexico City. I don't know what Don Juan will do. I don't know how to bring back Tezca. I don't know how to destroy the Dark Mirror. I don't know how to let go of this . . . this rage consuming me. I'm angry, *all* the time."

I shudder, running my hands over my face. "He's my mate, Martín. Even if I could somehow force myself to let him go, the bond between us is too strong. Time nor circumstance can break it. He is in my veins, in my heart. I can't be with him. I can't abandon him. I don't know what to do."

"Your bond—you say it's strong. Maybe it is stronger . . . than the Dark Mirror?" he proposes. "If you can find a way to reach him, to remind him of who he is—of who you are *together*—maybe that can bring him back. You have to be his light. If there's even a chance, you owe it to both of you to try."

Slowly, I nod. "And everything else?"

He sighs. "One step at a time."

"One step at a time," I repeat, letting his words settle my mind.

That night, I surrender myself to sleep.

In the morning, I have more work to do.

CHAPTER 48

La Señal

High above a little town in Cuernavaca called Tepotzlán, perched on a mountain, sits a small temple-pyramid devoted to the god of pulque. There, on that hill, surrounded by the thin air and the ancient stones, I kneel, offer my blood, and pray.

I beg Xochiquetzal to help me end Tezca's battle with the Dark Mirror, and I pray to Quetzalcoatl for a sign that I'm on the right path in the liberation for Mexico.

The sign arrives the next day.

I awaken to the commotion outside—voices, hundreds of them, rising in a chaotic chorus of revolution and resistance. I rush to the window and see the mass of people gathered at the palace gates. Two or three hundred, maybe more, all drawn by the same burning desire for change. I tear myself away from the window, frantically slipping into my black dress. I'm still buckling my belt as I storm down the corridors. Servants, guards, lords and ladies, move about the palace in a frenzy. No one seems to know what to do.

I find Martín alone in his bedchamber, lost in thought as he stares out the window.

"Martín," I say, breathless. "What's happening out there?"

"They've been arriving since dawn," he says, still peering through

411

the curtains. He turns to face me, serious. "Tales of your burning—or *unburning*—have spread. They think the gods have returned."

"Nonsense," I spit.

"You *are* a goddess," he reminds. "Leonora. You've given them hope."

"It's suicide," I grumble. "Don Juan will hear of this."

Martín bites his thumbnail. "The friars are chattering," he says. "Don Juan published a manifesto in Mexico City stating that the Cuernavaca Conspiracy was a mob of robbers, criminals, and assassins encouraged by . . . the monstrous masked witch Pantera."

I've been called worse things.

"You should go out there," he coaxes.

"For *what?*"

"Talk to them. They've clearly come here for you."

"No, *no*," I say. "We have to get them *out* of here. It's too dangerous. We can't risk their lives. I can't protect them all."

"No, you can't, but these people want to fight, Leonora. They believe in the cause, and they believe in you." He nods decisively. "I'll go with you."

We join the throng swarming the streets. The two of us stand at the gate, looking at the people, most of them Indigenous, but many mestizos too, maybe even criollos.

The Spaniards have fought since before my birth, and though we've had victory over them before, I don't know that this is a winnable war. I don't know if Tezca will be at my side again.

But, maybe, whatever happens, our names—mine, Martín's, Eréndira's, those who stand with us, will echo through the valleys and the hilltops. Tezca once told me we are like gods in that way, immortal.

And, maybe, this is the sign I prayed for.

Silence falls over the crowd as I move toward them.

"I know you want to fight," I tell them. "But this is not a time for reckless bravery. The Spaniards will not tolerate dissent. Every one of you here is at risk. They hang or imprison anyone involved in the conspiracy."

I raise my hands to calm their displeasure. "This is not to diminish your bravery or your desire for change," I continue, my voice firm yet sympathetic. "But if you stay here, you will be in grave danger. The Spaniards are already aware of the unrest, and they will not hesitate to strike down anyone who threatens their control. Your lives are too precious to risk in a battle we are not yet prepared for."

I swallow. "Please," I say, "leave now, while you still can. Return to your homes, to your families. We need to gather our strength and plan carefully."

Some shout, their voices filled with frustration.

"We came here to fight!"

Spanish guards appear at the edges of the crowd, starting to force them away from the palace gates.

"Stand down!" Martín strides forward, his authority commanding attention. "That is an order."

The guards obey, though reluctantly.

"You are not to escalate this situation," Martín says. "You will not use force against these people."

Martín is their marquess, but some of these men are more loyal to the Crown than to him. As he returns to my side, we trade a glance of understanding.

"How much time do we have?" I ask.

"Not much."

I try to regain control of the crowd. "Everyone, please listen! The guards are only here to maintain order. They won't harm you."

I can see the confusion in their faces, the uncertainty of who their true enemy is. They begin to settle down, their attention shifting away from the guards.

"Leonora, where are you going—?" Martín says as I walk back inside the palace.

He follows me to the strategy room. "What are you doing? The longer these people stay here, the greater the danger to their lives. The guards listen to me, but if this keeps up, I don't know what they'll do."

I rub my temples, trying to think. "I *know*! This wasn't supposed to happen, Martín! I asked for a sign, not for the battle to begin. This isn't some conspiracy anymore. It gives Don Juan every reason he needs to attack. I—"

Before I can say another word, a sudden, sharp crack rends the air.

Gunfire.

Martín and I look at each other horrified, before we rush outside to find the guards forcing their way through the crowd, muskets blazing. People are screaming and crying, scattering in every direction.

"Stop!" I shout, pushing through the multitude.

"We need to get them out of here," Martín says to me over the chaos. "Help me get them to the palace."

I nod, my heart pounding as I grab the arm of an elderly woman near me. "Keep moving. Follow me." I lead the way to the entrance, but there's a line of guards stoutly stationed at the gates. I release the woman's hand, counting ten men, all of whom have difficulty reloading their weapons—pouring gunpowder down the barrel, ramming it in place, and then trying to fit the lead shot.

The guards look to their leader for direction. Their corporal, a red-haired man with a pointed chin beard, surveys his men in such embarrassing disarray. He curses under his breath. "Shit," he grumbles, tossing his musket aside in disgust. Instead, he reaches for the sword at his hip and points it at me.

"Step aside, corporal," I say.

He starts to say, "Our orders come from the viceroy of New Spain—"

His words are cut off by a choked gurgle as I raise my hand, and my invisible grip closes around his throat.

"I'm not asking," I say, hoisting him into the air. "This is

Cuernavaca, and Don Martín is your marquess. Don Juan has no authority here. Tell your men to stand down. I will not repeat myself. Do you understand me?" I pause as he struggles for breath. "Blink if you do."

He blinks, gasping and sputtering as I release my hold, and he drops back to the ground.

"Stand down," he rasps to the men behind him.

The guards lower their muskets and clear our path. After ushering the elderly woman and others into the palace, I look about the gateway to see who the second fool will be to make a move against me. A familiar face catches my eye—the old man, Tezcamacatl, is being swallowed by the stampede of bodies. As I hurry over, he's shoved forward, and the crack of more gunfire freezes me in place. The bullet finds it mark. Tezcamacatl collapses.

"No!" I shout, my heart tightening.

The voices in my head are loud and clear. *Embrace the fury. Unleash it. They've earned it.*

The guard who fired the shot realizes his folly, his face pale, brow glistening.

Our eyes lock. His hand trembles on his weapon. My vision narrows, darkening at the edges until I see only him, the man who shot Tezcamacatl. The voices grow louder, a chorus demanding retribution.

My fingers tingle, then burn. Power crawls up my arms like lightning seeking ground. It builds in my chest, a pressure so intense I can barely breathe. The guard sees it happening. He steps back. Too late.

I extend my arms, then thrust them forward, unleashing a tonalli blast that sends the guards crashing against the stone walls of the palace. Bones and spines are snapped like twigs. Other guards positioned around the gateway remain standing, only for a moment, before scattering like frightened rabbits.

Their escape is cut short.

Twisting my wrists, I wrench stones from the palace walls and launch them across the gateway, one after the other, striking down the fleeing guards.

I find no satisfaction in this. The only thing that festers within me is hatred.

"Leonora, that's *enough*," Martín says.

I lower my hands, letting the stones drop, and rush to Tezcamacatl's side. His chest rises and falls with slow, shallow breaths—he's alive, only just. I examine the shoulder wound where the bullet struck, ready to heal him, but Martín stops me again. He takes my wrist. "The last thing you need right now is a bullet wound."

"I'll heal," I say, pulling away, but his grip tightens.

"Not fast enough."

I yank harder. "Let me go."

"No, *look*—we need to get him and everyone else into the palace."

I grit my teeth, swallowing my fury.

Martín carefully lifts Tezcamacatl, who winces in agony at the movement. As we hurry toward the entrance, I hear more and more boots scuffling, the smell of gunpowder drawing closer. I turn to assess the situation. The crowd is panicked; there's no way these people can outrun the soldiers, not without leaving some behind.

I won't allow that.

"Get them inside," I hiss to Martín.

"How?" Martín shouts, seeing the guards coming.

Taking a steady breath, I step forward with my hands raised. This time, I don't attack the guards with my tonalli—I've nearly drained it. Instead, I use *theirs*. Channeling tonalli is direct, blunt, like using the heel of your foot to kick down a door. But tonalli control is much more delicate, like threading a needle through an impossibly narrow space. It requires focus, a fine touch.

I curl my fingers and freeze them in place. Their weapons remain locked in mid-air as they struggle against the unseen force that holds them, faces caught in confusion and fear.

"Go," I say. "I can't hold them forever."

"Leonora."

"*Go*, Martín."

He carefully urges Tezcamacatl forward, shouting to the others. "This way! Move, quickly!"

The people hurry through the gaps between the immobilized soldiers. They move as quickly as their feet will allow them, but the strain of holding the guards in place is already wearing on me. Some of them have cold, weak tonalli, and my hands tremble with the effort, slipping through my grip like water.

Remember, the voices say. *Remember how they held you. How they pinned you down.*

Martín looks back at me from the entrance. "That's everyone. What about you?"

"Close the gates," I say, my teeth clenched as I struggle to hold their tonalli steady.

"For fuck's sake, Leonora—"

"Close them!" The strain is nearly unbearable, but the memory of that day—the helplessness, the humiliation—fuels me.

They won't take anything from me again. I won't allow it.

Martín hesitates for a heartbeat longer, then, with a grim nod, he turns and does as I say.

The heavy gates slam shut. My vision starts to waver, dark spots creeping in at the corners. *Make them feel what you felt. Break them,* the voices urge.

Through the noise, another voice slices through. Martín's. It's faint, but it reaches me. *What happens when you can't stop yourself?*

One of the soldiers breaks free, staggering forward with a gasp as my hold on his tonalli snaps. The others will follow soon if I don't—

Finish it, the voices demand. *Destroy them.*

I raise my hands, considering letting the fury consume me, to crush the guards where they stand. But something in me resists. Something that sounds like Martín's words. Something that still feels like me.

417

I push myself to focus—not on the voices, not on the rage, but on control. Not of tonalli. Of myself.

The gates are closed. The people are safe.

I release my hold on the guards, letting them drop in a heap at the base of the palace walls. I stumble back, shaky, drained, and push what tonalli I have left downward to lift myself into the air.

I soar, the wind rustling the edges of my black dress as I ascend to the roof of the palace.

Alone, on my high perch, I sink to my knees and let Tonatiuh renew me.

Everyone is gathered in the audience hall. Because I drew up plans of the palace, I know it's the largest room in the building, where Martín holds court, receives guests, and listens to petitioners.

Now, it's a refuge.

A woman cradles her child, her face streaked with tears. I hurry over and check the child's pulse. It's strong, but the child's breathing is labored.

"Is he hurt?" I say, pressing my hand against the boy's forehead.

The woman shakes her head. "Just scared."

I nod, offering what comfort I can.

Nearby, Tezcamacatl clutches his shoulder, grimacing. Martín is already there, surrounded by a few servants. I crouch before the old man to heal the wound.

For a third time, Martín intervenes.

I growl. "What in the Nine Hells is the matter with you? I can help this man."

"We've removed the bullet," Martín says, meeting my glare with one of his own. "What he needs now are stitches, and as you can see, we have people who can do that." A servant presses a cloth against the wound, applying pressure to stem the bleeding. "We'll get you taken care of, señor."

"His name is Tezcamacatl," I inform him.

Martín's sharp gaze softens a little. He puts an arm around my waist, and we move aside. "You can help this man," he tells me, "and everyone else here, by being a leader, not a healer."

I grumble. "Don't tell me what to do, Martín. I can be both."

"Yes, you can, but that doesn't mean you should. Let others handle the wounds. You're the one who can keep them safe. You *know* I'm right."

He is. That's why I grumbled.

"Hey. Look at me." He puts his hand on my cheek. His blue eyes pierce into mine, searching. "Are you good?"

Is *he*? Am *I*? Are *any* of us?

At first, I nod, tilting my head into his palm. The familiar comfort makes me want to believe, to pretend that everything is fine. That I'm still in control. But I know how close I am to breaking, how fragile it all feels.

I shake my head, the movement small but certain.

"It's all right," he says, his voice a quiet anchor. "You don't have to be."

His thumb brushes gently across my cheek. Just the touch, just knowing that I'm not alone, feels like enough.

"What if I lose control?" My chest tightens with the thought.

"Then I'll be there. I'll stop you."

I nod. I want to believe him, but the voices have been louder. Closer.

As I pull away from Martín, I approach a group of men and women huddled together, some of them nursing bruises, cuts, and scrapes.

"Is everyone all right?" I ask.

One of the women looks up at me. "Are they coming for us?"

"They are," I answer.

They're quiet, waiting for what I'll say next.

I go up to the dais, a raised platform where Martín often sits upon an ornate, gilded chair. The dais is several steps wide, and behind the chair hangs a large portrait of King Carlos on horseback. It takes up nearly the entire length of the wall.

I caress the arms of the chair, thinking about who should be sitting here. Not Martín, not the king it represents, not even the Mexica who conquered these lands.

A true Tlahuica ruler. Tezca should be seated here. He should be *here* . . .

Godsdamn him. Godsdamn everything. There are decisions to be made. Lives hanging in the balance. It's suffocating, this responsibility. I try not to sigh.

"You're safe here, for now. The fight is on our doorstep," I say. "The Spaniards won't give up easily. But neither will we. We have no choice but to arm ourselves. Gather whatever weapons you can find. Daggers, forks, pokers, vases, serving trays—anything that can be used to defend yourselves and your families. We don't let them take the palace. We fight for our freedom, for our lives, and for those who cannot fight for themselves."

A man near the front is the first to break a chair, using one of the legs like a club. Others move through the hall, heading off to find what they can.

"We have to wait for the others," Martín tells me.

"We don't have that choice, Martín. This is happening now," I say.

"Where are you going?"

"To get my sword."

CHAPTER 49

La Obscuridad

In my bedchamber, the noise in the palace rings in my mind like a death knell.

Footsteps pounding. Weapons clattering. Doors slamming. Voices—so many voices.

I sit with the Sword of Integrity, turning her tip absently on the floor. She has seen more blood than I can remember, but this battle feels different.

In the beginning, when I first donned the mask, I was a solitary creature. I fought alone, embraced the solitude. I hid. Then Neza called me to La Justicia, and everything changed. I had allies, comrades, people I could lean on. I came to understand that together, we could be greater than the sum of our parts. Since then, I've battled alongside friends. We've shared our victories. We've mourned our losses.

Now, though, it's only Martín and I, along with a handful of his loyal guards, defending ourselves, a land, a people, a vision.

I don't doubt myself, but doubt does coil around my heart like a serpent, hissing its venomous whispers. It's a strange thing to be so certain in oneself, yet so uncertain in outcome.

The night battles are always more challenging—my tonalli depletes faster without Tonatiuh shining. I'm at my best when he's high in the sky. Though I prefer to hunt in the darkness, I always find myself yearning for the dawn, perhaps also unknowingly longing for the Lord of Dawn himself, my father.

Battles don't wait for daylight, and neither can I.

The Sword of Integrity is ready. I'm not.

Nine Hells, I need Tezca. I need him by my side, not as a god watching from the Thirteen Heavens, but here, beside me, as the great warrior I know he is, as my mate.

Without him here, it feels like I'm missing a part of myself, as though I'm wielding a sword without an edge.

I refuse to accept that the Dark Mirror's hold on him is unbreakable. I've seen the man Tezca is, the one who fights not just for himself, but for others.

I grip the hilt of my sword tighter.

The darkness cannot win.

Resolve hardens within me as I leave my room. The hope, the desperate—perhaps pathetic—hope that he'll return, that our bond is stronger than the Dark Mirror, stays with me.

In the audience hall, Martín is overseeing preparations. The people have armed themselves as best they can. Their eyes meet mine as I walk among them, and I see the fear there but also a steely readiness.

"Everything's in place," Martín says as I approach. "We've barricaded the entrances with anything we could find."

"I can see that," I say, eyeing the bed wedged against the gate doors. "Is that . . . your bed?"

Martín smirks. "Figured if Don Juan breaches the palace, he might as well find somewhere to rest—permanently."

"That's one way to make him feel at home."

"Oh, come on, Leonora. It's poetic," he insists with a grin. "The windows have been reinforced with wooden planks and iron bars we pried from the stables. I've stationed men on the upper floor to keep watch. The kitchens have been turned into a supply depot—we've stockpiled food and medical supplies there, and the cooks are preparing to make anything we can carry with us if we need to retreat to the friary."

"The friary?"

"It's holy ground. The Spaniards wouldn't dare bring harm upon it," he explains. "We've filled every container we could find with water and sand in case they try to set fires. We've blocked off the lesser-used corridors to funnel any intruders into defensible areas. And the armory, such as it is, has been emptied and distributed among the people."

I exhale, letting go of some of the worries I've been carrying.

"And *that*?" I ask, eyeing a precariously hung chandelier.

He chuckles. "Rigged to drop at a moment's notice."

I smile faintly. "No news of our allies?"

"No," Martín answers. "We'll hold the palace. We have to."

I survey our group of defenders, a haphazard collection of people, and the serpent of doubt coils tighter around my heart. Half of them have never even *seen* a sword. The other half is just as uncertain, just as afraid. "If we can't?"

"Then I suppose we'll make sure our names are remembered."

Night falls. Stars twinkle. Crickets sing their lullaby. It's a perfectly balmy evening, almost magical, were it not for the promise of violence to come.

Martín finds me in the courtyard, sitting under the jacaranda.

Trees comfort me. They make me remember Zyanya, how the forest speaks to chaneques. They make me remember growing up in the verdant paradise of Tamoanchan, seeing the Flowering Tree every day, its blooms amulets of happiness, and listening to Master Toto share the wisdom of trees. Quetzalcoatl is the breath that rustles the leaves, the life that flourishes in their growth.

"Why does it seem like we're always waiting to meet our death?" I ask Martín.

When he settles beside me on the bench, a soothing warmth

radiates from him, grounding me in the moment. "You've been through a lot."

"So have you," I reply.

For a moment, Martín says nothing, his attention on the offerings at Ozomatzin's feet. Maize, cacao beans, and the basket of cotton are still there, but now new items have been added: a small carved figurine, a necklace of turquoise beads, and a woven cloth dyed in deep reds and purples. There's even a jaguar tooth. The offerings seem to increase every time I see them, and I wonder how many people hope or even believe that Ozomatzin will return.

The mix of simple and precious items speaks of a growing faith. Or maybe it's desperation. Right now, we're all feeling it. But each new addition feels like a prayer, a plea for something lost to be restored.

They've held on to this belief that Ozomatzin will return for over a hundred years. More than a lifetime of waiting.

"Do you want him to come?" Martín asks, his blue eyes gleaming with an unusual intensity.

"Of course I do. You know that."

"But you're afraid of him . . . the thought of his power."

"No," I say firmly, shaking my head. "He doesn't frighten me."

"Do you trust him to do the right thing?"

"What do you mean?" I narrow my eyes, noticing the way the moon casts a glow on his face, his features serious in the pale light.

"He's unpredictable, isn't he? Even as an ally, you never quite know what he might do. We need him, but . . . we don't exactly know what we're inviting."

I rub at my chest where my amulet used to rest. "Our bond is stronger than the Dark Mirror. I know it is."

"What if it isn't? What if you have to confront him? What will you do?"

"I don't have all the answers, Martín. Besides, you were the one who told me I had to be his light. Why do you hesitate now?"

He's about to respond when his eyes drift beyond the courtyard, toward the gate doors, almost like he's expecting Don Juan to burst through at any moment.

Then, the distant sound of hooves—many hooves—reaches my ears.

Martín brings me back to the conversation. "What if it's too late?" he asks. "What if the Dark Mirror has already taken control of him?"

My brows furrow. "You're very curious today."

"I don't want you to get hurt, Leonora. Do you really believe things can be the way they were again with him?"

"Yes."

"But he left you alone in Mexico City. He abandoned you."

"It wasn't what he wanted," I argue.

"So you understand, then."

"Do I understand?" I snort. "That's the problem. I've *always* understood. That's what makes it so painful. Tezca was born in the Third Sun. His tonalli is thousands of years old, and he remembers all of his lives—*all* of them. He's been everywhere, done everything, seen it all. Do you know how awful that is? To think he will continue being reborn and he will have experienced the most exhilarating moments on this earth, and also the worst, unimaginable horrors. I only remember this one life, and that is more than enough."

I pause, the words lodged in my throat.

"He is consumed by his memories. Memories that bring him pain and anger. And those two things feed the Dark Mirror. I know he stays away because it's the only way he knows to protect me." I inhale a sharp breath. "But if Tezca were here . . . if he was listening now, I would tell him that I don't need his protection. I would tell him that I'm not afraid of the Dark Mirror. I'd stand beside him, like I always have."

He doesn't want to be saved, the voices taunt. *He's chosen the darkness over you.*

"I would tell him," I whisper, more certain now, "that's he's not alone."

The distant beat of hooves grows louder. A drumroll heralding the approach of war. I can only think about this moment. I want to hold on to it and never let go. Nothing else matters.

I glance at Martín, noticing how he sits on the bench radiating a heat that doesn't belong to him, unless Martín somehow managed to cultivate an impossible reserve of tonalli in the past hour. At night, no less. My heart races. I reach out, resting my hand on his arm. The touch is so familiar it cannot fool me.

"Tezca . . . do you really think I can't tell it's you?"

His fingers twitch a little under mine.

I lift my eyes to his. "No matter what face you show the world," I say, "I'll *always* know it's you."

The way he holds himself, the slight narrowing of his eyes when he's deep in thought, the way he tilts his head when he listens, even the cadence of his breathing—slower, more controlled—everything about him is more intense, more alive than anyone else. Even now, the moonlight drenches him in a shimmering glow, as if Metztli herself refuses to let him remain hidden.

I knew all of this from the second I laid eyes on him on *La Capitana*, perhaps even before, when I sensed his tonalli for the first time. I didn't know then he was a sorcerer, or a god, but I knew there was something there, barely contained beneath the surface.

Tezca is quiet, his façade wavering just enough for me to catch the truth in his eyes—Martín's eyes.

"Why go through the trouble?" I ask him. "If you really wanted to know what I think, all you had to do was look inside my mind."

His voice, when he finally speaks, is not Martín's but unquestionably his own. It has that warm, deeper timbre that can both soothe and terrify. "I can't read your thoughts," he says. "I only know what the mirror shows me."

With him, the lines between reality and illusion blur. I'm not sure what's real. I don't know that I'm actually sitting here with him. If this bench is real. If the starry sky is something he's conjured for me. If the sound of the wind is no more than a whisper of his sorcery.

I can't even begin to fathom the reaches of his power.

"Are you really here?" I ask. "Or is this another dream?"

"I'm here."

"Tezca—let me see you," I say, my fingers sliding between his.

"You *do* see me. You've always seen me as I am."

"Stay," I say. "Stay with me." My fingers hover near his, desperate to pull him back, to keep him here with me.

"Leonora." I yank my gaze to Martín—the real one—barging into the courtyard with urgency. "Who were you talking to?"

I glance to my side, and Tezca is gone. Beneath my hand, I feel something warm and familiar. Lifting it, I find the amulet in my palm, where Tezca's hand had been moments before. I close my fingers around it and give it a squeeze.

"No one—myself," I murmur.

"They're here," Martín tells me.

"I know." I stand and slip the amulet around my neck.

As if we needed further confirmation, the gate doors shudder, dragging the bed fixed against it backward.

I hurry with Martín as he signals his men to prepare.

"Those who cannot fight are sheltering in the friary," Martín informs me as we rush to our positions. "They're safe."

"We hold the Spaniards here," I say. "They can't get in."

Martín looks at the doors as they rattle violently again. The noise on the other side grows louder, screams blending with the bark of orders. "Heave!" The command rings out, followed by another crash against the door.

"We have no idea how many are out there," Martín says.

My ears sharpen, picking up every distinct noise outside the door—boots thudding, shields clattering, helmet visors clinking, cloaks swishing.

I sift through the chaos until I have a rough estimate.

At least twenty soldiers are clustered directly at the door, but beyond them, I pick up ranks standing by. I can't be sure how many, but I let my hearing stretch and stretch until the jingle of chain mail stops.

I don't dare say the number.

"It doesn't matter," I tell Martín. "They're clearly desperate, and disorganized."

The wooden doors—and the bed—creak under the massive force pounding from the other side. The entire palace seems to quake with the impact.

"They're almost through," I say, more to myself than anyone.

A priest takes my side, wielding a large staff, knuckles white. It looks as unfamiliar to him as a crucifix would to me.

I raise an eyebrow at him. "And who might *you* be?"

"Padre Cipriano."

I jut out my chin, because that means nothing to me.

"Just a humble follower of the Lord," he adds, "though I suppose today I follow *you*."

I almost chuckle. "Ever taken down an armed soldier with a walking stick before, Padre?"

"There's a first time for everything."

Well, I certainly did not *ever* imagine leading a Christian priest anywhere—let alone into battle.

"God works miracles," he says.

The irony is not lost on me.

"Marquess, they're going to break through!" one of Martín's guards shouts.

"Go to the friary," I tell them. "Shelter with the others."

I take my place at the front and summon my tonalli, my vital heat pouring out of me as I slide the bed firmly against the doors, forcing them to lock in place. I close my eyes and grit my teeth, keeping my hands steady, my focus sharp. Gradually, the burden begins to ease, the crushing weight lessens, and I begin to wonder if the soldiers are retreating.

But then I open my eyes and realize it's not just me holding the doors.

It's Martín, Padre Cipriano, other priests, servants, the guards, men and women, many hands.

It's all of us.

"What are you doing?" I grumble to Martín beside me.

"Getting you out of trouble. Typical Tuesday."

"This is *not* the time for your jests."

He laughs, even as his arms strain.

The door holds. We hold. I feel the collective effort. The soldiers outside shout, the doors stop shuddering, and this time I hear boots fading. I start to believe we might just endure this siege.

Slowly, we lower our hands.

As first, there's silence, but then I hear chains and horses.

The hinges give way with a loud groan, the wood splintering. The Spaniards fastened chains to a wagon, and with the powerful pull of the horses, they've wrenched the doors wide open.

There's nothing between us and them now.

They touch their crosses. I touch my amulet.

And the Sword of Integrity sings.

The first line of soldiers reels back, blinded by her green brilliance. Martín is shouting orders, but his voice is lost in the chaos of battle.

My attention narrows. Blades swarm around me, the Spaniards raring in their attack. One soldier lunges, his sword barely out of its scabbard before the Sword of Integrity drops like a bolt from the sky, cleaving through his helmet.

A foolish move, I realize a second too late, because the scalp is the bloodiest when cut. The force of the strike drenches my face.

I blink through the torrent of blood, wiping my eyes with the back of my arm. As I do, something massive slams into me, knocking me back with the force of a battering bison. The air leaves my lungs in a sharp gasp. I shake my head, trying to clear the dizziness.

Through the blur, I make out a smudge of silver; every inch of my opponent is encased in armor.

I parry his blow clumsily, my feet sliding on the wet floor as he drives me backward. Up close, I can take in the full extent of his armor: steel breastplate, vambraces and gauntlets, metal plates protecting his thighs and shins, and boots reinforced with steel at the toes. A gorget wraps around his neck, guarding against any kind of strike to his throat. The only part I do see of the man are his eyes, glaring at me from behind the narrow slit of his visor.

The soldier presses his advantage. I duck, barely avoiding his whistling sword, and lash out with a burst of tonalli straight into his chest. He stumbles, though he remains standing.

He's a walking fortress, but fortresses have weaknesses. He relies on brute strength, not agility, and his visor limits his vision, forcing him to turn his entire body to track my movements.

As the soldier swings his blade, I pivot and slice the back of his knees, where his protective plates pull away from the greaves covering his lower legs. He staggers forward, and in a desperate attempt to disembowel me, raises his sword arm. With a shout, I drive the Sword of Integrity into his armpit.

He crumbles with a loud clank.

No time to breathe. For every soldier I cut down, two more take his place.

I can't hold them all.

I shift and run, all muscle and fur, my paws darting across the palace floor. I pounce on the nearest soldier as I round a corner, my claws raking through the gaps in his armor. He hardly reacts before my teeth go for the flesh beneath his helmet. He falls with a gurgling cry, but I'm already moving, leaping toward my next target.

I skid to a halt when I spot Padre Cipriano sweeping aside a soldier with his staff. I shift back to human form in an instant, panting as I rise to my feet, the Sword of Integrity still firmly in my grasp.

"What kind of priest are you?" I balk.

Padre Cipriano finishes his adversary by whacking him on his unprotected head. He wipes blood from his hands. "The kind who's walked through villages set ablaze, seen children torn from their homes. The kind who has given the last rites to prisoners with no eyes, no tongue, no fingernails, begging for mercy that never comes."

A mercy your brother never received.

Padre Cipriano's words fan the flames that are already burning inside me. I nod to the priest and move on, consumed by a mindless fury. All I can think about is how I want to let the Sword of Integrity take another life. I crave it, feel her trembling in my hand. I am nothing but anger and bloodlust.

Do it, the voices whisper, soft, seductive. *Let your sword do what it was made for.*

They're no longer in my head. They surround me, caressing me, coaxing me deeper into their embrace. The rage no longer feels like something I have to fight. It feels right. It feels like home.

I whistle as I go up the stairs, a tune that sounds strange to my own ears. "Anyone?" I call, moving down a lonely corridor.

This is who you are, the voices coo. *Don't fight it anymore.*

I allow one soldier, bold, stupid, or both, to sneak up behind me and press the tip of his sword against the back of my neck.

Curling my lips, I slowly turn to face him, forcing the tip to my throat. The edge digs in just enough to draw a thin line of blood.

Out of the corner of my eye, I see Martín rushing toward me from the other end of the corridor. I raise my hand to halt him, then I sheathe my sword.

"What are you waiting for?" I taunt the soldier, locking eyes with him. "This is your only chance."

I can see the doubt overtaking whatever pluck brought him this far.

Let go, the voices beckon. *Let go, and we will make you powerful.*

No more fear.

No more doubt.

431

Only strength.

Only blood.

"You should've taken the opportunity," I say and seize his sword from his unsure grip. It's in my hand now and aimed at him.

"Leonora, listen to me," Martín says guardedly, like he's trying not to spook a wild animal. "He's just a boy. You've unarmed him. You don't need to do this. Come with me to the friary."

I hiss. I don't see a boy—I see an enemy, one who raised a weapon against me.

Do it, the voices press. *No one will stop you. No one can stop you. Let us take you further. You're already so close.*

The soldier's frightened eyes dart between Martín and me, realizing just how precarious his situation is.

Martín steps forward, his voice more urgent now. "This isn't who you are."

Don't listen to him.

We will make you stronger.

We will make you invincible.

"You *really* have to stop telling me what to do," I snarl at him.

The soldier trembles. As I lean closer to sniff him, a small whimper escapes his lips.

"Next, time," I say, "don't hesitate."

Both my hands are on the sword's hilt, ready to drive it into his throat. But just as I make my move, the air around us ripples, like a pond disturbed by a stone.

Shadows begin to writhe at my feet, stretching and coiling like living things. Dark tendrils spiral upward, encasing me in a shroud of blackness. The soldier watches in disbelief as his blade, in my hand, begins to twist and bend, the metal turning molten. It drips onto the floor, pooling at our feet with a sizzle.

"Leonora, *no!*" Martín shouts.

"I'm not doing anything!"

The soldier looks at me in terror, but I can't even focus on him anymore. The shadows twist the air until everything is drenched in blackness. As the soldier tries to make his escape, the ground shifts, unstable as quicksand. The shadows expand, and the soldier's outline smears as though he's being obliterated from existence. He begs for help, but his hand passes through me.

I see a helpless boy then.

His screams are muffled, swallowed by the shadows that seem to devour him from the inside out.

The soldier is gone. No trace of him remains, as if he was never here.

Then, the shadows part. They make way for their master.

CHAPTER 50

La Luz

From the darkness, a solid form is birthed, a figure forged from shadow. The tendrils that wrapped around me now shift, curling toward their true source. I wonder if he even has a form anymore, if Tezca is still a man or something else entirely. If, before, he was only presenting himself as the man I love.

"Tezca . . ." I whisper achingly. "What did you do?"

He steps forward, but all I see is a dark silhouette that blurs at the edges.

I know it's him, but all I can see is what he's become.

"You see me now," he says, his voice low and resonant, vibrating through the blackness.

The shadows pull back, shifting, and slowly they peel away from him, until the corridor returns to view, and the Tezca I know is standing before me. But even as I see his human form, as I see the familiarity in his eyes, there's no mistaking that he's changed.

I stare at him, breathless.

For the first time, I see the Dark Mirror on him. It looks nothing like the one Ichcatzin wore, not even what once hung around my own neck. This version is much larger; it seems to be embedded in his torso, as if fused with his being. It's encircled by a gold chest piece

434

with layers of turquoise gems, complemented by a gilded belt, arm greaves, and high sandals, all encrusted with the same shimmering stones. His bare chest shows every sculpted muscle, every defined ridge. On his head rests a magnificent headdress, with feathers fanning out like a dark halo.

He looks both impossibly mesmerizing, and dangerously powerful.

"Do you prefer me like this?"

I take a shaky breath. "This . . . this isn't you."

"Isn't it? This is what I've become. What the Dark Mirror has revealed."

"You can still fight it."

"I don't need to fight it. I've embraced it, and I've become something greater because of it."

A piercing scream echoes off the walls of the corridor. I turn toward the noise, toward the battle still raging beyond us.

"Leonora," Martín calls, offering me his hand. "Come with me."

Tezca locks eyes with Martín for a moment, as if considering what to do with him. Finally, he exhales and says, "Get her out of here."

Martín moves quickly, his hand grabbing my arm as he tries to pull me back, away from the shadows, away from Tezca. "We need to go. Now."

"No," I protest, tearing myself away from him. "Don't you dare leave again, Tezca."

More screams reach us. Martín tugs at my arm again, more forcefully now, "Leonora, we *have* to go."

I can't move. I can't tear my eyes away from Tezca. My heart is being torn as I try to hold on to what's left of him. But before I can stop him, the shadows swallow him whole.

Nine Hells. I can't let the Dark Mirror claim him.

Fool, the voices scoff. *Can't you see? It already has.*

I shift.

I break into a run and leave Martín behind.

Desperation pushes me forward. I sprint faster. When I reach the stairs, I leap from the second level. All I can smell is the thick scent of blood, but I shove it aside, focusing solely on Tezca's trail. I vault over the bodies of fallen men, ours and theirs alike. My heart races, each step bringing me closer to him.

His presence grows stronger. He's close. *There.*

Tezca is in the courtyard, the beautiful garden now a ravaged battleground. His attention is fixed on the statue of Ozomatzin—what's left of it. It is a pile of rubble. His back is to me, and the Spanish soldiers surrounding the courtyard hesitate, weapons raised. They're not sure what to make of who—*what*—they're seeing.

Tezca wears no armor, carries no sword; Yellow-Beard isn't strapped to his back.

It's only him . . . and the Dark Mirror. It doesn't take someone with tonalli sense to feel *that* in their presence.

A soldier, acting on his superior's command, swipes at Tezca from the side with his blade. I'm there in an instant, throwing myself between them, deflecting the strike with a swift cut of my own.

Tezca's eyes blaze with outrage. Merely lifting his hand, a ribbon of fire erupts from his fingertips, searing through a line of soldiers. Their agonized screams echo through the air as flames consume them. The remaining soldiers are swept off their feet, tossed across the courtyard like chaff caught in a tempest.

"Stop it, Tezca!" I yell. "This is *exactly* what your father wants!"

"This is what *I* want."

"The more you surrender to your anger, the more control the Dark Mirror gains over you."

I turn to face him, and his eyes are no longer familiar. They're not even his. They're black pools.

The sky darkens, thick clouds swirling. Tezca lifts his hand again, and the earth shakes. Cracks spread across the courtyard, and from them, sharp obsidian spikes shoot up, piercing soldiers before they can even cry out.

As the crevices widen, chittering things start to crawl out.

Hundreds—thousands—of spiders and scorpions swarm, crawling up soldiers' legs and arms, finding gaps in armor, biting, snapping their pincers. Screams pierce the night, bodies writhing as the venom takes hold. I would scream too, if my voice wasn't trapped in my throat, frozen by the horror that grips me. It takes everything in me not to bolt as the web spinners and tail-flicking fiends scuttle across the ground. Such creatures have always frightened me.

Tezca watches the slaughter with an eerie calm.

The few who try to flee find no escape. Tezca's shadow stretches. It wraps around the legs of a retreating soldier, dragging him back. The shadow engulfs him, and his terrified shriek is cut off almost at once.

"Tezca, stop!"

If I don't reach him soon, there will be nothing left—not of the soldiers, not of the palace, and not of the man I love.

His gaze shifts to the gate, where reinforcements are pouring in, and with a single sweep of his arm, the entrance collapses, crushing those beneath it.

I channel my tonalli to clear a path through the chittering swarm. "Tezca, *please*." I plead. "I'm begging you. Stop."

The darkness around him flickers, and I see it—an opening. It's small, almost imperceptible, as the shadows retreat just a little.

"You don't have to do this," I croak.

"Isn't this what you wanted from me? To fight?"

"No," I say, shaking my head. "Not like this. Not with the Dark Mirror. Look around you. It's happening again. You're becoming the very thing people fear." I swallow. "What *Mia* feared."

Miahuaxihuitl. His daughter.

When Tezca and I bonded, he told me he saw our daughter. He wasn't looking into the future. He was looking into the past.

Ozomatzin waged war, which the Mexica won, and Mia married their emperor, becoming a queen of Tenochtitlan.

"You—you tried to protect her," I continue, "but it was Mia's fate to wed Huitzilihuitl. And it is fate that brought you back to this palace, so you could understand what led to all your choices and make things right. For the Tlahuica. For the Toltecs. For the Mexica. Most of all, for yourself."

"I'm doing what I have to," Tezca says, his tone now colder, harsher. "Get out of my way, Leonora."

"I *won't* let you lose yourself like this." I step closer, refusing to back down. "We were supposed to fight together, not against each other."

"Don't make me choose."

"I'm not trying to fight you, Tezca. I'm trying to *save* you."

Tezca is silent, but I'm desperate. If I stop talking now, I fear it will be over.

"A part of you must believe you can be saved," I insist, "if only a little tiny part of you. Otherwise, you wouldn't have taken Martín's form. A part of you has hope. I know it," I say. "I *feel* it. You're not a monster, Tezca. You're not the person the Dark Mirror is trying to turn you into."

Tezca tilts his head, looking over my shoulder. Martín is approaching from behind.

"Are you hurt?" he asks, and I shake my head.

I turn back to Tezca, and I see the intention in his black eyes. I *feel* it.

"*Not* him," I warn, my voice menacing. "Martín, leave. Now."

Tezca's shadow moves like a serpent, winding around Martín's throat. The darkness tightens its grip and lifts him off the ground, dragging him mercilessly toward Tezca's side.

"I said not him," I growl.

I raise the Sword of Integrity at the Dark Mirror. Her green brightness spills into the courtyard, reaching deep into the shadows of the palace, flooding everything. The light bathes Tezca, revealing the face and eyes I know, but he recoils, the darkness flinching from the radiance of the blade.

The shadow's grip on Martín falters, and he drops to the ground, gasping as air floods back into his lungs.

The last time I confronted the Dark Mirror, it hung around Ichcatzin's neck. I remember now, how terrified he was, how he immediately guarded it.

And I remember that fateful night, the Battle of the False God, and the words I uttered to Ichcatzin: "Gods can only be defeated by their own weapons . . . or those of other gods."

I knew this, yet recalling it now hits me like a whirlwind.

I *am* the Godslayer.

This is *my* fate.

"Tezca, I love you," I say, my sword still leveled at him. "Come back to me. You can still—"

I go quiet, hearing footsteps. A soldier steps into the courtyard, surveying his fallen brothers in arms, the scorpions and spiders creeping up the walls.

I frown.

It's the same boy from before, the one who challenged me with his sword.

How? I watched him disappear into a void. Tezca obliterated him.

"I don't understand," I say, bewildered. "You—you erased him from existence."

"No, I didn't," Tezca replies with a tenderness that both surprises and tears my heart.

"Why?" I ask, though as I say the words, the answer comes to me.

Tezca . . . protected him.

From . . . me.

I stare at the boy, and the truth settles in.

"You saved him," I murmur.

Tezca exhales a breath that sounds like it was inside him for a long time, waiting to be let out.

He comes closer to me, pressing himself against my sword until it meets his throat.

"Do it, Godslayer," he says in quiet resignation.

"You . . . know?"

"Since I remembered who I was," he says. "This only ends through you."

He pauses, searching my expression for understanding.

"I kept my distance to protect you. You wouldn't accept the truth, so I showed you those visions to make you fear me enough to raise your sword against me. It wasn't enough. I couldn't just share my memories with you. Then the darkness started to consume you.

"We're bound, Leonora. We share the same thread. My unraveling pulls at yours too. Had I known, I never would've allowed our bond to take place. I wouldn't have placed such a burden on you.

"There's nothing else left to do, Leonora. The only way to destroy the Dark Mirror is to destroy me. And the Godslayer—the sword in your hands—is the only thing that can."

My hand shakes as I try to hold the sword steady. Shadows swirl around Tezca, desperate to maintain power, but light pushes them back.

"The horses . . . Don Juan," I say, piecing it all together. "Was that you too?"

Tezca nods. "I couldn't let the darkness take you. If it had, it would've consumed us both. Then the Fifth Sun would fall into imbalance."

When Tezca said he was protecting me, it wasn't from others—it was from myself. He saw the danger I posed, even when I was blind to it. And despite everything, despite the Dark Mirror's hold on him, he chose to spare a life.

There it is—his humanity, still alive. There's more of him left than I dared to hope, but it's a dying flame. And the thought of it extinguishing terrifies me.

"In the joining of our blood," he says, "so too are our lives bound one to another. Bound we remain, until death's hand parts us."

The promise that we made to one another. The blood we shared. It wasn't just exchanging vows. It was a fusion of our fates.

My heart aches with the truth of his words. Our lives, our loves, our pain . . . even now, they mirror each other.

"This is the only way. The only way to free you . . . to free us both. Do it, Leonora," Tezca repeats, more forcefully this time. "I trust you with this, as I have trusted you with everything."

A plea and a command all at once, and I know that in this moment, he's surrendering—whether to me, to the darkness, or to fate itself, I don't know.

The Sword of Integrity's light illuminates the path I don't want to take.

"You are the light of my world, Leonora," Tezca says. "For you, I would endure every second of the darkness. In every lifetime, no matter the distance or fate, I would find you, choose you, and love you again and again, for eternity."

The tears I've been holding back finally fall. "I don't want to do this," I choke out.

"I know," he says, "but you must."

Though my heart aches, my resolve hardens. I wipe my tears and say, *"No."*

I lunge forward—not at Tezca, but at the Dark Mirror. I drive the Sword of Integrity directly into its cursed, obsidian surface, putting all my strength and will and fury into the blow. It does to Tezca what I thought it would—*nothing*, because the Dark Mirror is a parasitic power that cannot be what it is without him. As the mirror splinters, a faint light flickers in Tezca's eyes. Something human.

The Dark Mirror protected him, like it's done before. But the one thing I dare to desperately hope is that perhaps, Tezca can survive without it.

When the Sword of Integrity and the Dark Mirror meet, the impact is an earth-shattering force. Everything in sight—perhaps beyond—is thrown into disarray, except for Tezca and me. Both our weapons shatter in an instant. Tezcatlipoca's black tonalli bursts from the Dark Mirror, colliding with the green light of the Feathered Serpent.

The two forces spiral together in a frenzied, violent dance, twisting and merging as they vie for dominance.

That has always been Tezcatlipoca and Quetzalcoatl's struggle. Not ours.

Tezca and I are at the center of this maelstrom, and I can feel the intensity of the clashing powers. Neither force gives way, each as unyielding as the other, creating a spinning chaos. The distinction between light and darkness begins to blur, and from the center of this swirl, something begins to take shape.

Something new.

Creation and destruction entwine, and a dual-bladed weapon is born. It descends gently to the floor, as if guided by hands.

Then Tezca screams.

He clutches his chest where the mirror once hung, fingers digging into his flesh as if seized by a deep pain and his heart might escape or he'll fade away if he lets go.

My hands quickly find his. "I'm here," I murmur.

He takes a shuddering breath. I can see the effort it takes for him to nod, to accept that he can live without the darkness. I look into his eyes, and I see him—the man I love, free from the mirror's twisted power. I hold him tightly, wanting to shield him from the world, from the pain, from all that's torn him apart.

"It's over," I whisper. "We're free."

He takes me in his arms almost like he's afraid I'll disappear. "You saved me."

"*We* saved each other."

We pull away slowly.

"What took you so long?" he teases.

I smile through my tears. It's really him again.

"You know me," I say, "I like to make an entrance."

I tuck a lock of hair back from his forehead and adjust his head-dress, my fingers lingering to convince myself that he's truly here.

He leans in to my touch, pressing his cheek against my wrist. Only this exists, only us. But then he turns his head, and I follow his gaze to the dual-bladed sword lying on the floor. The sight of it yanks me back to reality, to what just happened, to what still lies ahead.

As I pick up the sword, the first thing I notice is how light it feels, more so than the Sword of Integrity.

It seems the collision has forged a weapon of opposing forces. Its body is a long golden haft, with curved blades at either end. One side radiates with light while the other is a void of darkness, casting a shadow. As I turn it over in my hand, I feel an immediate surge of power, both grounding and unstable, as if it's challenging me to maintain its delicate balance.

How fitting, given that Tezca is my mirror, reflecting my light and darkness. The Dark Mirror was never truly his own to begin with, and neither was the Sword of Integrity mine. I will miss her, undoubt-edly. She served me well through many battles and was a weight I grew to know by heart, like an extension of my arm. She had a purpose for me. She is still with me in this new weapon, but she's transformed into something else.

"I don't know how to wield this," I admit.

"You'll learn," Tezca says.

"Not the sword. This . . . power."

"You'll learn that too."

The duality of the blade is a push and pull that I can feel resonating through my entire being. I suppose, instinctively, I understand that to wield this weapon is to walk a precarious line; favoring one blade too much could unleash uncontrolled power. As always, the nepantla demands balance.

"Is it over?" Martín asks cautiously.

I breathe a sigh of relief. "Yes."

Martín holds out his hand to Tezca. "It's good to have you back."

With a nod, Tezca grips his forearm in return. "I'm sorry for—" he gestures to his neck.

"You did what you had to do," Martín says. "What now?"

"It seems Don Juan has pulled back his troops," I say, looking around.

A familiar laugh. A cruelly confident grin. "You're welcome," she says—Eréndira. She comes inside the palace, sliding her sword back in its scabbard.

Amalia follows behind her, shaking her head and rolling her eyes. "What a mess," she says.

Nelli strolls forward. "What did I say?" she remarks, surveying the battleground. "I distinctly remember saying not to start the fun without us."

"*I* remember," Tenamaxtli says, bringing up the rear with a chuckle that shows all his teeth. He claps Tezca on the back. "Lord Tezca! I was starting to think you were hogging all the glory, friend."

Zyanya is already immersed in tending to the wounded, her focus razor-sharp.

"Really? Not even a hello?" I ask.

She waves me off like I'm a pesky fly. "Can't you see I'm busy? There's much work to be done." She's a blur of concentration, snapping a man's arm back in place, but when she looks up at me, she asks, "What happened your hair?"

"Zyanya, no," Amalia chides.

"It's okay," I say. "I think it suits me."

"If you say so." She gives me the quickest of smiles.

"It's good to see you too, Zyanya," I tell her.

The last to arrive is Chipahua. "What did I miss?"

I bow my head. "We thought we'd spare you the effort, Lord King. But since you're here, perhaps you could lend a hand."

"Hmm," is all I get from the Great Speaker.

It's a small reprieve, but a precious one.

"I'm glad you all could make it, my friends," I say.

444

"Old *and* new," Tenamaxtli adds, nodding behind him where the Chichimeca and various other tribes have gathered outside the palace.

I laugh. It's good to battle. It's even better to battle alongside friends.

"Now," Nelli says, "where is my dear uncle?"

CHAPTER 51

El Comienzo

The Spaniards regroup, and so do we. Even though the fight is far from over, it feels good to breathe again. I'm not alone. Tezca is with me. The Dark Mirror is destroyed. My friends are here.

Everyone disperses to their tasks. The commanders to their commanding, Martín to the friary, Amalia to her strategizing, and Zyanya to do her healing. Tezca and I linger for a moment, watching as the others go about their duties, then we allow ourselves to make an escape.

When we reach my bedchamber, I close the door behind us, letting the rush of battle fade.

"Are you all right?" Tezca asks.

"I am now."

His hands come up to gently frame my face, his touch cautious as if he's still reconciling the man he became under the Dark Mirror's influence with the man he truly is.

"Nothing will come between us again," he promises. "We'll face everything together, as we should have from the start."

I nod, my heart full. "Together."

"Together," he echoes.

He starts to remove his headdress, then his neckpiece, and his jewelry.

446

"What are you doing?" I sing-song, raising an eyebrow.

"What does it look like I'm doing?"

I bite my lip. "We have a lot to tend to, my lord."

"It can wait," he says. "I have other priorities now."

"Oh? And what might those be?"

He lets his eyes travel down my figure, and without a single touch, the buckle of my belt comes undone, the belt flying off my waist. I gasp involuntarily.

So, he wants to *play*.

I smile in return and raise my hand. A small burst of tonalli pins him to the wall. "You think you can distract me that easily?"

That smug grin. "You think you can restrain me?"

"I'm pretty confident I can," I say. "I'm curious—how badly do you want to break free?"

"Oh, I could break free if I wanted to," he replies, his tone dripping with challenge. "But where's the fun in that?"

"So . . . you're saying you want to stay right where you are?"

"Only if you come closer."

Despite the hold I have on him, it only takes a flick of his wrist to draw me toward him. In an instant, I'm pressed against his chest.

"Cheater," I murmur against his lips.

He doesn't touch me, but he provokes me cruelly, with his smile, his eyes, his warm breath caressing my skin.

My cheeks flush. "You're such a tease."

"I'm going to play the hand I am dealt as well as I can."

When I can no longer resist, I release my hold on him, and he doesn't waste another second.

He claims my mouth and body then.

We lie together in the washing tub, surrounded by the soft glow of candles. Tezca is behind me, his arms wrapped around my waist, and I have my head resting on his shoulder. The water is warm, lapping softly at our skin. I trace my finger up and down his arm lazily. His leg brushes against mine beneath the water. There's love in my heart, but in my head, thoughts of war loom. Even here, in this beautiful moment we've carved for ourselves, the outside presses in.

"Don Juan will be back," I say.

He groans dramatically. "You're ruining the moment again, señorita."

I turn around in the tub, the water sloshing as I playfully slap his chest.

"*Ow*www," he exaggerates.

"Oh, stop it." I poke him in the side.

He squirms, dodging my fingers. "What are you doing?"

"I'm tickling you. Have you never been tickled before?"

"Stop it." He half-laughs, half-pleads.

"Ah, the mighty sorcerer has a weakness after all?"

He slides his arms around me and pulls me to him. I settle onto his legs, feeling the firmness of his thighs beneath me. My hands rest on his shoulders, and his find their way to the small of my back, holding me securely.

"Only one," he says, "and she's currently in my arms."

My heart swells. I close the small distance between us and bring my lips to his. "I suppose she's just as taken with you as you are with her."

"Good," he says, and he kisses me again, deeper.

As we part, I rest my forehead against his, then ask, "We'll get through this, won't we?"

"We will."

"And win?" I ask.

"I have you," he says, brushing my nose against his. "I've already won."

I rise from the tub and reach for a towel from the table nearby, where I left the dual-bladed sword.

Tezca watches me from the tub. He angles his head, intrigued and admiring, as I wrap the towel around me.

"You should give it a name," he tells me.

"What?"

"You once told me I had to name my sword, and that's how Yellow-Beard came to be."

"Speaking of which, where is Yellow-Beard?" I ask.

"Safe and sound, don't you worry. So, what will you call it?"

I look back at the sword, turning names over in my mind. "It'll come to me."

During the lull of battle, Martín summons everyone to the audience hall. The room is badly damaged; cracks run along the walls, and sections of the ceiling have caved in. There's blood and rubble all over the floor. Yet, despite the devastation, one thing remains unscathed: the gilded chair on the dais. Martín sits upon it now.

People file in. The room may be in ruins, but certainly not our resilience, not our resolve.

As the last person settles in, Martín clears his throat. He stands and steps forward. "We don't have much time before the enemy returns." He then looks at Tezca beside me. "My lord," he says, "I believe this is yours." He motions to the chair.

All eyes shift to Tezca, the room buzzing with hushed voices.

I smile, knowing the time has come to formally bridge the gap between Tezca and his people, to reintroduce the leader who has been so long absent, yet never truly forgotten.

Caught off guard, Tezca looks around, not entirely sure what to do. The Dark Mirror never revealed this to him; it didn't dare offer him hope.

I step onto the dais and begin, "Tonight, we not only reclaim Cuernavaca, but we also celebrate the return of a son of this land, a leader by blood, and by deed. For the first time in more than a hundred years," I say, "a Tlahuica will rule this territory." I gesture. "Lord Tezcacoatzin, King of Cuernavaca."

I say Cuernavaca because Tlalnahuac and Cuauhnahuac exist no longer. What this land has been, and what it will become under Tezca, is something new, something yet to be defined. We can't go back to the past. Our only path is forward.

The hall is alive with conversations.

My eyes sweep over the faces before me, and they land on Tezcamacatl, the old man seated at the back. His eyes widen in recognition. He's wounded, but still, he pushes to his feet and cranes his neck, as if needing a better view. Our eyes meet, and I nod, confirming what he already knows.

Tezcamacatl's gaze never leaves Tezca as the crowd parts, allowing him to ascend the dais.

"It cannot be . . . yet it is," Tezcamacatl says. "Ozomatzin? Is that you, my lord?"

Amazement spreads through the people.

Tezca smiles warmly. "You see me as I am."

Despite the old man's age and injury, he goes down on one knee. He presses a finger to the ground, then brings it to his lips.

At that, others begin to follow his example—servants, cooks, warriors, Martín, Amalia, and the others. Even the palace guards and the friars join in. They don't understand the greeting, but they understand what's happening.

"Ozomatzin has returned!" Tezcamacatl exclaims.

A collective cry rises, voices echoing through the audience hall, "Ozomatzin! Ozomatzin!"

Tezca looks about the hall, taking in the faces, many of whom have awaited this moment for so long. His smile deepens as he takes in the sight of his people welcoming him back with open hearts. More than a hundred years of a promise, a prophecy handed down through generations, kept alive by the faithful who never wavered— all of it has led to this moment.

"Tell me," Tezca begins, "where have you all come from?"

Eréndira is the first to speak up. "Michhuacan!" she yells proudly in her Purépecha language.

450

"Michhuacan shall be free," Tezca declares. "Who else?"

Another voice says, "Querétaro!"

"Querétaro shall be free," Tezca affirms.

Nelli, together with Tenamaxtli, says, "Zacatecas!"

Tezca nods at them. "Zacatecas shall be free."

More and more people join in, growing bolder. Tlaxcala. Veracruz. Puebla. Acapulco. The names of cities and regions fill the hall, each one met with Tezca's promise of freedom.

But when someone shouts, "Tenochtitlan!" the hall quickly quiets, the word heavy.

Chipahua steps up to the base of the dais. "*All* of Mexico shall be free."

Tezca gives Chipahua a nod of agreement. Two rulers, united by one man's vision.

"Our journey will be demanding," Chipahua continues, "but we will not rest until every city, every pueblo, every barrio, every inch of these lands is liberated. Mexico shall be free!"

There he is—the Great Speaker. *Mexico shall be free.* The cry is taken up by one person after another until it becomes a near-deafening chant.

Neza's dream is no longer just his; it has become our own. Tonight, a king has been welcomed back into his kingdom. We reclaimed Cuernavaca, but this is only the beginning. Tomorrow we take another step toward freedom.

We dine; it's a meager feast, not one befitting kings, much less gods. We make do with what we have: simple stews, roasted maize, and wild cherries from the orchards. We sit on the floor in the audience hall, everyone side by side, equal. There is no rank here, no finery, no ornate goblets. But pulque warms our throats, and our hearts. The taste of victory sweetens the meal, and so we raise our clay cups and toast to the day, to the freedom that now feels possible, what we have bled for tonight and will continue to fight for until it is ours in full.

There is laughter and merriment. We celebrate not what we have, but who we are—a people unyielding.

I glance at Tezca, who sits among us. He catches my eye and raises his cup, not to lead a toast, but simply to savor the moment with me. I've hated him, mourned him, lost him, hated him again, and loved him all the while. And it is the love that has endured despite it all. I don't know what awaits, be it joy or sorrow, triumph or defeat, but I do know one thing: I never want to be without him again.

"Fresh out of the forge?" Eréndira asks me, glancing at my sword. She gives an exaggerated sniff. "Mmm, nothing like the smell of a new blade."

I chuckle. "Something like that."

"What happened to the Sword of Integrity?"

"She's still with me," I say, "in a way."

"So, what do you call it?"

"I haven't decided yet."

"Well, think of something fast. You can't just go around swinging a nameless sword. That's how barbarism starts." I laugh, and she lifts her clay cup. "May it slice and dice with the best of them."

I raise my own cup. "Cheers to that."

Sitting beside Eréndira, Amalia tells me, "It's good to see you smiling again."

It *is* good to smile, to feel even a moment of lightness. To not hear the darkness anymore.

She turns her gaze to Eréndira, offering a smile of her own.

"And you," I say, not letting her slip by unnoticed.

"If my mother could see me now," Amalia muses, "I think she'd be surprised I've managed to survive this long without her."

"She'd be proud," I say. "Of everything you've done. Who you've become."

"Perhaps."

Chipahua and Tenamaxtli knock their cups together, laughing and shouting.

"Well," Nelli says, "if today's the end for us, we might as well savor our final moments."

"Here, here." Eréndira drains her cup.

Over the din of boisterous chatter, a gentle sound reaches me, my sharp ears catching it before the others. Zyanya. She's moving her hands, tapping them lightly against her thighs.

Her yellow eyes find mine. She says nothing, but I *know*. I know she hasn't allowed herself to feel the music, not since her village was set ablaze. The pain of that loss still weighs on her, but she yearns for connection, for life, in spite of everything.

I smile, encouraging her with a nod. Slowly, her body begins to move, her head tilting with the beat she's creating.

It starts with her hands, tapping her thighs, her chest, and soon she's tapping the floor too. Her feet join in. Even the way she breathes becomes part of the music, each inhale and exhale matching the tempo.

Zyanya closes her eyes; the music is calling to her, reminding her of who she is. This is something she hasn't allowed herself in so long.

The tapping becomes more confident, and the others quiet as the sound captures their attention. It not only invites us to listen but to *feel*. Every vibration seeps into the marrow of our bones.

Chaneque music. It has real power.

For a moment, we are carried away to Tozi. Back to the days when chaneques danced around a fire beneath the sky, free from the shadow of destruction, connecting to nature, but most of all, to each other.

Now, it is bittersweet. Happiness and grief together. The gods give us life in abundance. Again and again, we recognize the duality. Excitement and dread. Joy and pain. We can both mourn and celebrate. We learn to hold these contradictions within us. We can feel everything all at once.

Eventually, the music calls to all of us. Even the Christian priests are not immune. Though our beliefs differ, we are united by the same need to feel alive. Each of us is stirring in some small way, contributing. A shared pulse.

If anyone could get us dancing again, it's a chaneque.

Tezca and I lock eyes. His attention settles on me like a seductive caress. I push to my feet and reach for his hand. "Lord King."

His lips curve, and he stands. I slide my arms around his neck. We are not accustomed to such soft movements. Ours are shaped by battle. Yet here we are, bodies swaying. It's odd, this dance—this giving and receiving of touch without force, without the need to defend or strike. Tezca holds me, not like a weapon but with a different kind of strength. Vulnerability. Safety. Tenderness. In war, there is no room for those luxuries. We move as though this dance is a fragile thing, and it is, because neither of us knows how to navigate a world that doesn't demand we fight.

For now, we let the music lead.

We have our friends from the north, the Chichimeca of Zacatecas— the Red Sparrows and the Caxcanes—and those from as far as Puebla and Querétaro. We have our allies from Snake Mountain. We have the princesses Eréndira and Nelli. We have the Mexica and Tlahuica kings. The governors from the barrios. The brave chaneque Zyanya. The renowned warrior Tenamaxtli. The smartest person I know, Amalia. And my dearest friend, Martín.

Most of all, we have each other.

Don Juan returns in the morning. Our eyes meet across the palace gateway, and though our ranks stand behind us, the world seems to narrow down to just the two of us. In his gaze, I see the ambition— and arrogance—that has driven him to our doorstep once again. But I also see a fatal misjudgment. He underestimates the strength of our unity.

We all want him for ourselves. We decide it should be Nelli who has the honor.

Grinning broadly, she quips, "Finally! It's about time we had ourselves a little family reunion. I've been *dying* to catch up with my uncle." She unstraps her bow and arrow from her back, then reaches for the knife at her belt.

The battle is hers to begin, but it will be ours to finish.

Yet, we know, this fight isn't truly about Don Juan. Certainly, we have personal reasons for wanting to see his end, and he may be the face of our enemy, but he is just one man. We fight not to topple a single individual, but to dismantle the system he represents. When Don Juan falls, and he inevitably will, it will not be his demise that we celebrate. For every conquistador, every Don Juan, countless others have risen and fallen. The land endures. The people endure. He does not matter. He never did.

I try to imagine us wandering through Viceroyal Palace in Mexico City after this is all over. Who will live there, I wonder? It was my brother's home, but it was never mine. Not truly.

If anyone should be viceroy, it's Martín; as the heir of Cortés, the palace rightfully belongs to him. Yet, even as I consider this, I'm reminded that Hernán Cortés isn't its original owner. Besides, would we even remain a viceroyalty? Mexico is changing, the old orders crumbling. What kind of world would we emerge into? One still ruled by the distant hand of the Crown, a power stretching across the ocean to control a land it doesn't understand? Or will it be something different shaped by the hands of those who fought and bled for it? I imagine, then, Chipahua would be the most capable leader to guide all of the Mexica into a new dawn. Not far away in Snake Mountain, but in Mexico City. Under Chipahua's leadership, I can see us flourishing.

But before any of that can be decided, or become reality, there is the matter of the battle that presently demands our attention.

As Nelli steps forward to face her uncle, I look around at our warriors, and I see smiles—not of amusement but conviction. They believe in what we're fighting for. There's a sense of hope that is new, invigorating. Before, we fought to defend ourselves, to survive, but today, we're fighting for something bigger: not just to live, but to live long and well. This hope binds us together more strongly than fear ever could. From the palace walls, the ghosts of Hernán Cortés, Pedro de Alvarado, and their fellow conquistadors, must be scratching their heads. The victory they thought was secured is now coming undone, and the Indigenous people they believed they'd permanently subdued are now clamoring for independence.

This is just the start, we know. We are not the first, nor will we be the last. One hundred years from now, perhaps two hundred, long after our names have faded from memory and our descendants have lived and departed from this earth, the struggle we begin today will bear its fruit.

Mexico will be free.

The people of this land, our land, will live in the liberty we dream of now, and though they may not remember our faces or our names, they will honor the legacy of all who fought for their freedom.

It didn't start with us, and it won't end with us, but we shall gladly carry it forward.

Gently, I adjust my mask. I don't need it anymore. I don't need to hide who I am, or what I stand for. But I wear it today because Pantera means something to the people. It, too, gives them hope.

We hold our weapons a bit tighter and stand a bit prouder.

Tezca has Yellow-Beard, and I have the double-bladed sword.

It comes to me then.

"White-Tail," I say.

Tezca glances over. "What?"

"My sword," I reply. "It reminds me of the dragonfly's double wings. They're translucent with black bands. Each wing can fly separately, yet they belong to the same body. When one is up, the other can be down. So, it's very swift in flight. And, of course," I add, twirling the sword, "they're expert hunters."

Tezca nods, grinning. "Then let White-Tail guide your hand," he says, "and may it never falter."

456

White-Tail is a part of me now, as much as any name I could give it. This is the first time I'm wielding it, but it's already become an extension of my will, my resolve to fight for what I believe in. Naming it feels almost like giving it its fate.

He looks at me. "Together?"

I nod. "Together.

"¡Viva México!" shouts Martín. I smile, then join his cry, "¡Viva México!"

Finally, all, "¡Viva México!"

Glossary

NAHUATL

Ahmo – no

Ahuehuetl – cypress tree

Ahuizotl – a dog-like aquatic creature with a hand at the end of its
tail

Calli – a house or household

Chalalatli – a medicinal herb

Chicalotl – a medicinal herb

Chichyotl – sorcery of witches who can shift into owls

Chaneque (pl. Chaneques) – a small, sprite-like creature, guardians
of nature

Chichtli Mocuepa – owl shapeshifter

Coatl Xoxouhqui – snake weed

Cocoliztli – pestilence, plague

Cuetlaxochitl (pl. Cuetlaxochime) – poinsettia

Ihiyotl – animating force located in the liver

Iztac Colelehtli – white demon

Metl – maguey plant

Nagual – a shapeshifter

Nemontemi – the Dead Days, last five days of the solar calendar

Nepantla – in between, place in the middle

Octli – alcoholic beverage made from fermented sap of the maguey plant

Ololiuhqui – morning glory seeds

Quemah – yes

Tecpatl – sacrificial knife

Tecpillatolli – elegant speech spoken by Nahua nobility

Teocalli – temple

Teotl – a god, god tonalli, divine energy

Tepoztopilli – a type of spear

Teteoh – the gods

Tetonalcahualiztli – sickness, tonalli loss

Teyolia – animating force located in the heart

Ticitl – a healer

Tilmahtli – a cloak/cape worn by Nahua men, designed for various classes in society

Tlahtoani – one who speaks on behalf of a group, a king

Tonalli – life force made from teotl

Tonalpohualli – sacred calendar

Totomonaliztli – pustules, smallpox

Tzin – an honorific suffix attached to the end of a name, sometimes conveying affection

Tzitzimitl (pl. Tzizimime) a star demon, a destructive goddess

Xiuhpohualli – solar calendar

SPANISH

Ahuehuete – see ahuehuetl

Audiencia – highest governing council in New Spain

Corrida – a bullfight

Criollo – a person born in the New World of Spanish descent

Doña/Don – titles of respect attached to a first name

Glossary

Encomendero – the holder of an encomienda

Encomienda – a grant by the Spanish Crown to a colonist conferring the right to demand tribute and forced labor from the Indigenous inhabitants of an area

Gachupín (pl. Gachupines) – a Spain-born Spaniard, a Peninsular

Lechuza – a screech owl

Mestizo – person of mixed Spanish and Indigenous descent

Pulque – see octli

Virey/Virreina – the representative of the Spanish monarch in a region of New Spain

Dramatis Personae

Names marked with an asterisk are recorded in history, or in some cases, from folklore. While I have made an effort to faithfully depict their roles in history, I have taken significant creative liberties with their personal stories. Additionally, not all of them necessarily lived during the same time period.

Leonora de las Casas Tlazohtzin/Tecuani – The identity of the masked vigilante Pantera; daughter of Quetzalcoatl

Andrés de Ayeta/Tezcacoatzin* – Leader of the Tlahuica, son to Tezcatlipoca and Xochiquetzal

Martín Cortés/El Mestizo* – Son to Hernán Cortés and Malintzin; former usurper to Prince Felipe

Jerónimo de las Casas y Sepúlveda – Viceroy of New Spain, Leonora's half-brother

Nezahualpilli* – Former king of Snake Mountain, former leader of La Justicia

Amalia Catalina de Íñiguez y Mendoza/La Viuda – The Countess of Niebla

Felipe II* – King of Chile, son of Charles V and Isabella of Portugal, husband of Mary Tudor/Queen of England, future King of Spain

Dramatis Personae

Eréndira* – Purépecha princess, former commander of La Justicia, the Owl Witch

Chipahua – Member of the elite warrior order of the Shorn Ones

Ichcatzin – Former high priest of the Mexica, now King of Snake Mountain

Xico* –Tlaxcalan prince and war leader

Zyanya – A chaneque

Itzmin – Leader of the chaneques

Francisco Tenamaxtli – Leader of the Caxcanes, a Chichimeca tribe

Nelli Xicotenga – Daughter of Pedro de Alvarado, leader of the Red Sparrows, a Chichimeca tribe

Tomás – Captain Nabarres's former page

Iztla – A Nagual, follower of Ichcatzin

Diego de San Francisco Tehuetzquititzin* – Governor of San Juan Tenochtitlan

Diego de Mendoza Imauhyatzin* – Governor of Santiago Tlatelolco

Malintzin* – Mother to Martín Cortés/El Mestizo

Martín Cortés y Zúñiga* – Marquess of the Valley of Oaxaca, Martín El Mestizo's younger brother

Carlota de Sepúlveda y Olivares – Jerónimo's mother, former Viceregent of New Spain and Minister of Treasury

Hernán Cortés* – A conquistador, led the conquest of Mexico

Pedro de Alvarado* – A conquistador, brother of Juan

Juan de Alvarado* – A don and encomendero, brother of Pedro

Narcizo Nabarres – Former Captain General of New Spain and Minister of Defense

Bartolo de Molina – Minister of Development and Minister of Treasury, a don and encomendero

Rosendo Corona – Inspector General of New Spain

Cino Mondragon – Minister of Intelligence, a don and encomendero

Fray Anonasi – A Franciscan friar, Minister of Evangelization

Ruy Gómez de Silva* – Felipe's advisor

Nahua Deities – The Teteoh

Ometeotl – The dual-gendered god formed of Lord Ometecuhtli and Lady Omecihuatl, supreme creator of all that exists, creator of the four Tezcatlipocas

Quetzalcoatl – The White God, Plumed Serpent, god of light, ruler of the West

Tezcatlipoca – The Black God, trickster god of darkness and sorcery, ruler of the North

Tonatiuh – Sun god

Huitzilopochtli – God of war, ruler of the South

Tlaloc – Rain god

Metztli – Moon goddess

Xipe Totec – God of spring, ruler of the East

Xochiquetzal – Goddess of love, beauty, sexuality, vegetation, patroness of childbirth

Xolotl – God of death, double of Quetzalcoatl

Tzitzimime – Demon-goddesses cast from the Thirteen Heavens

Itzpapalotl – The Obsidian Butterfly, Queen of the Tzitzimime

Cihuateteo – Divine spirits who became goddesses after death in childbirth, servants of Itzpapalotl

AUTHOR'S NOTE

For the historically curious

The novel is not based on real events, but some events did happen, and the past continues to be a heavy presence in Mexico.

Those familiar with historical Mexico will know about the Chichimeca War, one of the longest conflicts in the Americas (1550–1590). After conquering the Aztecs in 1521, the Spanish pushed into northern Mexico, drawn by silver mines. To run these mines, they enslaved and exploited Indigenous people, leading to rebellion from the Chichimeca. The fighting only eased when the Spanish offered peace treaties. The war is not fiction, but my version is entirely invented.

Most of the major events happened; on June 8 of 1692, in Mexico City, a riot took place during the celebrations of Corpus Christi. In 1566, Martín Cortés, the son of Hernán Cortés and Malintzin, and his brother, also named Martín, plotted to overthrow the viceroy. The plot was discovered before it could be fully executed, but unlike how I've written it, both brothers were exiled to Madrid and were never allowed to return to Mexico.

I've shifted the timeline in a few places. I wanted to explore what might have happened if some key players lived in different times or interacted with each other in ways they never did in real life. I've also taken creative liberties with portraying the lives of those who did exist, like King Felipe II (Philip), who's based on the real Spanish monarch. Of course, Felipe "The Prudent" governed from Spain and never actually set foot in the New World. Indeed, he was regarded as a calculating ruler known for his patience and deep faith. The wealth generated from mining silver was crucial for funding his military campaigns and maintaining Spain's status as a global superpower.

Martín Cortés El Mestizo represents the blending of two worlds— Indigenous and Spanish—like Leonora, like over half of Mexico's population today. His early life is well documented, but he faded into relative obscurity. We do know that he was educated in the Spanish court as a young man and served as a page to Felipe II.

Francisco Tenamaxtli was a war leader in Mexico's early resistance against Spanish colonial rule, leading the Mixtón War in the 1540s in what is now the state of Jalisco, near Guadalajara. The Caxcanes, along with other Chichimeca tribes such as the Red Sparrows, joined forces to try to expel the Spanish from their lands. The conquistador Pedro de Alvarado did have a mestiza daughter, who was my inspiration for Nelli, but her personal journey in the novel is entirely fictional.

Nezahualpilli is remembered for his wisdom and leadership. He was the son of Nezahualcoyotl, a philosopher (tlamatini), a poet and a warrior, and like his father, Nezahualpilli was highly respected as a ruler. He lived through the early years of the Spanish conquest, witnessing the fall of the Aztec Empire. There was no better character to birth the ideas of freedom than Neza. Had he not died in 1515, I believe he could've been a real force in sparking early ideas of autonomy. Oh, if the timing had been just a little different . . .

Eréndira is a character that actually lived but most of her story has been passed down through tales. She was a Purépecha princess from what is now the state of Michoacán, Mexico, and is most famous for her role in resisting Spanish conquest during the early 1500s. There's a lot of speculation about her fate, and it's through this mystery that the idea of the Owl Witch was born.

Lastly, though far from least, Ozomatzin, or Tezcacoatzin, ruled the territory now known as Cuernavaca (Cuauhnahuac) in the late 1400s. He is remembered as a great king and believed to have been a great sorcerer.

The duology was born out of a simple question: *What if?*

We know Mexico became independent from Spain in 1821. My version rewinds history, imagining what could have happened if Indigenous leaders, renowned warriors, and even sorcerers had joined forces to organize a push for freedom back in the 1500s.

What if, indeed.